NEF HOUSE PUBLISHING

Remnants of Dusk
Dead Again: Book Three
Copyright © 2025 Bruce Jamison

ISBN: 978-1-965393-05-5

REMNANTS OF DUSK

DEAD AGAIN: BOOK THREE

BRUCE JAMISON

To my loving wife: The last three years have seen us grow as a family and as partners. This is the most challenging and best part of our lives so far. Thanks for letting me be a part of this journey with you.

To my boys: Just sitting on the potty won't get you marshmallows. We're on to your game. And be nice to your mom.

CHAPTER 1

Dafne's book slowly dropped into her lap. At sixty years old, she had trouble staying awake at such a late hour. The book she'd read a hundred times over couldn't keep her attention long enough to stop her from nodding off.

Books were hard to come by outside Ikrit's Citadel, so owning several was a mark of prestige. She'd collected nearly a dozen leatherbound tomes through her long life—stories of the young gods, the history of Ikrit, and chronicles of long-dead heroes were among the volumes she prized. The book currently splayed on her lap told the story of a man named Gerrard—a gladiator from ancient Jallfoss when it was just a fledgling nation. Gerrard led a group of dragon-blessed warriors on righteous quests to the far edges of the world. His exploits were legendary, even thousands of years after his death.

Dafne's weathered hands still held the pages open to the passage she had been drifting through. She read every night to pass the time now that her many children had grown, left, and had children of their own. It had been nearly twenty years since her home was filled late into the night with laughter from her children and their protests when her husband finally shooed them off to bed. Now, the only sounds in her cozy farmhouse were the crackling of fire and the loud snores of three massive worghounds that kept her company while her husband was away.

The fire in the farmhouse's brick hearth had already started to wane, but the stone would hold the heat and keep the chill from her home until morning. Dinner sat in a black cauldron still hot by the fire. She'd made her husband's favorite—green slaad stew—hoping that he would make it home soon. He was rarely late, but Dafne wasn't worried about the capable man she'd been married to for most of her life.

A loud *bang* shook Dafne from her sleep. The door to her farmhouse flung open, and her tardy husband rushed in. "The cart's already in the barn, but I can't stay long. Oh, somethin' smells good. Is that green slaad stew? I'll just have a few quick bowls, but then I'm back on the road."

"Yeorgious, you dusty old fart, don't you dare touch that stew without givin' me a smooch. And what are you talkin' about, *gettin' back on the road?* Put Truffle and Butternut to bed, and tell me what all herbs you've collected."

"No time for your wifely needs, I don't have a moment to spare. Jacoby is dead, along with a score of Acolytes." The old man's dirty, checkered vest and messy gray hair indicated he'd been on the road for several weeks.

"What are you goin' on about, Yeorgious? I think I remember Jacoby. He always wanted to be an Acolyte like his papa and his papa's papa before. Isn't he your third or fourth cousin?"

"*Was* my second cousin, once removed, on my mami's side. He just died in the Jallfoss mountains." Yeorgious pushed aside a bed at the far corner of the room and started going through boxes hidden beneath.

"Stop makin' a mess. You're not goin' anywheres tonight.

Acolytes die all the time, and that has nothin' to do with you," Dafne chided.

The old farmer overturned another container, dumping its contents on the wooden floor. "They don't die like these ones did. I picked up an injured boy on my way back from Jallfoss. He told some disturbin' stories. Stavros himself showed up for the boy's funeral, then sent five of his strongest Acolytes to the mountain. Some strange things are goin' on."

"Well, you best mind your business, Yeorgious. You always get in trouble when you don't mind your business. Did you get the trubulinias I asked for?"

"Of course, m'love. I found everything you asked for and more, but you'll have to unload the cart yourself. I'm taking Truffle and Butternut back to the mountain. I just came back to get this!" Yeorgious pulled an amulet from the contents he'd dumped on the floor. A thick, silver chain held a pendant made of a dark green stone, veined with red and violet. Characters from an ancient alphabet were etched on the ornament's face.

"Isn't that your grandpapi's medallion?" Dafne asked, racking her brain to remember the story behind the artifact.

"The very one, given to him by Lord Livadi himself nearly a hundred years ago, when my grandpapi was just a baby." Yeorgious hung the amulet around his neck, then scooped a ladle into the cauldron and filled a bowl. He spilled almost as much as he ate before returning outside.

Dafne followed close behind, shouting at her husband while he unhitched a heavy yoke from the draft ponies and causing chickens in a nearby coop to flutter and squawk. "Yeorgious, you old fool. What has gotten into you?"

Yeorgious held the slab of wood under a single arm and placed it on a holding jig, showing that the Strength of youth hadn't fled the man even at his old age. The farmer gave his wife a serious look. "Lord Stavros . . . I spoke to our Emperor for a long time. There's a darkness in him that I can't wrap my head around. Regardless, if I can help with whatever is going on in that mountain, I need to."

"You went on plenty of adventures when you were young. You deserve to rest. But you're like everyone else in your family, stubborn to a fault, and always trying to help. You just make sure to get back in one piece."

"My dearest wife, I'd almost think you like me," Yeorgious said, flashing a mischievous grin before walking back to the barn. Dafne gave her husband an angry look, trying her darndest to suppress a grin. She had always enjoyed their banter.

Yeorgious quickly returned with two saddles that looked more like the expensive ones that fancy, rich riders used rather than the more comfortable country mounts. They had narrow throats and no horn, with several extra straps rolled up and tied neatly in place. Yeorgious dumped one of the saddles on Butternut. The horse gave a snort of protest that sounded far deeper and more guttural than one would expect from a steed. It turned its head back toward the farmer, and the hair on its neck morphed into red scales.

"See, even the grulvorgs want to go to bed after two weeks on the road, and they're always itchin' for a fight."

Yeorgious gave the animal's hide an aggressive pat, and the scales returned to hair. "Knock it off, Butternut. We've got work to do."

While Yeorgious finished saddling the mounts, Dafne returned inside and packed a leather travel bag with food and other necessities, along with some of her strongest potions. If that stubborn man was going to pick a fight, she wanted to ensure he had every advantage. She handed the pack to her husband, and they exchanged a loving kiss.

"I'll have plenty more than snodbells for you when I get back." Yeorgious gave Dafne's backside a playful pinch, then climbed into the saddle before she could protest. With a wink and a coy smile, the old man spurred on his mount, seeing that even in the dim moonlight, his wife was blushing. He may be old, but he still knew what it took to keep his her interested.

"I'll hold you to it," Dafne said, waving as Yeorgious and his two grulvorgs began their long journey back to the peaks of Jallfoss.

CHAPTER 2

Henry steadied his gait, hiding any indication he was aware of the lurking danger. A shadow darted through the dark alleys and bound effortlessly across the rooftops. The monster had been stalking him and the other skeletons for at least a quarter mile. Jogging at a decent pace, the distance had only taken a few minutes to cover, but the anticipation of another battle dragged out the seconds for the undead warrior.

Henry's Perception, his strongest Attribute at **41**, allowed him to discern four heavily padded feet tipped with sharp claws that faintly scratched on stone and wood as the creature maneuvered itself for an ambush. This Sprig was stronger than the last dozen Henry and Beast had killed, by a significant margin.

Dread-bone boots padded softly on the empty sandy streets of another nameless city—just part of the hundreds of caverns and thousands of miles of tunnels that made up the inner structure of the mountain nation of Jallfoss. Henry's heavy gear should have slowed his progress, but with a Strength of **21**, he was twice as robust as an average human. Coupled with his Mobility and Fortitude in the low thirties, endurance wasn't a problem for the skeleton.

His armor had been created in the dwarven forges in Hjardharfell by Torbball, the last Master Blacksmith of Hraunfass. The dwarven smith fashioned Henry's armor using plates of golem steel and the durable bones of the Silent—the dread monsters that served as the Necromancer's minions. He also carried a shield and five javelins made of the same dread bones that could grow and shrink based on how much Health he siphoned into them.

At Henry's waist hung Slyngur, a doubled-edged xiphos forged from dwarven eversharp and enchanted with a Vitus-stealing flow crystal. The crystal had been salvaged from the destroyed Acolyte blade Henry used to help slay Smyrna's golem. The weapon could reform its keen edge with a bit of magic, and the dwarves boasted that even Henry would have a tough time breaking such a fine weapon.

Finally, the Drift Amulet taken from the first human he'd ever killed tinked softly against the inside of his ribcage as he ran. He hadn't needed it for the longest time since his Remnant Abilities began providing redundant Effects. The divination Ability, Haruspex, replaced the Amulet's Assess and Status Abilities, giving him detailed information about himself and the world around him.

Consume took the place of the Amulet's Essence Siphon Ability. The necromancy-based magic allowed Henry to trap a portion of the energy from a dying soul and add it to his own. He and the others had discussed the morality of using such magic to bolster their own powers. Still, as undead skeletons on a mission to rescue the destroyed mountain nation of Jallfoss, they didn't have the luxury of turning down the only source of power that had kept them from a second death.

Just thirty paces ahead, there was a slight change in the air current, an almost imperceptible puff of dust, and a faint shift in an alley shadow—all indicating to Henry that the Sprig had chosen a hiding spot for its attack. What gave the monster away completely was its aura—green, signaling it had originated inside the mountain, but the hue was a sickly off-color, like bruised flesh or stagnant swamp water.

Finally, Henry thought. He didn't mind fighting. In fact, he rather enjoyed it. The prospect of testing blade and skill against tooth and claw sent a shudder of adrenaline through non-existent veins. Far more motivating than the excitement of battle, he was tired of running and thankful the Sprig had offered him an excuse to rest. Henry waited for the last possible moment to draw his sword.

The Sprig launched from the shadows like a bolt from a crossbow. Its form resembled that of a panther, though several times larger. Black and green skin as rough as bark covered its body. Four powerful, pawed legs were tipped with vicious black claws that seemed too large, even for the oversized creature. Its head contained clusters of eyes on either side and a mouth that unhinged far too wide, revealing multiple rows of sharp, hooked teeth. Three whip-like tails with razor-sharp spikes at the end curled above its body, ready to strike. Like all the other Sprigs they'd fought, it was a horrible mockery of a living creature. They were putrid, disfigured monstrosities, plucked from a nightmare and dropped with irreverence in the undead cities of upper Jallfoss.

Haruspex

Type: Sprig, Tainted Cougar
Health: 128/128
Vitus: 19/19

Attributes:

    STR: 29

    MOB: 48

    FOR: 15

    ACU: 12

    PER: 22

    RES: 8

Resistances: Bludgeoning

Weaknesses: Acid, Cold

Lore: Tainted Sprigs are the creations of the corrupted forest god, Ghara. They can be extremely dangerous and should only be fought by groups of trained warriors

As Henry suspected, another Sprig. The monsters were frequent and dangerous enough to pose a significant threat. Like the other, weaker versions, the creature before Henry was susceptible to acid and cold damage. Unfortunately, they couldn't take advantage of those vulnerabilities with Buddy out of commission and Beast's daggers drained of their frost enchantment.

Thorodd had described Sprigs as abominations created by a corrupted elven god. *Or was it a forest Primal?* Henry couldn't keep the terms straight and realized he was more tired than he'd thought. He needed to kill this monster and find a spot for him and others to rest.

Blitz

Henry accelerated forward with Slyngur cocked for the strike. His favored Ability was based on transmutation magic and allowed him to use his Vitus to speed up the movement of his bones to an extreme level. He'd learned to meter that increase based on the ratio of finesse to raw power required by each situation.

Henry ducked under the Sprig's outstretched talons and open jaws, then ran his xiphos along its underbelly. Its skin was more robust than boiled leather armor, but the eversharp blade had no trouble opening the monster and spilling its innards on the sandy street.

Henry skidded to a stop and heard the Sprig roar in agony. The sound was a high-pitched yet guttural growl that showcased the creature's pain and anger. The Sprig pawed at the ground and snarled as dark organs and viscous black blood continued to dribble from the wound.

Blitz

Henry didn't give the monster a chance to recover. He propelled himself forward, aiming for vital spots on the Sprig's neck. He aborted the thrust just inches from impact as his Perception picked up the tainted cougar's counterattack and sent waves of alarm through his psyche. Barbs on the ends of the Sprig's tails shot toward the skeleton like darts from a blow gun.

Other Sprigs had attacked with various levels of poison, giving Henry reason to assume the barbs were similarly endowed. His Skeletal Body Status Effect stated he was immune to poison, but he was reluctant to test that Resistance against whatever this more-powerful version of a Sprig could produce.

Sacrifice

The dread bones that made up Henry's shield and javelins required an offering of Health to expand. Henry's Sacrifice Ability did something similar. It allowed him to pull Health from his bones and use it to resupply the Vitus in his tempest core. Henry had learned to reverse the flow of Sacrifice so that he could channel Vitus, in the form of Health, directly into the dread bones, but he still lacked the skill to heal himself. Buddy had theorized that Henry's Perception Threshold, the bonus one received when their Attributes reached a certain number, which stated that he could transfer transmutation Abilities to his equipment, was the catalyst that enabled the process. Magical theory wasn't Henry's strong point, so he could only trust Buddy's assessment without question.

Though ignorant of magic, he was no novice when it came to melee. Henry forced Vitus into his dread shield, expanding it from the size of a small buckler to a full kite shield. The flying barbs bounced harmlessly off the bone before Henry ducked under another heavy swipe of the monster's paw. He lifted his xiphos and expertly severed muscles and ligaments before dodging another round of darts.

The cougar's arm hung limp as it lunged and snapped at the skeleton. Henry eyed the Sprig, determining the best way to finish the maimed creature, but he was too slow.

The Sprig aimed its barbed tails at Henry once again. Three blue slashes ripped through the air and severed the whip-like appendages before they could fire. Beast appeared on the creature's back and buried a dagger in the base of its skull. The Sprig died instantly and silently. The skeletal elf leapt from the monster's back as it collapsed to the ground. She spun in the air and landed gracefully on her feet, then started running without acknowledging Henry.

"I had that one," Henry yelled. Beast didn't respond.

Heavy footfalls pounded in the sand from behind Henry. He started running and glanced back at his approaching companion.

"Ox, how's Buddy?" Henry asked. The massive armor-clad warrior held Buddy in his arms as he ran, making the full-sized mage look like a child beside Ox's huge frame.

Ox had to weigh several hundred pounds with his complete set of dreadmail, but as he ran, he managed to keep his gait smooth and prevent Buddy's body from jostling too much. "Sleeping like a baby, Harvey. He hasn't stirred since we left Ammerthall. His Health is fine, but his Vitus is still negative."

"Ghakk, Ghakk," Gator clacked, as though the animated skull added valuable context to their conversation. The amalgamator seemed happy to be back on his perch on the shoulder plate of Ox's dread armor. While battling Jaromak, the Master Acolyte, Gator separated from Ox and animated the huge skeleton's dreadmail. Even with the Ability to puppet Ox's armor, the two had ultimately lost to the Acolyte's superior battle prowess.

"And you?" Henry asked, ignoring Gator. "We've been keeping up this pace for miles. You haven't had time to heal yourself. I can still see the cracks in your bones, and Haruspex shows your Health is very low. Your Vitus is even worse." It wasn't just Ox's Health that worried Henry. They had come across several extremely hostile monstrosities. Each was a different disfigured and putrefied creature that looked like a twisted version of an insect or an animal. Henry's Haruspex identified the monsters as various iterations of tainted Sprigs. *At least Thorodd had been right about that threat.*

Beast and Henry had gained enough Soul Essence from the battle with the Acolytes to advance a Tier and put them halfway to **14**. Their Health and Vitus had been fully restored, but the same was not true for Ox. Since the group was out of charged healing crystals, Beast and Henry had taken the lead and quickly dispatched the Sprigs that attacked them. The formation allowed Ox to protect Buddy, but Henry feared stumbling across something more powerful that could get past them and harm Buddy and Ox in their vulnerable state.

Henry wanted to stop earlier, but he hadn't found a safe place, and they all agreed that getting as far away from the ramp battle as possible was their safest bet. After the fight with Jaromak and the other Acolytes, they had run for their lives from the destructive and persistent magical attack that Buddy had released. With the mage incapacitated, none of the skeletons were sure how much damage Buddy's magic would continue to inflict on the city and how long it would last.

"Don't worry about those little cracks, Herbie. Sometimes I leave them for fun," Ox said, but Henry's Perception easily picked up on the tired strain in the huge skeleton's voice.

The sound of cracking bones rang clear from the giant skeleton every few steps. Even though Ox had a massive supply of Vitus, Henry knew Ox must have been spending it as fast as it rejuvenated just to keep himself from falling apart, though Ox would never admit weakness. In any case, they all needed to stop and rest, at least to make sure Buddy was alright.

"That huge building up ahead. We'll camp there and attend to Buddy," Henry suggested. They'd been running through several cities and curving tunnels for what felt like hours. Each location had its unique hue of stone, but as they went up, the masonry got lighter, the sun globes got brighter, and the dwellings got more and more immaculate, likely indicating the wealth of the former residents corresponded to an increase in elevation.

One thing hadn't changed: there were still thousands of skeletons. There was no lack of the undead and their green auras. However, it seemed like the undead had been pushed out of sight of the main pathways, likely by the humans to ease their travels. Henry had no idea the correct route, so they had elected to follow the cleared roads.

The city they were currently in was nearly a mile long and half that wide, with stone ceilings two hundred feet high. The cavern was stretched and curved, with a bulge in the wall near the city center. A large tunnel on the far end had sunlight shining through. The prospect of breaking free from the mountain excited Henry, and he felt they were on the right path, but they still needed to rest. Also, Buddy was the only one who had taken the time to sketch a map of upper Jallfoss, so Henry wanted to consult the mage's tome before continuing.

CHAPTER 3

The main feature of the cave city was a massive building that could have been a palace or a cathedral. It connected to the wall and ceiling behind and above and looked like it had been carved from the mountain itself, though huge white stone blocks with veins of black and red made up the structure, betraying Henry's monolith theory.

Dust and black scorch marks marred the building's exterior, much like the rest of the upper cities of Jallfoss, though several of its stained-glass windows were still intact, depicting various scenes of winged humanoids. Tiered stone steps led to giant wooden doors at the entrance. A cobblestone plaza about a hundred feet wide and lined with stone dwellings and abandoned shops sat in front of the huge building. It seemed as good a place to stop as any.

"Beast, hold up," Henry shouted. The elven skeleton had gotten further and further away as they ran. After a few strides, she slowed and halted but kept her back to Henry. She hadn't said a word since the last battle, and her demeanor was even more sour than usual. Henry had been too concerned with fighting the Sprigs to worry about her, and he assumed her disposition stemmed from the series of fights and exhausting run.

Ox carried Buddy up the steps and gently laid the mage on the landing before slumping against the oversized door. Henry followed Ox up the stairs but immediately reconsidered choosing the site for a camp when he noticed signs of a recent battle—scratch marks on the landing and scuffs from metal on the stone steps that disturbed decades of settled dust. Claw and boot prints led from the steps to the other side of the plaza to a destroyed building front containing nearly a dozen skeletons that had begun piecing themselves back together. Judging by their state of regeneration, it had been over a day since they'd been destroyed. Henry wanted to take a closer look but decided to attend to Buddy instead.

Henry watched as Ox's Health and Vitus slowly ticked back up, then he Assessed Buddy.

Haruspex

Name: Buddy
Race: Human Skeleton
Tier: 12
Health: 93/93
Vitus: -6/384
Attributes:
    STR: 16
    MOB: 18
    FOR: 28
    ACU: 84
    PER: 38
    RES: 31

Status Effect: Vitus Drought (Severe)

Henry ignored the Resistances and Status Effects, save for the mage's Vitus Drought. Buddy had previously explained that the Effect resulted from an Ability that allowed him to go below zero on his magic. However, it came at a cost, which is likely why the mage was still unconscious and showing negative Vitus. Henry couldn't discern any more details from the Status Effect since he wasn't experiencing it himself, like how he couldn't delve into an item's Abilities unless he handled it.

Henry also noted that the mage's Acumen was nearly as high as Ox's Strength. *No wonder he could cast such powerful magic,* Henry thought. After examining the mage, he used the calm moment to take stock of his own Status.

Haruspex

Name: Henry

Race: Human Skeleton

Tier: 13

Health: 109/109

Vitus: 112/116

Attributes:

    STR: 20

    MOB: 33

    FOR: 31

    ACU: 24

    PER: 41

    RES: 37

    MIG: 6

    AFI: 9

    HAR: 5

Resistances: Lightning, Poison

Weakness: Fire, Bludgeoning

Status Effects:

    Soul Anchor

    Skeletal Body

    Fourth Path of the Desert

The information flooded through Henry's view. Magical characters appeared before him that looked like they'd formed from natural stone. He had little trouble simultaneously focusing on both the glyphs and the world around him, though the information did annoy him when he kept his Status actively displayed. Since his Haruspex was now Tier IV, he had learned to display only his Health and Vitus bars, as well as the circle indicating his Tier progression at the top of his vision, while collapsing the rest of the display. He focused on his Desert Path Status Effect and expanded the description.

Fourth Path of the Desert. By entering a realm forbidden to most of the mortal world, you have embarked on a dangerous course. Where will your journey take you, and will your metal prove worthy when you reach the end? STR -12, MOB -12, FOR -4, ACU -4 Health -20, Fire Resistance -20, Lightning resistance +20

The Effect's description had expanded since the last time Henry viewed it. It was now more of an ominous warning than an explanation. He wanted to avoid traveling to the Desert again, but he knew that it likely held answers to the questions caused by his foggy memory and the mysteries of the dead nation of Jallfoss.

Henry's desert visions were even more mysterious than being a human-killing skeleton. He had discovered that his mind would be transported to another world when subjected to an increasingly large amount of lightning. His body was restored in that place, but his magic was gone. He'd traveled through a scorching desert and ravaging sandstorm that turned into a massive tempest, then taken refuge in an outcropping of jagged, towering stone. There he'd found a man in a prison of yellow glass-like rocks. Soon after, he was attacked by a huge monster he could describe as nothing less than a dragon. Henry escaped the dragon by taunting it to attack him, then jumping down a hole it had created.

Upon every return to Jallfoss, Henry found no time had passed. Also, he grew increasingly weak, as shown by his severely degraded Attributes. However, on his last two trips, he'd been granted particular Abilities that proved extremely useful.

Spark was evocation magic that allowed Henry to enchant weapons and armor with lightning. An additional, more useful perk of the skill was that it also increased the Tier of the affected item's Abilities.

Taunt allowed him to directly connect to an opponent's mind and attempt to goad them into attacking. He likely gained the Ability from provoking the dragon. The third Ability was more of a warning than a skill.

Primal Urge I (Enchantment). You toe the line between courage and recklessness, a madman who would dare to challenge a dragon. You have confronted a Primal and survived . . . for now

Henry had tried to use the Ability a few times, but it failed, and he received a message that there were no valid targets. Henry continued to rest and examine various aspects of his Status until Ox spoke up, jarring him from his thoughts.

"I had no idea Benny was capable of such a powerful spell. I thought the Acolyte had him for sure." Ox cleared his throat and added, "Also, I appreciate you pulling me off the battlefield. It wasn't necessary, but I may have underestimated my opponent."

Henry chuckled to himself, not letting it show. "So many unknowns—this crazy world, our undead bodies, and on top of that, we're dealing with Remnants, Primals, and gods. Where do we fit in?"

Clinks and snaps under Ox's dreadmail indicated more broken bones were fusing. "Thorodd said that Remnants receive their power from Primals, and in turn, the Primals were created by the young gods. As the emperor, it would make sense that I'm also a Remnant, chosen to rule this mountain by the divine. Perhaps in your past life, you were also an emperor, though of a much smaller and weaker nation than mine. Fate may be leading you back to your kingdom via your Desert Path."

Henry shook his head. "We can't allow fate to determine the future of this mountain. We'll stop Stavros and his Acolytes. We'll revive the Empress and save Jallfoss." He stared into Ox's dark eye sockets.

Though no flesh clung to the animated skull, Henry had become familiar with the subtle mannerisms of his companions, and he knew Ox was smiling when the huge skeleton said, "Spoken like a true emperor, Herbie. I'm glad you're taking my mentorship to heart."

Turned his attention to the unconscious mage, Henry remarked, "I knew Buddy was capable of very formidable magic, but whatever he did to end that fight was beyond powerful. He stole all the Acolyte's Vitus and used it to make that spell, though he lost control when he passed out. Who knows how much destruction it caused after we fled? I feared the mountain would cave in on us. We're safe now, I hope."

Henry knelt and dropped Buddy's pack. The jostling roused Muji, and the trogold climbed from the unsecured top flap. The furry creature rubbed sleep from his eyes with tiny, human-like paws. When Muji caught sight of Buddy, the Trogold scurried over to the mage, laying his chin on Buddy's chest and watching with concern as he waited for his chosen skeleton to awaken.

"We shouldn't have survived that fight," Henry said, and he knew it was true. The skeletons had nearly been defeated in the battle at the Ammerthall ramps, and all four had been beaten to within an inch of their afterlives.

Buddy had gotten trapped in an anti-magic dome for most of the fight. Beast freed him just in time for the mage to intervene in the contest between Ox and the Master Acolyte, Jaromak. The Acolyte would have ended Ox, but Buddy revealed that Jaromak was the brother of the first human the skeletal mage had killed. The man flew into a rage and engaged Buddy in a magical duel that caused enough destruction to make Henry and the others flee up the ramps and into the higher cities of Jallfoss.

While Buddy and Jaromak were fighting, Henry used his last Health crystal to stabilize Ox before freeing Gator from the stone prison, along with Ox's dread armor. Gator had learned how to take over the dread armor—combined with weapons, armor, and broken Acolyte body parts—and pilot the mass of flesh, metal, and bone as though it were part of him. Henry was thankful that the amalgamator left behind the putrid mix of Acolyte gear and gore, and joined Ox's dreadmail back with the giant skeleton. Ox didn't seem to mind that his armor was once again covered in dirt and bloody carnage, or perhaps he was just too exhausted from the battle and subsequent retreat that he didn't care.

Henry could do little more than stare in awe as Buddy and Jaromak had fought. Stone met fire, ice, and lightning in such a violent collision that Henry felt the two would tear the entire mountain asunder. Their armies of elementals clashed, and their exchange of evocation magic destroyed stone houses like they were made of paper.

The duel raged through the landing between the ramps. Eventually, Buddy faltered, and Henry thought the Acolyte had won. As the massive human stood over Buddy, Henry pumped Vitus into his bones and prepared to intervene, but before the warrior skeleton could attack, a spinning mass of blue fire erupted from inside the man. Buddy's spell tore the Acolyte apart before Jaromak could even scream, and it didn't stop there. Waves of heat, nearly as hot as the dwarven forges, blasted through the battlefield like the scorching winds from Henry's Desert Path. The spell picked up speed and turned white, sending bouts of blue flame in violent eruptions, and unleashing a roar like a tornado—deep, frightening, and just as loud as Beast's Vitus-fueled scream.

Stone melted like wax, but Henry managed to retrieve Buddy and carry the mage to safety. Henry and Ox followed Beast up the ramp and out of the city, with the destructive spell tearing apart Ammerthall behind them. After hours of running, the roar of the spell ceased and no longer echoed through the caverns. Henry couldn't tell if it had stopped or if they had just gotten far enough away that they could no longer hear it.

Buddy's cough interrupted Henry's recollection of the battle and subsequent destruction.

"Beak, beak!" Muji squeaked, bounding around the mage as Henry helped Buddy sit up.

Buddy groaned and rolled his head. "Uggh."

"Oh, he's got 1 Vitus! We're in business," Ox said as he propped up the mage's head.

"The Acolyte . . . is he . . ." Buddy's wheezing voice trailed off, and Henry helped the mage scoot back and prop himself against one of the wooden doors.

"Torn apart by your spell, and likely most of Ammerthall along with him."

Buddy took a moment to collect himself. "Ah, yes. That may have been . . . excessive, but I had to ensure it would take him out. Where are we?"

"We're safe, for now. Several cities up," Henry assured the mage.

Satisfied with Henry's explanation, Buddy stared straight ahead. After a moment, Henry saw through his Haruspex that Buddy's Health and Vitus instantly regenerated. His Tier changed to **13** along with an impressive Attribute jump. However, the Vitus Drought Status Effect didn't disappear.

"That's better, but it will take several days for me to recover fully. Though my Health is full, my mind and body are still weary." Buddy leaned his head back against the door and put a skeletal hand on Muji, who had curled up on his lap. The trogold chirped and rolled on his back, exposing a soft underbelly for the mage to pet.

"Glad to see you're fine. We'll rest here until you've recovered. We need to be at full strength in case we run into more Acolytes, or something even worse. Beast, did you see the sunlight in the far tunnel?" Henry asked. He hadn't seen or heard the elf approach, but somehow, his Remnant Attribute, Harmony, made him aware of her presence.

Henry turned to find Beast standing at the top of the steps with her back to them. He thought she hadn't heard him, so he asked again, "Beast, did you—"

"What, Henry? What do you want?" She snapped and swirled around to face him. Her fists were clenched tight at her sides, and the sharp tone in her voice radiated an anger that Henry hadn't seen from her outside of battle.

"I, um, was just wondering if you saw that lit tunnel," Henry stammered. "We'll check with Buddy's map, but that might be the right way to go."

Beast Blinked directly in front of Henry. "Yes. It's probably the right way to go so we can keep murdering people."

Ox grunted and brought himself to his feet. "Calm down, grumpy minion. We have plenty of battles ahead of us. Your eagerness to fight is admirable, though."

Henry marveled at Ox's inability to read emotions. Though the huge skeleton was very knowledgeable in matters of biology, he was far from mastering the art of interpreting sentiments. Beast had never been happy about killing humans, and she was obviously worked up over the ordeal. Henry tried to assuage her. "They ambushed us. We had no choice."

Beast crossed her arms over her chest and leaned forward within inches of Henry's face. She was close enough that Henry could clearly see the lines on her skull and the empty darkness behind her hollow eyes. "And why do you think that is? Maybe because we murdered *all* their friends?" she asked, still not trying to mask her anger.

Henry struggled for words, but the elf's ire made him more uneasy than fighting an army of the Silent from the dwarven Underdeep. "They're killing skeletons. They're killing *us*."

"We can't die, you idiot. We're already dead. What does it matter if they're fighting a few skeletons?"

Buddy's aged voice crept into the conversation. "Beast, you're aware that their leader is the Necromancer. We're left with very few options but to fight the Acolytes."

Her head snapped toward the mage as she yelled her reply. "Oh really? We know that because *why*? Because Henry keeps having visions? Some lady yelling his name? Necromancers stealing souls? Dragons in the desert? Give me a break."

Beast swiveled back around, and Henry noticed that a large leather case had replaced the metal box that housed the dwarven explosives.

"What's that?" Henry asked and pointed to the item, hoping to change the subject.

Beast looked down at the pack. She pulled it free from her hip and tossed it to Henry. "Useless junk. I had to switch it with my solofurnos to kill the Acolyte mage."

"Clever," Henry noted as he opened the leather case. He found rows of glass vials, metal and stone containers, various herbs, and several other materials neatly organized. His vision immediately lit up with glyphs.

Haruspex

Item: Sulfur Spark (Uncommon)

Description: Alchemy ignition source. Concentrated sulfur packed tightly around a miniature detonator. Commonly used to initiate reactions

Item: Silverbane Acorns (Epic)

Description: Alchemy Reagent. Rare seeds from a silverbane tree. Used to prevent Status Effects from garonels and related venomous creatures

Item: Powdered Parlood Root (Superior)

Description: Alchemy Catalyst. Ground herbs used to extend the duration of alchemical Effects

There were dozens more, and even though the descriptions stated the uses of the various materials, Henry was sure he knew less about alchemy than he did about magic and had no idea what to do with the items. "Ox, do you know what any of this is?"

Ox peered into the case momentarily, then said, "Of course. They're obviously alchemy ingredients, Harry. Can you not read?"

"Obviously . . . thanks," Henry agreed without arguing, handing the case back to Beast. "This stuff will probably be useful if we figure out what to do with it."

Beast snatched it back and secured it to her hip. "Yes, a case of ingredients we don't know how to use instead of high-powered explosives. I feel much safer now."

Ox gave Beast a curious look. "You're more grumpy than usual? We're saving this mountain, all the humans and dwarves and everything else. That, mixed with the opportunity for battle, should entice even the most irascible of dead elves."

"Don't give me that virtuous boulovar dung, you oaf. You're not a hero. We're not heroes. We're either fools or monsters. Likely both."

Henry let out a long sigh. Even though Beast had a point, she wasn't the one that experienced Stavros's evil magic. The Ikritian Emperor—the Necromancer—had taken his own Acolyte's life in order to peer into Henry's mind. Henry couldn't promise that the skeleton's mission would bring everyone back, but he chose to hope it would. "You're right, Beast. We almost died, and yes, we just killed a bunch of humans. That doesn't change the fact that this entire mountain is counting on us. If we can get to the Empress, maybe we can save everyone that died, including everyone we've killed."

Beast's anger fled in an instant, like air leaving a balloon. A sad tone took its place. "Or maybe we'll just make everything worse."

"I don't think it can get worse," Henry said with a chuckle.

"Skreeeaww!" A hoarse squawk pierced the quiet cave-city, quickly followed by a loud *thunk*, and the voice of a young boy shouting. "Rat, attack! Die, Sprig. Die!"

Muji's ears perked up, and the trogold let out a low growl. The skeletons turned to locate the source of the noise.

"Acolytes?" Ox asked in a hushed but excited voice.

"I don't think so. I hear the fighting but not the sound of swords and armor," Henry said. The squawking grew louder, and a red aura burst from around the far bend in the road.

Status Effect: Enraged (Minor)

CHAPTER 4

Status Effect: Enraged Resisted

Henry focused his Resolve. Fighting off the rage Effect induced by the red auras was getting easier with every point he gained in the Attribute. However, the urge to murder those who produced the crimson emissions never completely receded until the auras entirely left his vision. "Someone is in trouble. Let's check it out. Buddy, can you walk?"

"I believe so," Buddy grunted, slowly pulling his body up.

"The red aura reveals that the person is no good citizen of Jallfoss," Ox offered.

Henry replied, "It's a child under duress; we have to help."

"You just can't leave well enough alone, can you?" Beast let her shoulders slump and released a loud sigh.

Henry focused through the rage-inducing radiance and onto the aura's owner. The cries were coming from a young boy, and a . . . skeleton? And they were fighting a Sprig? Though over a hundred yards away, Henry's Perception easily identified patches of ugly feathers on black, swollen skin. The monster's body resembled that of a hawk, with a bloated form and crippled wings and talons that should have prevented it from flying. Somehow, it overcame its deformities and hovered in the air, attacking the elf with the grace of a hummingbird.

Henry couldn't make sense of the spectacle. Up to that point, he hadn't noticed skeletons and Sprigs interacting. So why was the skeleton attacking one instead of the red-aura-clad child? Even more worrisome, the boy was about to come into view of the gaggle of skeletons in front of the destroyed building across the plaza, and Henry had no idea what would happen then.

"I won't let a child fight a monster while I sit and watch," Henry said, drawing his sword.

Beast made no indication that she wanted to join the fight. "That fool isn't our problem."

"I thought you wanted to be a hero, grumpy minion. Here's your chance," Ox chided. He and Buddy gathered themselves, and Muji scurried back into Buddy's pack. The trogold peered from under a flap and seemed intrigued by the commotion.

"I've had enough fighting for one day," Beast sighed, still not moving.

"I'm always ready for battle," Ox bellowed, launching himself down the stone steps. Henry followed behind Ox, springing from the platform just as the boy moved into view of the gaggle of skeletons. As Henry feared, they immediately noticed the boy's aura, and the horde charged. Not all had fully regenerated. Some ran and others pulled themselves along the ground, thrashing forward with the sole intent of extinguishing the boy's life force.

The skeletons were almost on top of the boy before the child noticed them. Henry felt the child was doomed, but the boy didn't run; he held his ground. His hands began to glow a brilliant amber, and suddenly a creature appeared in a burst of light. Though half the boy's size, it had a menacing presence. Dark red skin covered sinewy muscles. Its four wiry arms were tipped with sharp black claws. Several ebony horns jutted from its head where hair and a beard should have been. An evil grin, much too large for its face, parted black lips and revealed jagged yellow teeth.

Strangely, the red-skinned monster sported a dark green aura. It tore into the skeletons like a ravenous needle-tooth ankheg, and cackled with laughter as it chomped on brittle bones.

The horde of charging undead wasn't interested in the creature. They parted around the snarling defender, paying the monster little heed, and stampeded toward the child. Henry was determined not to let them reach their goal.

Blitz.

Forcing Vitus through his body, Henry launched himself forward and covered the distance between him and the charging skeletons in a blur of speed. Brittle bone did little to resist the keen edge of his eversharp xiphos. He destroyed the undead in a flurry of precisely aimed slashes.

Henry ignored the Soul Essence notifications as glyphs flashed in his view. He also tried to overlook the thought that he had just rationalized killing the very skeletons he swore to rescue. Yes, they would return, but was it any different from what the Acolytes were doing? He didn't have time to parse out his conflicting feelings as the battle turned dire.

The one skeleton that was fighting the Sprig landed a blow with a sword against a taloned flank. Black blood sprayed from between patches of feathers. The creature screeched and chomped at the skeleton's neck, severing the skull from the body. Then the Sprig turned its attention back to the boy.

Two, three, four more skeletons fell under Henry's blade

as Blitz carried him forward. The red-skinned creature, some sort of imp, Henry thought, was locked in a grapple with one skeleton, but the last two were nearly on the boy.

With a quick spin of his sling, the boy took the head off one of the skeletons, then readied another projectile. Distracted by the undead, he didn't see the Sprig swooping from his side until it was too late. Henry was fast, but the Sprig would reach the boy before he could. The child stepped backward and tripped as the final skeleton and hawk Sprig descended upon him. Henry was too late.

A series of slashes pierced the air above the boy as the skeleton crumbled and the hawk's head tumbled to the ground, quickly followed by its body. Beast cut through the enemies with such speed that they were destroyed before they knew they were being attacked . . . before Henry's Perception and Harmony could pick up the skeletal elf's movement.

The boy had covered his eyes and was doing everything he could to scoot away from the battle. Henry and Beast approached the boy. Ox followed, smashing the two legless skeletons that continued to claw their way forward, though he didn't bother interrupting the fight between the imp and the last remaining skeleton.

They all stood over the boy as he moved his hands away from his face. Four skeletons looming over him must not have been what he expected. He let out a cry and pushed himself further back over the cobblestone street.

Though the red aura still tempted him, Henry tried to say something to calm the boy. Before he could speak, the child—an elf, Henry realized—held up a hand and shouted, "Hold!"

Status Effect: Hold Undead. No actions may be taken without the direction of the caster. Command Link Established 923/1200

Henry tried to move, but his bones wouldn't respond. Whatever spell the elven boy had just cast, it held him tight.

CHAPTER 5

"Hold! Hold!" the elf continued to shout as he scrambled to his feet. It wasn't necessary—the skeletons were already restrained under the spell's Effect. Henry could only watch as the elf tripped over himself trying to get away. He was young, just an adolescent, with fair skin, dark brown hair, and matching eyes. Leather clothes and layers of fur that looked well-made, yet indicated years of wear, covered his body, and he wore thick fur boots on his feet. He looked ready to brave winter chills, and Henry realized they must be getting higher in altitude if the outside required such protective layers.

The boy had a sling in his left hand and still held up his right as though the motion would keep the undead in their place. While Henry struggled against the spell, he couldn't help but notice that the elf's aura was different from the normal red blazes he'd encountered. From a distance, Henry thought it was of the same variety as those of the Acolytes. Now that he was close to the boy, Henry could see that the swaying emission resembled a coniferous tree, with wispy branches forming around the elf's body.

"Harvey, I can't move," Henry heard Ox's booming voice and saw the elf's eyes grow even wider.

"Neither can I," Buddy added. "Either necromancy or enchantment, this boy's spell is very effective."

"You will release us, now, or I will flay your skin from your bones," Beast growled. The anger in her voice had returned, or perhaps it had never left.

"You . . . you can talk. How?" the elf asked, scooting even further back after Beast's threat.

"We can do more than talk. At least, we could until your spell captured us," Henry said, finding that he could project his voice as usual from inside his skull, but he couldn't get his jawbone to move. Luckily, the mountain's curse never required movement as a prerequisite for undead vocalization.

The boy looked around and took in the battlefield carnage for the first time. The hawk Sprig had already begun to dissolve, melting into itself as its skin turned into an ashen husk and released vile black wisps. Hundreds of bones lay scattered across the plaza, but his attention turned to the summoned creature.

The imp sliced through the bones of the skeleton it was battling with a gusto befitting a rabid animal, then calmly turned to face the boy. Its eyes narrowed in an angry scowl just before it vanished in a flash of amber light.

The boy turned to the skeletons and began to speak with a quaver in his voice. "Y . . . you saved me. But why?"

Beast spoke up, the violence in her voice barely hidden under her annoyance. "These three were convinced it was the right thing to do. I disagreed."

"Who are you, young elf, who possesses such powerful magic?" Buddy asked, ignoring Beast's angry tone.

"My . . . my name is Jai," the elven boy responded, "and

it's not really my magic." Jai reached up and touched a dark yellow bead tied to his head by a braided circlet. "I'm not quite sure how it works. I was barely able to control Lord Rattlebones." Jai motioned to the headless skeleton that had fought beside him against the hawk Sprig. "But it worked easily on all of you. It barely took any of my Command Link to Hold you."

"In that case, it should be easy for you to release us in repayment for saving you," Henry suggested while reviewing the notification that confirmed what the boy was saying.

Jai didn't seem to hear Henry's request as he pulled a Drift Amulet from beneath his furs and scrunched his eyebrows at them. After a second, his eyes widened again, but this time with excitement instead of fear.

"Oh, wow!" Jai exclaimed. "You have Tiers. *Lots* of Tiers."

He stepped forward and looked at Ox, Buddy, and Beast in turn. "**94** Strength, **87** Acumen, **76** Mobility . . ." he said before getting to Henry. "And you're quite strong as well!"

"Not strong enough," Henry said, thinking back to the severe beating they had recently taken from the Acolytes, and how a child's spell had just snared all four of them. Still, Henry couldn't disagree with the boy that his three skeletal companions were powerful. They'd been impressive from the time they'd awoken from their undead slumber, and had made substantial progress and power gains every step of the way. Henry only hoped to find a way to remove his Desert Path Attribute degrades and catch up to them.

Jai shook his head. "No. You're plenty strong. This changes everything. You're more powerful than any Guard that's ever existed."

"I am no man's guard. I am the great emperor Ortegus Oxendine," Ox said.

"Well, now that you're under the Hold Effect, technically, you *are* my Guard," Jai replied, his confidence slowly growing.

Though Henry wasn't pleased with being immobile, Jai's words piqued his curiosity. "What exactly is a *Guard?*" he asked.

Jai furrowed his eyebrows, indicating Henry had asked a dumb question. "A Guard is a group of skeletons under the control of a Sentinel. We elves use them to fight off Ghara's Sprigs."

"You fight the putrid monsters that occupy the upper cities? Then you are a warrior worthy of being one of my minions," Ox said with a deep belly laugh.

Jai lowered his eyes and stared at the cobblestones. "No. I'm not supposed to have a circlet. I . . . got it from a friend. Only high elves are allowed to be Sentinels." Then he smiled. "But now that I have you, Bharat will *have* to let me in the ranks. Maybe you're strong enough to stop Ghara from sending her Sprigs to torment us."

The boy was dropping a lot of information that Henry had trouble sorting. Ghara, Sprigs, Guards, Sentinels. The boy seemed to have no intention of releasing them, and it sounded like he planned to use them to fight Sprigs. Thorodd had warned the undead that elves were trouble, and Henry was beginning to understand why. "We'd love to help, but—"

"Of course you would, Henry," Beast interrupted.

"We'd love to help," Henry repeated, ignoring Beast, "but we're busy trying to save Jallfoss. We don't have time to work for you. The Necromancer is coming."

Jai gave Henry another confused look. "Lady Destria banished the Necromancer back to the Underdeep a hundred years ago, and the undead keep the humans at bay. The real problem is Ghara and her Sprigs. Her monsters keep getting stronger. With you, I might be able to stop Ghara forever. I'll redeem my sister's name and send the high elves back to their stone castles."

"If you're not a high elf or a Sentinel, what were you doing here fighting a Sprig?" Buddy asked.

"I was training my Guard, Lord Rattlebones. I'll call him Rat for short." Jai motioned again to the headless skeleton. "We could have taken it . . . if those other skeletons hadn't attacked. I didn't expect a huge gaggle to be in the plaza. The Acolytes normally keep the main paths cleaned out." Then his eyes narrowed. "Speaking of skeletons. Why *do* you attack us?"

Henry considered his options and quickly decided that answering the boy's questions could result in his release much more rapidly than resisting. "We can sense your aura. Those from outside the mountain appear to us as blazing red. It drives us into a rage. Even now we're being urged to rip you apart, though our Resolve has grown strong enough to resist that impulse."

Jai gave them a wary look but seemed increasingly comfortable that the Hold spell would protect him from the skeletons.

"Child," Beast grumbled, "take the ring off my finger and put it on yours."

Jai furrowed his eyebrows. He was clearly most afraid of Beast and the continuous threats she'd cast at him.

"That's a good idea, Beast," Buddy said. "Do not fear, young elf. The ring is enchanted with dwarven illusion magic. It will conceal sight, smell, and sound. Most importantly, it will shield your aura from our view."

Jai took a hesitant step toward Beast and slowly reached for her hand, then asked, "Don't you need it?"

"No. These three idiots have large auras that need concealing. However, I am much more advanced in the clandestine arts, and the ring doesn't benefit me as much. Now, hurry and take it. I can't think with your red blaze before me."

Jai grabbed the ring on Beast's finger and pulled. With a little effort, it came off, and Jai rolled it over in his hand. "It's definitely dwarven," he said before sliding it on. His aura faded instantly.

"Much better," Henry remarked, relieved to be free of the mental urges. "Now, you should be safe from skeletons. You can return the favor by letting us go."

Jai looked up from the ring and frowned at Henry. "I'm sorry, but you might be my only chance to save Amera. I'll bring you back and make them see. It's time for us to finally confront Ghara. But first, I need to test your strength . . . and mine."

CHAPTER 6

"Go ahead with your update, soldier," Thorodd grumbled and stormed down the hall. Two dwarven messengers struggled to keep up with the Elder's quick footsteps. The tunnels were alive with activity; Hjardharfell citizens of all sorts were shoring up defenses, organizing resources, and doing whatever they could to assist the warriors on the front lines.

The first messenger read from a scroll as he followed. "Captain Craggitt is reporting all three choke points are secure. They've only suffered three casualties in the last several days, all of whom were those retrieving ore from the uncovered storeroom. As of late last night, it's been completely cleared. The flood of cave creatures has slowed to a mere trickle, but the Silent have only increased in number. They're throwing themselves at our ranks. Luckily, our new equipment has allowed us to hold the lines, and our Geists can now easily block the Fear Effect."

"How long until we're ready for the push to Lundarbrekka?" Thorodd moved past two dwarves and an orc loading a cart with newly forged golem-steel shields.

"That's hard to say, Lord Thorodd. The three clusters are

holding the choke points, despite the manpower issues. It will stretch us thin, but Craggitt is finalizing plans to lead a cluster of five cells and set up a stronghold at Lundarbrekka. Once we've blocked the Silent from pouring into the upper tunnels, we can establish supply lines and start clearing them out. We expect it to take several years before we're ready to make an assault any further into the Underdeep."

"We'll only be sending two cells," Thorodd said, continuing to wind his way through the maze of tunnels.

"Lord Thorodd, I must object. We don't know how many Silent have filled the tunnels between here and Lundarbrekka, but based on the number that have reached us, it must be hundreds. Not even Captain Craggitt could make the push with only two cells under his command."

"Four skeletons made the trip, there and back again, with shoddy gear and only a handful of Tiers between them. Two cells of elite dwarves sporting the finest arms and armor known to the world should have no trouble. Also, Craggitt will not be leading the charge."

"Who then? Who could possibly be more fitting to command our troops than your lead Captain?" the second messenger asked.

Thorodd ignored the question and stopped in front of a set of heavy iron doors several times his height. The ring of hammers on metal and the smell of sulfur and argon emanated from the room beyond. "Tell Craggitt to have two cells of his best warriors ready to go in the morning. I'll see them off myself. Dismissed."

The messengers acknowledged their orders and departed silently, leaving the dwarven Elder with his thoughts. "Your time has passed, old dwarf," Thorodd whispered, and a smile parted his thick white beard.

The Elder pulled a deep breath through his nose and pushed on the heavy iron doors. They groaned on geared hinges and opened to reveal the workshop beyond. He thought the chaos of engineering on a timeline was a lovely sight, though he put on an angry expression to conceal his approval.

The chamber was a large dome, fifty feet across and just as high. A lava forge sat in the middle of the room and radiated heat. Four partial golems stood throughout the room—inert and half torn apart down to their inner workings. Ropes of flow crystal were attached from points on the walls to the golems at various spots. The rest of the room was filled with ladders, scaffolding, and gnomes . . . so many gnomes. All worked vigorously, tightening and loosening bolts, lubricating gears, arguing over schematics, and performing several other tasks that Thorodd didn't bother to discern. In the middle of it all, high on a ladder, stood a dwarf working on a large flow crystal hung from the ceiling by several chains and supporting beams. Directly below sat a collection of golem steel plates fashioned together in a large machine that looked more like a flayed salamander than any instrument of war the Elder had ever seen.

"Torgga, you've been in here for days. What do you have to show for it?" Thorodd roared.

"Father!" Torgga greeted and climbed down from the ladder. "Your timing is perfect; we're just finishing the last few touches." She pulled a set of dark-lensed goggles from her eyes. Her cheeks were burnt from the heat of the lava forge, but her smile and friendly giggle indicated no discomfort.

"All this for a golem heart. Where did you get that thing? And why bother when we can't even use our golems to mine until we've cleared out the Silent."

"For your information, *Lord Thorodd*, Buddy gave it to me." Torgga was the only person in Hjardharfell who could give the

Elder sass and not suffer the repercussions. "And this flow crystal isn't just a golem heart. It came from a control unit—one of the automatons used to organize and manage other golems."

"Fracking magic users," Thorodd muttered.

"That *magic user* brought us the magma blaster and restored our forges. Because of him . . . all of them . . . we repelled the Silent. If Buddy succeeds and revives the Empress he will regain his body. I believe him when he says he'll return to help. Once we've beaten the Necromancer's forces for good, who knows what he'll choose to do after that."

"Careful putting your faith in humans. They're almost as bad as elves." Thorodd had met plenty of good humans in his life, and maybe two decent elves, but the betrayals from Bharat and Livadi were beyond forgivable and had soured the Elder against their kind for the last century.

His warning came not as a father trying to protect his daughter, but as a dwarven ruler advising his progeny. Torgga would one day govern Hjardharfell and the dwarven Underdeep, and Thorodd wouldn't always be around to protect her. He almost laughed, thinking about how he was more concerned about her fancy toward a skeletal human than the legions of the Necromancer's Silent she was about to face.

Torgga giggled and gave her father a warm smile. The dwab knew Thorodd could be grumpy and rarely changed his mind, but she also knew the old dwarf was grateful for the skeletons' assistance.

"Lady Torgga, we're ready when you are," a gnome shouted from a high basket connected to a system of chained pulleys.

"Excellent," Torgga replied. "Get everyone in position, and we'll show the Elder what we've been working on." The gnomes sprang into action, disconnecting flow-crystal chains and pushing back scaffolding and platforms.

Thorodd ignored the gnomes and put a hand on his daughter's arm. When Torgga's eyes met his, she was taken aback by the sad look that haunted his aged face as he spoke. "Torgga, you and I are the last descendants of the Oxendines. It will be up to you to carry on the celestial legacy when I'm gone."

Torgga blinked several times, clearly surprised by the sullen tone of her father's voice. After a moment, she touched his hand and gave him a warm smile. "That will be unnecessary, Father. When Buddy revives my cousin, she can return to her duties as Empress, and I'll have a chance to focus on my illusion studies. Regardless, we now have the resources to push back the Silent and reclaim the Underdeep."

"We can't rely on Destria to break the curse, especially if the skeletons are right and Stavros is the Necromancer. If they fail, you'll be the last to carry on our legacy. You need to start thinking strategically, not just about winning a single fight."

"You can't win all the fights unless you win the next one," Torgga countered. She broke her father's gaze and started pressing buttons and pulling levers on a nearby panel as dozens of gnomes climbed from their workstations.

Thorodd shook his head and did his best to suppress a proud grin. "You're too much like your father. The next fight is what I wanted to talk to you about. I want you to lead the charge and secure Lundarbrekka."

"I know," she said bluntly.

Thorodd's grin quickly faded to a scowl. "How do you know what I'm thinking?"

"As the Elder of Hjardharfell, your priority is protecting the citizenry. That means you need to leave most of your troops at the choke points, which includes your most capable Captains. Then, you need to send someone who has experience with the tunnels between here and Lundarbrekka.

"All clear, Lady Torgga!" The gnomes had moved from the workspace and assembled around her, each nervously examining the mechanical creation.

Torgga continued, "That person will only have a few of the most capable warriors at her side, so she'll need to have both magic and engineering at her disposal. That only leaves you with one option . . . me."

She flipped a large switch in the middle of the panel. "Besides, the army I need is already there." The flow chain holding up the golem heart illuminated and began to pulse as magical power surged through its links. Gears smeared with thick, lubricating grease began to spin as the loud hum of operating machinery filled the workshop.

"Ahh," the gnomes choired in approving unison, pleased to see their handywork coming together before the dwarven Elder.

The golem heart quickly lowered into the pile of golem steel. It radiated a violet light as plates of metal lifted into position and encased the flow crystal. A low *whirr* reverberated from the construct, like a bee hive that had been disturbed by a hungry toglebear.

"Minoa's curled toes . . ." Thorodd gasped as he realized what Torgga and the gnomes had created.

CHAPTER 7

"Of. I'm strong, but I can't walk through a stone wall, tiny elf," Ox said after smacking into the dwelling's exterior for a third time.

"No, no. Just walk straight down the path, like I told you," Jai said, clearly frustrated. It had been an hour, and they had only traveled a few hundred yards. Jai tried to get them to move forward, but he was having trouble communicating in a way that allowed the skeletons to execute his commands.

Whenever Jai gave an order, the skeletons were automated by an unseen force, like a puppeteer controlling a marionette. The problem was that the force moving them seemed drunk and only half paying attention. Something as simple as "walk forward" sent the skeletons scattering in random directions.

"Try being more specific in your instructions," Buddy offered.

Beast disagreed. "No, our bodies are revolting against your coercion. The orders need to be more general, or better yet, free us, and I'll make your death painless."

Jai released a long sigh. "I don't understand. Rat does exactly what I ask. He follows me, goes where I tell him, and fights how I need him to." Jai's original Guard, Lord Rattlebones, had retrieved his severed skull and stood motionless beside the elf, like he was judging the other skeleton's inability to adapt to the spell. "Holding you four with the spell was much easier, but now, I can't figure out how to control you. Big guy, come back to me."

Ox bounced off another wall. "My name is Ortegus Oxendine, and I am your emperor. You may call me Ox, but not *big guy*."

"Fine. Ox, come to me," Jai said. Unexpectedly, Ox pivoted and walked directly back to the elf.

"I think you're on to something," Henry said from the other side of Jai. "Call us by our names. I am Henry. The mage is Buddy, and the one threatening you is Beast."

Jai turned to Henry and gave the order a try. "Henry, draw your sword."

Henry's left hand gripped the hilt of his sword and awkwardly drew it. Though it was with the wrong hand, the order worked.

Jai summoned all four skeletons to him by name. The elf looked very pleased with himself as they gathered around him. "We're making progress, but at this rate, I'll never be able to fight with you. Talji doesn't use words to command her Guard. She's been a Sentinel for several decades and is one of the few who can do it with just her thoughts."

"Who is Talji?" Henry asked.

Jai scrunched up his face like he'd eaten a sour jallopear fruit. "Taljipura is the favored Sentinel of our leader, Bharat. She's the most beautiful elf in the world, but she's meaner than a cornered kenku ape. She's especially nasty to me. I don't understand why Bharat loves her so much, or how she's so good at controlling her Guard. I just wish she'd go away forever."

"Controlling magic does not come easily, young elf. I've seen that you are a master with the sling. How many stones have you thrown?" Buddy asked.

"Thousands," Jai said, proudly puffing out his chest.

"How many skeletons have you . . . held, if that's the correct term?" Buddy left the question hanging.

Jai looked back at the cathedral. They hadn't come far enough to put the building out of view. "Well, five, including you four."

"Aren't both a skill that requires practice?"

Jai unwound his sling and spun it in his hand a few times. "I guess you're right, but I don't have time to practice if I'm going to fight with you as my Guard."

"You mean, *force* us to fight for you?" Beast objected.

Buddy released a wheezing sound that could have been a chuckle. "You are correct, Beast. However, learning everything we can about a *Hold Undead* Ability may come in handy if we intend to fight a Necromancer."

A grumpy *hmph* was Beast's only response.

Satisfied he had assuaged the skeletal elf for the time being, Buddy turned his attention back to Jai. "I also witnessed you summon an imp to fight for you. Conjuration magic is no simple art." Buddy's patience with the elf surprised Henry. The mage had never been so kind in his explanations before. Perhaps, as with Torgga, Buddy had a soft spot for another magic user.

A tiny smile formed on the corner of the elf's lips. "I'm not much better at summoning than controlling a Guard. I have no idea what manner of animal or monster will appear, and I can never control them. I always feel like my summon wants something from me, but I can never figure out what it is."

"Are you telling me you've never been taught how to use

your conjuration magic, but you can still call a being of another plane into your service? I am impressed, young elf," Buddy said.

Jai's smile grew at the compliment. "Bharat doesn't allow forest elves to use magic, so I have to practice on my own."

Buddy scoffed. "I will not have magical potential go to waste. There is a metal tome on my left hip. Open it to page seventy-eight."

Jai did as instructed, removing Tekşan's spellbook from Buddy's leather holster and flipping through the pages until he reached the intended spot.

Buddy began his instruction, and Henry imagined the mage would be waving his hands, were they not held tightly to his side. "As you can see, conjuring has three parts—connection, contract, and fulfillment. I can't help you form a connection to this or any other plane, as conjuration isn't my specialty. However, if you are requesting the services of a sentient being, you must be willing to provide something of equal value— most common is the use of your Vitus. Then you may allow that creature to tap into a certain amount of your magic for a period, manifesting as reduced maximum Vitus for hours or even days. A more powerful summon will take more Vitus or permanently seize Health or Attributes."

Jai listened intently to the mage's words and read through the pages describing the magic. "It says here that the contract is a mental connection. That sounds like the Hold Undead spell I'm using on you."

"Indeed. The finer aspects of magic in different schools can be surprisingly similar. Elements of conjuration, enchantment, and even necromancy overlap in this case. Give it a try."

Jai flipped through the pages again. "I will, but how do I know what I'm summoning in the first place?"

"This is painfully slow," Beast snapped. "I'll take it from

here. Child, what do you visualize when you pull Vitus from your mind?"

Jai looked back and forth between Beast and Buddy and eventually said, "A waterfall. I see a small stream rolling off a cliff and into a lake."

"Good," Beast affirmed, her voice still sharp. "In the same way you reach into your mind, go the opposite direction. Stretch your awareness and reach far, far away."

Jai sat quite for a moment, then his hands began to glow a deep amber. "I'm doing it. I see a jungle. The trees are so close together. They're covered in vines and flowers."

"Focus. What creature do you see?" Beast probed, her voice dropping low and slow.

"It might be a rabbit, but it's flying. It senses me too," Jai said, his excitement growing.

"Stay calm. Now, beckon it toward you and pull it into this world."

Jai's face scrunched as he followed Beast's guidance. Suddenly, an amber sphere formed on the ground just in front of Jai. Then, in a burst of light, a dark brown rabbit appeared. It was smaller than Henry expected, but it fluttered around with white, feathered wings and chirped happily at Jai.

"I did it!" the elf exclaimed.

"Not yet," Buddy interjected. "Keep the connection you made, but turn part of your attention back to the waterfall in your mind. Offer your summon part of that magic, then will it to execute a simple task."

Jai's face scrunched as he focused, and after only a short pause, the rabbit lit upon Ox's shoulder, directly on top of Gator's mantid helmet. The Amalgamator was under the same Hold Effect as Ox, so he could do little more than look dumbstruck. With another flash of light, the rabbit disappeared.

Jai bounced excitedly, his face flushed with pride. "You were right. I have a Status Effect that says my max Vitus is down by 2 for an hour. It's strange, though. I don't understand why other summons would fight for me without a contract."

"The contract binds the summoned creature's service to your offering and allows you to connect to them again for a future conjuration. More powerful creatures may attack you if you bid them to serve without a contract or don't fulfill your end of the bargain. The more contracts you fulfill, the more your Abilities will grow, as will the aspects of your summons."

"That makes sense," Jai said, flipping through more pages of the metal tome until he got to the last section of the spellbook.

"Here's some different writing," he said, then started to read aloud. "Unlike the rest of the dwarves of Hjardharfell, Lady Torgga is quite becoming. I must admit that I have conflicting feelings as I am drawn to a dwarf of such intellect. Her—"

"Ehemm," Buddy interrupted Jai with a loud cough. "That's enough for now. You can replace the tome in my pouch and try summoning again."

Ox barely suppressed a laugh. "No, Barney. I believe the boy is just starting to understand your wise insights. Please keep reading, tiny elf."

After skimming the following few lines silently, Jai's cheeks flushed red. He quickly closed the tome and avoided eye contact with the skeletons.

"Alright. Let me try again." As before, Jai extended his awareness past his body and into a distant plane. A few seconds faster than the previous time, another amber circle appeared on the ground, and a flash of light revealed the summon. The creature could have been a puppy, were it not for its clawed feet and spikes jutting down its back. Short brown hair covered its body, and its tail wagged happily as it bounded toward Jai with a loud *yip!*

Beast let out a low growl, but Henry recognized it as the same sound she made when she cuddled Muji. He had to agree; the summon was very cute as it jumped happily and licked Jai's face.

"I've never had one that was so friendly." Jai laughed and failed to stop the creature from covering his face in slobber. The elf brought himself to his feet and found a nearby broken piece of wood. "I've got a task for you," he said as he waved the stick over the creature's head. It responded with another loud *yip!*

"Fetch," Jai shouted, throwing the stick as far as he could.

"Very good, young elf," Buddy said.

"You'll be summoning nine-headed hydras to fight for you in no time," Ox lauded.

"I hope—" Jai began, his words cut short. A flash of green and black pounced on Jai's summon before the creature could pick up the stick.

It was fast enough that Henry's Perception didn't pick it up until it was too late. Coiled muscles flexed below dark green skin and black quills. A long, curled tail covered in more quills flitted angrily as the Sprig crunched down on the summon's neck. The creature released a painful yelp, then disappeared with another flash of amber light.

Confusion and agitation crossed the monster's fanged maw and black eyes. It resembled a squirrel in shape and movement but was larger than Jai, sported powerful, mangled limbs, and had a misshapen body.

Jai stared in horror as the Sprig's attention went to the elf and his skeletal Guard. The monster's tail flitted quickly. Its disfigured body lowered, preparing to pounce.

Henry couldn't use his Haruspex on the Sprig, but he could still tell it posed a danger. Maybe not at their normal power, but as the Hold Undead spell restrained them, it could deliver significant damage. From the corner of his vision, Henry saw Jai load his sling and start to twirl it. "Jai, I hope that lesson helped, because that Sprig is much more powerful than any we've come across yet."

CHAPTER 8

The air around Jai's sling hummed as he spun the cord and launched the stone projectile. His aim was true, and the rock smacked into the side of the Sprig's face with a *thud*. The monster reared back and released a cry that was something between the screech of an eagle and a bear's growl. Black ooze squirted from its face, but Henry could tell the wound was superficial and wouldn't stop the monster's attack. That attack came quickly.

Black eyes narrowed as the Sprig focused on Jai. Powerful legs launched so forcefully that the sand beneath its clawed feet flew backward.

"Henry, Ox, kill it!" Jai screamed.

Henry was impressed that the elf kept enough composure to give them orders, even if Jai's control over them had only increased marginally. Henry and Ox drew their weapons and lumbered forward. The Sprig was on them before their bodies could move to strike.

The corrupted squirrel leaped into the air and plowed directly into Ox's torso, easily dodging the hammer's slow arc. Ox was still much larger and heavier than the monster, and the massive skeleton held his balance. The Sprig latched on and climbed him like a tree, rending with sharp claws and biting with jagged fangs. Ox's dreadmail protected him from getting mauled as he flailed in vain and struggled to catch the agile attacker.

Henry's response was just as slow and frustrating. His Perception picked out dozens of vulnerable spots on the monster: throat, spine, bloated, protruding organs, and thick tendons. His Strength and Mobility screamed at him to thrust. A quick activation of Blitz would give him all the speed he needed to end the monster, but the Hold spell only allowed him to swing his sword awkwardly. Unfortunately for Ox, Henry's eversharp xiphos was a much better weapon than the Sprig's claws, and a slash buried deep into Ox's dreadmail.

Henry didn't have time to apologize or even attempt another attack. The Sprig vaulted from Ox and climbed onto Henry. It bit hard into Henry's armor, but like Ox, Henry's dreadmail held strong. Henry heard the monster's teeth and claws scraping, and even a few cracking, under the force of the Sprig's vicious gnawing. Henry's Health stayed at full—until Ox's hammer caught him square in the ribs.

Though the force magic in the weapon hadn't been activated, the blow from the maul under Ox's Strength was enough to shatter bones and send him tumbling.

Status Effect: Broken Ribs (Minor) MOB -10%

Henry skidded to a stop, dismissing the notification as his body slowly righted. The force had separated him from the Sprig, allowing the monster to turn its attention to the elf.

"Beast, shoot your bow," Jai cried, unleashing another rock from his sling.

The rock hit the monstrous squirrel, causing minimal damage. Beast's arrow went wide and shattered against Ox's chest plate. Once again, the monster sprang forward, screeching with murderous intent. The Sprig closed on Jai quickly, and Henry saw that the elf had neither the time to evade nor the room to fire off another rock.

Instead of doing either, Jai held his ground and gave another order. "Buddy, use magic."

In the span of a breath, the calm air of the underground cavern roared to life with the intensity of a tornado as a blast of wind shot from Buddy and sent the Sprig reeling. The air current carried the monster and smashed it into and through the nearest building wall. It sat there, limp and sticking halfway out of the crumbling dwelling.

"We did it," Jai shouted, but his celebration was cut short. The sound of cracking bones and tearing flesh rang from the Sprig as its body rolled and contorted. Bones ripped through green skin, and black blood sprayed in all directions. Jai stared with mouth agape as the mass of corrupted flesh pulled against itself, separating then reforming into four smaller squirrel Sprigs.

"Don't just watch. Tell us to attack, you idiot," Beast cried.

"Oh, yes. Everyone, attack the squirrels," Jai ordered, realizing the fight wasn't over.

Fireballs and arrows whizzed through the air; Henry and Ox charged. Even Rat rushed forward to meet the tainted contingent. The smaller Sprigs were even faster than the original. They zigzagged forward, letting out high-pitched squeaks and easily dodging the incoming attack. They ignored Henry and Ox, rushing at Beast, Buddy, and Jai.

An arrow caught one, and a ball of acid hit another. Rat descended on the screeching, acid-covered Sprig and began stabbing it with his rusty sword.

The other two Sprigs continued their charge, one going for Buddy and the other for Jai. The first Sprig reached Buddy and latched onto him with a flurry of biting and clawing. Elemental bolts of every type launched in all directions, eviscerating nearby stone structures, though luckily avoiding the undead.

The final Sprig lunged at Jai, snapping and biting with a rabid ferocity. Henry wanted to join, but with the Hold Undead spell hindering a rapid response, he could only wait for the Sprig to maul the boy. The monster's attacks never landed.

Jai pivoted, avoiding every swipe, lunge, and bite, and countered with stabs from a humble-looking dagger. Henry hadn't used Haruspex to Assess the elf, but felt his Mobility must have been relatively high to allow him to dodge and strike so proficiently.

While Jai defended, Buddy's robes were getting clawed and shredded. The jostling disturbed the inhabitant of Buddy's pack. With a snarl and a whirl of brown and white fur, Muji sprang from the leather flap and collided with the squirrel. They were roughly the same size, but **15** Tiers gave the trogold a considerable advantage. Black globs of blood showered the area, and the Sprig was dead before it and Muji hit the ground. Muji landed with a heavy thud, shaking his head and clawing at his face to get the putrid taste out of his mouth.

"Muji, follow us from a distance. We'll need you later," Buddy said in a quiet but forceful voice. The Trogold cocked his head and gave the skeletal mage a curious expression.

"Skat!" Buddy said a bit louder. Muji scurried off and disappeared into a dark alleyway.

A few yards away, Jai was quickly tiring. "Beast, help," the elf gasped between breaths.

Beast ran forward and grappled the Sprig. It retaliated by

tearing into her. "No, you idiot. Tell me to use my daggers," she hissed.

"Beast, k . . . kill it with your daggers," Jai stammered.

The words had barely left his mouth when Beast's blades slipped from beneath her cloak and deftly removed the squirrel's head. It died with a shrill gurgle. Beast stood over the tainted Sprig's body as it slowly began to ash and whisp away.

—

"Beak . . ." Muji quietly chirped, narrowing his eyes and rebuking the ungrateful Protector. He couldn't quite figure out what all the sounds made by the skeletons meant, but he knew that *skat* meant *go away*, and Muji instantly hated the sound.

All the trogold wanted was to help the Protector—help, and play with magic things, of course. What trogold wouldn't want to play with magic things? Muji had always been the best when it came to magic because he could see how it moved between creatures and objects, and in most cases, he just knew how to make it work better. Making magic things work better was the most fun, and as the skeletons kept finding fun magical things for him to play with, Muji was happy to keep helping them in return.

The next best thing to helping and playing with magic things was eating lizards and bugs and other tiny crawlies, but only if he could pounce on them first. Now that Muji was really strong, he could even eat the big crawlies with no problem, except for ones with green and black skin that had gross magic flowing through them. The one Muji had just killed left a nasty taste in his mouth that he hoped eating a delicious lizard would remove.

After helping, playing, and eating, Muji's next favorite thing was cuddles, and the smallest skeleton was the best creature for cuddles. Her bones were pokey, like those of the other skeletons, but she would wrap Muji in her cloak and tickle his belly and give him happy sounds whenever he made cute noises. He was very good at cute noises. Muji really liked that, and he made sure to return that affection by pretending to bite at her bony fingers, but not very hard, because Muji didn't want to hurt her.

Besides the Protector and the lady skeleton, Muji thought the other two undead were just fine. The big one was a bit loud, but he'd killed more lizards than anyone else. Anyone who liked to kill lizards couldn't be bad. The last skeleton always made sure to roast lizards over the fire, then give them to Muji. Something about lizards being slightly burnt made them taste even better, so Muji decided he liked the fourth skeleton, too.

The skeletons had everything Muji liked, so he knew he wouldn't stay mad at the Protector for long. Even spited by the *skat* sound, Muji was loyal and would continue assisting the Protector and his skeleton friends as long as possible. Muji felt he would need to stay close to the Protector as something strange had happened to the skeletons.

A child was using an interesting type of magic that Muji had never seen before. Muji could sense different types of magic flowing through things and environments. It wasn't sight, but more like an awareness that he chose to interpret as varying intensities and shades of color. The magic affecting the skeletons came from a flow crystal tied to the child's forehead. It emitted a faint cloud of yellow and brown that wrapped around the skeletons and clung to their bones, allowing the child to tell the Protector and his friends what to do.

That seemed silly. Why would the Protector let a child's magic affect him? The sorcerer should be able to dispel it with a flick of his hand, even if the child had pretty good magic as well? Just like with things, Muji could sense magic potential in beings, and even if the child wasn't very good at using his magic, he still had a lot of it. Not nearly as much as the Protector, but still a respectable amount.

It seemed so long ago that the Protector had saved Muji from becoming a meal to the giant, mean lizards. Muji had accidentally gotten himself trapped on a ledge, and the walls behind him were too smooth to allow him to climb to safety. Back then, he was too weak to bite through the monsters' thick skin, and with no way to fight back, he was sure they would snatch him from the cave wall and devour his poor little self.

Out of nowhere, lightning, ice, and fire destroyed his attackers. That was the first time Muji saw the Protector—a skeleton in blue robes that commanded phenomenal magical powers with no effort at all. The undead had more magic than any creature, especially any skeleton, Muji had ever seen. In that moment, Muji swore to help the Protector until he had paid him back for saving Muji's life. He had even tried to give the Protector the great honor of becoming Muji's thrall, but the skeleton refused every time Muji extended the offer, much to the trogold's displeasure.

They were an interesting group for skeletons, but they would have been in big trouble several times over without Muji's help. Because Muji was so good with magic things, he managed to kill a big rock monster with the firestick. It was one of the best magic things Muji had ever found, and after being so brave and saving the undead, Muji had hoped the Protector would let him keep the firestick.

Instead, the Protector gave it—along with the super magic gloves—to the smelly dwarves. Muji found that very strange, because the Protector didn't like dwarves . . . except for the nice dwarf lady. The Protector seemed to like her very much. Probably because she was really good with magic, too.

Muji was unhappy about losing the firestick, but soon after, the dwarves gave Muji and his skeletons plenty of magic things in return. That made the loss much more bearable, and he currently wore one of those magic things.

Muji rubbed his long fingers over the magic rock at his chest, held in place by a high-quality leather harness. It was very comfortable, and the fact that it was made from dead lizards made Muji like it very much. It was a great gift, and Muji had some ideas on how to attach more magic rocks to make it even better, though he hadn't quite figured out how to do it.

There were many magic rocks hidden in the caves, and Muji had come to learn that they could be modified to contain certain spells. He had even helped put spells in many of the magic rocks his undead now used. However, the magic rock at his chest was much different.

It contained strange magic that made Muji stronger and smarter whenever he killed an enemy, and it was also the reason he would occasionally see strange things. He had first thought what he saw were small bugs, and he got very frustrated when he couldn't pounce on them. After several failed attempts, Muji realized they were like the markings in the book that the Protector spent so much time looking at. Maybe if Muji stared at the book too, he would become even stronger, making it even easier to help, thus earning Muji more magic things, more snacks, and of course, more scratches.

Muji sat quietly, lost in thought, until the child and the skeletons finished talking and started moving again. Still unsure what was going on, Muji scurried after, making sure to stay hidden. He was really good at hiding.

CHAPTER 9

"That was amazing. I think I'm getting the hang of controlling you," Jai said, sheathing his dagger and stowing his sling.

Globs of black ichor that clung to Beast's torn cloak had already started to dissolve into smoky ash. "Any of us could have stopped that weak monster, were we not constrained by your spell."

With no more enemies to fight or orders to carry out, Henry stood still with sword in hand. "She's right, Jai. You could have died. You need to let us go so we can get to Destria before the Ikritians. If we can break the spell, we'll return to help the elves."

Jai considered Henry's request, but after a moment of staring at his feet, he gave the skeleton a sad look. "I want to let you go, and I would if Ghara weren't a bigger threat than the humans. It's not just about stopping her. I need to be the one to do it, and I can't without your help."

Though Beast had been splattered in Sprig gore, Ox was absolutely dripping in the remains. The carnage would eventually whisp away, but in the meantime, he looked like a giant sludge monster. He seemed to be enjoying himself and not at all resentful of being controlled by the adolescent elf. "As much as I love smashing these abominations, why does it matter who stops your angry god?"

"No forest elf has ever Held *living undead*, if that's what you are. If I don't use you now, I may never get the chance to prove my family's worth to the high elves."

Ox bellowed loud enough to alert the entire city of their presence. "Don't dismay, tiny elf. You've proven your worth right here. When the squirrel charged, you held your ground and fought back like a true warrior. Does it really matter what intoxicated elves think about you?"

"Intoxicated?" Jai asked, looking somewhat puzzled.

"Yes, the high elves' opinion seems of little consequence," Ox answered.

Beast let out an angry scoff. "You idiot. *High* describes the race of the elves. It doesn't mean they're under the influence of narcotics."

"Hmm, I'm not so sure . . ." Ox mused.

Jai scrunched his face, still looking confused. "I don't know what you're talking about, but what the high elves think means everything in elven society. My family is disgraced. Even among forest elves, we're outcasts. It's not our fault, though. I was just a baby when my sister betrayed the elves and helped Lord Livadi attack the mountain. Since then, Bharat has made it a point to ostracize my family. If I prove that a forest elf can once again become a Sentinel and save us all from Ghara, I know I can make amends for her betrayal."

"What stops forest elves from becoming Sentinels?" Henry asked. He was starting to understand why the dwarves weren't so fond of elves. Not counting the flood of deadly Sprigs, most of the elves' problems seemed to come from internal politics and arbitrary rules.

"Bharat's blessing is required for almost anything in our society. My parents told me the original Sentinels were forest elves. The Sentinels would protect Amera from goblins and trolls. Of all the Sentinels, my sister was the strongest. She had powerful Abilities, and she could kill any monster in the blink of an eye." Jai held back tears as he told his story. "I don't know why she would betray us, but now, Bharat only allows high elves to be named Sentinels. He gives them these," Jai said, pointing to the circlet on his forehead, "to create skeletal Guards and fight Ghara's Sprigs."

Buddy's robes were torn in a few places, but he seemed to have recovered from his skirmish just fine. Now that the talk had turned to magic, he became interested in the conversation. "An enchanted flow crystal. How does the magic of your circlet work?"

Jai shrugged. "I have no idea. The Sentinels have used them for decades to keep us safe. Bharat even grants lesser circlets to a few forest elves out of necessity to protect our villages, since there aren't enough Sentinels to manage the entire valley. Those Guards are far less effective than those of the high elves. When we arrive, you'll see bare skeletons guarding huts and farms.

"You don't arm them?" Henry asked.

"We try, but weapons are hard to come by. Some elves occasionally venture into Jallfoss to find a recently killed Acolyte that's already armed. As you can see, going into Jallfoss is dangerous and few return. The high elven armories lie buried under rubble in the former mountain city. Bharat gave the few remaining armaments to his personal escort. There was dissent when Bharat restructured the Sentinels, but the forest elves were grateful for the protection after a few waves of Sprigs ravaged the valley. Sadly, that protection is rarely the Sentinels' primary interest."

"Shouldn't protection be a Sentinel's main job?" Henry wondered aloud.

"They only protect the villages that shower them with gifts. Those with Bharat's blessing are given the best housing, plenty of food, weapons, and whatever else they desire. Sentinels even get to choose their own mate, but that doesn't matter much because we're not allowed to mix between forest and high elves. The worst part is that Bharat only allows forest elves to choose a partner if they pay a satisfactory penance to him."

"You're barely one hundred years old, far too young to care about finding a mate. Focus on training your skills to become worthy of a woman," Beast scolded.

Her advice made Jai snort. "I agree. I don't need some girl telling me what to do," he said, then his face turned somber again. "More than anything, I want to prove to Bharat and Talji that I can be a Sentinel, and that my family and I shouldn't be treated like outcasts."

"An admirable goal, tiny elf," Ox said with a tone of approval.

Jai walked over to the ashen remains of a squirrel Sprig and stomped it with his boot. "Elven children play a game called *Guards and Sprigs*. On the rare occasions they let me join, they always make me be the Sprig. I hate being the Sprig. Ghara's monsters are evil, and I just want to stop them."

Back to the forest god again, Henry thought. He couldn't tell if Ghara was truly the source of Jai's woes, or if the young elf saw slaying it as a way to improve his situation. Henry couldn't deny that the Sprigs were terrible monsters. If he hoped to revive the skeletons of the mountain, he would eventually need to deal with that threat. "What can you tell us about Ghara?" he asked, hoping to glean any information he could about a potential enemy.

"Only what Bharat teaches us. The elves were originally drawn to the mountain tops long before the humans and dwarves started mining. Ghara is a powerful god of life we've worshiped for nearly five thousand years. She created all the animals and insects of the world and sent them out to provide for the elves. She was a symbol of balance, life, and prosperity. The forest elves built their homes in the high valleys, while the high elves created their castles alongside the humans.

"However, Lord Livadi and the Necromancer attacked our home. Whatever evil magic they used, it corrupted Ghara. Where she once supplied the forest with life, she now creates evil Sprigs that flood into the mountains and forests. Without access to our armories, we were nearly defenseless.

"The elves inside the mountain all died fighting Livadi's fire army, but those in the surrounding forest weren't attacked. On our own and without the protection of Jallfoss, we had to fight the evil Sprigs and prevent them from spreading. Many elves died until Bharat learned how to take control of the animated dead and make them fight on our side. He created the Holding circlets and allowed the Sentinels to use skeletons as frontline fighters. They can stop the Sprigs with their skeletons whenever they're not showing off to each other in the Theater. We've been slowly losing ground and fighters over the years. Everyone I know is constantly at risk of being killed by Ghara's monsters. They're vicious and cunning; we're never sure what form they'll take or when and where they'll appear. The more I talk, the more I understand that I don't even know what I'm doing. How can I hope to stop a god and an army of Sprigs?"

Jai let out a deep sigh, finally realizing the direness of his situation. Buddy caught on to his demeanor and assured the boy. "The situation of the elves isn't hopeless. Thorodd, the dwarven Elder, told us Ghara is not a god, but a lesser being called a Primal."

Jai scrunched up his face like Buddy was trying to force-feed him bitter schmekenroot. "No. Ghara is the god of life. You shouldn't listen to dwarves. They're liars and scoundrels who will take everything from you at their first opportunity."

"Are those your words or Bharat's?" The patience in Buddy's voice surprised Henry. "While I would agree that dwarves are scoundrels . . . some dwarves . . . I don't believe they have a reason to lie about Ghara's nature."

"What *is* a Primal?" Jai asked, ignoring Buddy's question.

"A spriggan, to be exact. A powerful being similar to a dragon or a giant. Though created by the gods, Thorodd claims most have been killed off, indicating that they are not immortal. However, I don't know if beings like us can dispatch such a force. Between the Necromancer and Ghara, the high elves were fortunate to make it out of the mountain alive."

"That's what I don't understand," Henry chimed in. "You said the high and forest elves don't get along. What were high elves doing outside the mountain when the Necromancer attacked?"

"Bharat never speaks of it, but my parents often told me the story before bed. If you keep going up from here, you'll find the destroyed remains of the high elven city." Jai pointed toward a mountain peak several miles away. "Before the Necromancer came, there was a smaller . . . happening. A troll destroyed most of Bharat's castle and the surrounding area. A few high elves who'd lost their homes chose to move into the valley, still preferring to live with forest elves rather than humans and other non-elves. A few weeks later, Lord Livadi used his fire army to kill everyone inside Jallfoss. The several hundred high elves outside the mountain were safe—at least until the Sprigs started attacking. The Sentinels have slowed the tide, but are more concerned with showboating in the Theater. So many forest elves have died waiting for a Sentinel that never came. If Bharat and Talji don't have the courage to stand up to Ghara, I guess I'll have to."

"Jai, that's the second time you've mentioned a Theater. Is it like the arena in Ammerthall?" Henry probed, surprised by his own excitement. The thought of an arena grabbed his attention, enticing him with the prospect of further testing his combat Abilities. There was something about melee—facing down a stronger opponent with the odds stacked against him—that felt familiar and comforting to Henry in a way that probably shouldn't have. As much as he wanted to get to Destria, he wasn't completely opposed to following Jai for a bit longer.

Jai touched the circlet on his forehead, confirming it was securely in place. "I've heard the human arena is spectacular. Thousands of people would stack on top of each other to cheer for their favorite fighters. Our Theater is simple in comparison, but that's where I'm taking you to make our point. It's a few days' walk, and we'll come across dozens of Sprigs on the way. That will give me plenty of chances to practice with you."

"Now you're talking, tiny elf. Let's go pick a fight!" Ox exclaimed, mirroring Henry's excitement.

CHAPTER 10

21st Day of Summer's Dawn, 4285

All is quiet, save for the scratches of quill on this tome's parchment—a gift from Mathis. It is an ancient collection of spells, bound together by a mage long dead. I once thought the Ikritian sorcerer intended me to study the rudimentary magic contained within, but I now realize the tome's blank pages were his true gift—void of spellcraft and yearning for a new author. The revelations I have made, and my progress controlling my magic, can thus be documented.

My latest discovery has changed my perception of the Primals completely. They are commonly depicted as forces of wrath and vengeance that the young gods used to wage war on each other. I believe their true purpose is much more subtle. The foremost Ability that a Primal bestows on their Remnants is Consume, but the name is misleading. First, let us look at what the Remnant is consuming: Soul Essence. Contrary to what the term implies, Soul Essence is not an integral part of one's actual soul. It is the collection of energy that a being has accumulated over their life. Love, loss, joy, despair—all the emotions experienced as one goes through the tribulations of existence are intertwined with the soul, building into a deposit that, upon death, is used to transport the soul to the realms that the young gods have created for us.

The act of killing creates a connection between the two parties involved. Upon death, the Consume Ability channels that energy into the Remnant, leaving just enough Essence to carry the soul to its destination. The important part to understand is that the soul itself is not devoured in the process.

As I examine this Ability, I find that it would be difficult, though possible, to modify it in such a way that the Remnant could ingest the actual soul and transform it into much more power than could be originally gained from mere Soul Essence. The fact that Primals don't allow this of their Remnants tells me those beings are more concerned with order than power. I find the practice almost respectful of the dead.

Mathis calls this type of magic necromancy and is very concerned that I approach its study carefully. He believes that these spells I created could lead to catastrophic outcomes in the wrong hands. He has encouraged me to guard these writings as a mother would her child.

My mentor believes putting thoughts on paper will ease the burden on my mind. Though I've filled this tome with my own spells—spells that I agree no mage should ever possess—my distress comes not from my ruminations, but the intrusive sentiments of those around me that burrow into my consciousness. Sometimes I wish I could silence them all, just for a moment's serenity.

For three years, Mathis has guided me. He gave me control over my domain, and I am genuinely grateful for that. He taught me to endure, even enjoy, existing among the living once again. Another hour scribbling my musings in this tome, and I may even look forward to rejoining the busy world of Jallfoss.

My progress is slow, and I still find a welcome reprieve in the isolation of my family's crypt. Here, the only thoughts in my head are my own. The blank dispositions of my long-dead ancestors have a way of drowning out the noise of the living. Maybe the silence is what draws me here. Perhaps the silence gives me the strength to endure the world's noise.

I can sense that even babies in their mothers' tummies have tiny thoughts. Does Destria know? Should I tell her it's a boy?

—

"Spells that no mage should ever possess . . . should I tell her it's a boy . . ." Stavros read the passages aloud, then closed the ancient tome. A small fire crackled before him, holding back the cool nip that preceded dawn. He could toss the cursed book in the flames and watch as the pages turned to ash. It wasn't the first night he'd contemplated such an act. The Ikritian Emperor ran his fingers over the rough leather. So many memories were trapped in the volume that it hurt to think of parting with the spellbook, though it pained him just as much to keep the damned thing.

A gust of wind rattled the bare branches of the trees around him, hardly masking the rhythmic crunch of his horse lazily chewing the sparse fall grass. Stavros had stopped just before dawn to let his horse graze a few paces off the main road.

This night was clear with a hint of fall chill, enough to keep most travelers home at such a late hour. It was a well-traveled thoroughfare, one of recent upkeep that saw hundreds of merchants, farmers, and craftsmen spread prosperity throughout Ikrit. It was also one of the safest roads in the known world, as Stavros ensured that both bandits and monsters were dealt with severely enough to keep the byways of his kingdom clear of any obstacle that would hinder commerce.

Stavros almost wished for someone to talk to, anything to keep his mind off the sentient undead that had murdered his Acolytes. It was hard for him to forget the skeleton's mind.

Henry was the skeleton's name. His spirit was young and filled with determination. The few seconds of connection left no doubt that the skeleton sought to revive the apparition. Henry acted under his own free will, but the fool couldn't possibly conceive of the catastrophe his actions could create.

Cirilo and his Acolytes had hopefully reached the ghost by now, as the Bastion was much closer to Jallfoss than Ikrit City. Stavros should have been home days earlier had he not taken his time. He should have hurried, as he had important work at the Citadel, but his body was old, and what he needed to do when he got there would require more than a man his age should have to endure. He wanted to say his reluctance to press his horse was because the journey was arduous on his old bones. That was a lie. The life force he'd stolen from Koş, the only Acolyte who had survived the slaughter in Jallfoss, had invigorated him enough to make the trip a dozen times over.

The truth was that Stavros dreaded what he would have to do if Cirilo failed. The Great Lord hoped it wouldn't come to that. Cirilo was alive—that much Stavros knew with certainty, as the Acolyte's Soul Essence had not been transferred to him.

The sun was starting to rise. Stavros could just make out the spires of his capital stretching toward the morning sky like the splayed fingers of Jallfoss's peaks a hundred miles to his back. He put the tome away, mounted his grazing horse, and started the last leg of his journey.

CHAPTER 11

Muji hadn't eaten a lizard in several days, which left him rather cross. Not that he was hungry; plenty of creatures were hiding in the shadows and under broken pieces of wood. Most had beady eyes and sharp teeth. The city creatures were much smaller than Muji, and though they were fast and good at hiding, the trogold found them easy to kill. Crunching their tiny bones wasn't the problem. No, it was their fur. Wiry, dirty, and often full of mites, it stuck in Muji's mouth and left behind a terrible taste. Perhaps they would be more palatable with their fur removed and roasted over the fire, but as the skeletons were preoccupied with the child, there was little for Muji to do but endure his mediocre snacks.

On top of having to eat the furry creatures, Muji had gone far too long without scratches. He'd grown accustomed to the good life of being praised and cuddled whenever he did something cute. Now starved of affection, Muji decided he'd had enough.

The lights had long since dimmed, and the skeletons' campfire was dying down. The undead sat around the waning flames, and the child had lain down and fallen asleep. Muji crept as quietly as he could until he stood just outside the firelight. If he made the right noises and rolled on his back, the lady skeleton would have to oblige him, wouldn't she?

"Beak," Muji chirped softly to avoid waking the child.

"Muji," the Protector whispered, then said a few more quick words. Muji knew his own name, but the other sounds didn't make sense. Sometimes, Muji could get the gist of what the skeletons said based on their movements, especially when they involved magic things. As they were strangely still, the trogold had no idea what they wanted. Fortunately, Muji knew how to get them to move: overwhelming cuteness.

He rolled on his back and chirped, twisting and scooting until he was within reach of the lady skeleton. Instead of giving him scratches, the skeletons only whispered. That was fine. He would just have to up his game.

Muji rolled back to his feet and growled playfully. Then he pounced on the large skeleton's boot, aggressively biting it and clawing with his back feet. Surely that would get a reaction.

Much to Muji's disappointment, the skeletons just whispered a bit louder. Fine, he would pull out all the stops—he would be *annoyingly* cute. He jumped on the Protector's lap and started playing with the crystals in the leather strap. Muji knew he wasn't supposed to play with those, but getting scolded and possibly zapped was way better than being ignored. Muji pulled one of the crystals free. It was charged with fire magic and made his tongue tingle. Instead of getting a response from the undead, the child began to stir and started to wake up.

"Skat," the Protector said in a rather mean voice. Muji knew what that sound meant. He didn't like it, but if that's what the Protector wanted, Muji would reluctantly comply. He ran away before the child opened his eyes, hiding in an alleyway without getting any cuddles.

Frustrated by the strange situation, Muji made himself comfortable in a dark corner and resorted to playing with his harness. He still had the crystal he took from the Protector, but more importantly, he had an idea.

Working carefully, he bit a small hole in one of the harness straps until it was just big enough to fit the crystal snugly. Then, he infused some of his magic into the harness, using the leather as a medium to create a link between the two crystals.

The Drift Amulet and the fire-charged flow crystal contained drastically different types of magic, and Muji could easily tell the spell inside the Amulet was much more powerful. One would think connecting the two wouldn't work, or could potentially be dangerous, but Muji was confident in his artificing . . . even if he wasn't sure exactly what he was making.

Muji directed more of his magic into the connection, carefully metering the flow to prevent damage to the harness. He instinctively knew what he was doing, something all trogolds had in common, though his skills were now on an entirely different level. Before meeting the skeletons, Muji would put all the Vitus he had into any magic things he found, often resulting in the thing breaking or exploding. That was always fun, but now that he'd learned to control his magic, he found that there were better ways to apply magic than all-at-once.

Both crystals began to glow, the fire-charged crystal turning a bright orange and the Drift Amulet radiating blue and red. Energy surged from the Amulet, threatening to overwhelm the weaker fire spell. It started to get very hot and was just about to explode, but with Muji's new expertise in the field of artificing, he knew just what to do. He carefully formed a small magical barrier around the Amulet, making it not quite strong enough to hold the spell entirely. The barrier acted as a metaphysical membrane to meter the Amulet's output.

With the flow in check, an equilibrium formed between the crystals, and both instantly stopped shining. Muji wasn't quite sure what would happen if he tried to use the two crystals in tandem, but he knew it would be much stronger than either alone. That made magic things interesting—they were inherently greater than the aggregate of their individual pieces.

Satisfied with his work, Muji turned his attention to the symbols that appeared and flashed in front of him. Just like the sounds the Protector made, the symbols meant little to Muji, and he quickly dismissed them.

Muji continued to pay with his harness, tweaking the link and adjusting the crystals until he drifted off to sleep. He spent the next day hunting furry creatures and trailing the undead until he followed the skeletons through a bright tunnel. There he found something he never knew existed, and something he instantly hated—the world outside the mountain.

—

"Tiny elf, we must enter that building," Ox grunted as he strained against Jai's spell.

"Why do you want to go in there?" Jai asked, stopping mid-stride. He'd been leading the enchanted skeletons for nearly two days, and only Beast had given heavy resistance against the spell's bonds. Ox seemed to enjoy the constant battles with Ghara's Sprigs, even under the restraints of the Hold spell, so the elf was clearly surprised by Ox's impulse.

"I implore you, tiny elf. Let me go in for but a moment, and I will fight the next battle free of charge!" Ox grunted again as he struggled to move toward a building near the outskirts of another cave city. Daylight shone through a nearby tunnel, allowing Henry to make out the shape of trees on the other side. They had finally reached the exit from Jallfoss's cave cities.

"You should let him go in," Henry said. "He'll wail and lament if he finds a pub without going inside."

Jai shrugged his shoulders. "Fine, Ox. You can go explore."

Ox squealed like a child set free in a candy shop—a large, undead child—and ducked into the building's entrance, loping awkwardly as he trudged ahead, still within the confines of the Hold Undead spell.

"The Nipp and Cuddle," Henry read the sign above the business's entrance. "Emperor Oxendine is drawn to pubs like a moth to flame." It was a large single-story building with no windows. The establishment's name had been chiseled in fancy writing on the stone exterior. Half the name was blackened under a scorch mark, and the rest was outlined with flaking red and white paint.

"Strange name for a bar. Let's get this over with," Beast said.

"Pubs are a center of commerce. We may find something useful here," Buddy proposed.

Jai started walking toward the doorway with Rat close behind. The un-woke skeleton stayed close to Jai like a watchful friend. The boy hadn't used Rat much in combat since the other four were much stronger, but Jai had an easier time getting the mindless skeleton to follow his orders.

Henry, Buddy, and Beast followed. Though still awkward, the elf's control over them had grown sufficiently that the skeletons could obey the blanket command: *stay close*. Even Jai's most recent instruction toward Ox allowed the huge skeleton to venture into the pub nearly under his own will, though his movements were still spastic and unregulated.

As the boy walked, he pointed to the chiseled letters. "There are hundreds of pubs like this inside Jallfoss. You can always tell by the strange names. I used to follow Sentinels on their trips through the cities, and they would often go in for a drink even though Bharat frowns on elves drinking alcohol. One time, I overheard Mayur and Talji talking about this pub's name. Apparently, it's an insult to elves, but I don't understand how."

Inside, they found the burnt remains of what had once likely been a quaint drinking establishment. Wooden floors, wall paneling, and several wooden chairs and tables were charred black and nearly destroyed. In some parts, only the stone structure of the building remained intact. A heavily lacquered bar and a few surrounding wall decorations on the room's far end had mostly avoided destruction, though a mirror in its center was completely smashed. Three skeletons, likely former patrons, stood in watchful silence around the tables and chairs. Jai froze when he saw them. When they didn't react, he proceeded cautiously. The muffle ring that Beast gave him hid the boy's red aura sufficiently to avoid the wrath of the undead, but the young elf was still apprehensive.

Ox was already behind the bar where dozens of bottles were scattered on the floor. He rummaged through shelves and cabinets in search of any preserved stock. "All broken or empty. Something must have survived," Ox muttered as he ripped through solid wood with no more trouble than a normal being would have pushing aside a window's drape.

"The scorch marks are the same as those found in Ammerthall. The further we climb, the worse the fire damage becomes," Henry said aloud as he surveyed the destruction.

Jai ran his fingers over the charred remains of a table. "Bharat says that Lord Livadi's army of fire soldiers was responsible for killing most of the people in the mountain. Once everyone was dead, the army just smoldered until it eventually disappeared like a dying campfire. That was long after Livadi had been cast out of the mountain, and the Necromancer retreated to the dwarven Underdeep."

Henry cringed as he thought about fighting a legion of Acolytes covered in fire. "I wonder how Livadi got enough fire soldiers to kill everyone in the mountain. Buddy, where do you think he found an army like that?"

". . . Buddy?" Henry asked, suddenly aware that the mage had been strangely quiet.

"What? Oh, yes . . . I have a theory, but not enough evidence to arrive at a useful conclusion," Buddy replied, then sank back into his thoughts.

The sound of snapping wooden planks rang through the pub as Ox started pulling up floorboards still in search of alcohol. Henry's Strength was at **21**, which made him twice as strong as a normal person, but with Ox's Strength approaching **100**, the brute could inflict severe damage with little effort.

Beast ignored Ox's rampage and addressed a faded poster on the wall. "What's this?"

The large print depicted a drawing of the Ammerthall coliseum with fancy lettering at the top that read: *The 3,434th Annual Gladiator Supreme Games.* Smaller lettering at the bottom read: *Now open to Ikritian citizens. Featuring the heated rivalry between the Taliskers and the reigning champions, the Bloodbeards.*

"It looks like the whole mountain was enjoying the games when the Necromancer attacked," Henry said. "Those names are familiar. We saw them on bronze plaques in the coliseum."

"I wish I could have seen the games," Jai replied, suddenly animated. He pulled the knife from his belt and slashed it through the air. "From what I've heard, the games were always amazing. The strongest warriors in Jallfoss would battle before cheering crowds of thousands."

Whenever the subject of the arena or the elven Theater came up, the thought of fighting a worthy opponent before a throng of spectators gave Henry an unexpected rush of adrenaline. "What all do you know of the games?"

Jai gave a slight shrug. "Only what I've caught from the stories old elves sometimes tell to pass the time. It started as an actual fight for control of Jallfoss. The winner became the Emperor of the mountain. That didn't last long, however. They realized that the strongest warrior wasn't always the best ruler. The Oxendines took control of the mountain, but the games continued as individual combat that often resulted in death. Over the years, they introduced group combat and a complicated scoring system. The games became an annual contest between factions. Points were allocated through individual and group events. The winning faction always received vast wealth from various merchants and nobles. Most importantly, they got to apply for the royal security division, one of the highest honors available to a warrior."

"How many warriors participated in the contest?" Henry asked.

"Thousands. Anyone from Jallfoss was allowed to enter, though the tournament's first few days always eliminated most of the novices. The middle part of the games were faction events. Everyone had their favorite faction: Hellhounds, Toad Knights, Volkhard Rebels. But the two most popular were the Taliskers and the Bloodbeards.

"The Taliskers were mostly human and were said to be part of an ancient family of warriors. The Bloodbeards were a mixture of several different races. Most of them were brutal mercenaries who spent years fighting in foreign wars. The final contest was always between the two fighters who had emerged from the tournament brackets. It was the most watched and worth the most points because the winner would be named *Gladiator Supreme*. I don't know who won the last contest. The Betrayal happened soon after the final fight, and word of the victor never got to Amera."

Beast unexpectedly offered the boy an account of what they had found in the Ammerthall Arena. "The champion was named William Talisker, at least according to the bronze plates in the Gladiator Supreme chamber."

"Good," Jai said with a smile. "I wish I could have seen it. I knew the Bloodbeard guy had won the previous year. I heard he was a real monster who fought dirty. I remember hearing that William Talisker was one of the youngest faction leaders ever, and his skill with the sword was unmatched by anyone in the world."

A crash of splintering wood and breaking glass rang through the pub. Ox accidentally knocked over the entire bar, and it slammed onto the wooden floor. He didn't acknowledge the demolition as he reached into the newly exposed support beams and lifted a single bottle filled with dark liquid. "Ah ha! I have a nose for treasure. No hidden whiskey can escape me."

Henry eyed the bottle and acknowledged the glyph that hovered over it.

Haruspex

Item: Bulette Trail Whiskey (Superior)

Description: Consumable. This rare vintage whiskey from the distant land of Begard is made from corn and rye. It is named after the bulette, a ravenous armored creature that once roamed freely through the lands the distillery and surrounding farmland now occupy. Though only aged for five years in blackhedge barrels, the warm, humid climate of Begard allows for quick maturation. ACU -1, PER -1, RES +2

The bottle in Ox's hand had a faded label with fancy writing in a language Henry didn't understand, and the top was sealed with wax. Ox suddenly stopped moving, freezing in place with the bottle still displayed for the group to see. "It appears I'm done investigating," the giant skeleton said.

Henry realized that Jai only told Ox that he could explore, so when Ox found the whiskey, the spell decided that was the end of the order and ceased to allow him to move further.

Being held in place didn't stop Ox from talking. "Fine whiskey is meant to be drunk in good company. The outcome of the next battle is never certain, and an enemy can't enjoy an empty bottle. Tiny elf, you may join us in a toast. Herbie is our best bartender, so please order him to pour us all a round."

"I . . . um—" Jai stammered before Beast cut him off.

"You will not give whiskey to a child, you idiot. You got what you wanted, now let's get moving," she snapped.

"The boy is on a quest, and a quest always starts in a pub," Ox countered.

Henry heard an angry growl emanate from Beast, so he decided to interject before the tensions escalated. "I feel like I couldn't properly enjoy our last drink at the Jolly Squid. Why don't we save it for when we get our bodies and tongues back?"

"Very well, Hank. This bottle is probably far too valuable to pour down a skeleton's gullet. We shall enjoy it after we rescue the mountain."

With Ox satisfied, Jai led them from the pub and toward the exit tunnel. The sun had changed its angle enough that it wasn't so bright. Henry could now clearly see a pine forest and barely make out mountain tops in the distance.

"This leads to Amera, the elven valley where we'll face the

Sentinels. With five skeletons by my side, I know I can convince them to join me." Jai's words carried confidence, but his voice wavered with uncertainty.

"Four skeletons," Henry said, bluntly.

Jai gave Henry a puzzled look. "But I have five of you."

"Rat isn't alive. You shouldn't bring him with us."

"I can give him a Drift Amulet, and then he'll come back to life like you," Jai offered.

Buddy dismissed Jai's claim in a solemn tone. "The Drift Amulets didn't give us life. They only transfer the Soul Essence from another being. We're only alive because someone else died."

Jai looked at Rat but didn't respond. Henry could tell the boy had grown attached to the skeleton, so he tried to explain the situation. "Rat would have to kill someone to bring himself back to life. We've only seen it work with humans. We don't know if it works with other races, animals, or monsters."

"There's no other way to bring him back?" Jai asked.

"Maybe there is. We won't know until we revive the Empress. We're doing this to save all the undead in the mountain."

Jai considered Henry's words for a long moment, then nodded. "Once we defeat Ghara, I promise I'll help you wake up Lady Destria. Lord Rattlebones saved my life several times. It's the least I can do for him."

"I'm glad *Lord Rattlebones* has your eternal gratitude," Beast said with a grumble.

Jai started to respond to Beast, but instead turned to Rat and gave his orders. "Rat, go back into the pub and wait. I'll return after we save the mountain."

The skeleton immediately turned and walked back to the entrance of the Nipp and Cuddle. Jai watched Rat follow the order, then the boy turned and started walking toward the exit tunnel. "Alright, Guard. Let's go!"

"On with the quest!" Ox shouted as the four skeletons followed Jai out of Jallfoss and into the elven valley.

CHAPTER 12

Muji quickly concluded that the world outside the mountain was terrible. Everything was covered in several inches of a strange substance—*snow*, he overheard the skeletons calling it. That was another word for Muji to hate.

The snow was like dirt, but white, and wet, and . . . cold. It hurt Muji's fingers and toes, and the trogold sank into the powdery substance with every step. It clung to his fur and made him regret following the skeletons from his warm, comfortable caves.

To make matters worse, the single sun globe in the high blue ceiling was much too bright. Being used to navigating in the dark caves of the Underdeep with little more than the dim lumimoss, the brightness hurt his eyes and made hiding much harder.

One part about the outside world Muji did like was the trees—tall and brown with rough exteriors that made them easy to climb. He'd found something like them in one of the caves deep in the mountain, but there were thousands of trees in the outside world. Most were close enough together that Muji could travel across their larger branches, making it much easier to follow the skeletons high above the wretched snow.

Muji sprang from a tree branch and landed heavily on another, steadying himself by digging clawed fingers and toes into the rough bark. Before he could launch forward again, the swish of pine needles from a nearby branch caught Muji's attention. A small, fluffy creature with a twitching tail looked at him and chittered. Muji let out a growl and gave chase.

To Muji's surprise, the small creature easily evaded his pounce. In a flash, it was high above him on another branch, chattering aggressively and taunting the trogold.

"Beak!" Muji retorted and leaped after the creature again. Before he arrived at his target, the creature had already retreated to a further branch.

Muji bent his legs and prepared for another attack but quickly stopped himself in an impressive display of self-control. Even though he was much faster and stronger than before, Muji realized there was no way for him to catch the creature. It could run around the trees much more deftly, and the tiny branches that couldn't possibly support Muji easily held the little creature's weight, giving it several escape paths that weren't available to Muji.

He refused to let the tiny tree dweller get the best of him. He was a mighty trogold, who could defeat any enemy. Besides, Muji had been waiting for the perfect opportunity to test his harness.

He focused the energy between the two flow crystals, taking the flame aspect of one and mixing it with the soul-targeting properties of the other. The Drift Amulet was too powerful to use directly, but Muji had figured out how to use the Siphon Ability to alter the discharge of the flame crystal. Such a use would quickly drain the flame crystal of its stored magic, rendering the array useless until Muji either got it recharged or replaced it with another evocation-type flow crystal.

The crystals' magic combined with Muji's, building until a small sphere of flame appeared just in front of the trogold. Then, he focused on his target and felt the Drift Amulet's magic lock onto the creature.

Sensing that something was happening, the creature halted its chattering and scurried behind the nearest tree trunk, peaking its head around the side and resuming its mockery.

Perfect, that was precisely what Muji wanted. Muji released the magic, and the flaming sphere zipped forward. The creature jumped behind the tree to avoid the attack, but the tiny flame altered its course and arched directly at its target. When the magic sphere reached the tree trunk, it shot straight through, completely unhindered, and impacted the creature, immediately setting it ablaze and launching it from its perch. It was dead before it hit the snow with a quenching *hiss*.

Muji sprang from the tree and landed in the snow, not even caring about the cold and wet, and bounded through it to get to his prize. He found the creature's burnt body and chomped down excitedly. The meat was juicy and delicious, and the flame had burnt off most of the fur.

Muji was quite proud of himself, not only for the successful encounter with the tree creature but also for modifying his harness to allow him to combine aspects of variously enchanted flow crystals. In this case, he had gotten the flame spell to lock onto and track the soul of his target, completely ignoring anything tangible except for the annoying creature. The Protector would be very proud of Muji's accomplishment, and the trogold was excited to show off his creation . . . whenever the skeletons were finished playing with the child.

Finishing his meal, Muji examined his harness and found enough magic in the fire-charged crystal for two, maybe three more attacks. Unfortunately, he couldn't recharge it himself and would need the Protector for that. More importantly, the skeletons would likely need him and his newly improved magic to help them.

Speaking of the undead, where are they? Muji wondered as he realized he'd gotten lost while chasing the tree creature. He climbed the nearest tree, happy to get back out of the snow, and began searching for his lost skeletons.

—

Jacoby found that fighting in fresh-packed snow was much harder than on the cobblestone paths and sandy streets of the cities in Jallfoss. His boots slid in the powder, and his frozen fingers barely maintained their grip on the cold hilt of his blade.

The possum Sprig screeched and lunged at him. Jacoby lifted his forearm and jammed his iron bracer into its mouth. A few yellow teeth broke, but many more pierced the metal and dug into muscle. Jacoby drove his sword deep into the monster's torso, though the creature twisted at the last second and avoided a fatal thrust.

"Use Auric Palisade!" Talji shouted. It sounded like she was cheering for him.

He focused his Vitus into the sword and let magic erupt from the chipped blade. Golden magic wrapped around his weapon and tore into the Sprig with a quick slice. Jacoby could hear flesh sizzle as his spell melted through the monster. It screeched again and bit down harder. Jacoby twisted his sword, and the tainted possum died, releasing its bite and slumping to the ground.

Tainted Possum Killed, Soul Essence Claimed

Just before the fight, Jacoby told Talji the name of his Ability. He was grateful that the elf could allow him to use magic, but also that she chose to employ his Ability before he suffered further damage.

With the battle over and no further orders to follow, Jacoby stood in a mixture of snow, dirt, and black Sprig blood. His heavy breathing quickly calmed.

"Not bad for a human." Talji's soft voice floated like a schmetterflueg on a gentle breeze. Those were the kindest words she'd said to Jacoby so far, until she added, "Not bad at all, for a filthy savage."

There it is.

"You're getting better, Talji. I've never seen any Sentinel able to activate magical Abilities through their Guard," Lata said. She and Surat stood beside Talji and watched the entire scene, just as they had all the previous fights. They hadn't yet lifted a finger to assist him.

"This connection is strange," Talji said. "It's simple, almost effortless to Hold him. I could bear a hundred like him with my Command Link. However, now that I have control, it's taking all my mental energy to compel him, even with the simplest order."

"You mean it's exactly the opposite of normal undead that are easy to command, but we can only Hold three or four at a time. Why do you think that is?" Surat wondered.

The elves were behind him, so their red aura didn't affect Jacoby. That didn't stop real anger from welling in his mind. He hated being under Talji's control, and with every fight and every dismissive comment, his discontent only grew.

"It's his mind. Because he has thoughts, it's much easier for me to gain a foothold on his psyche. However, I must wade through those thoughts to get him to do anything. With normal undead, holding them is like laying siege to a castle. You have to fight through soldiers and batter down the portcullis to gain entry, but once you get inside, the hardest part of the battle is over, and you can easily take control. It's the opposite with this dirty human. The front door is open, but all the soldiers are standing guard inside, just waiting to fight back against my every move."

"Is he resisting?" Lata's words took on a dangerous tone, and Jacoby imagined her sneering as she asked the question.

Jacoby didn't hear Talji's steps, but the red blaze of her aura immediately caught his attention as the elf moved into his view.

Status Effect Resisted: Enraged Dismissed

"Are you resisting me, human? Do you think you're anything more than my subject?" Talji looked into his eyes, inches from his face. She squinted just enough to make tiny lines form on her perfect skin.

The question loosened Jacoby's tongue, allowing him to respond to the elf's query. "Try restraining me with your hands instead of your magic, and you'll see how much I can resist."

The elf moved so fast that even if Jacoby could have reacted, he wouldn't have been able to stop the strike. She hit him hard enough that Jacoby felt molars shatter and his eardrum rupture. He didn't care about the damage—the resurrection Effect would heal him quickly enough. He was just satisfied knowing that he got a reaction.

Despite the heavy blow, Jacoby kept his eyes locked on Talji's. Even through the pain, the ringing in his ear, and the rage induced from her aura, Jacoby couldn't deny the woman's beauty. That made him despise the elf even more.

Talji smirked a wicked grin, and the tip of her pink tongue

danced behind her teeth. "I would cut out your tongue if I didn't have further need for it." Then she shouted to the other elves. "Lata, Surat, let's move."

CHAPTER 13

Countless dead Sprigs and broken skeletons lay scattered around the three Master Acolytes. One final tainted monster charged the group. It galloped like a horse and had thick, powerful limbs, standing nearly eight feet at the shoulder. Horns jutted from a sleek skull that sat on broad shoulders. The monster had to weigh over a ton and was covered in rough black and green plates. Its hooves looked like the gnarled roots of a pesimelli tree, and it gained speed quickly as it approached. Black flesh sprayed like fountains under the monster's feet, its charge crushing the mangled corpses of its fellow Sprigs.

Tainted Barrow Yak, Eudora read as the monster thundered toward them. The Sprig locked its black eyes on her Commander, Master Acolyte Cirilo, and lowered its horns to skewer the offending human. Her first instinct was to launch a volley of summoned weapons at the Sprig, but that wasn't necessary. The foolish monster had chosen to attack one of the most powerful warriors Ikrit had ever produced.

Cirilo's sword was as long as a normal-sized door and half as wide. The solid sheet of metal weighed more than the man himself, but the Commander cocked it back with a single hand like its bulk was no more than a kitchen knife. The tainted yak lowered its horns and lunged for the kill. Cirilo bent his legs, then shot forward. Eudora's Perception was high, but she barely caught her Commander's movement. She only heard the impact of the sword on the plated carapace and saw the explosion of gore spewing like waves in Cirilo's wake.

The Commander stopped thirty feet from where he had begun his thrust, with his massive sword extended in front of him like the ornament on the world's most deadly weathervane. Not a drop of black ichor was on the Acolyte, though the buildings on either side of the street were painted with the remains of the tainted yak.

Cirilo calmly turned his head to either side. Satisfied that no more enemies remained, he hefted his greatsword over his shoulder and started walking back toward Eudora and Mersin.

Seeing that the battle was done, Eudora began gathering her gear. She held a large glaive made of Boromite steel, and dozens of weapons were scattered around her. With a wave of her hand, swords, axes, spears, and several other summoned weapons vanished from the battlefield and returned to the storage vault in the Bastion, hundreds of miles away.

"Disgusting . . ." Mersin said, flinging Sprig blood from his hands. His aversion to being dirty, his high-pitched voice, and small stature would have made Eudora laugh if she hadn't been aware of how deadly the Acolyte could be. Because the man fought with his bare hands, he usually ended up covered in his enemies' blood after every battle. The man rarely employed weapons, as his limbs were more effective than most warriors with any blade. He wore light leather armor and sported a thin black beard, with a leather cap covering his bald head.

Eudora retrieved a flow crystal from a pouch at her waist and tossed it to Mersin. "Here, I have a few extras."

Mersin caught it and immediately activated the magic within. A mixture of wind, water, earth, and just a small amount of fire magic swirled around him, exfoliating the grime from his body. "Thank you. I never seem to bring enough."

Eudora nodded, then looked around the cavern city. They'd been traveling upward through the mountain for days. She hadn't spent much time in the upper caverns, having transferred to the infantry shortly after completing her training as a Junior Acolyte. Now that she was responsible for teaching Junior Acolytes of her own, she would need to learn everything she could about the mountain's layout and the myriad dangers within.

The city they were currently in was smaller than most others, but they'd followed winding tunnels and fought their way through so many city-caverns that Eudora wasn't sure exactly where they were. A quarter mile ahead, she could see three tunnels that led out of the city. Two had white writing over the top, but the tunnel on the right was surrounded by red marks, indicating danger.

"Which one of those are we taking?" Eudora asked.

Mersin let out a squeal that barely passed as a laugh. "Obviously not the *right* one, Master Eudora."

"Why is that?"

Cirilo stopped his approach within a few paces of Eudora and Mersin. He took a short swig of water from his flask, then chinned toward the tunnels. "That exit is marked to prevent you from accidentally entering *the Lair*." He lowered his tone and drew out the last words.

Eudora's eyes widened. "So, that's where the Fiends live? I remember hearing about them in my training. I don't recall much, except that they're best avoided by all but the strongest Acolytes."

"They're not much of a threat to us, but any Acolyte below Tier **20** should not enter their city. Still, the danger they could pose to our mission isn't worth the risk."

"Can simple skeletons really present that much danger?" Eudora wondered aloud.

Mersin snorted again. "They're unique skeletons, much like the three on the Ammerthall level. However, the problem with them is threefold. First, they are still equipped with potent magical gear that we haven't managed to strip from them. Second, even if we manage to kill one, they somehow work together to protect each other. Finally, the layout of their cavern is mostly vertical, making it nearly impossible to hide from them or gain any sort of tactical ground. If you ever take your Acolytes this far, you should avoid the Liar at all costs. Too many have died trying to conquer the Fiends and take their gear."

Eudora pursed her lips, disappointed not to test her mettle against more powerful enemies, but ever mindful of the wise Mersin's warning. "Noted. Back to the task at hand. Are we getting close?"

"No, the cave cities of Jallfoss are not convenient for quick travel."

"Is there another way, like the switchback pass that takes merchants around the range and directly to Amera?" she asked.

Cirilo finished draining his flask and placed it back in his pack. "No, that would add a week to our trip. We could go for one of the exits to Amera and follow the elven valley to the Empress, but that would take us almost as far out of the way. This is the fastest path. We won't leave the mountain caves until we're ready to transition to the highest peak."

Eudora lowered her head in a slight bow. "Forgive my

ignorance, Commander, but I don't completely understand what we're doing? I know we're going to the Empress's ghost. I've heard of her suspended beauty, but why must we protect her from the skeletons? I was told that no magic or weapon could affect her."

"Stavros spoke to Koş just before the boy died. Our Emperor learned that the skeletons have returned to life and are headed to kill the Empress's ghost. 'She is the only thing holding back the Necromancer. You must stop them at all costs,' he told me before ordering me to gather my team and head out immediately."

"How does he know that? Just based on a Junior Acolyte's tale?"

Mersin shook a finger at Eudora and gave her a stern warning. "You would be wise not to question the Great Lord. Even in his old age, his power is beyond your comprehension."

Eudora bowed further. "I apologize, Commander. I only sought to understand so that I may better serve."

Cirilo gives her a warm smile. "No offense has been taken. Mersin asserts that Lord Stavros's knowledge of the workings of this mountain far exceeds our own understanding. We must trust in his guidance."

"I trust his guidance, but how does a man know such things? I know the former Emperor, Livadi, tried to save the mountain from the Necromancer a hundred years ago. Does that have something to do with our mission?"

Cirilo gave Mersin a knowing smile. "Tell me, Master Eudora, what do you know of our nation's history?"

The question caught Eudora off guard, and she did her best to recount the lessons from her youth. "Well, for most of its existence, the vast plain we now call Ikrit was a collective of small farming towns. Anytime a settlement got too big, Varanasi would invade, plunder the harvest and livestock, and kill everyone. Ikrit was founded several hundred years ago when the first Emperor, Efendi, unified the plane and repelled the Varanasi. He organized farmers into a defensive force that picked apart the invaders over many years until he finally pushed them out, establishing the entire plain as the nation of Ikrit. We've been in different states of war with the Varanasi ever since. The Emperors of Ikrit established trade with other nations, developed our infrastructure, and took steps that led to prosperity. All the while, the greedy Varanasi slowly weakened, finally culminating in our most recent war and subsequent victory. Stavros completed the task that Efendi began all those years ago."

Cirilo nodded as she spoke. "Much of Ikrit's history has been omitted. It's not surprising; we were farmers for thousands of years before we became famous as scholars, probably before the first dwarves sank their picks into this very mountain. The Varanasi raids left the farmers struggling to survive. They had little time to create vectors of knowledge. Civilization, and with it, record keeping, started with Efendi. That's where the written account of our history began. The Ikritian Emperors have always been driven by a quest for knowledge, likely resulting from the lack of documentation before Efendi's time. One of the first things he did after chasing out the Varanasi was establish the Citadel and begin filling it with the world's collective knowledge. What you may not know is that Lord Stavros is a direct descendant of Efendi, as were all the subsequent Ikritian rulers."

Eudora gave him a confused look, allowing Mersin to comment. "A little wine and a post-battle fire does wonders to loosen the tongue."

"What Mer—" Cirilo started to say, but his voice caught in

his throat. He began coughing and nearly dropped to a knee. Eudora moved to offer assistance, but the Commander held up a hand and righted himself. "I must have caught a bug down the wrong pipe." He cleared his throat and continued his thoughts. "What Mersin means is that we've spent much time, years, in my case, by the Great Lord's side. He's told us much about his family."

Eudora knew it would take more than a bug to cause Cirilo to falter. She'd heard stories of the man fighting his way through a nest of ice mephits and coming out unscathed. What concerned her more was the tiny trickle of blood that now sat at the corner of her Commander's mouth. She pushed away the concern and instead addressed Cirilo's comment. "That explains Stavros's thirst for knowledge and adventure, but I still don't understand his obsession with Jallfoss."

"Jallfoss is more than a training ground for our Acolytes— it symbolizes Livadi's only failure. Ikrit and Jallfoss had just become allies, and Livadi was in the mountain for the Gladiator Supreme games as a special guest of Lady Destria. When the Necromancer attacked, Livadi was one of the few who made it out alive. Despite all his power, he couldn't save the mountain. Livadi made it his mission to reclaim Jallfoss, and Stavros took up that banner when he became Emperor. Neither of them could ever overcome the evils that lurk in the mountain, especially when the threat from Varanasi loomed at our doorstep." Cirilo tugged on a chain around his neck and pulled his Amulet from below his armor, clearly displaying the dark **44** on its surface.

Eudora knew that every Tier was exponentially more challenging to gain than the last, and with each level came a tremendous amount of power. There was much more to one's clout than Tiers alone, but the fact that her Commander had reached such a high number indicated that the man was likely one of the strongest beings ever to live.

Cirilo continued. "The flow crystals we collect from Jallfoss and the Soul Essence we Acolytes gain through Stavros's Drift Amulets have been enough to make Ikrit the most powerful nation in the known world over the last hundred years."

Eudora listened intently but was still taken aback by the revelation that all Ikritian rulers came from a single lineage. It was rare for such knowledge to be imparted, even to a Master Acolyte, so she pressed for more. "Where did Efendi come from? Was he a powerful wizard from a faraway place? And why is it not common knowledge that Stavros is related to the first Emperor?"

Cirilo smiled and shrugged his shoulders. "As far as I know, Lord Efendi was just a simple farmer. Stavros said he had more magic than a normal person, but it was his drive to protect the weak that led him to greatness. That drive persisted through his progeny, with every generation becoming stronger and stronger sorcerers. They kept the knowledge of that lineage silent to prevent it from being exploited by the Varanasi."

"I always knew that the Emperor named his successor, but I didn't realize they had all been a family. I assumed Lord Stavros would name either you or Commander Alicos . . ." she trailed off.

"A bold assumption, Master Eudora," Mersin chirped, giving her a stern look.

"Bold, yes, but a fair question," Cirilo said. "Though our Emperor is aged, Stavros's mind is sharper than any blade. He will be around for several more years. Livadi never had children, so he passed the throne to his nephew, Stavros, who is the last of their line. Stavros will name his successor, but Commander Alicos would be a good choice to carry on Efendi's legacy.

Regardless, I will serve whomever Stavros chooses to the best of my abilities."

"Why did Livadi and Stavros never have children?" Eudora asked.

"Love and loss affect us all differently," Mersin replied. Eudora gave the man an angry look. Though he was several years her senior, she was getting tired of his cryptic interjections.

Cirilo was much more open to answering her questions. "The Great Lord and I are very close. Even so, I only know what he chose to tell me. Sometimes those with the weight of responsibility feel they don't deserve the simple happiness a loving spouse and a child's laughter can bring to one's soul."

"So, our Emperors are an increasingly powerful line of mages that will end with Lord Stavros?"

"As far as I am aware, yes. You know many of the famous sorcerers that Ikrit has produced, but you're probably unaware that, like our Emperors, most also come from Efendi's lineage." Cirilo started waving his massive sword around as he recounted the tales of Ikritian heroes. "Emir the Just was the only known man to look a basilisk in the eye and survive. If you believe the stories, he held its gaze until the monstrosity submitted to his will and became his thrall. You can find multiple volumes dedicated to his many heroic deeds in the upper spires of the Citadel.

"There is also Haşim the Vengeful. Two centuries ago, he destroyed an entire legion of Varanasi Centurions. The blast was so powerful that it created a hole in the earth that later filled with water and became the great lake Çaraso. He died in the process, but it took the Varanasi several decades to recover."

"You can't leave out Sorcerer Exalt, Mathis, the most powerful evoker to ever live. Entire universities worldwide are dedicated solely to his theories on magic." Mersin had been apathetic to the conversation up to that point, but now his voice held a tinge of elation. Eudora was aware of Mersin's great admiration for the mages of times long passed, especially the famed Sorcerer, Mathis.

"Wait, Stavros and Mathis are related?" Eudora asked, her eyes growing wide and matching Mersin's excitement. She had always been fascinated with the great mage, long before she knew of Mersin's regard for the sorcerer. Though she specialized in conjuration, she had always dreamed of attending one of his schools.

Cirilo nodded. "Distantly, but yes. Mathis was the only sorcerer in our history, in the history of the known world, who was possibly stronger than Stavros. That claim is based on the power Stavros displayed at the battle of Duşon Bay, forty years ago. Our Great Lord's prowess has grown by fathoms since then."

Eudora thought for a long moment before she asked, "Is Stavros truly that strong?"

Cirilo gave Eudora a look that told her the claim was no embellishment. "I've seen the man perform feats so vast that even the young gods themselves would marvel at his power."

CHAPTER 14

Jai picked at singed hairs on his forearms. Crispy bits pulled against his skin and looked like tiny gnats under the flickering light of the campfire. The ground below him was wet, but like the hair on his arms and eyebrows, the dead vegetation that had once been under a foot of snow was now nearly burnt away. Perhaps using Buddy's magic to start a campfire wasn't the greatest idea.

"My evocation is not a toy, nor is it to be used for convenience." This wasn't the first time Buddy cautioned Jai about haphazardly employing the mage's craft. Fortunately for them all, only Ox had suffered wayward blasts of various elements.

"I know that, but starting a fire with wet wood takes forever. It's almost morning, and I wanted warm food to help start the day." Jai put a handful of sticks on the tiny blaze.

"You still had to start it with flint, and now anyone near knows exactly where we are," Henry warned.

Ox chimed in. "Let them come, it's been several minutes since our last fight, and I'm getting bored. Besides, Herbie, this was nothing compared to what Barney's magic did to the ramps." Buddy's jaw was set in a stern scowl, and he didn't respond.

Jai smiled, happy to have Ox's support. "Buddy is right, his magic is too difficult for me to control. Even Beast is too hard to command in a real fight, but in a different way. I'll just stick to Ox and Henry until I gain a few more Tiers in the Hold Undead Ability." A chunk of wood shifted, and a bout of embers rose on the heated air current and spun high above them.

Jai followed the embers with his eyes and scanned the expanse above him. He pulled a stick from the fire and pointed the still-burning end at twin moons. "You're lucky. It's a clear sky, and you'll be able to see all four. You can look."

"Four moons? What are their names?" Henry asked, turning his head upward after Jai's go-ahead.

Jai gave Henry a curious expression. "I have to remind myself that your memories are fuzzy. You know so much about certain subjects, but very little about others."

The elf turned his attention back to the sky. "Bharat taught us that each moon is one of the young gods that ascended from this world after their wars. The white one is called Ezerath, and the blue one is Golos. The other two moons should be rising shortly in that direction." Jai pointed to the horizon. "You'll see the red one first. Its name is Heraclion and is much slower than the others. Shortly after the sun rises, the orange moon, Sereph, just slightly faster than Heraclion, will start its journey, catching the red moon just as the two hit the far horizon."

Henry listened intently to the boy's description. "This is the first you've mentioned any god besides Ghara. As adamant about religion as the elves are, it surprises me to hear you talk about other deities."

"Bharat taught us about the other young gods and their failings so we could identify their shortcomings in ourselves and avoid their influence. It's not that the young gods are evil; they are just immature and misguided. They're not pure . . . like Ghara," Jai explained.

"So, there are five gods in this . . . world . . . where are we exactly?" Henry wondered aloud.

Jai laughed. "It must be hard not having your memories. There are eight young gods, and the world around us is called Rahka. A human farmer taught me the Ikritian word for it, but it was an ugly word, and I can't remember how to pronounce it. He taught me lots of other words, mostly ones that you're not supposed to say unless you're mad . . . or if you're talking to your wife, whatever that means."

"You should never speak to a woman with inappropriate words," Beast muttered.

"What if a young lady enjoys such words?" Ox asked in a coy tone.

Jai scrunched his eyebrows at Beast and Ox's banter, unsure what the two were getting at, and returned to his explanation. "There are also hundreds of other religions, but Bharat says they're all idol-worshiping savages."

Buddy also chose to ignore Beast and Ox. "Eight. That matches Thorodd's account. Jai, what can you tell us about the young gods?"

"That's easy," Jai said, flashing a smile. "I've had to listen to Bharat preach about them my whole life. I can tell you everything you'll ever need to know about the young gods."

"Please, enlighten us."

Jai didn't hesitate to show off his knowledge. "In the beginning, Jallfoss created the world, and from it grew a giant tree. From that tree sprouted Jallfoss's children, the eight young gods. Seven were disobedient and left their father. Stricken with loneliness, Jallfoss's tears rained down and mixed with the dirt, becoming all the plants and animals of the world. He ultimately died of sorrow. Ghara was the only one of his children who stayed to watch over her father's body as her seven brothers and sisters spread across world. Ultimately, three stayed here on Rahka, including Ghara. Four became the moons, and one left completely.

"The first child was Veletos. He was lazy. He spoke slowly and liked to sleep all day. He kept walking downhill until he could go no further. Then he lay down, and his body became the oceans. Bharat hates people who live on the water's edge, using boats and nets to catch giant fish instead of grabbing them by hand like elves do in rivers and streams. I don't care what the Sage thinks, I love hearing stories about giant boats made of trees that float people on top of the water and carry adventurers to distant lands. I hope to visit the ocean one day.

"Aside from Ghara and Veletos, the only other god that stayed on Rahka was Zuriel. She lurks in the shadows, stealing gold and hoarding it for herself. No amount of wealth can satisfy her thirst for what others possess. Her followers are thieves and tyrants who prey on the weak."

"That doesn't match any god or Primal that Thorodd spoke about," Henry said. "I wonder if there's a connection that we're missing?"

Buddy never missed an opportunity to comment on the denizens of the Underdeep. "Most dwarves only care about their machines. It doesn't surprise me that they would have conflicting knowledge of religions. Fortunately for their race, certain dwarves possess a poise and elegance which redeems the others."

Jai continued. "Bharat doesn't speak of the dwarves often, but when he does, it's usually derogatory. Most of his sermons are about how our lack of faith keeps Ghara in her corrupted state, and only by shunning the faults of the other young gods can we restore her. He especially likes to talk about the four gods who left Rahka. Sometimes they were allies, and sometimes they were enemies, but the wars they fought with each other ravaged the world.

"The first is Ezerath. He was considered the strongest god, but that power made him pity all other beings. Most of the humans in Jallfoss worshiped Ezerath, including the Oxendines, but many also followed his brother. Heraclion was a giant serpent with bat-like wings and huge, vicious claws." Jai splayed his fingers and growled, his excitement growing as he told the story. "He couldn't control his fury. He spewed fire from his mouth and almost destroyed Rahka. His rage led to most of the wars between him and Ezerath."

"The third god, Sereph, took to the sky on golden, feathered wings. He was the most beautiful of all the gods, but even so, he was jealous of Ezerath and Heraclion's power. He never earned the glory or prestige of his elder brothers, but he cobbled together his followers from the aftermath of destruction. Those who worship him are among the rulers of the world's most prosperous and dangerous nations.

"And finally, there was Golos. He was mean and sullen, and was said to be bigger than the largest mountain. He would eat and eat, until there was nothing left to consume, then he would conquer another place, just to eat it as well."

"How does anything exist after such terrible gods ravaged the world?" Henry asked.

Jai shrugged his shoulders. "Ghara pleaded with them to stop. She spoke with such love for the world that all their hearts broke. They saw the evil of their ways and begged the world to forgive them. The lesser beings of Rahka obliged, and the weight of their crimes lifted from their souls. The four gods became lighter than air and ascended into the sky. They transformed into the four moons, forever watching over the world they had nearly destroyed."

"That's only seven," Beast remarked, urging the young elf to continue.

Jai nodded, proud that Beast had been following his account. "The last young god was Solaire. She was actually the first to leave Jallfoss. It's said that she fell in love with the sun and flew toward it, never turning back to the family she had left behind. Bharat says that her followers worship debauchery and lewd behavior, but I haven't been able to get anyone to explain to me what that means."

"A child is not ready for such exposure," Beast said bluntly.

Buddy sighed before responding. "The four moons correspond to the Primals that Thorodd told us about. Ezerath goes with the celestials—Heraclion, the dragons. Sereph most likely begot the archons, and Golos was a giant. The fifth group of Primals is the spriggans, which link with Ghara. Thorodd mentioned that Veletos went to the bottom of the ocean, and Solaire went to the stars. That only leaves the Raven . . ."

"Zuriel . . . ?" Henry wondered aloud.

Jai opened a pouch on his belt and placed a few round nuts near the outside part of the campfire. "I told you all about my friend, Mayur. He and I used to eat moosel nuts together, and he would tell me stories about my sister. We'd talk about the gods and what Jallfoss was like before the Necromancer killed everyone inside. Mayur was the only high elf who was ever nice to me. He's dead now, but I hope I can make him proud."

Jai threw another stick on the fire and took a deep breath. "Anyway, dragons and giants are just monsters. We worship Ghara because she stayed to comfort her father in his time of need, and she saved the world from the wars of her siblings. We must emulate her if there's any hope of her boon returning."

Buddy replied, "I was not questioning your beliefs, merely remarking on the similarities between dwarven archives and elven religion."

While they talked, the first rays of sunlight began to touch the highest tips of the great pine trees. The previous day, with the remaining daylight, they had traveled a few miles through pine forests before setting up camp in an elevated spot. With the lightening sky and a decent vantage point, Henry could see the snow-covered forest stretching to another mountain range dozens of miles away.

To Henry's far left and right, along the ridges of Jallfoss, he saw huge bouts of steam rising into the air. *Those must be from the air-circulating systems that turned on with the dwarven forges,* Henry thought. The swirling air masses were much larger than Henry expected, but it made sense if it was designed to service a mountain nation of hundreds of thousands.

"Welcome to the high valley, home of the forest elves . . . Amera," Jai said with pride as the horizon began to brighten.

Compared to the dim light of the sun globes and drab stone that made up the tunnels and cities of Jallfoss, the scene before him was breathtaking. White snow, pure and untouched, blanketed the forests and meadows before them. The mountains just past the treetops failed to hold back the rising sun. "Another mountain range?" Henry asked.

"Yes, the valley lies between two ranges. Though that one is much smaller than Jallfoss, the mountains continue toward dawn for several hundred miles before they meet the ocean."

"It's gorgeous," Beast said, just above a whisper. Henry couldn't argue. After spending all his life that he could remember underground, the pine forest was a stark contrast to the dwarven Underdeep.

"It's home," Jai replied.

In the city where Jai had captured Henry and the others, sunlight came from a tunnel entrance. Instead of using that exit, Jai had elected to take the skeletons through Jallfoss for several more days. The boy stated that no regular elves, and only the occasional group of Sentinels, ventured into Jallfoss. Staying inside the mountain was their best bet at keeping the skeletons secret for as long as possible.

Jai's control had grown substantially over the two days of travel through the mountain, and he even learned to give Henry a bit of free rein, though he couldn't automate Henry's Abilities without a direct order. Jai shied away from using Buddy and Beast, since the boy hadn't learned to control either without severely damaging everything in the vicinity. Buddy's spells were uncontrollable, usually flinging random magic blasts everywhere. Luckily, only Ox had been on the receiving end of one such uncontrollable attack.

"This is your last chance to turn back, Jai. Once they see you with us, you'll have no choice but to move forward with your plan," Henry advised, wondering if Jai would release them so they could proceed to the Empress.

Jai hesitated for a second, then said, "I know. I've already made up my mind. There will be a few Sentinels training in the arena, and several forest elves watching them. Word will spread quickly when I show up with you and issue my challenge."

"You plan to fight anyone who shows up? Then what? They join you, and we all go together to battle Ghara? That's the dumbest strategy I've ever heard." Beast scolded Jai, but the boy gave her a defiant look in return.

"It's the best plan I've got. You're the strongest beings I've ever seen, and I'm getting much better at controlling you. My Hold Undead Ability is at Tier **2**. If I can get it to Tier **3**, I should be able to control Buddy's magic and your temper."

"We'd be far stronger if we weren't under the spell," Beast replied with a grumble, but there was a resignation in her voice that said she was done trying to persuade the boy.

"That's true," Jai admitted, "but I must learn to control you if I want to become a Sentinel."

Henry couldn't blame the boy. Jai saw a chance in the skeletons to correct a wrong in the elven world, and he was taking a considerable risk to see it through. However, the boy was replacing his faith in his own Abilities with that of Henry and the others. "Jai, you said that Sentinels existed long before the Betrayal?" Henry asked.

"As far back as elven memory goes."

"Until the last century, the Sentinels never had a Guard— your sister never had a Guard. If I knew anything about elven warrior classes, I've forgotten the knowledge. However, from what you're telling me, it's not the Guard that makes the Sentinel."

Jai was silent for several moments. He pulled a few moosel nuts from the fire and set them on a rock beside him to cool. Eventually, he said, "Mayur used to say the same thing. Though he was one of the Sentinels in Talji's group, he was like a big brother to me. I took his Drift Amulet and circlet after he died. He always encouraged me to get better. Whether it was my sling, my knife, stealth, or even my magic. The problem is that I'm out of time to train. We've only half a day's walk before we reach the arena. What do I focus on, if not control over my Guard?"

Ox hadn't spoken as much as usual since leaving the pub.

He'd been somewhat more reserved since they'd departed the dwarven keep at Hjardharfell, but he seemed to be fond of the boy and eager to encourage him, despite being under the elven spell. "You have minions to protect you because you're weak. I have minions because I'm strong and handsom. You need to train to build your muscles. Try picking up bigger and bigger rocks until your muscles bulge and the elven women swoon."

Beast had few gentle words for the young elf, but she found it hard not to counter Ox, especially regarding his advice on women. "No, stealth and your sling are your best assets. You're a hundred years away from being full-grown, so there is no need to worry about your muscles, and you're two hundred years away from finding a suitable wife."

"Your conjuration will be a valuable addition to your repertoire. I recommend you develop your magic to the point where you can summon something much stronger than four simple skeletons," Buddy suggested.

Ox, Beast, and Buddy would have continued to argue if Henry hadn't interjected. "All those pieces are important, but none of them will matter unless you can bring them together under a single purpose."

Jai popped a few of the cooled moosel nuts in his mouth as he listened intently to the advice. "I'm sorry, Henry. Ox is stronger than the largest Sprig, Beast is fast and deadly, and Buddy's magic might even be greater than Bharat's. You're weaker than all of them. Why would I follow your advice?"

Henry's degraded Attributes from his Desert Path frustrated him, but even without those limits to his development, he would still be struggling to keep up with the other three. He wasn't offended by the elf's question. "Tell me, Jai, why are you taking us to fight the Sentinels?"

"To save Amera from Ghara's Sprigs."

"Close, but not exactly. You're bringing us there to get the elves to follow you in your quest. Your strongest asset won't be us. It will be your ability to lead the elves."

Jai scrunched his eyebrows. "I can't train persuasion like I can train my muscles."

"You've been doing it this whole time. Your magic, your weapons . . . those help you accomplish your goals. The important thing is understanding how to use those tools to accomplish your objective. You said you've been an outcast your whole life and are trying to overcome your family's tarnished reputation. You could have done that in many ways, but you chose to put yourself in danger and fight to save your fellow elves. When your weapon breaks, when your Vitus runs dry, even when your breath leaves your body, that purpose will always cling to your bones. Show someone you're willing to die for them, and they'll follow wherever you lead." Henry didn't know where the words came from. They seemed to pour from his mouth like he'd said them a thousand times. He pressed his mind to search for their source, but the fog of his memories churned and broiled, only getting thicker.

Jai considered Henry's words carefully, still unconvinced. "What you're saying makes sense, but how can any amount of charisma overcome a Strength as huge as Ox's. Even if I had every elf in Amera on my side, would it even matter compared to a force that strong?"

Surprisingly, Ox was the one to counter Jai. "You are right to be awed by my physical prowess, tiny minion. However, recent events have shown that even a Strength as great as mine cannot conquer every adversary alone." Henry didn't expect unsolicited humility from Ox. The beating he'd taken from the Acolyte, Jaromak, must have had a profound and lasting impact on the massive skeleton.

Jai still didn't look persuaded and opened his mouth to argue, but Beast added sharply, "In a fair fight, no magic or weapons, Henry would beat Ox."

Ox's support for Henry faded under Beast's words. "Well, I wouldn't go that far, grumpy minion. Henry is very small and breaks easily."

Henry felt everyone's attention on him and wasn't quite sure how to respond. Luckily, Buddy broke the silence. "I agree with Beast. Ox fights well against large groups of weak opponents or single, powerful adversaries who are unskilled. However, Henry excels at one-on-one combat and would likely use Ox's Strength against him."

"How would you do that?" Jai asked, turning to Henry.

Every enemy Henry fought had a weakness. He was drawn to their vulnerabilities and knew, almost instinctively, how to exploit them. He was grateful that the other three skeletons had accompanied him on the adventure, and he had never consciously considered fighting them. However, now that the question had been asked, his mind couldn't avoid the thought. Buddy's blind spot and casting rate, Beast's minor disorientation after teleporting, and Ox's overreliance on Strength—all were weaknesses that, as a group, the other skeletons helped compensate in battle but could be taken advantage of by an observant enemy.

"It depends, and no two fights are the same," Henry said. "Attributes play a huge role in the outcome of a fight, but terrain and weapons are also factors. When you add magic, all bets are off. The important thing to realize is that no opponent is invincible. If you can exploit a weakness, your chances of victory increase dramatically. It all comes down to training, preparation, and experience. I'm inclined to pick up on vulnerabilities in the same way that Buddy knows the perfect spell for every situation. My body knows how to fight in ways my mind can't seem to remember. After thousands of practice rounds with your sling, your hands don't think when you load it. In the same way, my bones execute while my mind is plotting the broader strategy."

Jai pulled his sling from his waist and loaded it with a rock. "Maybe you can show me? Could you two spar so I can see what you mean?"

Buddy said, "That wouldn't make sense. With them under the hold spell, you'd only be fighting yourself."

"That's a good point. Buddy, hit that open space with a small fireball." Jai pointed to a flat patch of snow just before the forest's edge. Buddy held up his palm and released a mass of blue fire that impacted where Jai was pointing with a thunderous explosion. All the snow within a fifty-foot radius melted instantly under the extreme heat.

Jai held up a hand to cover his face from the heatwave. "That wasn't little, but much better than last time. Henry, Ox, leave your weapons and gear here and stand on opposite sides of your new arena."

Henry and Ox did as they were ordered. As Henry made his way over to the cleared patch, he wanted to advise Jai that this was a bad idea, but part of him was growing increasingly excited at the chance to spar with an opponent as strong as Ox. He noticed all the vegetation had been burned away under the heat of the magical blast, forming a concentric circle inside the larger outline of melted snow. Buddy's flame had even been hot enough to evaporate most of the moisture and leave the ground baked and somewhat hardened. There was a clear demarcation where the vegetation started again.

"Are you ready to prove yourself a worthy minion?" Ox asked as he and Henry took their places in the ad hoc battlefield.

"As long as you're ready to look bad in front of the others," Henry returned in jest, even as a lump formed in his non-existent throat. He'd seen Ox tear apart enemies much stronger than himself with his bare hands. If he was going to prove his point to Jai, he couldn't let the giant get a grip on him. Twenty feet in front of Henry, a two-headed giant, covered from skull to toe in dread platemail, stared him down.

Jai approached close enough to scan the makeshift battlespace. "Here are the rules: no weapons and no magic. The first skeleton incapacitated or knocked out of the center part of the arena loses. You can start as soon as I release you. Ready?"

"I am ready, tiny elf," Ox boomed.

Released? Henry thought. Buddy had made the suggestion, but Henry hadn't expected the boy to completely release the spell just to see them fight. This was his opportunity to free himself and the others. If he could use Blitz to get to Jai's circlet before the elf could cast the Hold spell again—

Status Effect: Hold Undead Dismissed

Ox launched himself forward as soon as the spell broke. His heavy boots pounded off the fresh dirt. The massive skeleton raised a gauntleted hand to deliver a heavy strike.

There goes our chance to escape.

Ox's speed left Henry only a split-second to create a plan. There were numerous options to incapacitate a living opponent. He knew dozens of ways to cut off the blood flow to the brain with a strangle, and hundreds of joint locks that could disable a limb, regardless of an enemy's Strength. Unfortunately, the undead had neither arteries nor tendons and ligaments, and Henry didn't have the power to hurt Ox with strikes through his dreadmail. Could joint locks still work? There was only one way to find out.

Ox lunged at Henry. The huge skeleton had an arm span large enough to wrap around several warriors of Henry's size.

Henry dropped his body to a low lunge, feigning a duck under Ox's grasp. Ox took the bait and lowered his arms to block Henry's escape. Instead of dodging, Henry leapt forward and thrust a knee directly into Ox's face.

The attack connected and staggered Ox. Henry launched into a series of punches and kicks as soon as his feet landed on the ground. Most of Henry's strikes were ineffective, but he noticed that a kick just inside of Ox's knee caused the joint to buckle slightly. Henry noted the movement as Ox recovered and dropped a double hammer fist.

Henry narrowly avoided the heavy blow as baked dirt exploded under the force of Ox's attack. Henry threw two more punches into Ox's ribs, but none affected the giant. It was like punching the mountain itself. Henry would likely hurt himself more than Ox if he kept up his melee tactic. *Time to switch it up.*

Henry ducked under a heavy backhand and wrapped his arms around Ox's massive thigh. He forced his head into Ox's side and lifted with all his Strength, hoping to catch the giant off balance and force him to the ground. *An opponent's Strength is much less dangerous when they're on their backs,* Henry thought as though he were instructing someone through the take-down that his bones remembered far more than his mind.

Unfortunately, Ox was even stronger than Henry expected. The giant skeleton grabbed Henry by the dreadmail and lifted the warrior into the air. Before Henry could protest, the giant turned and flung him away. Henry shifted his body at the last moment, preventing Ox from sending him into the forest.

Henry skidded to a stop just inside the arena boundary and recovered to his feet.

Ox was already charging with a heavy right hand raised to strike, presenting a significant threat Henry didn't want to get caught with. Henry knew exactly what to do. He would step inside the punch, spin around, and use Ox's momentum to send the giant skeleton flying outside the dirt circle. Henry stepped forward to set up the throw when he noticed something was off. Ox's shoulders were square with Henry, not rotated to the right as one would expect from a punch.

Ox's left jab nearly took off Henry's head—if Henry had noticed the feint a second later, it would have. Henry barely parried the jab and pivoted to Ox's left just in time to avoid being run over by the charging skeleton. Now almost behind his opponent, Henry wrapped his hands around Ox's waist, planted his feet, and lifted.

Henry recalled from his previous experience moments earlier that Ox was much heavier than expected, but Henry knew just where to move his bones to align his center of gravity directly under Ox's. Henry flexed his legs and lifted the giant as high as he could, then pulled hard to accelerate the drop.

"Ghakk!" Gator croaked as he and Ox descended.

Henry released his grip on Ox's waist and switched it to the giant's arm while maneuvering just outside the path of the falling skeleton. As soon as Ox's back hit the ground, Henry put a shin in Ox's armpit and threw the other leg over his face. Now wrapped around a huge arm, Henry fell backward and extended his hips.

Ox's arm bones were massive, especially covered in armor, but Henry had no trouble finding the giant's elbow. Henry arched his back, putting enormous pressure on Ox's joint and stopping just short of where he felt the arm would snap. A regular opponent would be screaming in pain. Ox wasn't a normal opponent.

As though Henry wasn't wrapped around the limb, Ox curled his arm and started standing. "Not bad, Herbie."

Henry didn't wait for the giant to stand to his full height. He released the arm, dropped to the ground, and reached for Ox's legs. He wrapped an arm around one ankle and put his heel behind the other. Ox's stance was wide enough that Herny had to stretch to span the gap. He planted his other foot in the crook of Ox's waist and kicked as hard as he could.

Ox couldn't keep his balance, and he toppled over backward again. Henry wasn't about to give Ox a chance to recover. Henry sprang to his feet as the giant fell, still holding on to Ox's ankle and lifting it into the air, which forced Ox's shoulders to the ground.

Henry circled to Ox's side, avoiding flailing arms. He placed a knee on Ox's chest and prepared to rain punches on his opponent's face, when a small detail caught his attention. Ox's shoulders were flat on the ground. It wasn't a significant detail, but it made him think of Ox's faint with the jab moments earlier.

Like a spark igniting a flame, Henry realized he'd seen Ox's ploy before, but not in his current life. This wasn't the first time Henry and Ox had fought. Henry froze with his fist raised.

The delay was a mistake.

Ox reached and grabbed Henry by the chestplate with one hand, and gripped his foot with another. Henry tried to punch, but Ox was too strong. The skeleton muscled Henry to the ground with minimal effort, then kneeled on Henry's chest with all his weight. The massive skeleton lifted his arms in the air, preparing for another double hammer strike that Henry had no hope of dodging.

Ox's fists stopped just inches from Henry's face.

"Hold!" Jai screamed.

Status Effect: Hold Undead. No actions may be taken without the direction of the caster. Command Link Established 115/1600

The curved horns of Ox's dread helm loomed above Henry's head as Ox stared down at him like death itself. For many opponents, this had been the last thing they'd seen. Henry considered himself fortunate.

Henry focused on the numbers of Jai's Command Link. When Jai first cast the spell on the skeletons, he had **1200** points in his Ability, but it was now up to **1600**. The boy was getting stronger. Henry was grateful the elf saw fit to stop the fight. The number of used Command Link points had dropped, indicating that Jai had released his control over Rat.

"You almost had me, Harvey," Ox said with considerable admiration in his voice. "Keep practicing and you may even have a chance."

Henry didn't respond. Now that he was back under the Hold Undead spell, his chance to free himself and the others was gone. Regardless, it was a good fight.

Jai ran to their side. "That was amazing. I can't have you two killing each other, so I had to stop it. You can both stand up. That was way closer than expected. I can't believe Henry won."

"What?" Ox asked, releasing Henry and rising to his full height.

Buddy and Beast followed close behind Jai. The skeletal mage had an amused tone in his voice. "That is correct, Lord Oxendine. When Henry tripped you the last time, you landed outside the designated boundary. According to the rules set by Jai, Henry is the winner."

Ox couldn't move his skull, but Henry knew the giant was looking around. "I . . . guess that is so. Congratulations, Harry."

Henry pulled himself off the ground. His armor stuck in the dirt just a bit as the weight from Ox had driven him into the soft earth. He saw that he had been lying just outside where the vegetation started, indicating that before Ox had thrown him to the ground, he had successfully tripped the giant outside the arena. It was challenging to maneuver the fight around without Ox noticing what was happening, but Henry had successfully distracted the brute enough to pull it off.

Jai pulled a clump of mud and grass from Henry's armor. "I didn't think you could do it. I thought Ox would crush any opponent with his Strength."

"He almost did," Henry said with a chuckle.

"If you can stand against him with no weapons and magic, you'll be fine against any Sprig, Guard, or Sentinel we'll face. Grab your gear. It's time to get going."

Jai led the skeletons into the forest and toward the heart of Amera. When Henry got close enough to Ox, he said, "Thanks for holding back."

"I don't know what you mean," Ox said.

"Yes, you do. Your last punch stopped *before* Jai cast the Hold spell."

Despite his lack of skin, Henry knew Ox held a proud grin. "There were several times in that fight that you could have broken an arm or a leg. You could have even ended me with that first knee to my face, if you wanted. I wasn't the only one holding back . . ."

CHAPTER 15

Jacoby sucked in sharp breaths. Sweat mixed with black and green ichor ran down his face like mountain spring water. The dead creature before him resembled a toad, though it was covered in dark spikes and was nearly the size of a full-grown simian hog. The monster would have swallowed him whole, had Talji not ordered him to activate his Auric Palisade just before its tongue impacted his chestplate and sucked him into its mouth. Bits of the overgrown amphibian now lay scattered around him in a wide circle, while most of the monster's mouth clung to his armor.

It was the tenth Sprig he'd killed in as many hours as the elves marched him through the snowy forest. Jacoby wondered how the monsters could endure the cold and remain so hostile. However, the fact that he was an undead human being controlled by an elf made it less complicated to suspend disbelief—the exhaustion from constant fights made it even easier.

"Better." Talji's soft but menacing voice hummed as she walked into his view.

Status Effect Resisted: Enraged Dismissed
RES +1

He moved his eyes to look at hers. It was the only voluntary movement he could make without her orders. She'd had him under her control for nearly two days, and they had barely stopped to rest between trekking and fighting. He was bloodied and slightly wounded, but he'd garnered **2** Tiers and successfully learned to push back the aura's Effect.

Talji noticed that, too. "So, you've conquered that little quirk. No longer wanted to claw out my eyes?"

Jacoby felt the question unlock his jaw and allow him to speak. "I've suppressed the urge, but that doesn't mean the thought has left my mind." Jacoby tried to put as much threat behind the words as possible, though he had little hope of resisting the Hold spell, let alone actually harming her. As far as Jacoby could tell, the spell had no weaknesses he could exploit, and the elf's capacity to control him had grown rapidly. She could now issue him blanket, enduring commands, like the one that allowed him to speak if he was answering one of her questions. She had even given him free reign to attack how he liked during fights, though she refused to allow him control over his magic.

Her eyes fluttered over him just a moment before the corners of her mouth twisted up in a pursed smile. "Over there. Build a fire, human. You may use magic to start it." She motioned with her head to a small clearing in the forest. Without hesitation, his body trudged through the snow toward where she indicated. He grabbed a few downed limbs along the way and piled them in the center of the clearing.

The autonomy he'd gained in carrying out her commands had grown substantially over the last day. He'd sustained considerable wounds from the first battle where he could barely swing his sword, though she allowed him to use a healing spell on himself. Now he was executing precise tasks based on her intent. If the Hold Undead spell was a skill like his Auric Palisade, then she must have gained a Tier or more from the few days commanding him.

"I can't believe it. The filthy mongrel is stronger than every other Guard combined, and you're controlling him nearly as well as Bharat could." Jacoby recognized Lata's voice. The woman was slightly more petite than Talji, but the venom in her words when she spoke about Jacoby was so thick he could almost see it drip from her mouth.

"Yes, and I feel he's capable of so much more. Though I have no idea how he's alive and undead at the same time, or how he is able to have and gain Tiers," Talji replied.

The elf could command him to talk, but she couldn't control his honesty, which was the one advantage he held over her. He'd told her everything about waking up and killing Acolytes, but he'd managed to keep his Drift Amulet a secret. As far as he knew, Talji thought his words were complete truths.

Raze

His prismatic Dazzle Ability had evolved into Raze, and it now had a scalding Effect in addition to its original blinding cone of light. The dry twigs and logs before Jacoby ignited in a blaze. Surat had been the one to suggest using Jacoby for chores like making camp and hunting for food. Jacoby hated the male elf for his smug grin that came with every one of Talji's commands.

"Human, continue to feed the flames. Lata, Surat, we'll rest here until morning, then make our final leg."

"What do you think Bharat will say? He told you to go to the dwarves, and now we're returning with a human in tow."

Jacoby had no idea what Lata was talking about, though he had gathered the elf named Bharat was their leader. *Where did dwarves fit into what was going on?* He wondered.

Though Jacoby's back was to the elves, the uncomfortable silence told him all he needed to know about their exchange. Talji hated being questioned, and even though he couldn't see her, he knew she was giving Lata an angry stare, and the subservient elf was lowering her head and looking away. He would have chuckled, had he the freedom. Instead, he continued plowing through the knee-deep snow, collecting fallen pine limbs, and adding them to his fire until he had a small blaze.

"Human, sit. Warm your ugly self," Talji commanded. Jacoby was grateful for the order. The boots and metal armor were not meant for the chilly weather outside the mountain. He began to shiver now that the sun had gone down and the sweat and Sprig blood had rapidly cooled. Jacoby sat in the snow as ordered and soaked up as much warmth as he could.

"You two can go kill something for dinner. I have more questions for the Acolyte," Talji said. Surat and Lata left quickly and silently in response, leaving neither track in the snow nor sound of footsteps behind. Their proficiency in stealth impressed Jacoby, though he didn't want to admit it.

"Now, human, before I introduce you to the High Sage, I need to know a few things."

Though Jacoby could resist the Effect, Talji's aura still assaulted his senses like waking from a deep sleep to find the sun in your eyes. It was nothing like the blazing auras of his fellow Acolytes, but the thick vine-like streams that wrapped around her bones caused him only slightly less distress. Talji must have noticed both his anger and his shivering because she walked behind him, out of sight. "Pitiful human. You'll probably freeze to death tonight."

Thick fur draped over his shoulders, and the elf's earthy, yet sweet scent filled his nose.

Item Status Effect: Warmed (Cold Resistance +3)

The act of kindness was unexpected, but even more so was the sensation when she sat behind him and put her weight against his back.

"Tell me, human, what are the Acolytes trying to accomplish in this mountain?"

Jacoby's mind went to the first experience he could remember. The sorcerer, Stavros, killing a boy . . . a skeleton trying to get to the top of the mountain. He didn't know what his fellow humans were doing, but he knew he needed to get to that ghost. Warm or not, there was no way he could reveal that information. "I've already told you my memory is gone. I know not what the humans are doing, and I didn't have the mental acuity to ask them."

"Instead, you ran . . . up and straight to me. How . . . fortunate." She toyed with the last word, letting it dance on her tongue like the last drop of an expensive wine. Jacoby found himself struggling to parse her intent while focusing on the melodic tones in her voice.

"You're old for an Acolyte. You must have gained so many Tiers after endless trips through this mountain. How strong do you think you were?"

"You could shut off your spell, and we could find out."

Jacoby expected a blow to his head after such a statement, but Talji lowered her voice instead. "Don't tempt me with a good time."

Talji seemed to catch herself, and her tone returned to its icy bite. "But that won't happen. I don't know what else

I can pull from you, but hopefully, you will be useful to Bharat. While we wait for food, you may ask me a question, human."

Jacoby knew he needed to gather as much information on his situation as possible. There was so much of the elven culture that he didn't understand. "Why do you worship a god that sends these Sprigs into your home?"

"Ghara has protected this mountain long before we elves arrived. We serve her, and if our faith is strong enough, she will bless us again."

After a long pause, she said, "You may ask me another question."

Jacoby wasn't ready for the follow-up opportunity and blurted out his query before he could think it through. "Am I your first human. I mean, the first human you've captured?"

Jacoby felt Talji's back rise and lower in a silent chuckle, and her soft tone returned. "You're the closest a human, alive or dead, has ever been to me." Jacoby felt her relax against him. It almost felt good. "But capturing the undead was never my intended profession. When I was young, I wanted to be an herbalist—what you humans would call an alchemist, I believe. That never happened, as my family pushed me toward the sword and away from the pestle. A few hundred years later, and here I am. If the troll hadn't destroyed my home prior to the Necromancer's attack, I would be dead in the mountain like the rest of the high elves."

A moment later, she spoke again. "You may ask—"

"All we could find was a scrawny rabbit. It will have to do." Surat's voice rang through the quiet of the campsite like the gong of a grandfather clock at the darkest hour of night. Jacoby hadn't even heard him approach. Neither had Talji.

She was on her feet before the first word left Surat's mouth and was not pleased. "You chose to return with a meal that can't feed one, let alone four!"

"Four? I didn't think the undead needed to feed. And why is the human wearing your furs?" Lata asked.

"Well . . . we can't bring him to Bharat if he's frozen and starved," Talji snapped, then quickly added, "and he's more useful alive than dead again."

Jacoby wanted to laugh, but more than that, he wanted to ask Talji another question.

CHAPTER 16

Jai stood at the forest's edge with the four skeletons behind him. The boy's leg bounced nervously as he stared toward the large clearing. The arena wasn't fancy, nothing like the multi-tiered arches that composed the coliseum in Ammerthall, but it served the elves' purpose. A dirt square, thirty paces wide and thrice as long, lay at the base of a pine-covered hillside. Twenty elves with blonde hair and relatively fine fur clothing sat in rough seating carved into the hillside and padded with pine needles. Across the arena from the high elves, a gaggle of fifty or so forest elves stood or sat beyond the wooden logs that marked the battlefield. Their clothes were modest but still looked comfortable in the chilly morning air.

On either end of the arena stood a series of logged cages. Some held skeletons, and others confined prowling Sprigs, though the logs were too thick for Henry to make out anything other than green skin, long dark spikes, and black eyes.

"This is where the high elves force skeletons and Sprigs into combat?" A tinge of excitement rolled through Henry's bones as he imagined the elves on either side cheering for their favored Guard to trounce its foe.

Jai gave a quick murmur of assent. The boy had his hand on a tree trunk, and Henry realized the elf was nearly trembling—likely a combination of fear, uncertainty, and excitement.

"That's the problem with knowing the time and place of your next battle. The added preparation comes with anxiety. It's both better and worse than being caught unaware," Henry noted, more to himself than Jai.

Jai didn't take his eyes from the arena. "I don't know if I can do this. Once I walk out there, there's no turning back."

From behind Henry, Beast huffed. "You've wasted enough of our time. Either release us, or let us get this over with."

"The grumpy minion is correct," Ox said. "I thought we came here for a fight."

"Intent turned to action leads to consequences. The fallout of your decision will exist no matter what you choose. You will likely regret inaction over boldness." Even Buddy seemed eager to get to the encounter. It could have been the red auras of nearly a hundred elves coaxing them to violence, but Henry knew their Resolve had grown enough to allow reason to overcome rage. Whatever they had been in their past lives, the skeletons were now battle-hardened warriors. They had faced far worse dangers below and weren't about to shy away from the Sentinels, Guards, and Sprigs that awaited them in the dirt rectangle.

A cage at the far end of the arena opened. A giant Sprig, shaped like an anteater but with vertical plates extending from its back, burst from the cage and charged a single skeleton at the arena's center. Matted hair that looked like it was covered in an oily sludge clung to the monster, and a barbed tongue flicked from its mouth like a snake testing the air for prey.

The skeleton wasn't a match for the Sprig. The undead's

sword clattered harmlessly against rigid plates as heavy claws ripped the Guard apart.

Loud *boos* erupted from both sides of the arena as high elf and forest elf alike jeered the victorious Sprig. The monster didn't hesitate after its battle with the skeleton. It reared and charged the group of high elves.

Before it reached them, thorned vines sprang from the ground and wrapped around Ghara's spawn. It roared in protest as more vines lifted it from the ground and dragged it back into a wooden cage. Heavy bars slammed shut as the Sprig continued to howl in protest.

Sounds of dissent were replaced with applause as the magic returned the Sprig to its confinement.

Two elves, likely Sentinels as they were adorned in white armor and thick furs, met in the center of the arena. As the crowd quieted down, Henry's Perception picked up their dialogue.

"A skeleton is never stronger than a larger Sprig. You must wear it down first," one elf said to the other.

Uncertainty wavered in Jai's voice, rooting the boy's feet to the ground. "This is too hard. How do I know what's right?"

"You don't. If this was easy, someone would have done it by now. Luck is the crossroads of opportunity and preparation. You have both here." Henry could have easily defeated the Sprig, though under Jai's control, the feat would have been much more difficult. Even so, the decision was now in the boy's hands.

Jai seemed to pick up on Henry's tenacity. The boy lifted his chin and pulled in a deep breath. "I'm ready. Follow me."

Henry and the others joined in step behind the elf. As soon as they left the forest, a hush rolled over the arena like a dark cloud. All eyes were on them within seconds, and not another word was spoken. The only sounds were the snarls of Sprigs locked in their wooden prisons.

The elves in the center of the arena stopped their conversation and turned toward the approaching coterie. What started as harsh whispers quickly evolved into sharp words and angry shouts.

"What is Jai doing with a Guard?" asked one elf.

"Traitor, like his sister," Henry heard another say, though he couldn't tell if it came from the high elves or the forest elves.

Jai kept walking, but he managed to ask Henry, "What do I do?"

"Now is when you train your leadership muscle," Henry encouraged.

The advice was just what Jai needed. The boy rolled back his shoulders as he approached the center of the arena. He looked to both sides of the dirt battlefield, then started what he'd likely practiced in his head a dozen times over the past two days. "You have no reason to trust me, but these four skeletons are our only hope for a better life."

The whispers turned into discord louder than the *boos* for the victorious Sprig.

"Keep going," Henry urged.

Jai raised his voice, but it barely rose above the growing jeers. "I'm not your enemy; the Sprigs are. And as long as Ghara is sending her Sprigs to attack us, she is our enemy as well."

Shouts erupted from both sides of the arena. "Blasphemy!"

Jai began to yell back as he tried to overcome the crowd's noise. "It's the truth. With these skeletons and your help, we can finally stop the Sprigs and live in peace."

The Sentinel of the fallen guard at the center of the arena approached and gave the boy an angry snarl. "No elf would ever join you on a fool's errand. Turn these skeletons over to me, and I'll let you walk away in shame."

"No!" Jai barked. The Sentinel froze in his tracks and gave

the boy a wary look. Jai took a step forward. "I am done with your shame. If you won't join me against Ghara," he looked to Henry and gritted his teeth, "then you better get ready to fight me!"

"That's the spirit, tiny elf!" Ox cheered.

CHAPTER 17

"A human stands in my hut. Not just any human, but a filthy Ikritian Acolyte like the ones that brought evil to this mountain so many years ago." Bharat's eyebrows twitched and his nostrils flared as he struggled to hold his temper. Talji knew the Sage despised guests and hated surprises even more. However, she believed showing the man to Bharat was worth facing his wrath.

Bharat paced before the rigid human, fidgeting with his robes and shaking his head. "I asked you to find out what had disturbed the dwarves. You ignored that request and brought this man into my very dwelling instead. My patience is thin, Taljipura. You will explain yourself."

Jacoby struggled to move, but the spell held him tight. No amount of will or muscle allowed him to do more than breathe without Talji's command. No matter what he did, resisting even her smallest decree was impossible.

The last several days of fighting had worn him ragged. Talji had struggled to command him at first, but she quickly learned to control him with relative ease. By the time Jacoby had killed two dozen Sprigs, he felt like he was able to execute the intent of her commands, instead of just the literal interpretation. The automation allowed him to fight almost as well as he could have, were he not under her influence.

"*Was* an Ikritian Acolyte, Great Sage," Talji said with a knowing smile. She pulled a dagger from her hilt and held it up to Jacoby's face.

Her sweet scent of pine and fresh snow, soft voice, and beautiful face couldn't overpower the red blazing aura that emanated from her. Their auras, though more subtle than those of the humans, were almost as hard to resist as the Hold spell. After being forced to endure them, however, Jacoby had been rewarded with several points in Resolve and could now force away the Status Effect with significant focus and mental effort.

Bharat gave Talji an agitated look until she pressed the blade into Jacoby's skin. A bead of red flowed from his cheek and into his beard. Jacoby focused so hard to suppress the red aura's Effect that the pain of the blade almost didn't register with him.

"Was?" Bharat drew out the word like a hiss leaving a snake. The Sage's curiosity had been piqued.

"He is under the influence of your magic, Great Sage." Talji practically sang the praise as she wiped the bloody dagger on Jacoby's tunic.

Bharat stopped his pacing and faced Jacoby. His eyes narrowed, and he tilted his head to study the man. "Hold Undead cannot affect the living. I have tried to modify the magic many times and have never been successful. Are you telling me you found a way to make it work on this disgusting human?"

"If you would but Assess him, Great Sage," Talji said, trying to suppress a smug grin.

Bharat stared at Jacoby for a second until realization rolled across his face. "Impossible. My Drift Amulet tells me that he is an undead human. How is this so?"

"That I don't know. But he flies into a rage upon sight of us, just like the legions of skeletons. I asked him how, but his memory is blank. He couldn't provide a useful explanation. Though he's less offensive than I would have imagined for a human."

"He can speak, even as an undead?" Bharat's eyes grew wide, and an expression bordering on excitement unfolded on his wrinkled visage. He reached up with a gnarled hand and squeezed Jacoby's face.

"He speaks, and much more. We've had several conversations," Talji replied.

I wouldn't call it a conversation, more like a violent interrogation, Jacoby thought with an internal laugh. Talji had been far from gentle with him until she learned that she had to walk out of his view to remove the enraged Effect and allow him to speak with a clear mind, though her chat with him the previous night had been almost pleasant.

"What use do I have for a talking human, Taljipura?" Bharat's question interrupted Jacoby's thoughts.

"His talking isn't what interests me. I'm more concerned about his Tier. I found him at **5**, and after a few days of fighting our way back here, he gained **2** more. When we came across him, he dispatched a huge Sprig and tore through our entire Guard like it was nothing. He attacked with the rage of the undead, so I Held him. To my surprise, he only occupied **38** of the **2300** points available in my Command Link. If we can figure out how this happened, we can control an entire army and march to Ghara's cave. We will never again fear Spri—"

"Hold your tongue, Taljipura. I will tolerate no one, not even you, to propose sacrilege in my presence. I will allow no being—elf, human, or other—to assault the lady of the mountain. We do not fear the trials that Ghara imparts on us. We merely endure. Do not forget that, and do not forget your place." Bharat's weathered scowl warned her against pressing the matter further.

Talji opened her mouth to apologize to the Sage, but a blast of wind and snow cut her words short.

Lata rushed in, leaving the door to Bharat's hut open, and began frantically spouting her words. "Talji, Great Sage, you must hurry to the Theater."

"How dare you interrupt us. You know better than to let yourself into Bharat's private quarters." Talji considered striking her insolent fellow Sentinel, but Lata's desperate expression made her hesitate. With a quick nod, she allowed the intruding elf to speak.

Surat bolted in just behind Lata. "Jai. It's Jai. He has a Guard." Bharat's forehead wrinkled further, changing from anger to annoyance and finally to confusion.

Talji's curiosity overcame her irritation. "What are you blabbering about?"

"Jai has four skeletons in his Guard, and they're strong . . . maybe stronger than us," Lata explained.

"How is that possible?" Talji asked.

Bharat's voice creaked like a howling wind. "I thought it curious that you didn't recover Mayur's circlet and Drift Amulet. Now we know where they went."

"Ugh," Talji growled. "Surat, what is the traitor's brother doing now?"

"He's at the Theater, showing off and raving about going to fight Ghara."

"We have tolerated the boy's insolence out of pity for his sister's betrayal, but this is beyond forgivable," Bharat said.

"Go. Teach him a lesson. I will be right behind you. I need to address the gaggle and reaffirm their faith after we . . . reapportion . . . these new skeletons."

"Understood, Great Sage." Talji turned and shoved Lata and Surat out the door.

Bharat called after her. "Talji. I will understand if you must do more than hurt the boy."

CHAPTER 18

Another skeleton exploded under the force of Henry's shield bash. Bones scattered across the dirt arena as the undead's green aura vanished. He didn't need to use Blitz to destroy the weak enemies, though Jai enjoyed having him trounce every Guard the high elven Sentinels put before them. Despite being controlled by the young elf, Henry enjoyed fighting in the makeshift arena—standing across from an opponent, knowing that it was nothing but his skill versus theirs and listening to the gasps from the onlookers. The last kill had even brought Henry to his next Tier.

Skeleton Killed. Soul Essence Claimed. Tier +1
STR +1, MOB +2, FOR +1, ACU +2, RES +3, PER +1

Surpassed first Acumen Threshold. Attribute bonus applied
ACU +10%, Vitus +1 per Tier

Power welled through his nonexistent veins. The additional Tier and the mental bump that came with the Acumen Threshold invigorated his body and mind. Though he hadn't taken enough damage nor spent enough Vitus to need the recovery that the new Tier brought, the Acumen Threshold and accompanying Vitus expansion were a welcome boost, considering the deficiencies from his Desert Path still held him back. With the additional **10%** added to the Attribute, his thoughts seemed to move just a bit quicker. Much to his satisfaction, his Perception picked up the shocked faces of the elves around him.

All attention was on Henry as quickly whispered words and anxious glances passed between forest and high elves alike. Henry assumed he must have been a fearful sight—a skeleton adorned in dread armor and wielding an eversharp blade, having just annihilated the elves' only protection from their god's corrupted forest creatures.

At least Henry wasn't invoking the sheer terror that Ox and Gator, with their dread fullplate and Silent-skull helmets, had imparted on the populace. When Jai brought the four skeletons to the center of the arena and issued his challenge to any Sentinel in Amera, the elf initially used Ox. However, the massive physical damage the brute dealt to the Theater, along with the fear he inflicted on the elven spectators, was so severe that the boy had quickly switched to Henry. After more than an hour of fighting, every skeletal Guard in the vicinity had been downed, and their Sentinels looked on in shock.

His complete victory secured, Jai approached Henry with a look on his face somewhere between conviction and relief. He smiled at the gaggle of forest elves, then turned to the seated high elves and the Sentinels near them. The boy's confidence had grown with every Guard he defeated. He addressed the elves on either side of the arena who had grown increasingly hostile throughout the fights. "We've been under the assault of Ghara's Sprigs for my entire life. I'm tired of it, and I know you are, too. Now that I have these skeletons, we no longer need to fear her Sprigs. Come with me to her cave, and we can stop her once and for all."

Three Sentinels in shining elven armor gripped their swords and prepared to unsheathe them, but Jai didn't back down. "Buddy. Fire."

Blue flames appeared around the skeletal mage's hands, and the Sentinels stopped their advance. Gasps and cries of fear erupted from the collected elves, but there was something more. A few sporadic and isolated cheers rang out from the side of the forest elves.

Encouraged by the small showing of approval, Jai went to speak again, but a woman's voice from the woods cut him short.

"Betrayal is a family characteristic, I see. I'm not surprised that you would turn the undead on your fellow elves." Three elves with a human in tow emerged from the tree line and deftly made their way down the hill. From Jai's description, Henry assumed it was Talji, Surat, and Lata, of whom the boy has spoken frequently with no small amount of disdain. What concerned Henry more was the human they had with them. Henry's Perception quickly picked out bloodied Acolyte armor. His newly powered Acumen took in the man's strong jaw and slightly thinning, sandy red hair—Henry recognized the man.

If Henry had a throat, a lump would have formed. This was the first man he'd killed—the man who had given Henry life, but also the undead with whom he'd connected when Stavros killed the Acolyte boy and entered his mind. *Did the Necromancer raise this human? Would the other Acolytes he'd killed return as well?* Henry wondered.

Jai was equally taken aback, but more so at the words of

Talji, though the boy collected himself quickly. "I would use magic to defend myself and my fellow forest elves. From both you and the Sprigs."

"Admirable, but foolish," Talji quipped dismissively, then turned to one of the other Sentinels on the arena's edge. "You let him defeat you? You call yourself a Sentinel. You should be embarrassed. How did you get so weak that a boy could trounce your Guard?"

The Sentinel's face blushed with anger. "Talji, we could do nothing. He controls skeletons at Tier **14**, higher than any of us."

Talji ignored the elf's excuse, brushing past and approaching Jai and Henry. Jai took a step back and started fidgeting with his sling strap. Henry noticed the boy's trepidation and offered a stern warning. "You've come this far, Jai. Either run or fight. Now is the time to make your choice."

Jai looked at Henry and nodded. "Buddy, Ox, Beast. To me. Weapons out!" The three other skeletons approached—hammer, daggers, and fire brandished. Talji's group halted, and Henry could tell by the purposeful look in her eyes that she was Assessing them.

"I don't fear you anymore, Talji. And I don't fear Bharat. I'm here to save Amera. With or without your help," Jai cried, the creaking in his voice betraying feigned confidence.

Talji narrowed her eyes at Henry. She had heard him speak but was less surprised by that capability than he expected. A threatening smile parted the beautiful elf's lips, revealing perfect white teeth and a pink tongue that flickered on the edge of her mouth as she directed her attention back at Jai. "I see you've gained a few Tiers as well, Murenjai. You have a Drift Amulet and one of Bharat's circlets. Where did you come across such treasures?"

"I don't need to answer any of your questions. Are you going to help me or . . . or fight me?"

Talji's eyes fluttered innocently. "Me? What reason would I have to fight you?" Her voice turned harsh and stern. "Maybe because you stole from Mayur's dead body? Because you threatened your fellow elves with a Guard you don't deserve? Or could it be that you're controlling a dead elf? You truly have surpassed your sister's betrayal."

Murmurs came from both sides of the arena as the elves whispered. All color flushed from Jai's face as he turned and looked at Henry. "You're an elf?"

Ox's booming voice silenced everyone. "If you want your beautiful face to hide your snake tongue, you shouldn't talk so much. Either join us or fight. Or, if you prefer, I would be willing to calm you down with my own tender hands."

Now it was Talji's turn to flush with anger. "Enough of this. A skeleton will not taunt me. Jai, if you think you are a Sentinel, then prove it. That one against mine." She pointed at Henry, then thumbed at the Acolyte behind her. Henry saw the human's eyes darting around, but he hadn't moved since he'd arrived with the elves.

He's under the Hold spell, too, Henry thought. *He must also be undead.*

"If I win, I'll take those four skeletons, and you are banished from Amera. Forever!" Talji growled.

"But if you lose, you will denounce Bharat and pledge your loyalty to the boy," Beast answered. Though her voice was barely above a whisper, it penetrated the Theater, carrying a threat of violence and a weight of authority that took even Henry by surprise.

Talji's eyes widened with fury, and Henry wondered if the elf saw a Status Effect in her own vision. She gave Beast a menacing scowl before her eyes went to the alchemy broach on the skeletal elf's hip. "Fine," she snapped, "but cage the other three so they don't attack if you lose control."

Then she spun and shouted at the human behind her, unsheathing the blade at her hip. "Take my sword and prepare to fight, human." The Acolyte took the elf's weapon, and a golden sheen began to radiate from the blade. The man's eyes locked onto Henry's. Talji stomped off toward the high elves with Surat and Lata in trail.

Jai looked up at Henry. "The human is only Tier 7, you can take him, right?"

"I can if you release me, but her control over the spell is much greater than yours. I can easily tell that by the man's reactions to her commands."

Jai glanced over at Talji, who had reached the arena edge and stood fidgeting in agitation. He turned back to Henry and shook his head. "No, I have to prove I'm worthy of being a Sentinel. I know I can do this."

"You hear that, Herbie. It's about to get rough," Ox said with a laugh.

Henry looked back at the Acolyte. The man's stoic expression hadn't shifted, though his eyes darted over Henry. Henry could tell the man was an adept warrior, picking out weak points to prepare for the fight. "Jai, don't let me kill that man, I need to talk to him. Also, don't let him kill me."

"I'll do my best," Jai said, then ordered Beast, Buddy, and Ox into one of the empty cages at the arena's edge.

"Don't fail us, Henry. I despise that elf already and would rather have this imbecilic boy control me than that wench," Beast demanded as she walked away.

CHAPTER 19

Twenty paces apart, Jacoby stared down his opponent. The skeleton's bone armor and rainbow metallic sword were unbelievably high quality, even if Jacoby couldn't use his Drift Amulet to Assess them at that moment. A man who had no knowledge of fighting would be a significant threat in such adornment; a proficient foe could be insurmountable. Jacoby could tell by the skeleton's jerky movements that the elven boy had far less control over his Guard than Talji commanded. That would hopefully be enough to see him through the fight.

The vulnerable spots in the skeleton's armor were few, but they were still there, and Jacoby would need to exploit every last one if he wanted to come out of the fight alive. This enemy was by far the most powerful he'd faced yet. However, there was something strangely familiar about the skeleton, though Jacoby didn't have time to dwell on that impression.

"Ready?" Lata shouted from the side of the arena. Talji and the elven boy had positioned themselves before the high elves on the terraced hillside. Jacoby could tell the boy had somehow acquired the skeletons in such a way that it aggravated the high elves. There was severe animosity between the elven factions, and now, Jacoby and this other skeleton would solve the grudge by proxy.

"Ready," Talji said flatly, like she was hurrying to get the fight over.

There was a brief pause before the boy, Jai apparently, replied, "Ready."

"Fight!" Lata roared before the boy had even finished the word. The elves on both sides erupted in cheers, replacing the solemn atmosphere of the Theater with the roar of a crowd eager to witness the spectacle. This wasn't just a fight between Jacoby and the skeleton, or even between Talji and the boy. There was a rift between the high elves and the forest elves—a chasm that separated the two cultures. Jacoby stood on one side of that division; his adversary was planted firmly on the other.

"Human, destroy that skeleton," came Talji's orders, and Jacoby's body sprang forward, sword radiating with his Auric Palisade. With Talji's sword and his magic, he hoped to gain an early advantage and overcome the skeleton's higher Tier and superior equipment.

"Henry, equip your shield. Attack with Blitz," Jai shouted over the crowd's jeers.

Jacoby watched as the buckler on the skeleton's arm grew to the size of a full kite shield, then the undead blurred forward so fast that Jacoby's Perception had trouble following the movements. It was a straight-line attack that Jacoby barely managed to dodge. Had it struck, it likely would have ended the fight.

Jacoby sidestepped and sliced with his sword. The magic from his Ability exploded with a shower of sparks, but the sword rebounded from the armor, leaving little more than a scuff on the bone plate.

This won't be easy, Jacoby thought as the skeleton's bash stopped ten paces behind him.

The elven boy continued to order his skeleton. "Henry, attack with your sword." The undead quickly obeyed, turning and advancing on Jacoby.

Henry, Jacoby thought with an inward chuckle, *what a name for a necrotic monster.*

The skeleton ran forward on unsteady legs, brandishing the sword and delivering a series of broad, telegraphed swings. Jacoby ducked under the wild slices and struck, aiming at the tiny spaces between bone plates. His magic detonated with enough force to crumble granite, but again, the blade rebounded, leaving little more than scorch marks. The skeleton swung again, seeming to have forgotten the shield in its off-hand and barely able to keep its balance.

Jacoby danced outside the skeleton's blade. It would have been easy to mistake the prismatic metal for a ceremonial or decorative weapon that would shatter under the first impact, but Jacoby was no fool. The blade wielded by the skeleton was far superior to the one Talji had given him. Even though the skeleton was slow and awkward, a single misstep would see that weapon end him.

He avoided blow after blow, thankful for the automation Talji allowed him and for the elven boy's inexperience. The gap in control between the two elves gave Jacoby room to set up an attack. His best option was the open face of the skeleton's helmet. Jacoby dodged another strike and cocked back his sword, charging Auric Palisade and preparing a thrust.

The voice of a young man reverberated from the skull. "Human, are you awake? Can you hear me?" The words caught Jacoby off guard. His thrust faltered and glanced off the side of his opponent's helmet in a spray of light and sparks.

Drat, I'm almost out of Vitus, and did that skeleton just talk? Jacoby realized he'd heard the skeletons speak earlier but was too focused on Talji to consciously note that as significant. He mentally kicked himself and searched for the voice's origin. He found only darkness behind the skeleton's eyes. Jacoby's body, however, continued to attack.

"Ah, you can't move your jaw. I'll just talk then, and maybe we can figure this out before one of us kills the other." The skeleton, Henry, continued the monologue as they exchanged blows in another shower of golden embers. "I don't know if you remember, but we've met before. Twice actually. I somehow killed you and took your Soul Essence. Your death gave me life, and then your last thought helped guide me. You were thinking: what a fitting way to die, battling in the dungeon you'd spent your whole life exploring. You regretted not finding your father and grandfather. You knew you would never make it to the lowest level of the dungeon, nor destroy the Necromancer and break the curse."

The revelation shook Jacoby to his core. He tried to focus on the fight and push out the skeleton's words, but somehow, Jacoby knew he couldn't refute the claim.

His sword banged harmlessly against the skeleton's bone armor, still completely ineffective. The undead continued to talk as though he were used to having such a conversation in the middle of a fight. "I'm trying to save all the undead in this mountain by reviving the Empress, but the leader of the Ikritians, Stavros, is the Necromancer who caused this evil. I saw the truth when he took the boy's life, and I know you did too."

His opponent spoke the truth—the skeleton searching for a ghost, an old man taking the life of a boy, the haunting feeling that came with Jacoby's first memory. What kind of world was this, and why couldn't he remember anything? Had he truly been a soldier in the Necromancer's army? Had he known the evil nature of his leader and willingly followed?

"I hope the movement of your eyes indicates that you know I'm right. Now we need to figure out how to get out of this situation," Henry said.

Jacoby struggled against the Hold spell, but his efforts were futile, and the fight dragged on, neither able to land a decisive blow. Then, from the corner of his vision, he saw a hunched elf emerge from the trees and join the high elves on their terraced hillside. Bharat had arrived, and there was no telling how the leader of the elves would react.

CHAPTER 20

"Beak," Muji chirped, more out of boredom than anything else. He watched the warrior skeleton fight dozens of other undead from his perch on a low pine branch. It wasn't particularly interesting, and he found himself dozing off.

Over the past day or so he quickly adapted to the outside world to the point where he was pretty comfortable. He'd modified his harness array to emit a blast of heat that instantly dried his wet fur. Though the crystal was now out of magic, he learned to physically remove snow from his coat with frequent shakes before it could melt, keeping him effectively dry. He'd even started using his tail as an insulating cushion to keep his hands and feet warm—a simple comfort that made a world of difference to the trogold's morale.

Muji even caught a few of the annoying tree-dwelling creatures by pretending to be slow until they risked getting too close. He couldn't outmaneuver the tiny animals, but he learned that a quick burst of speed would usually catch them by surprise.

Maybe the outside world wasn't as terrible as he initially thought. He could do without the snow and the super bright sun globe, but for the most part, he could tolerate it. Perhaps he could get the Protector to recharge the fire crystal in his harness array? Yes, that would do nicely.

The fighting almost became interesting when another group showed up, and the warrior skeleton started fighting a human instead of other skeletons. The human had interesting magic that sparkled brighter than the sun globe on the blue ceiling. It coated his body and weapon in a powerful barrier that had both offensive and defensive properties. Muji followed the exchange, noting that the two combatants were closely matched, until his attention once again flagged and his sleepy trogold eyes began to droop.

Muji had almost fallen asleep when the magic in the air changed. Malice in the guise of dark energy permeated the area and suppressed all other forms in the vicinity. A chill ran across Muji's body. The trogold's instincts brought him to his feet with tail bushed and teeth bared before he was fully aware of the change.

Another person had arrived and cast an ugly spell over the area. To Muji's eyes, it appeared as a sickly brown and green miasma that hung in the air and concentrated around the undead. The new person wore a flow crystal on his head, like what the child used to enchant the Protector, but much more powerful.

Muji felt danger exuding from the new person and doubted his skeletons could do anything without the trogold's help. He scurried down the tree and stealthily approached the wooden cage that housed the undead. The strange things had gone on too long. He was going to help, whether the Protector liked it or not.

—

"It will take us several hours to get to the top. Should we rest? Maybe in that cave over there?" Eudora asked, dismissing her floating lance. It vanished in a flicker of red magic, and the globs of black Sprig blood on it fell to the ground with a loud *splat*. She'd killed dozens of the putrid monsters and hundreds of skeletons on their journey through the mountain. After days of fighting through the horrors of Jallfoss, she was happy to stand at the base of the final ascent with Master Mersin and Commander Cirilo.

At Tier **20**, she was one of the most powerful warriors in the Ikritian empire, but the journey had still taken its toll. She was low on Merq, down to her last few Health crystals, and ready for a slight reprieve from the endless battles.

"If you're looking for a rest, you won't find it in that cave," Mersin replied with his high-pitched voice.

"Trolls?" Eudora asked, eyeing the massive opening. It was a hundred feet high and three times that wide. Her Perception was **34**, but it couldn't pierce deep enough into the cave to see what lay within. She did, however, pick up a few rotting carcasses of some unfortunate animals just inside, and a deep red glow that seemed to pulse like the beat of a dying heart.

Cirilo put a hand on her shoulder plate. His voice was kind, but it carried a seriousness that she dared not question. "The mountain troll is a vicious creature. Even the strongest Acolyte would be tested to her limits against a lair of the brutes. However, I would prefer to face an army of trolls rather than set foot inside Ghara's burrow."

"Ghara," Eudora repeated the word and looked from the cave to the twisting path that led up to the craggy mountain top. "I had no idea the Sprig mother resided just a few thousand feet below the Empress's ghost.

"The high peak was once a beacon of power for the rulers of Jallfoss. The Oxendines were crowned in that spot for thousands of years. Ghara was once a symbol of prosperity—a peaceful being of nature that the Oxendines defended fiercely. That protection kept the elves happily under their rule for millennia, until the Necromancer destroyed most of the living things inside Jallfoss. The elves call Ghara a god, but Lord Stavros calls her a Primal."

Mersin let out a whistling snort. "A god is a being of great power that shapes the world. They gather worshippers and dole out blessings and punishment as they see fit. I would argue that a Primal fits that description."

"As always, your logic is wise beyond your years, Master Mersin," Cirilo acknowledged. Eudora knew Cirilo's words were not in jest, but the knowing look in the Commander's eyes betrayed the hidden knowledge of a man who had learned too many secrets in his time.

"You are too kind, Commander, but logic will not serve us well, were we to be caught in the open by a horde—be it Sprigs, trolls, or skeletons. Might I suggest we make our way to our destination?" Mersin said, indicating with his chin to the top of the mountain.

"Of course," Cirilo agreed, hefting the six-foot chunk of metal that served as his sword over his shoulder, and began trudging up the mountain path. Suddenly, the Commander dropped to a knee. He clutched his chest and let out a series of gasping coughs.

Eudora ran to his side. She'd never seen either a monster or a man inflict *any* damage on Cirilo, so for him to stumble was extremely worrying. "Commander?" she asked as she approached. She thought she heard the man wheeze, but as quickly as he had dropped, he rose back up.

"Not as sure-footed as I was a few decades ago," Cirilo joked, but Eudora noticed the color had drained from his face. She'd observed him wincing occasionally throughout the trip, but this episode was the most severe yet. Cirilo began the hike again, not allowing Eudora the chance to question her leader.

Mersin followed Cirilo, then turned back to Eudora and said, "Don't worry, Master Eudora. Plenty of time to rest when we're dead. Ha!" He let out a loud cackle, clearly tickled by his joke. Eudora eyed the craggy peaks of Jallfoss's highest mountain, unwilling to return Mersin's jovial sentiment.

CHAPTER 21

Bharat heard cheering from the Theater long before he arrived. The shouts were much louder than typical for the elven arena, though far from the roar of crowds long past in the Ammerthall coliseum.

The applause brought him back to the Gladiator Supreme games a hundred years prior. While he didn't enjoy traveling into the depths of Jallfoss, he had to admit that watching humans bash in each other's heads was usually worth the journey into the squalor. On his way to the earlier matches of the Gladiator Supreme games, he'd learned of the emergence of evil from the dwarven discovery, and the Sage had been forced to return to the elven forest to prepare. Missing the final days of the games had been a small price to pay for keeping his life, but he still wondered if the Talisker boy had won. *He was undoubtedly talented, even for a human.*

Bharat thought it ironic that his move to the pine forests of Amera had saved his life when the Necromancer's curse, along with Livadi's fire soldiers, extinguished every living soul above Hjardharfell. Had that damn giant and troll not destroyed his beautiful home, he would now be one of those undead, mindlessly roaming the halls of his former castle. Though thankful to be alive, he still lamented that he'd had to live the last hundred years away from the comfort of his high-elven home.

Another round of cheers rang out. Bharat exited the line of trees at the clearing's edge and approached the hillside seating from behind. A few elves noticed him and bowed, but with a simple gesture and a kind smile, he encouraged them to continue enjoying the fight. They returned their attention to the arena, though eagerly parted to allow the Sage to pass through. At the arena's edge, Bharat found Talji and Jai. His anger flared again at Talji's inability to follow his instructions. He thought he'd clarified that Talji was to handle the situation. Instead, she had engaged the boy in a Guard duel. Bharat stopped several feet behind them and watched. He'd found that a thoughtful moment of reflection was always better than a rushed reaction. A part of him was also quite eager to see the capabilities of Talji's human.

It was indeed an entertaining battle. A skeleton, clad in horrifically powerful armor and bearing a sword and shield that would put all but the finest elven armaments to shame, fought Talji's Acolyte. She had far superior control over the man than Jai had over his skeleton, but the skeleton's superior equipment and high Tier proved more than the human's attacks could overcome. *So, it's true. The skeleton does have Tiers. This is . . . unexpected.*

Bharat would let the crowd have their fun. Then, regardless of the outcome, he would simply overcome Jai's Command Link and take control of all the undead.

Bharat glanced casually around the arena as though he'd come to enjoy the spectacle. The forest elves had worked themselves into a frenzy and were cheering wildly every time the skeleton pushed back Talji's human. *Simpletons. I could protect and guide them for the next thousand years, but they wouldn't understand loyalty, no matter how stringently I forced the lesson upon them.*

"Surat," Bharat barked, loud enough to summon the elf, but quiet enough not to distract Jai or Talji.

The sentinel rushed to the Sage's side and bowed his head. "Yes, Great Sage."

"You said the boy brought other skeletons. Are they as powerful as this one?" Bharat asked. He was sure Lata had mentioned more skeletons in Jai's guard, but he highly doubted the boy had the means to control one skeleton, let alone synchronize an entire Guard. Either way, he would punish Jai severely for taking Mayur's circlet and thinking he could become a Sentinel. As the Great Sage, Bharat had to set an example for the forest elves on the other side cheering for Jai.

Surat bowed even further. "Far more powerful, great sage. But what is most remarkable is that they are completely sentient. They can talk as though they were alive." Surat pointed to the cages at the far end of the arena.

"Henry, kick him!" Jai shouted. The human had knocked the skeleton to its back, but a powerful kick sent the man flailing through the air.

Bharat ignored the fighting and looked at the cages that Surat was pointing at. He saw the wooden structure that apparently held the rest of Jai's undeserved Guard. Though his vision wasn't what it used to be in his youth, he saw a massive skeleton that had to hunch just to fit in the cage, as well as one in blue robes, and another small one in a black cloak. "Sentient? What do you mean?" Bharat asked, though his voice nearly caught in his throat as he forced his mind to deny the connection it was trying to make.

Surat snorted with a derisive laugh. "They talk just like

normal beings would. One is a giant, one is a mage, and Jai even had the gall to Hold a female elf."

Bharat's skin ran cold as he mouthed the name . . . *Harshmira.* He pulled an immense amount of Guile from his core and forced it into the circlet on his forehead.

Hold Undead

Command Link Established 12,085/39,000: 33 undead added to Guard. 61 undead available to command

"Hold!" the Sage shouted, pushing his aged voice to its limit. Bharat's spell spread through the arena and most of the surrounding valley as he took control of every undead in the vicinity. The human and skeleton fighting in the arena froze in place.

Bharat's magic was formidable, beyond the imaginations of any living elf. In all his years, he'd only come across one single being, a human mage, whose skill with magic could outclass his. He'd spent a thousand years perfecting his craft, but only the last hundred developed the spell he now blanketed over the high valley. Even so, controlling so many undead pushed his vast power to its limit. The strain on his aged body and mind forced his Guile to dip lower than it had in ages.

"Lata, restrain the boy. This charade is over," the Sage ordered, his body shaking under the force of magic that flooded from his mind.

Every elf turned toward Bharat as their cheers died down to murmurs. Talji spun, her face flushed red. "Great Sage, I was about to win and take these powerful skeletons. I—"

"These skeletons are beings of pure evil, sent directly from the Necromancer. They must be destroyed and returned to the bowels of the filthy mountain." More Guile welled from

Bharat's core and spread into the destroyed skeletons scattered throughout the arena. It was a spell he didn't use often or lightly, as it came from the same pages where he'd garnered the Hold Undead spell. The fear of the identities of the caged skeletons forced him to disregard caution and lock every nearby undead in Amera under his control.

Reanimate

Command Link Established 17,220/39,000: 23 undead added to Guard. 84 undead available to command

Black, green, and yellow waves surrounded Bharat's out-stretched hands and snaked across the ground like a monitor hunting for prey. The magic entered and revived the entire field of broken skeletons. Dozens of defeated undead pieced themselves back together and stood, awaiting Bharat's orders.

"Sentinels, destroy Jai's skeletons," Bharat ordered.

"No!" Jai screamed as Lata and Surat held the struggling elf tightly. "That's my Guard!"

"Those abominations are not yours. They are evil beings that must be destroyed. And you, boy, are a vile outcast that I should have dealt with long ago!"

Jacoby, along with dozens of skeletons and a handful of elven Sentinels, converged on Henry.

CHAPTER 22

"**B**arney, this is bad. I don't think that old elf cares much for us," Ox said from the center of the thick wooden cage. Its bars were sturdy and woven together as though they'd been grown. It would have held any Guard and most of the Sprigs securely, though Ox could smash his way out handily, if only he could break free of the elven spell. The new notification in Buddy's view made that seem quite unlikely.

Status Effect: Hold Undead. No actions may be taken without the direction of the caster. Command Link Established 17,220/39,000

Beast let out a resigned sigh. "The Elven Sage is powerful. He just revived all the skeletons that Henry destroyed, and I'm sure he just ordered the elves to kill us. I told you all to mind your business, but *no*, you had to help that pathetic elf."

"Your analysis of our circumstances is correct, Beast. Though it lacks a viable course of action." Buddy said, though he agreed that their situation looked increasingly hopeless. The skeletal mage tried for the hundredth time to force Vitus into his hands, but the Hold Undead spell prevented any action on his part. He looked out at Henry, standing frozen in the arena as fifty skeletons and twenty armed elves converged on the warrior.

"I was planning to die smothered beneath the bosoms of my lustful concubines. Perhaps in the next life, minions," Ox said with such a jovial tone that one could have assumed he was welcoming the horde of elves and undead before them.

Beast nearly shouted in anger. "You oaf. We're about to get torn apart, and all you can think about is your made-up harem. At least you could—"

"—Beak," Muji's squeak cut her off. The Trogold clung to the bars of the cage and reached in as far as he could with tiny, splayed fingers.

Ox's laugh got even louder. "Ha! Hello, tiny friend. We should have let you keep the magma blaster. I fear there's little you can do to help, even if you were to gnaw through this cage."

"Unghh, beak," Muji grunted and pushed his hand a bit further into the cage. He extended claw-tipped fingers as far as he could, mere inches from Buddy's skeletal hand.

Now it was Beast's turn to laugh. "Looks like you don't have a choice, old mage."

"What choice is that?" Ox asked.

From the arena, they heard Henry's shout as an army of skeletons and elves converged on him. "Buddy, I need a spark!"

Buddy heard Henry's desperate request and knew what had to be done. The mage glanced down and saw the determination in Muji's eyes. The trogold's tiny paw swiped closer and closer to his hand. Once again, Muji was putting himself in danger to assist him, despite Buddy doing everything he could to push the creature away. Buddy felt like he had done nothing to deserve such loyalty and devotion. He was thankful that his skeletal features were incapable of showing emotion. "Very well, Muji. You have earned my respect. I am honored to call such a brave trogold my thrall."

"Beak!" Muji grunted and stretched as far as he could until the pad of his tiny finger brushed the exposed bone of Buddy's hand.

—

"Henry, kick him!" Jai rang through the arena.

Henry's leg shot upward and booted Jacoby hard in the center of his torso. The huamn's chestplate absorbed the blow, and he tumbled backward, giving Henry enough space to recover to his feet. Henry stepped forward to continue the attack but froze in place.

Status Effect: Hold Undead. No actions may be taken without the direction of the caster. Command Link Established 12,085/39,000

Slyngur tumbled from his fingers as a will far stronger than Jai's seized his bones. Dread filled Henry, and the elven cheers faded, silence washing over the arena. He directed his attention to where an old elf had arrived, likely the source of the new Hold link. *Bharat.*

One of several cages held his friends, fifty paces before him, on the arena's far boundary. His Perception picked up the tiny shape of Muji clinging to its side. He knew those cages were robust enough to hold the strongest Sprigs. Even at Tier 15, it would take Muji a long time to gnaw through the thick bars.

"Sentinels, destroy those skeletons," Bharat shouted.

Jai screamed in protest as two armed elves restrained the boy.

The new Command Link increased again, indicating Bharat had taken control of even more skeletons. All around Henry, broken undead reformed themselves as wisps of black and green magic wove the corpses back together. The undead and their elven Sentinels began to converge on Henry. Jacoby brought himself to his feet and brandished his sword as he readied an attack.

Henry pressed his Resolve against the magical connection, but it wouldn't budge. There was a wall between his mind and body that he just couldn't overcome. There had to be a way around the barrier, another path he could take . . . The idea hit him like Ox's maul smashing into a salamander's skull. Henry shouted, projecting his voice as far as he could. "Buddy, I need a Spark!" Henry could do nothing but hope that Buddy would figure out how to fulfill his request. It was unlikely that even the mage's huge Acumen could overcome the Hold spell. Henry had to trust his friend would find a way.

Jacoby loomed closer, and a golden glow from the man's magic emanated from his sword. The Acolyte cocked back the blade and prepared for a thrust.

Henry's savior arrived in a flash of brown and white fur.

Muji darted between Jacoby's legs, moving so fast that even Herny's Blitz would have had trouble matching the creature's speed. Henry saw arcs of blue lightning dancing along Muji's fur. The tiny cave dweller launched into the air and hit Henry directly in the chest.

Just as quickly, Muji rebounded off him and sped toward the high-elven seating at the side of the arena. Henry heard the crackle of electricity as blue light welled up and enveloped him.

Lightning Resistance applied: 20/68 damage negated.

Health: 48/115

The tip of Jacoby's sword rushed toward Henry's face. The arena began to dim. Lightning seared his bones, then everything turned black.

CHAPTER 23

For the fifth time, Henry traveled to the desert. Maybe traveled wasn't the right word—visited . . . dreamt? He expected the darkness to recede and, hopefully, not reveal an attacking dragon. After a few breaths in pitch black, Henry wondered if Jacoby's sword had struck, and he was truly dead.

No, he thought, as the rush of sensations hit him. He was face down on a bed of rocks. They were uncomfortable and cold. The air was damp and smelled of mildew. He listened, but no sound beyond his breath and beating heart came into his awareness.

Beating heart . . . at least he was alive.

Slowly, he reached out and started to explore the area around him with his hands. He stood and extended his arms upward, but couldn't reach the ceiling. He was walled in on three sides by piled rocks and boulders. The fourth side, however, sloped down steeply.

He pursed his lips and let out a whistle. The sound echoed along the decline and returned after several seconds, indicating a long tunnel stretched before him.

With no other option present, Henry carefully descended, placing unsteady feet on the damp stone. It was a tunnel about eight feet tall and just as wide. Henry couldn't quite tell but thought it might have a slight curve to it.

He slipped twice and landed hard on his back, though he managed to stop his fall before tumbling down the steep grade. Sharp rocks tore into his skin, leaving superficial wounds. Henry welcomed the pain that he'd been sorely missing as an undead skeleton.

One wary step turned into countless more as Henry trudged down the dark tunnel. Slick, wet walls guided his descent, and only the echo of his own foots steps and breathing kept him company. As frustration began to set in, a dim halo emerged from the darkness.

Another hundred steps down, the corona formed into a tiny fire on a small candle, providing just enough illumination for him to see. The single wax torch sat on a small natural ledge on the side of the tunnel. Someone had come before Henry and left the candle. Was it meant for him?

Black and grey stone with veins of yellow and blue made up the rocky enclosure, similar to what he'd found in the stoney outcropping above. However, there were no signs of yellow dragon glass from either Raynott's cage or the blue dragon's horns and spikes. He also noticed the smooth decline had started to waver, almost forming into steps.

Henry took the candle and continued down the path. His footsteps softly padded on the damp stone. He was grateful for the illumination and for the steadier footing. The minutes dragged on as Henry continued down the featureless tunnel, and his mind began to wander.

The weight of saving an undead mountain was a lot to shoulder. Without the memory of his former life, he had trouble parsing out his own motivations. Henry had lectured Jai on being a leader. The words he'd told the young elf were valid and what the boy needed to hear at the time. However, Henry's guidance felt hollow without a clear way ahead or a purpose of his own. He was trying to save the mountain, but what did that mean? What did he really want? What was he missing?

Fighting made him happy; it filled him with an intense thrill of pitting his swordsmanship against that of another. Though it had been interrupted, the current battle in the elven arena had given him that satisfaction. Jacoby was a superb swords-man, and Henry wanted to fight the man on even grounds—similar equipment and no elves controlling them. It would be a great match.

He'd already fought the Acolyte once and killed him. Now Jacoby had returned, proving there was a chance to save all the undead. But at what cost? Henry had killed Jacoby to regain his own life. That meant someone had to die for Jacoby to re-gain his. Was it the boy, Koş? Did the Necromancer resurrect Jacoby? Henry thought such evil was the essence of necro-mancy—bringing the dead back to life, though at an unknown toll. Buddy would probably clarify the specifics of the magic more conclusively, but that was a good enough explanation for Henry.

Searing pain shot through Henry's finger, and the light around him snuffed out. The candle had burned through while he was lost in thought. The ache lingered on the burnt skin and hurt in a far more severe way than could have been expected from such a tiny flame. Could his susceptibility to fire still exist in his Desert Path? That meant the lightning Resistance was there as well.

His eyes started to adjust to the dark, and another dim light emerged further ahead. After several more steps, Henry found a second candle. This one was larger and in a metal sconce. In the dim light, he noticed the waving stone decline beneath his feet had become terraced, most likely hand-carved, steps. If the tunnel was natural it was well-traveled enough to require masonic crafting. Henry wondered if he was back in the Dwarven Underdeep.

He hesitated, looking back up and into the dark tunnel, then down the staircase. *I guess I'll keep going.*

As he descended, he came across several more sconces holding candles, each slightly less rudimentary than the previous. The walls had begun to straighten into flat vertical surfaces, and the uneven steps became more regular.

Henry continued to let his thoughts drift until the sconces started appearing at regular intervals of about twenty feet and on either side of the staircase. He stopped to examine one and found it was made of a black metal that formed into a swirling design.

Just past and on the right, white markings were drawn on the walls. It looked like someone had used their fingers to create the rudimentary design, but he could make out what was meant to be the outline of a dragon with wings, a long tail, and an open maw spewing something, though the drawing was heavily faded.

Henry found several more sketches as he walked further down: dragons and monsters, animals, and even humanoids in scenes ranging from peaceful natural settings to intense and bloody battles. Each drawing was more elaborate and more detailed than the previous. The now-smooth walls made an acceptable canvas for the multicolored paintings.

He ran his fingers over one of the murals, taking in a scene of a tentacled sea creature spilling out both sides of a large ocean. The paint was old, and some of the pigment crumbled on his fingertips.

A faint noise came from above as Henry rubbed the paint flakes between his fingers and thumb. It was a raspy sound that could have been a door creaking or a tree limb groaning in the wind. A cold chill ran over Henry's skin, and he felt goose bumps forming on his neck. Henry saw the candles flicker ever so slightly.

He looked up the stairs and into the fading darkness. Seconds passed like hours as he waited for the sound to repeat, but it never came, and Henry had to convince himself he'd heard anything.

The sound didn't come again, and after several long minutes, Henry gave up and turned his attention back down the tunnel. With nowhere to hide from anything coming down the staircase, he could do little more than direct a portion of his Perception upward and stay prepared for a fight.

He looked around and realized the steps he walked on now had a carpeted strip loosely adhering to the center of the stairs. The runner was torn and very dirty, but looked like it had once been elegant. It felt soft and welcoming under his bare feet, and for a moment, he considered stopping to rest. The image of his friends trapped in the elven cage and Jacoby's sword screaming toward his face cut that desire short.

After another hour of walking, the walls, steps, and ceiling slowly became pristine marble. The drawings evolved into highly detailed paintings hung with elaborate wooden frames. The sconces were now made of brass, and each was in the shape of a different creature, most of which Henry couldn't recognize. He continued, torn between paying homage to the beautiful artwork before him and wanting to hurry to see what else he might find further down.

Hundreds of steps later, the sconces became gold and in-laid with jewels of every sort. The carpet now had a woven design and tightly followed the marble steps. What caught his attention, though, was that the paintings began to repeat a common theme. There were mostly dragons, but also men with feathered wings and shining armor. There were people in forests with antlered heads, and creatures that seemed to be made of bone. Most of the paintings had become scenes of epic battles. *Dragons, celestials, spriggans, archons . . . Primals,* Henry supposed. Sometimes the Primals were fighting each other, but sometimes they were on the same side, fighting other monsters and men.

Up ahead, Henry saw a landing. A woven silk rug covered the ten-foot square space, and across from the steps were a pair of double doors set firmly into a marble wall. Neither wood nor stone, the doors were composed of the same dragon glass as Raynott's cage and the dragon's horns. There were brilliant blue and gold veins running through the material, as well as streaks of green and red. The glass, if it was glass, was opaque with no light penetrating it from the other side.

Henry cared little about the material. His attention was fixed on the figures carved into it. On the left, a woman with long hair wearing a summer dress walked toward him. Suspended in the relief, her mouth held a smile, but her eyes seemed to hold back tears. She glanced down and to Henry's right, where her delicate hand held that of a child's. A boy, just old enough to walk, smiled up at his mother. His feet wobbled in the unsteady canter of a toddler while the woman provided just enough sup-port to keep him balanced.

Though carved in the yellow stone, the detail of the relief was so precise that Henry had to look twice to ensure the two weren't moving. The woman's face held such love for her child that Henry's heart ached, and he wished for them to come to life so she could sweep the boy into her arms and hug him tightly. Henry reluctantly dismissed the emotion and refocused his attention on the doors themselves.

He searched but couldn't find handles, key holes, or hinges. He studied the doors, then looked around. On opposite walls on either side of the doors hung two huge paintings. The one on the left showed eight beings of different sizes and shapes, likely more Primals, standing before a towering monstrosity. Clouds obscured a colossus the size of an entire mountain as it loomed ominously over them. However, he could clearly see the monster's eyes—dark voids that seemed to bore into his soul, so vast and oppressive that it could have originated from the very space between stars. The detail was fine to the point that Henry couldn't make out brushstrokes, and it gave him the impression that the painting had been created from something other than the artist's mind.

To the right of the doors, another painting showed a dragon and a warrior clad in brilliant white armor engaged in an epic battle against a monster formed of black bone. The similarities between the monster and the Silent from the dwarven Underdeep were unmistakable and gave Henry all the evidence he needed to call them *archons*, though the painting depicted a creature many times larger and more horrifying than those he'd fought. In the painting's background, lightning struck from the sky, and fire spewed from the ground like the earth itself was joining the clash. Henry could have stared at the scene for hours, but the situation's urgency forced him away from the canvas.

Henry approached the yellow doors and ran his fingers over the intricate carvings. He wished he had longer to study the artwork, or better yet, someone to tell him their meaning and origin, but he was in a hurry. He raised his palm and banged on the door. The sound echoed loudly through the tunnel, but there was no response. He tried to push, and the door refused to budge, more solid than the surrounding marble.

Well, this is the only way forward. Henry stepped back, raised his leg, and kicked as hard as possible. He didn't expect the doors to kick back.

A wall of sheer will rebounded through his leg and flung him backward. He landed hard against the steps, thanking the tunnel's designer for the soft carpet that only mildly blunted his landing.

Henry sat up and studied the doors, contemplating the sensation that forced him back. It felt like the mental block that the Hold Undead spell presented to him when he forced his Resolve against it, just in physical form.

The loud rasping sound from before pierced the silence above Henry, shaking him from his focus on the doors. That time, he knew for sure he hadn't imagined it.

CHAPTER 24

Henry quickly rose to his feet, looking for a weapon but finding none. He strained his vision up the steps as the sound congealed into a voice and got louder. It was laughter mixed with a harsh whistle, but there was no questioning that it came from some being. After a moment, a figure emerged from the shadows above.

The man from the cage in the desert slowly hobbled down the steps.

"Old man . . . Raynott. Is that you?" Henry asked, just above a whisper.

"No need to hide your voice down here, warrior. The dragon can't fit in this staircase," Raynott replied with labored breath.

Henry bounded up the carpeted stairs. The old man looked even more frail than he had in the glass prison, as if he would collapse and roll down, likely dying before he made it to the bottom. "You're alive! I didn't know what to do to get away from the dragon, but I'm glad you made it," Henry greeted, holding out a hand to assist.

"More alive than I've been in ages, warrior," he wheezed,

taking Henry's hand and leaning his weight into him. The man was surprisingly heavy for nothing more than old bones and skin.

"You're Raynott? One of the men who defeated Malek and founded Jallfoss?" Henry asked.

"I was many things, though few of them matter anymore." Raynott pointed a shaky finger at the painting on the right. "I was once a warrior like you, yearning for battles the likes of which this world has never seen." A sense of nostalgia and memory rolled over the old man's eyes.

"Of course, that's the battle where you and Osirian defeated Malek and founded Jallfoss. I don't understand how you went from that fight to being trapped in a cage. What were you doing in there?"

Raynott coughed as much as he laughed. "Rotting. What else is there to do in a prison?"

Henry tried not to let his frustration show. He needed answers from the man if he wanted to help his friends. "What is this place? Why is there a dragon trying to kill me? And what in Minoa's rosy hosiery are you doing here?"

They reached the bottom of the staircase, and Henry motioned for Raynott to sit, but the old man waved him off. "This place is one of the many worlds the young gods created. It became my prison when a necromancer trapped me here. The Primals sometimes use it to test their Remnants.

"I'm being tested?" Henry asked.

"You're being forged, warrior. But like any ore, if you are weak in quality, you will crack under the pressure and be nothing more than a broken implement."

"Broken? Like Thorodd?" Henry asked, remembering what his Haruspex had revealed of the dwarven Elder.

"If this Thorodd is a Remnant who failed to complete his Path, then yes, broken."

Raynott's words provided more information than Henry previously had, but it still didn't help him. "I don't have time for a test. I'm in a forest outside the Jallfoss mountain range. I'm a skeleton without a memory, trying to revive the mountain from the Necromancer's spell, likely the same evil being that imprisoned you. But right now, I'm fighting for my life and under the control of an elven spell. I came here searching for a way to break free from that spell and save my friends."

Raynott's gaze drifted as though he were reliving an old memory. "Your body and your mind are gone. All that's left is your soul. You were right to come here in search of help." His eyes snapped back to Henry, and his dark pupils narrowed. "Yes, warrior, I will assist you with this valiant task. Together, we will find your body and mind, defeat your necromancer, and so much more. But first, we must kill your dragon."

Henry shook his head and chuckled a humorless laugh. "That's impossible. It's a dragon. I still don't know what this place is, but I get weaker every time I go back and forth. If you know something, tell me so I can eliminate this Desert Path Status Effect."

"If you want to get stronger, you must defeat the dragon. He is the Primal guarding this Realm. You have come too far to run, warrior. A fate worse than death waits for failed Remnants. Fight warrior, like your life depends on it. Because it does."

Henry looked at the doors and studied the woman and child carved into them. "How do I fight a dragon?"

"How do *we* fight a dragon? Is the correct question." Raynott pointed to the glass doors. "The answer is the same way we get through those."

"It's no use. There are no keyholes or handles. I tried to kick it down, and it blew me back."

Raynott raised a frail hand and stopped just short of

touching the door. "The young gods created the rules of this world. When they left, the Primals maintained the keys to their power. Those Primals then distributed it to mortals they deemed worthy of protecting that legacy. Sadly, some of those protectors interpreted their duties differently, resulting in my lengthy captivity."

"Are you saying a Remnant is the keeper of godly power?" Henry asked.

Raynott let out a cackle that turned into an uncontrollable cough and back into laughter. The old man nearly collapsed, and Henry had to help him sit on the stairs. When Raynott recovered, he gave Henry a once-over and smiled a rotted, toothy grin. "If you were to fill a stein with salt water, you wouldn't say you've harnessed the power of the oceans. Few Remnants have learned to sail those waters, and fewer still have dove into its briny depths and returned to speak of what lies below."

"But you have?" Henry asked, searching for meaning in the man's words.

"For the better part of five thousand years."

"You still haven't told me how you got here."

"Betrayal, by my closest friends. Jealousy, greed, and lofty ideals will often overcome the bonds of trust. You want to save your companions, but would they do the same for you? Discard your earthly chains, warrior. The two of us can conquer Jallfoss, and then we can reshape the world as it should be. All you need to do is open the door. You already have the keys. You just need to use them."

Henry had no intention of abandoning his friends, but he felt that five thousand years in an otherworldly prison justified the man's bitterness toward whatever former allies he referenced. Regardless, Raynott's words made Henry realize what he needed to do, and no amount of physical or magical force would work.

He stood and faced the doors, spreading his awareness past his body and using his Harmony instead of sight or thought to sense the surrounding area. It started as a faint sensation in the distance, but the more Henry focused, the clearer the feeling became. He felt a strong connection to the doors, like they weren't a barrier from passage, but rather a bridge to something else, something calling for him. He solidified that connection with his Affinity, then with his Might, he formed it into a mental span from where he was to where he wanted to go. With a loud *click*, the doors moved just a bit, no longer restrained by their locks.

"Good, young warrior. Now, let us enter and I will show you the true power we possess," Raynott croaked.

Henry didn't move. Raynott's tone made him wary of the man's intentions. "At our last meeting, you talked about the Necromancer and Malek, but you implied they are not the same being. How does Stavros fit in? Before I let you through, I need to know what you know about each of them."

Henry heard the old man's feet shuffle on the carpet. "Once we get out of here, I'll tell you everything you need to know."

Henry hadn't yet dampened his Harmony, and Raynott's words sent a black cloud through his mind, too close to the feeling from the aura of the Silent for Henry to ignore. "You'll tell me everything right now or spend another five thousand years locked away."

The man's voice lowered to a tone Henry didn't think it capable—a bass that pushed away any hint of age and weakness. "You will not threaten me, warrior. I've spent a hundred lifetimes prying ancient secrets from Jallfoss himself. Osirian and Raynott were fools to—" The old man cut himself off, but it was too late. His identity had been divulged.

"—Malek," Henry whispered. A cold chill ran down his spine. He couldn't tell if it was his Remnant Attributes that alerted him, but he felt Malek's anger fill the landing like searing magma pouring into Hjardharfell's forges. Henry sensed a wave of pressure bearing down on him and ducked just in time. A gnarled fist slammed into the dragon glass, passing through where Henry's head had been a moment before. Like a gong being struck, a resounding thud echoed as lines of black light arced through the door before dissipating.

Henry's fighting instinct kicked in, and he threw an elbow backward, smashing into a jaw that felt sturdier than Ox's. The old man's face should have been crushed under Henry's blow, but Malek only took a small step back and glared before thrusting with a knee.

Henry rolled out of the way toward the stairs, barely missing the decisive blow that would have crushed bone. Physically, the old man hadn't changed; his skin still clung tight to atrophied muscles, though he now stood with the confident demeanor of a young fighter in his prime. His eyes were still sunken, but the fearful expression had changed to one of fury. Henry didn't want to chance a fight without knowing more about the old man. A peaceful resolution seemed unlikely, and Henry had to get around him and through the doors.

"You could have ruled the mountain under me. Now you will serve as one of my pawns for eternity." Malek turned and pulled hard. The door budged just a bit, and light gushed into the room.

It looked like avoiding a fight was out of the question. Henry rushed forward and struck as hard and fast as he could at Malek's rib cage. Malek swung with a heavy backhand, and Henry ducked under while landing a hard kidney punch. The blow would have destroyed the internal organs of a normal adversary, especially a geriatric, emaciated prisoner, but Henry's fist pounded against the man's torso like he'd hit a solid barillo tree.

Malek followed up with a heavy right hook. Henry parried a blow and landed an upcut on Malek's jaw. Malek's head lifted just slightly under the force of Henry's attack, enough to allow him to grip either side of Malek's neck in a hard clench. Henry thrust with a knee to whatever part of the man's body would happen to get in the way.

Malek responded with a headbutt so quick that Henry barely had time to steady his neck. Stars flashed in his eyes, and when they cleared, he was lying on the carpeted steps with Malek glaring down at him.

"You Degonharts never knew when to quit. But I thank you for allowing me into the Dragon Realm." Malek turned and reached for the doors.

Whatever was on the other side of that door was for Henry and Henry alone. He knew if Malek got in there, it would be terrible for not only him, but for his friends and all of Jallfoss. He had to get through and lock Malek out, and he didn't have much time. He searched through his awareness, wading through the murk that was the connection between him and Malek, strengthened it, and forced the taunt into the old man's mind. "I think Raynott imprisoned you out of pity. I doubt he could have brought himself to kill someone so pathetic. You probably weren't worthy of a warrior's death."

A low growl formed in Malek's throat. "I was worthy of EVERYTHING!" He snarled and turned back to Henry. The man lunged forward with death in his eyes. Henry was ready. He grabbed Malek's wrists and put his foot in the man's stomach, then rolled backward. He used Malek's momentum and his own powerful legs to launch the old man up a dozen steps.

Before Malek landed, Henry was on his feet and sprinting toward the doors. He gripped the edge and pulled. Blinding light hit Henry's face, but he didn't need to see to make his way through the portal.

"No!" Malek's rage turned to fear.

Henry saw the old man running down the stairs. In the same way he'd opened the doors, Henry used his Remnant Attributes to seal the portal, slamming them shut and locking Malek on the other side.

Henry stared at the yellow glass and breathed heavily. His head ached from Malek's attack, and his wrists and hands hurt from where he had struck the man.

Old man, Henry thought with a painful laugh. *I hope I'm that sturdy when I hit five thousand years old.* A blast of wind caught Henry in the face. It was salty and wet, and the air smelled of brine and was chilly. Henry didn't dare turn away from the doors until he was sure they were sealed, but when he was satisfied that Malek couldn't follow him, he looked around.

The doors were at the base of a steep rocky cliff that went up hundreds of feet before vanishing into a thick cloud base. Green moss clung to rocky outcroppings, and hundreds of gulls swooped in and out of nests, cawing to one another as they flew. The cliff face went right as far as he could see, but curved away and disappeared a quarter mile to his left.

A black sandy beach sloped gently down into heavy waves. Henry strained his eyes, but the whitecaps disappeared into mist within a mile. A low cloud ceiling stretched in every direction and signaled an incoming storm.

Henry marveled at the beach and assumed that after hours of walking down the staircase, he would be deep underground and not at the edge of an ocean. He stepped forward, and his toes squished an inch deep into the coarse, gritty sand.

Thunder rumbled in the distance as Henry took a few steps toward the water. The gulls' screeches above him grew frantic, and Henry looked up to see the birds fleeing around the bend in the cliff. A swooping sound from above told him why.

The clouds swirled around a descending shape with blue scales, and yellow horns and claws. The hurricane-like force under the dragon's wings arrested its descent, sending sand blasting in all directions.

The dragon was even larger than Henry remembered and easily took up the entire stretch of beach. Its heavy back feet and winged fore-claws sank into the sand, and its crystal blue eyes pierced into Henry's. Henry saw a fresh wound on the dragon's face and dark, congealed blood from a few large gouges in its wings. Those wounds were likely from Henry sending the monster into Malek's cage. The presence of injuries meant that the beast could be hurt.

Predatorial intent flowed across the channel between the dragon and Henry before he could cut off his Remnant Attributes, and the guttural sound that came from the dragon's throat told Henry everything he needed to know about the monster's objective.

The dragon took a step forward and Henry took several back. His hands touched the yellow doors, and a shock rippled through his body. It didn't hurt, but Henry knew he had accomplished what he needed. He saw the dragon open its giant maw and release a colossal roar. Blinding white and blue coalesced in the back of the dragon's throat as everything faded to black.

CHAPTER 25

The darkness around Henry receded, and the arena came into focus. The clearest indication he had returned was the tip of Jacoby's sword speeding toward his face. He ignored the glyphs flashing in his vision and pulled Vitus from his core. He reached with his Harmony, searching for the connection. It appeared instantly in his awareness, like a beacon pointing from the elven Sage directly to Henry. He could also feel connections going to his companions and to the other undead—much weaker, but still there. Henry's Vitus swirled in his mind, and he used his Affinity to form the link between him and Bharat into a doorway. Then, with his Might, he slammed it shut, blocking out Bharat like he had Malek.

Remnant Gateway

Status Effect Dismissed. Hold Undead Command Link Severed

AFI +1

MIG +1

HAR +1

Henry's hands shot up and grabbed the blade. Chunks of bone splintered from his fingers, and his arms cracked under the force of the Acolyte's thrust, but he held firm. Several glyphs continued to flash, demanding attention. Henry ignored them. He could feel his entire body was weakened, and he knew this Desert Path's Effects were the most severe yet. He'd lost a few Thresholds again but gained what he needed to break the Hold Undead spell. Now for the hard part.

Jacoby pulled back his sword and prepared for another jab, but Henry didn't give him the opportunity. Releasing the elven blade, Henry grabbed Jacoby's forward ankle and planted his other palm as hard as he could in the center of the man's chest plate. Henry lifted and pushed, forcing the Acolyte off balance.

Jacoby landed hard on his back, and Henry was on him before the man could recover. Henry stepped on Jacoby's wrist, pinning his sword hand and weapon to the ground. Jacoby's throat was exposed, along with half a dozen other kill points. Instead of finishing his opponent, Henry kicked him hard in the head. Not enough to kill him, but easily enough to take him out of the fight. *Hopefully, brain damage doesn't last with the undead.*

Henry swept up his sword and took in the chaos in the arena. All the skeletons he'd killed had reformed, and now they, along with all the elven Sentinels, rushed toward him. Perception was still his highest Attribute, and with the few seconds he had to spare before the undead were on top of him, he turned his attention to his Status, wanting to see how harmful the new Effects were.

Haruspex

Fifth path of the desert: STR -20, MOB -20, FOR -10, ACU -10, PER-10, RES -10, Health -50, Fire Resistance -50, Lightning Resistance +100

MOB below first threshold. Attribute bonus removed

ACU below first threshold. Attribute bonus removed

**Ability Discovered: Remnant Gateway I (Enchantment). Portals be-
yond the physical realm can now be affected by your Remnant
Attributes. Open and close connections to your mind at will.
RES +5, Mental Resistance +10**

**Ability Discovered: Taunt II (Enchantment). Pit your Resolve against
your target and goad them to attack you. Increased effective-
ness against Remnants. RES +3, MIG +1, AFI +3**

The damage to his Attributes was severe, but at least he'd
freed himself. The Ability that helped him shut out the Hold
Undead spell was the same one he used to open the glass doors,
then seal out Malek. Somehow, whatever was testing him in the
Path gave him what he needed to succeed. On the other hand,
Malek was a problem he would eventually need to deal with.
First, he had to get himself and his comrades away from the
elven arena. Shouts from the side of the dirt battlefield inter-
rupted Henry's thoughts, and he turned his attention to where
Jai and Talji had been controlling the fight.

"Impossible, how does it resist your spell?" Henry's
Perception picked up Talji's question. Bharat stood beside her,
and Henry's Harmony allowed him to confirm the old elf as
the source that had taken over Jai's Hold on him. Henry could
still feel the threads of power connecting the ancient elf to the
other undead.

"Kill him, now!" Bharat ordered. Talji drew a sword from
Lata's belt and started toward Henry.

"No, they're *my* guard," Jai shouted. Lata and Surat were

restraining him, but a quick punch to his stomach made him slump over.

As the skeletons came into striking range, Henry saw something else. Flashes of brown and white fur nimbly maneuvered around the high elves, forcing their attention away from Henry and the arena. Muji was harassing them and doing a great job. Henry wasn't sure how the trogold had delivered Buddy's lighting to him, but he was thankful for the intervention.

Talji struck at the cave creature. The crowded seating area made maneuvering difficult, and Muji darted behind and around the other elves, grunting and flashing with arcs of Buddy's lightning magics. *Looks like the little fella has that covered.* Henry turned his attention back to the skeletons surrounding him.

Blitz

Henry spun, cutting down Tier **1** undead like they were paper targets. Though his Attributes had taken a hit, he had become proficient enough with Blitz that he made quick work of the attacking skeletons, cutting through bone like dry kindling and absorbing enough Vitus with his sword to keep himself charged. Within seconds, bones lay scattered across the arena.

Skeleton Killed x38, Soul Essence Claimed

With the undead dispatched, there was nothing between him and ten Sentinels that had started circling him. Haruspex revealed they were all between Tier **10** and **15**. Though their Attributes were similar to his, their equipment was far inferior. Even so, Henry didn't want to allow them to overwhelm him. He needed their fear to slow their attacks, and he knew just how to elicit that emotion.

Half of the elves drew near, brandishing swords and

wearing armor that had likely been taken from dead Acolytes. Five more elves stood back, either nocking arrows or weaving their hands through the air to prepare spells. *This will make them think twice.*

Spark

Blitz

Henry forced his lightning magic into his sword, and the blade lit up with blue arcs of electricity. The Sentinels halted their advance, and Henry surged toward the nearest foe. He kicked hard with his boot, catching the elf just below the knee. The joint buckled backward, and the elf cried out in pain. Before his opponent could topple over, Henry thrust with the electrified blade, piercing through armor and flesh with little more resistance than the skeletons had provided.

The body slumped to the ground, the wound immediately cauterized by the lightning magic.

Elven Sentinel Killed, Soul Essence Claimed

A wild spear thrust nearly struck him. To avoid the attack, Henry had to release his xiphos, still stuck in the dead elf's torso. He parried the pole arm across his body, grabbed the elf behind the bicep with his free hand, and pulled the elf off balance. Henry threaded his free arm under the elf's armpit and to the other side of the elf's neck before wrapping his wrist in the crook of his own elbow and securing the lock. *If this doesn't intimidate them, I don't know what will.* Henry stared directly into the eyes of the nearest Sentinel, then opened his mouth and roared as loudly as he could.

Sacrifice

Henry willed his Vitus into the dread shield at his wrist. It was in buckler form and directly below the elf's neck. The dread bone absorbed the magic and tripled in size instantly, severing the struggling elf's neck and arm still held firmly in Henry's lock.

Blood sprayed in a ten-foot arc around Henry. He let the arm and head thump into the dirt, then he cast the body aside as gore dripped from his armor, not breaking eye contact with the closest Sentinel.

The intimidation tactic did the trick, as every elf stopped their approach and looked at him in shocked horror. Two elves had been slain by a skeleton far more potent than they were used to confronting, and the shaking grips on their weapons said they didn't want to be next. They'd seen what Henry could do, and they were rightfully cautious to attack a skeleton wearing dread armor and wielding a prismatic lightning sword.

They're not warriors that fight together like the Acolytes, Henry thought, *they just use the undead to fight for them*. Without their Guard, the elves were now in a position they hadn't prepared for. The circle around Henry widened as the Sentinels took hesitant steps backward.

Henry retrieved his sword for the torso of the first fallen elf. He pointed the tip of his blade at the elven Sage and shouted, "Bharat! We're not here for you. Free my friends, and I won't have to kill your Sentinels."

The old elf narrowed his eyes, and his face flushed with anger. Henry supposed the elven leader was not used to being challenged, and Bharat's response proved that assumption correct.

The Sage's hands lit up with a bright green radiance. It flickered like Buddy's flame, and orbs of magic pulled off the spell like it was dripping wax from a candle. Seven balls formed and hovered around the sage briefly, then shot up and back toward the forest.

"I don't think he's giving up!" Ox shouted from the cage. He was right.

The orbs each found a tree and smacked into its bark, infusing into the structures. Trunks and branches shook violently, sending birds scattering away. Then, with deafening *cracks*, the trees shook and split apart. Splintered wood chunks separated from the central trunks, forming a semblance of arms and legs. Henry Assessed the new threat as the twenty-foot-tall tree monsters uprooted themselves and began lumbering toward the arena.

Haruspex

Type: Forest Elemental (Greater)

Health: 520/520

Vitus: 23/23

Attributes:

  STR: 85

  MOB: 8

  FOR: 72

  ACU: 2

  PER: 8

  RES: 2

Resistance: Physical, Environmental

Weakness: Magic (Fire)

Lore: The very forces of nature, anthropomorphized and formed into a bipedal state. Greater Elementals of all types are very unpredictable and are far more powerful and dangerous than their lesser brethren

The ground shook as the trees bound toward him, trenching huge divots into the hillside with every heavy stride. Fearful shouts spread through the area. Forest and high elves alike ran for cover.

"Henry, those are greater forest elementals, and very powerful. Be careful!" Buddy warned, the tone in his voice giving Henry more pause than the tree monsters' Statuses.

The Sentinels around Henry exchanged hesitant looks, then turned and fled from the battlefield. Henry didn't blame them. The elementals charged with little regard for what was in their paths and would likely crush any elf unlucky enough to be in their way. He looked for a vulnerability in the monsters but couldn't find one beyond the weakness to magical fire stated in their description.

Henry cycled through his Abilities, trying to find something that might assist. Buddy's fire or Ox's hammer would make quick work of the wooden monsters, and Beast could Void enough chunks to maim them. With his allies still restrained, his xiphos and Spark Ability would have to do.

The magically altered trees made quick work of the distance with their huge strides, and they were in the arena in seconds. Log arms thicker than Henry's torso smashed into the ground. Their attacks left craters that even Ox would have trouble matching with his maul. Henry decided his best option was to copy Muji's technique for fighting larger opponents. As the elementals crowded around, Henry dodged heavy strikes and rolled between them, avoiding being crushed by sometimes less than a few inches.

Blitz

His Vitus trickled down, though the elemental's low Mobility made dodging the lumbering attacks not extremely difficult. His sword had little effect on the thick wood, but he directed his adversaries' wide, swooping strikes into each other through perfectly timed feints and dodges. Splintered shards of exploding pine shot through the air like ballista bolts while the elementals continued their relentless attack, unresponsive to the damage they were both giving and receiving.

More shouts of frustration came from the side of the arena. Henry would have laughed at what he saw if he hadn't been facing a contingent of animated tree monsters. Muji had climbed Bharat's robes, aggressively biting and scratching the Sage, and forcing Talji and Lata to assist their leader. The three elves flailed helplessly as the trogold continued his assault. Nearby, Jai had recovered and struggled ferociously to free himself from Surat's tight hold.

Muji and Jai couldn't last forever, and neither could Henry. The Desert Path had diminished him, and his endurance began to flag significantly. His subdued Strength and Mobility caused Blitz to drain his already low Vitus pool, and he knew he couldn't dodge the elemental's relentless attacks for much longer.

Bharat's frustration boiled over as Talji finally knocked Muji from the Sage. Bouts of green magic spiraled around his hands, and three of the elementals turned and started toward the cage holding Buddy, Beast, and Ox.

Blitz

Spark

Henry rocketed forward, dodging more tree limbs that fell around him like an avalanche. He jumped as high as he could, latching onto what served as the back of one of the departing elementals, and wedged his xiphos into a split section of wood. Spark bumped up the Tier of his sword's Drain Ability, sucking magic from the monster and channeling it back into Henry's core. The elemental spun, trying to knock him off, but it crashed into the other two racing toward the cage.

Harden

Henry was slammed between two colliding tree trunks. His

bones snapped, barely managing to hold their form as Henry channeled Vitus into his body and armor. He used every last bit of his magic to keep himself intact while the trees smashed together in a tornado of spinning pine. Henry felt his sword pull the last of the Vitus from the forest elemental and channel it into his damaged bones. The tree ceased its rampage and toppled to the ground.

Forest Elemental Killed x2, Soul Essence Claimed

In its thrashing, the tree monster had destroyed one of the other elementals and nearly crushed the third. Henry jumped from the falling mass, landing just in front of the cage holding his fellow skeletons. His Harden Ability had saved his bones from being crushed, but it had nearly drained his Vitus, and four more elementals were rushing toward him.

"Henry, get out of here, you idiot. You can survive this," Beast urged.

"Yes, sing our exploits loud and proud. May a thousand lonely women lament my heroic passing with cries of sorrow and lust!" Ox bellowed.

You want to save your companions, but would they do the same for you? Malek's words echoed in his mind.

Henry twirled his sword and took a step forward. He had enough Health left to use Sacrifice and recharge some of his Vitus. Henry refused to abandon his friends in the middle of a fight—Malek be damned. "I think I'll stay. This is just getting fun."

"I have a better idea," Buddy said with an unexpected amount of calm.

CHAPTER 26

M uji bound in and out of Talji's range. With so many other elves running about, he easily dodged between their legs and avoided being struck. Being chased was a fun game, especially with his high Mobility, though he didn't have time to play. The elven spell was still holding the Protector.

Buddy . . . that was the Protector's name, and the angry old elf was trying to hurt the mage. Muji wouldn't let that happen.

Everything made sense now that Muji and Buddy had combined their power—the skeletons' mission to revive the long-dead Empress, their susceptibility to the Hold Undead spell, and the looming danger of the Necromancer. Additionally, the trogold could now easily understand words and the strange glyphs that appeared before him.

Status

Name: Muji
Race: Trogold (Thrall)
Tier: 15
Health: 46/52
Vitus: 42/96

Attributes:

STR: 8

MOB: 32

FOR: 13

ACU: 19

PER: 29

RES: 8

Status Effects:

Skeletal Thrall: A powerful mage has granted you the honor of serving as his thrall. You are forever bound to this individual, and your life is tied to his. You may access a portion of his power to carry out your service. (ACU +7)

Abilities:

Evocation I (Thrall Ability): Your Protector specializes in evocation magic. Choose two elements and one vector to cast as your own

Element 1: Lightning

Element 2: Unchosen

Vector 1: Remote Sigil - Detonate

Trogold's Oath I (Thrall Ability - Passive): You have chosen to devote your existence in servitude to a being of great power. As a Thrall, you may communicate telepathically with the Protector and access 10% of his Vitus. (ACU +1, Vitus +10)

Magic Item Affinity III (Artifice - Passive): Trogolds have a natural affinity for items containing magic. You have developed a deeper understanding of those items and can manipulate them easily. (MOB +1, ACU +2)

Charge Item II (Artifice): As a natural conduit of Vitus, you may channel raw magic and even spells between beings and items more efficiently. (ACU +1)

Tinker I (Transmutation): The physical limitations of items are of little concern for the proficient artificer. Make minor modifications to the physical structure of a magical item of uncommon rarity or lower

Muji could understand the words. He could understand many things now that he had been granted several points in Acumen from his Trogold's Oath, though he found it slightly annoying that the words indicated he was Buddy's Thrall, and not the other way around. However, now that he was connected directly to the mage, Muji could see the full extent of Buddy's magic, and the trogold was taken aback by just how powerful the Protector truly was. His mind couldn't fully grasp the range and depth of Buddy's magical prowess, so Muji quickly dismissed his concerns about who the Thrall was. The massive amount of power now at Muji's disposal made the compromise well worth it.

It would take him a while to parse through the rest of the information displayed in his Status, but what he did know was that he could now use the Protector's evocation magic, and Muji loved magic more than anything. He had already chosen *Lightning* as an element and *Remote Sigil* as a vector. Buddy had used the mental link from his Trogold's Oath Ability to direct him to hit the other skeleton, Henry, with lightning.

With that done, Muji intended to harass the old elf until he released Buddy. He dove between more frantic elven legs and brought up his choices for elemental magic. The Protector had a huge variety for him to choose from, but Muji knew what he wanted.

Element Chosen: Fire

Every few steps, Muji drew power from Buddy and forced it into the ground.

Remote Sigil: Fire

Remote Sigil: Lightning

He would have only been able to cast the spell once or twice with his own magic, but with only 10% of his protector's Vitus, the ground below him hummed with magical energy. Eventually, that stockpile ran low, and once Muji was out of Vitus, he turned his efforts to physical attacks. Two more jaunts around a female elf, just to get her riled up, then he climbed up the robes of the old elf and started biting. He only got in a few good chomps, but he sank his teeth as deep as he could. The old elf cried in pain. Before Muji could rejoice, another elf caught him with a glancing blow and sent him tumbling. Muji quickly rolled to his feet and bared his teeth, preparing for more biting. A message from Buddy made him stop.

Now, Muji. It's time.

Muji had nearly forgotten why he had planted all the magic spots while evading. "Beak," he chirped threateningly at the elves one last time before he darted away, getting as far from the magic he'd laid as possible. A few seconds and a dozen strides later, he released the spells.

Remote Sigil: Detonate

Flames and arcs of lightning seared his hindquarters as he ran, but he ignored the bit of pain and rushed toward the living trees. Panicked and pained elven screams rang behind him. His tummy began to rumble, and the thought of eating delicious lizards entered his head.

—

Surat broke a few of Jai's ribs. That didn't stop the boy from fighting the larger elf. Everything turned into chaos as soon as Bharat had shown up, and Jai was furious. The old Sage took away his Guard, and now Bharat used his magic on the forest, turning the trees into monsters and sending them to attack Henry and the others.

Somehow, Henry freed himself from the spell, but there was no way he could take all those monster trees by himself. Jai needed to free himself from Surat's hold and do something to help.

Lata and Talji were struggling to pull a giant squirrel off Bharat. That made Jai smile, knowing even the forest animals had turned against the Sage, though the creature's attacks did give Jai an idea. He pulled Guile into his hands and reached out, searching through the various planes to find the most powerful summon he could. He felt an answer, but fire and lightning erupted all around before he could offer a contract. The magical blast hurt and brought his Health down by nearly a quarter. The explosion forced Surat to release his arm, and Jai fell to his knees.

"Kill them now!" Bharat screamed, erupting into a fury Jai had never seen from the old Sage. Green and black magic swirled around him like a giant bonfire. Whatever spell the sage was casting would likely be very bad for him and his skeletons.

Jai pulled his sling free and loaded it in one smooth motion, just like he'd done a thousand times before. Bharat looked at him, and Jai could tell the Sage was about to unleash the spell.

More reaction than intent, Jai spun his sling and sent the rock directly at Bharat's forehead. From the distance of a few feet, there was little the Sage could do to dodge. The sling rock hit with a solid *whump* on the yellow circlet stone.

Blood sprayed, and Bharat's eyes rolled to the back of his head.

"What have you done!" Talji screamed, looking more enraged than the Sage had been a moment earlier.

Jai was already running. He didn't know what he could do to help, but he had to stop the trees from killing his Guard. He'd gotten them into this, after all.

Just a few steps into the arena, Jai realized there was nothing he needed to do. The cage holding the skeletons exploded outward.

Blue fire enveloped two elementals, roaring skyward and blasting Jai with intense heat from fifty paces away. Branches and pine needles disintegrated as their splintered trunks and limbs dissolved into ash. In the same instant, Ox caught a third tree center mass with his hammer. A loud crack pierced the battlefield, and the elemental buckled in half and tumbled to the ground.

Beast spiraled up the trunk of the last monster, leaving behind vacant spheres in its body the size of bollomomo fruit. With nearly half of its structure removed by Beast's Void Ability, the monster collapsed under its own weight.

Jai ran up to the skeletons, avoiding the still-burning piles of dead elementals. "We have to go before they rally and come after us."

Four undead skeletons turned toward him, and Jai realized he no longer controlled them. They all took a step toward him, and Jai held up his hand. "Hold."

Henry blurred forward faster than a skeleton should have been able to move. The undead lifted a skeletal hand inches away from the boy's head. Jai realized his foolishness and resigned himself to death.

Instead of killing him, Henry plucked the circlet from his forehead. "No more of this," the skeleton said.

"I . . . I'm sorry," Jai stammered. "I didn't know what else to do."

"We'll handle it from here." Henry dropped the circlet into a pouch on his belt. "Your fear is misplaced, Jai. We'll make quick work of them." The four skeletons started toward a contingent of elves gathered around Bharat.

Jai realized what Henry was going to do. "No, please. Don't kill them. This is all my fault. I'll do whatever you want."

Henry stopped and looked at the boy. "You have a kind heart, Jai. Would you have us spare your tormentors?"

"Please," Jai begged. "Without their Guard, the elves will be unable to defend themselves." He looked around the arena, taking in the destruction from the battle. "What have I done?"

Ox placed a massive hand on Jai's shoulder. "We've already won. The boy fought bravely. I say we allow him and the others to live." Then he leaned down to Jai's level and added, "Just remember, tiny elf. Mercy is a luxury only afforded to the victors."

Beast scoffed. "Mercy is the choice someone makes right before they get a knife in the back. I say we flay the skin from these pretentious elves while we have the chance."

"No, I'll take you straight to the Empress," Jai pleaded.

Henry considered Jai's appeal and looked toward the high elves. The contingent of Sentinels had formed a protective line between them and Bharat, staring warily at the skeletons. "They'll be much easier to deal with now than after they organize. And I'm sure they'll be coming for us . . ."

"Our fight is not with the elves," Buddy said with a calm tone that carried a heavy note of wisdom.

Beast grunted and sheathed her daggers, the closest form

of agreement that Henry felt she would offer. Henry looked down at his sword, then at Jai. "I hope this doesn't come back to haunt us. Very well, Jai. Show us the way."

"Follow me. Hurry!" Jai urged, trying to lead them away from the Theater.

"One thing first." Henry pointed toward the unconscious Acolyte in the center of the arena. "Come on, Ox. We're taking him with us."

———

Bharat's eyes fluttered open. The four healers around him, as well as the group of Sentinels, all breathed a heavy sigh of relief.

"You're awake, Great Sage. Ghara truly blesses us," Lata chimed like she was proving she was the most joyed at his improved state as she made to assist the Sage.

Bharat slowly sat up, pushing away her help. "What happened? Where are the skeletons?" he asked, carefully touching the swollen gash on his forehead.

"Gone," Talji replied from a nearby seat. "Jai took them and ran, after he tried to kill you."

"My circlet," Bharat said, looking around quickly and wincing in pain. The healers tried to attend to him, but he pushed them away as he had Lata.

Talji opened her hand to reveal the shattered remains of the flow crystal. "Destroyed, but its sacrifice likely kept your skull intact."

"How will we protect ourselves from the Sprigs without Bharat's circlet?" Lata asked.

Talji gave her an angry look that warned her against further interruptions. "Bharat can still cast the spell but must concentrate to sustain it. Our circlets should continue to work, though to a far lesser extent."

Bharat let out a long, labored sigh. "We'll force the dwarves to make a new one in due course. What is important now is stopping those skeletons before they reach Ghara and do her harm. And you, Talji, why did you not lead the charge against them?"

Talji looked around, unsure how to respond, until Bharat's scowl forced her to cobble together an excuse. "Great Sage, what could we have done without our Guard? They destroyed your elementals like they were dead saplings."

"You three," Bharat indicated to Talji, Lata, and Surat all in turn, "allowed a filthy forest elf and a trogold, of all things, to attack me. Guards don't make Sentinels. I do. I have entrusted you as my wardens, and you have failed me."

The three Sentinels lowered their heads in shame. Talji's anger flared at being chastised before the other elves, but she couldn't refute the Sage's claim.

Bharat slowly drew himself to stand on unsteady feet, further refusing help from the healers. He hobbled to the edge of the arena and surveyed the battlefield. The smoldering remains of his elementals, along with the bones of several dozen skeletons, lay scattered before him. The slain bodies of two dead elves lay among the destruction.

"A single dead elf is too many, though the price for our lapse in faith could have been much worse. I will not allow us to fail again. Fortunately for you, the undead human has inspired me." Bharat raised his hands and drew forth his remaining Guile. Just above his raised palms, orbs of green and yellow magic swirled together, turning a dark brown before dimming to a black so dark it seemed to draw in the light around it. He lowered his hands, and the orbs dropped to the earth. The magic splashed on the ground like Bharat had just dumped out a water pitcher. Instead of diffusing into the dirt, the orbs spread out and began undulating toward the arena, like a school of trout skimming the top of a lake in search of flying insects to eat. The spell swept over the bones, dead elves, and elemental remains, pulling them into the ground as the dark magic sank into the arena.

After a moment of silence, loud grunts came from the cages holding the Sprigs at the far side of the battlefield. The grunts turned into snarls, then twisted into howls of pain. The cages shook, and the sound of snapping bones and tearing flesh roared from the enclosures.

Wooden slats bulged and creaked, then all three cages burst apart. Gasps escaped from the Sentinels and healers as they stared in horror. The monsters that emerged were no longer Sprigs.

The hulking forms stood twelve feet tall and nearly as wide. Dark brown skin with the texture of rotting bark clung in patches to bulging muscles colored a sickly, pale green. Several skulls sat bunched on top of massive shoulders, connected by a webbing of moss and necrotic flesh. Huge claws dripping a black ichor drug on the ground as the monsters bounded more than ran toward the elves.

"Stand your ground," Bharat ordered when the Sentinels made to flee. They obeyed, but the elves' fear grew with every heavy thud of the monsters' advance.

Within a few strides of Bharat, the monsters slid to a halt and prowled before him like wolves eager for a hunt. The bunched skulls raised, revealing rows of jagged bone teeth that looked more like a collection of saws than a mouth. A black tongue, long and thin as an arm, emerged from their mouths and dripped with thick strands of yellow saliva.

"Cryptids . . ." Talji whispered, afraid to move.

A grotesque smile parted Bharat's lips, just a bit wider than it naturally should have. "I introduce you to the *Wendigo*, your new Guard. Close enough to dead, they should serve you far better than skeletons. Now Hold them and follow me. We depart for Ghara's cave at once."

CHAPTER 27

"How did you teach magic to a squirrel?" Jai laughed as he ran, struggling to hold the squirming Muji in his arms. The trogold demanded belly scratches while Jai fed Muji the last of his roasted moosel nuts.

Buddy jogged alongside Jai and Muji, free of the Hold spell's Effects. They ran hard for several miles but slowed when Buddy and Henry's endurance began to flag. "He is not a squirrel. He is a trogold, and while magic is intrinsic to these cave-dwelling creatures, he can use certain aspects of my Vitus because he is my Thrall."

"What's a Thrall?" Jai asked.

Ox chuckled from the rear of the group. "Yeah, Barney. What is Thrall?"

After a few steps, Buddy replied, "A Thrall is a lesser creature, magically bound to a higher-powered magic user."

Jai wrinkled his forehead as he considered Buddy's explanation. "So, if he can do magic, why didn't you have him help you escape while I was sleeping?"

Henry could tell by the subtle movements of the mage's skull that Buddy was getting annoyed by the questions about

Muji. He almost laughed but decided not to agitate the mage any further.

"Because he wasn't my Thrall until recently," Buddy said bluntly.

Jai seemed satisfied with the answer and continued to scratch Muji's upturned belly. "Does he have a name?"

"Yes. His name is Muji."

Jai halted in his tracks and looked at Buddy with wide eyes. "Did you say *Muji*?"

"That's what Beast named him shortly after we saved him from some giant cave salamanders," Henry said.

Muji continued to squirm, and Jai had to heft the trogold to his shoulder to get a better hold. The excitement on the elf's face beamed as he addressed the skeletons. "That's my name. I mean, it's my nickname. Jai is short for Murenjai, but my parents call me Muji. That's what my sister used to call me, too!" Henry, Buddy, and Ox all turned and looked at Beast.

"I knew it. You're Harshmira, you're my sister!" Jai accused.

Beast rolled her skull in a sarcastic motion and kept walking. "I am *not* your sister."

"No, it all makes sense. You didn't betray us. You died trying to save us. Everything Bharat told us was a lie. You—"

"Quiet," Beast snapped. "I am no hero, and I am *definitely* not your sister. Once I get my body and memory back, I'm leaving here forever. The last thing I need is you trying to create a back story for me."

Buddy's serious tone cut off Beast's anger. "Regardless of your origin, Beast, we need to address the problem at hand," he said, attempting to change the subject. "Bharat can raise and control the undead. Henry, in your vision at Hjardharfell, you claimed that Malek and the Necromancer were different people. How do you think Bharat fits in with them?"

Henry realized he'd been so busy with the battle that he hadn't had a chance to review what happened in his most recent Desert Path vision. He tried to explain what he'd seen. "It's more complicated than that. The prisoner wasn't Raynott—he was Malek. We fought, and he tried to get me to let him through a doorway, but I managed to seal him out. He didn't say anything about the elven Sage. It makes me wonder, though, what if Bharat is the Necromancer and was the one that teamed up with Malek and Livadi, not Harshmira?"

Beast crossed her arms over her chest. "That makes no sense, you idiot. You're the one who says Stavros is the Necromancer."

"Maybe Livadi or Malek taught Stavros and Bharat their magic?" Henry offered, struggling to fathom some explanation. Those four were somehow involved with Jallfoss's downfall, but just how that happened still eluded Henry. He was no expert in magic, but he felt that Necromancy was a very uncommon type of magic for elves.

As though he were reading Henry's mind, Buddy chimed in. "The crux of Necromancy is that it allows the mage to be influenced by forces that have escaped the bonds of the physical. Our minds are locked within the constraints of our bodies, limiting our thoughts but also protecting our frail cognizance from warping into something beyond our control."

Buddy pulled the red mage's metal tome from the leather straps at his waist and thumbed through the pages. "With enough discipline and guided training, a careful mage could avoid the worst consequences. I believe Bharat's hubris will force him to exceed those limitations . . . if he hasn't already."

A loud groan came from Ox's direction. Everyone turned and looked at the man slumped over his shoulders. Ox shifted so they could get a better view of the human. Jacoby placed a hand on his temple where Henry had kicked him. "Ugh, my head."

Gator rotated on Ox's opposite shoulder and addressed the Acolyte. "Ghakk."

When Jacoby saw the skull, he cried out and started to scramble like Muji, trying to escape Ox's grasp. Ox dropped him with a less-than-gentle *thud*. Jacoby rolled away and jumped to his feet, looking ready to fight.

Henry pulled Talji's bare sword from his belt and tossed it to the man. It spun on the long axis, and Jacoby caught the hilt with a deft grip. "Apologies for knocking you out, but I'm sure you prefer that over me killing you."

Henry pointed toward the highest mountain peak that loomed twenty or so miles away from them. "Long story short, we're headed toward that mountain to revive a dead Empress. We escaped from the elves, and I didn't want to leave you. You're free of their spell, so you're welcome to join us, or go your own way."

"How do I know you?" Jacoby asked, lowering his sword just slightly.

"Funny story, that. Somehow, I killed you and got revived by your Drift Amulet. Your death might be a good thing for you, though. Your leader is a man named Lord Stavros, but he's actually the Necromancer who killed this entire mountain. If we revive the Empress who turned his undead against him, we can save all the skeletons . . . maybe. The dwarves and humans believed the Necromancer had been sent back to the Source Crystal, where he came from, but according to the vision that you and I shared, he went to Ikrit and took over the nation after the previous Emperor, Livadi, died. Bharat, the leader of the elves, is also involved with the dark magic, but we're not yet sure how."

Jacoby looked at the sword in his hand, then back at Henry. "Ikrit . . . the Acolytes. I killed my friends . . ."

The look on Jacoby's face spoke volumes, and Henry felt pity for the man. While the four skeletons had each other to rely upon throughout their journey, Jacoby had to brave the dangers of Jallfoss on his own. Isolation was one thing, but feeling like he'd betrayed his fellow Acolytes would be an onerous burden to bear. Henry did his best to comfort Jacoby. "Don't blame yourself. The red auras are tough to deal with until you get your Resolve high enough."

"If I'm an Acolyte, then I'm one of the men who would try to stop you from reviving the Empress. How do I know you're telling the truth about Stavros?" Jacoby asked, taking a firmer grip on his sword.

Buddy took a step forward to address Jacoby. Henry's Perception caught a subtle twitch of the mage's fingers, indicating Buddy was prepared to meet the man's weapon with overwhelming magic, should the situation escalate. "Henry's vision and the Acolytes' assault on the mountain are our only evidence. Stavros's intentions are a mystery to us, and we still don't know how Bharat, and now Malek, fit into this equation." Then the mage looked at Henry. "The fact that Malek is alive, at least in your visions, is very concerning. Even more so since he tried to deceive you."

Henry shrugged. "I don't understand, either. After I freed Malek from his prison, he wanted to follow me wherever my Path was leading . . . the *Dragon Realm*, he called it. Luckily, I blocked him out, which gave me the Ability I used to stop Bharat's spell. Both Malek and Bharat are likely not very happy with me."

Henry turned to the Acolyte. "You know as much as I do. We saw the same thing. Stavros took the boy's soul and used it to peer into our minds."

Buddy motioned to the high peak looming over the valley. The setting sun lit up half the mountain, casting a dark shadow on the far side. Bright red and orange clouds filled the sky as the day ended. "Our mission is to revive the Empress. Since no ruler would want an undead kingdom, her goals are logically the same as ours, making her our greatest ally and best chance to save our fellow skeletons."

"And if we can't convince the fair lady, I can always seduce her," Ox added, quite pleased with himself and his contribution to the discussion. Beast grumbled under her breath and started to walk away.

Jacoby lowered his sword. "I don't know what to believe. However, I don't want to get caught by the elves again. I'll join you, but I still have so many questions."

"Good," Henry said. "We've wasted enough time. Let's get moving, and I'll give you the full story along the way."

—

They made quick time, though Henry and Buddy were the limiting factor. A **20**-point deficit in Strength and Mobility and **10** in Fortitude put a massive hamper on Henry's endurance and speed, bringing those Attributes almost as low as the mage's. Henry's body still made him gasp for breath in an attempt to fill nonexistent lungs, like his soul yearned for its lost flesh. Henry explained the ordeal to Jacoby while they ran despite his labored breathing.

"If a dragon is trying to eat you and keeps making you weaker, why do you insist on returning?" Jacoby asked.

"Great question," Beast quipped, lightly jogging beside Henry and barely exerting effort. The skeletal elf used her Blink Ability and her high Mobility to glide along the treetops as quietly as she did over the ground. Only once did Henry's Perception pick up the sound of a snapping twig from Beast passing just overhead, but he felt she had done it on purpose.

When Jacoby put Henry's plight in such simple terms, Henry entertained the idea of abandoning his Path for the first time. It would be simple to avoid the Dragon Realm, as Henry supposed that each trip required him to exceed his lightning Resistance. Now that he could take **100** points of damage from an electrical source before losing any Health, nothing short of Buddy's most potent attack, or an actual lightning bolt, could send him back. However, he had come too far to consider giving up as a feasible option. The only problem was that Malek specified Henry would need to kill the dragon if he wanted to succeed, which seemed no less impossible than defeating the Necromancer himself. "Thorodd and Malek both indicated that the Path is a test of sorts, but I think it's trying to assist in a way. I've learned several Abilities that have helped us get this far, including the one that blocked the Hold Undead spell."

"Sprig ahead!" Ox shouted.

The off-beat sound of stomping hooves approached, and a corrupted moose charged them. Ox had barely uttered the words before a series of blue slashes maimed the monster. It slumped to the ground, and Ox dashed ahead. The moose stood and bellowed a challenge until Ox's maul crushed the Sprig before it could pose a threat, spreading green and black monster parts in a wide arc.

"If that's the best this forest god can do, these Sentinels should have fixed the problem a century ago." Beast Blinked back into the formation near Henry and sheathed her daggers.

"Faced directly and one at a time, the Sentinels and their Guard have little trouble defeating even the strongest Sprigs. However, the monsters don't fight fair. They can show up anywhere and anytime, and the Sentinels have the entire valley to protect." Jai had said little over the past several hours of running, besides giving directions toward the mountain to help them avoid elven settlements. Henry assumed the boy was embarrassed for having used the skeletons for his own means. Or perhaps Jai was thankful they didn't kill him. Either way, the boy was mostly quiet while keeping a watchful eye on Beast.

They ran for several more miles as the sun set, killing another dozen Sprigs along the way. Jacoby recounted his journey—everything from waking up in a room full of undead, to fighting Acolytes and Sprigs, and eventually getting captured by Talji. Henry found it notable that the man had almost nothing to say about his time under the elf's control.

Eventually, they drew close to the base of the mountain. The elven valley was a long, narrow stretch of pine forest between the Jallfoss range and a lesser collection of mountains. Though Jallfoss extended in both directions and faded into the far horizons, the colossal peak before them towered high above any other mountain.

According to Jai, the lower peaks were once home to various human and elven cities. All had been under the rule of the Oxendine empire, off and on, since the founding of Jallfoss five thousand years earlier.

Jai explained that the other side of Jallfoss dipped drastically several thousand feet into the Ikritian planes. The boy claimed the lush Ikritian farmland stretched hundreds of miles before it met the nation of Varanasi. Those two countries had been at war for a while, but all of Jai's information came from a single human farmer who frequented Amera to collect herbs and trade with the elves.

The last rays of sunlight vanished, silhouetting the dark mountain against a backdrop of starry sky. Two moons, the red Heraklion and the light blue Golos, crested the horizon and began their journey across the sky. The moons' radiance sped through the twilight, casting shadows on the various mountain crags that looked like the open maw of goliaths rising from the earth and lunging toward the fabled young gods. Reminding Henry of the mountain-sized monster from the painting in his most recent visions, the landscape gave him an unsettling feeling that Jallfoss was far more than a pile of rocks.

"I see a cave ahead," Jacoby said. They had arrived at the base of the mountain. With the sun down, they could see a dim red glow from a huge opening off to the side of their approach. It didn't match the illumination cast from sun globes and was far too steady to come from torchlight.

"A settlement?" Henry asked.

Jai's voice shook as he spoke. "No. Ghara's home. I've never been here at night, but Bharat says the red is from the blood tears she cried after the Necromancer killed the mountain."

The sound of snapping tree branches and heavy thuds rang in the distance from where they had come. Henry drew his sword. "The elves are not far behind, and it sounds like they've brought more forest elementals."

"No. The living trees were loud, but they ran on two legs. I hear a gallop from three sources—far too large for horses, but still smaller than the elementals," Beast offered.

"If they're that close, we don't have time to waste," Jai said, then pointed to a path of stone steps that switch-backed its way up the mountain. In the moonlight, it looked like a series of scars cut into the rocky face with a huge knife.

"I've never been up there, but that path should lead to the top, where you'll find the Empress's ghost. I'm sorry for getting you involved in my troubles. I hope you find what you need to fix the mountain." Jai gave them a sad look, then lowered his eyes and turned toward the cave. He unstrung his sling and loaded a rock, then trudged toward the tunnel at the mountain's base that looked like the open jaws of an angler toad waiting to lure and devour its prey.

"Where do you think you're going?" Beast Blinked in front of the boy with her arms crossed, blocking his path.

Her sudden appearance should have startled Jai, but he just looked up at her with a resigned expression. "Ghara is in there. I have to find a way to stop her," he said bluntly and made to step around her.

Beast blocked his way again. "What can you do to stop whatever is in that cave? You have a sling, a knife, and basic conjuration. Against a Primal, you'll get yourself killed."

Jai looked over his shoulder at Henry, then back at Beast, and sighed deeply. "When I found you, I thought I would be the hero to save Amera. I would be the brave Sentinel who freed all the forest elves from both Ghara's Sprigs and Bharat's rule. I failed at that, but at least I learned one thing: The Guard doesn't make the Sentinel, nor does Bharat. What makes a Sentinel is their drive to protect their fellow elves."

Jai narrowed his eyes, and his voice rose, louder and more forceful. "That's what my sister stood for, and so do I. If you won't help, then get out of my way. I'm going in that cave to fight Ghara, and there's nothing you can do to stop me!" Jai pushed Beast out of the way and stomped toward the red glow of the enormous cave.

The skeletons and Jacoby watched in silence until Ox spoke up. "What's going on? I think I'm still under the spell. Oh no, I guess I'll have to go fight, too." Ox caught up to Jai in a few lumbering steps, pretending to stomp awkwardly like he had little control over his movements.

"Beak." Muji leaped from Buddy's pack and followed Ox and Jai.

Beast gave Henry a look that said, "Stop him."

Henry shrugged his shoulders in response and started toward the cave. "The boy's made up his mind."

"Buddy?" Beast said, turning her hands up and cocking her head.

The mage looked at Jacoby, then the two of them fell in behind Henry. "The Empress has been dead for a hundred years. A bit longer won't hurt her. The elves and Ghara, however, pose an immediate threat."

Beast stood alone, watching them walk toward the cave. After a moment, she unsheathed her daggers and grumbled loudly. "Ugh, fine."

CHAPTER 28

"Hurrugh!" Lata spewed black vomit. She staggered and nearly fell. Her face had lost all color, and strands of yellow hair were matted to her clammy skin, but she kept stumbling forward as quickly as her wobbling feet would take her. Surat looked even worse. He hadn't thrown up, but he could barely keep his legs moving.

Talji grabbed Lata by her armor and pulled her back into a run. "Get yourself together, we're almost there." Though she prodded the other two Sentinels along, it was everything she could do to keep the waves of nausea under control. *If they're feeling as bad as I am, no wonder they're having trouble.*

The Wendigo plowed forward just ahead of the elves, knocking over trees, boulders, Sprigs, and anything else that stood in their path. The hulking monsters plodded with heavy strides, using their massive arms as much as their legs to propel themselves forward. The destruction they left in their wake was nearly as bad as what the cryptids were doing to Talji's mind.

The thoughts of skeletons were blank, aside from the rage that seeing a living being elicited from them, so there was nothing much to overcome. Jacoby's mind had been jumbled, and Talji got little more than sporadic emotions from their connection. The psyche of the Wendigo, however, was a landscape of horror. They were dead on the inside, but they were driven by a vile, sadistic madness that crept through the Hold spell and burrowed into Talji's skull like a jackal ripping into its prey.

She didn't know if this was a punishment from Bharat for failing him, or if this was what he deemed necessary to stop the skeletons. The four undead that Jai had brought to Amera were powerful, and if they had Jacoby on their side, Bharat would have no hope of stopping them without the Wendigo. The twenty or so Sentinels that had joined them all had Tiers in the low teens, but few had sufficient battle experience beyond controlling their Guard. *Safety in numbers,* she tried to laugh, but it came out as a gurgled wheeze.

Jacoby, Talji's thoughts wandered to the human Acolyte, between bouts of nausea. She didn't think she would miss the man, but their conversations were easy, and anything was better than the cryptid burrowing its evil thoughts into her mind.

"Focus, Lata. Steady your mind, and the Wendigo will bend to your will. They are powerful and will serve us well . . . if you keep your faith strong, of course." Bharat ran just behind them, barely seeming to exude effort. The Sage wore a fur hood that cast a shadow on his face.

"Yes, Great Sage," Lata managed, just before another bout of vomit spurted down her furs and armor. A bit of it splashed on Talji, and she nearly gagged. It smelled like Lata had drunk Sprig blood mixed with ten other forms of rot.

Talji focused on the path before her. The tracks of the giant skeleton were easy to follow, as were those of Jai and the two male skeletons. About ten miles back, another pair of footprints appeared, which she immediately recognized as Jacoby's.

Her heart leapt for just a second before she pushed the excitement away. He was alive. He had joined the undead instead of getting killed by them. *What a joke. An Acolyte teaming up with the undead.* Even though she had forced Jacoby under her will, she still felt betrayed that the human had run away and joined Murenjai.

A pile of ashes lay up ahead, indicating a Sprig had been killed within the hour. The skeletons were close, but the elves would be hard pressed to get to them before they arrived at Ghara's cave.

Every mile or so, they would come across dead Sprigs. Jai and his Guard had no trouble running through Ghara's monsters, though Talji felt something was missing. There should have been another skeleton with them, but Talji couldn't find a single indication of its passing. The skeletal elf should have left something for her to track. No Sentinel was *that* good.

There. Talji saw a single snapped twig, high in a branch just over their path. It was obvious to Talji's trained eye. *Had the elf done that intentionally? Is she taunting me?* Talji's mind flooded with anger. The Wendigo seemed to pick up on her emotion over their connection, and she felt a sharp tug on her thoughts, like the creature was trying to pull her insides directly through the mental link.

Talji gritted her teeth, forcing out her Guard's hideous nature, though the Wendigo still prowled just outside her consciousness like it was waiting for her will to falter.

She saw a dim red light looming in the distance, like the dying embers of a neglected hearth. Few elves would dare go near the Spriggan god's den during the day. To enter the cave at night was a dangerous act that Talji had never even considered, knowing one likely wouldn't survive the venture.

—

Ox led the way into Ghara's cave. Henry and Jacoby flanked him with enough room to remain clear, wary of the broad reach of his maul. Buddy and Jai followed closely behind, with Beast taking up the rear. The creepy ambiance of the cave kept them on high alert.

Since his last Desert Path, Henry had gained a deeper understanding and control of his Remnant Attributes. They were primarily used to sense and interact with the world around him. He felt the most powerful connection through Ox, likely because the huge skeleton was a Remnant . . . whatever that entailed.

However, Henry felt a completely different sensation coming from the cave. It was much more powerful than what he felt with Ox, but it was . . . off. It was like listening to a song where some of the notes were out of key. Henry tried to use his Affinity to tune in the connection, but after several failed attempts, he decided to use his Might to dampen the link to a tolerable level.

The cave's opening was large, but it only got bigger as they went further in. A huge tunnel expanded into the heart of the mountain for nearly a quarter mile before it meandered around a curve and out of view. Massive roots, some thicker around than Henry was tall, wove their way among loose boulders and uneven ground. The roots looked like they were rotted entirely, but as the group made their way over and around, they found the vegetation was sturdy and nearly as hard as the stone around it.

Large lacerations streaked the roots like open wounds, dripping a thick, bubbling sap that pooled on the ground. Jai poked at the ooze with a stick, and it clung to the tip like tar.

Strangest of all, hundreds of small trees with umbrella-like canopies were growing from the roots. Each one had tiny leaves that glowed with a dim red radiance. Together, the trees lit up the cave with an ominous maroon that reminded Henry of the lumimoss in Lundarbrekka. He analyzed the trees.

Haruspex

Item: Spriggan Sapling (Legendary)

Description: Alchemy reagent, commonly used as a powerful additive in healing potions. While typically green, the properties of a red Spriggan Sapling are unknown

Lore: Spriggan saplings can only be found connected to the root system of a Spriggan Magnolia. These trees and their saplings facilitate a stable ecosystem wherever they grow. Be wary, as the Magnolia and its saplings are always protected

Henry stopped his fingers from touching the glowing leaves as he read the warning in the sapling's description. "That's ominous, but why is it glowing?"

Ox plucked a single leaf free and rubbed it between his fingers. "Unlike the lumimoss below that lures insects, the leaves of a Spriggan Sapling nourish animals of all sorts." Everyone turned and looked at Ox, wondering where that bit of trivia had come from. Ox shrugged his broad shoulders. "I guess you all should have paid better attention in school."

"Ghakk," Gator squawked in what Henry could only assume was agreement.

Jai poked the sapling with his stick, and a sparkling rain of pollen scattered from the leaves and settled to the ground.

"Jai, leave that alone, it's probably poisonous," Beast scolded.

"You're not my sister, remember. You can't tell me what to

do," Jai said with a hint of derision. Beast gave the boy an angry stare but said nothing further.

"Come on, you two, let's get going," Henry coaxed. Beast looked like she wanted say something else to Jai when Buddy cut her off.

"What's that hanging above?" The mage pointed to thick branches that snaked their way along the ceiling. They sported huge leaves that glowed brighter than those of the saplings. Dangling from the branches, green pouches with rough, barky skin hung like a gourd or a melon. There were dozens, ranging in size from less than a foot to larger than Jai in diameter. All dripped with the same black goo that oozed from the roots.

Haruspex

Item: Spriggan Berry (Legendary)

Description: Fruiting body of the Spriggan Magnolia

Lore: The fruit of a Spriggan Magnolia is thought to provide the world with abundant life. Like the saplings, these fruits are always protected

"Fruiting body . . ." Henry read. "I don't suppose those are edible."

"Anything is edible with enough perseverance, but I wouldn't recommend munching on these. I'll give you three guesses where the Sprigs come from." Ox held out his hammer, pointing to where one of the berries had fallen and smashed open. It was hollow inside. A puddle of more black ooze surrounded it, and hoofprints were leading away.

Henry eyed the broken pouch, then turned his attention back upward. Though faint, his Perception picked up on a tiny movement from one of the berries shaking ever so slightly.

"I can hear flowing water up ahead," Jacoby said, giving the cracked berry a wide berth. Henry also heard the sound, and it only got louder as the group continued down the tunnel. The opening narrowed slightly and curved just a bit, but for the most part, it led them directly into the center of the mountain. After nearly a mile, they saw the mouth of the tunnel open into a cavern.

"Everyone, on your guard. No telling what we'll find in there," Henry whispered, expanding his dread shield. The roots, branches, saplings, and berries indicated they would come across a tree, but Henry wasn't prepared for what he saw beyond the tunnel's opening.

The cavern was a half mile across and several thousand feet high. So high that the dark above disappeared into a layer of clouds. Small waterfalls streamed from somewhere above the veil. After a few thousand feet, they crashed into various pools of water at the round cave's exterior. Natural terraces covered in dead shrubbery led up a massive dirt mound to a center dais that held the largest tree Henry had ever seen.

"Ghara," Jai murmured, taking in the magnificent view.

The Magnolia was easily as tall as the thousand-foot mushroom trees in the dwarven Grunischwald, but its branches spanned from the tree for hundreds of feet. Four huge branches shot out from the main tree. One terminated at the far exterior of the cave, and two others dug into the ground near the far water pools. The fourth snaked overhead and wound down the tunnel the skeletons had entered.

The entire structure was covered in huge glowing red leaves. Each leaf cast an individual radiance, and with so many sources, it should have been exceedingly bright. However, the leaves barely provided enough illumination for Henry to see. From each branch hung dozens or even hundreds of rotten berries, and the ground was littered with broken husks.

"If all of these were to hatch at once, Sprigs would over-run the valley and likely kill every last elf," Henry said. It was just an observation, but Jai was close enough to hear Henry's assumption.

The boy's face went pale. "We have to stop this tree. We have to protect the elves," Jai pleaded.

"Then we'll need to speak to the local arborist," Buddy said, pointing to the base of the Magnolia where a figure was attending to one of the lower hanging berries. Not much could be discerned from the distance, besides the being's red and black adornment, but Henry could see whisps of green aura flaking off from the person before fading away.

"Is there a chance we can resolve this peacefully?" Jacoby asked.

"Maybe," Henry said, sheathing his blade. "If so, we probably shouldn't sneak or do anything threatening. Henry reduced his shield to the size of a buckler, and the others followed suit, putting away their weapons. They approached quietly but directly up a winding path. As they followed the dirt trail and ascended the terraced structure, they could see the area had once been well taken care of, though it had now fallen into disrepair. Cobblestone pathways that looked more natural than constructed were lined with withering plants and small trees of every sort. There were no animals or insects throughout the withered foliage.

They made no efforts to hide their approach, but the cavern's resident either didn't notice or didn't care. Within a hundred feet, Henry could tell the figure was tall and humanoid, wearing tight-fitting black and red clothing covered in vines and leaves that looked like they had been grown rather than donned. Antlers jutted from each side of the being's head, large enough to be from a full-sized buck. Judging by the shape of the body, it was female. An approving grunt from Ox said that he thought the same.

Henry noticed the side profile of a woman's face when they were within a dozen steps. She was beautiful, with soft features. Her eyes were hidden by shadow.

Haruspex

Name: Ghara

Type: Primal—

—Error

Henry's Ability cut off before he could gain any information beyond a name and the confirmation that she was a Primal. Much in the same way Thorodd had blocked his Haruspex, Henry felt Ghara sever the connection, but instead of feeling like a pair of shears cutting a taut string, it felt like a guillotine had severed him at the nape.

Henry pushed away the feeling and cleared his throat. "Ghara. We're here to help. The Sprigs—"

Ghara raised her hand and extended a single finger. The tip glowed a bright red as she traced a line from the top to the bottom of the berry. Then she turned and walked away.

"He said—" Ox's words were cut off by movement from the fruit. With a loud *crack*, it split open along the red seam. Black ooze-covered limbs and a segmented body spilled out and plopped on the dirt with a sickly *splat*.

The creature unfurled itself and shook off the goo. Armored limbs creaked as they expanded, growing several times over until the Sprig was larger than a horse. Two pairs of insectoid wings stretched out and lifted a dark yellow thorax and abdomen. It had a round head with black faceted eyes and sharp, crooked mandibles. Its clawed feet twitched with agitation, and a stinger longer than Beast's daggers curled under its body and pointed at Henry.

"And that, children, is how Sprigs are made," Ox said, powering his maul with force magic.

No one else thought Ox's joke was funny, especially the Sprig. Its wings buzzed and lifted the distorted body higher into the air. Henry's Haruspex labeled it a Tainted Hornet, with a high Mobility and other Attributes comparable to those they had recently faced.

Beast buried three arrows into the monstrous insect, and Buddy hit it with dual blasts of ice and lightning. The Sprig crumpled and fell from the air, dying with a gurgling screech.

Ghara turned and looked at them. A blank expression resembling apathy crossed her face as she held up a hand. All her fingertips blazed with a red glow like giant angry fireflies.

Loud cracks came from all around. Dozens of putrid berries burst open and dropped their contents onto the mound below. Some fell several hundred feet, and many landed in the pools of water.

Ox rolled his shoulders and cracked his neck as a horde of Sprigs flooded toward them. "Not the worst welcome I've received from a pretty lady."

CHAPTER 29

An army of Sprigs roared toward Henry and the others. Giant animals and insects of every sort ran, flew, crawled, and slithered forward in a frenzied sea of claws and fangs. Henry recognized some of the creatures, but most were too disfigured for him to identify properly. He was far more concerned with fighting for his life than categorizing the tainted creations. Henry began pulling Vitus from the tempest in his core when a flurry of white enveloped the area around him. Strength surged through his bones as his Harmony quickly identified Ox as the source of the unexpected boost.

Temperance Aura: +5 Health Regeneration per Hour, STR +5

The blizzard didn't obscure his vision, and the bump to Henry's weakest Attribute indicated Ox had removed Torgga's ring and unleashed his aura. Henry welcomed the much-needed Effect and was happy that it had the opposite influence on the wave of Sprigs. Though they didn't falter, their movements grew sluggish, and their approach slowed.

A ring of blue fire formed around the skeletons and

expanded outward in a violent blast, taking out the first row of Sprigs. Flesh and bones melted under the intense heat as Buddy readied another round of elemental attacks. The mage released a clasp at his belt, and five bronze dwarven bucklers, wrapped in various elements, began orbiting around him.

Magical bolts, arrows, and sling rocks followed closely behind, dropping, or at least wounding several of the monsters. Despite the heavy barrage, for every Sprig that fell, two more hatched from the Magnolia's branches and joined the fray.

Not to be left out, Henry, Ox, and Jacoby met the approaching Sprigs head-on. Henry blurred between enemies, slicing and jabbing with his xiphos and bashing with his dread shield. His sword easily soaked up enough magic to keep his Vitus topped off, but that did little to bolster his weakened physical Attributes, and he found it necessary to pace himself to avoid the risk of breaking under the force of his own attacks.

Golden sparks erupted from Jacoby's blade, and arcs of light blinded large swaths of charging monsters. Ox simply smashed his way through the Sprigs, paying little heed to their fruitless attacks. Even Muji engaged the few Sprigs that found their way to Jai and Buddy at the center of the destruction. The trogold would bait Sprigs into chasing him, then lay down an elemental mine and detonate it just as the monsters crossed over top, ripping apart the creatures in concussive blasts of fire and lightning.

As they whittled down wave after wave of monsters, Ghara calmly strode toward the trunk of the massive tree. When she got to the base, she turned and sat on an elaborate wooden throne shaped from the roots and branches of the Magnolia itself. The Primal calmly watched the chaos before her unfold, not changing her blank expression.

Before long, the onslaught had waned to less than a handful

of Sprigs. Jai and the undead took minimal damage in the short exchange, but Henry's endurance had certainly flagged. He pulled his sword from the skull of a tainted badger and looked up at Ghara. Henry tried to expand his awareness to form a connection with the Primal, hoping to use his Attributes in the same way he had with Ox or with the Dragon in his Path. His Harmony seemed to rebound against everything surrounding him, and it failed to locate his target through a jumbled mix of sensations.

Ghara must have detected Henry's efforts because the giant branches of the Magnolia began to shudder. The leaves shook like the tree itself was being uprooted. A *crack* louder than a lightning bolt rang from within the mighty canopy. Two masses, each the size of Smyrna's Golem, dropped to the ground on either side of Ghara, cratering into the dirt with resounding *thuds*. The two largest Sprigs Henry had seen yet began unfurling themselves. The first was a colossal bear, covered in a black, plated carapace. Its jaws were big enough to crush even Ox's skull in one bite with plenty of room to spare.

Haruspex

Type: Greater Sprig, Tainted Grizzly
Health: 502/502
Vitus: 118/118
Attributes:
    STR: 112
    MOB: 28
    FOR: 76
    ACU: 12
    PER: 11
    RES: 8

Resistance: Physical (Piercing), Cold

Weakness: Fire

Lore: Greater Sprigs are infused with large amounts of magic over long periods. Far more dangerous than their lesser brethren, these creatures act as the guardians of Spriggan Magnolias

The second Greater Sprig was a tainted tarantula. Brutal, razor-sharp spikes covered its body and legs, and its mandibles looked strong enough to crush stone. Instead of attacking, the greater Sprigs held fast, sentries protecting their monarch. Ghara stared ahead, like she was waiting for something. It didn't take long to find out what that was.

"You abominations would dare to attack the mother of the forest?" Bharat's voice rang through the cavern, far louder and more forceful than an aged elf should have been able to project.

Henry spun to find a force even more intimidating than Ghara and her sentries. Though smaller than the greater Sprigs, three horrifying monsters pawed at the ground just in front of a contingent of two dozen elves. Henry recognized Talji and her two fellow Sentinels behind the monsters. They stared blankly at the ground, and even from the distance, looked downtrodden and emaciated. The auras of the monsters, as well as that of the three Sentinels, were a cloying yellow that rolled inward on their owners like a collapsing sinkhole.

"We'd rather not fight, but she's leaving us little choice. Don't worry, we can handle this. Why don't you go on home?" While Henry shouted while Assessing the sordid monsters the elves had brought.

Haruspex

Type: Cryptid, Wendigo

Health: 480/480

Vitus: 83/83

Attributes:

    STR: 98

    MOB: 73

    FOR: 48

    ACU: 12

    PER: 11

    RES: 8

Resistance: Physical (Piercing), Mental (Immune)

Weakness: Unknown

Lore: The Wendigo is a creature of nightmares, assumed to be the most dangerous and terrifying of all cryptids. This undead monstrosity relentlessly hunts its prey, adding the form of its victims to its horrific shape. One of the few intelligent undead, the Wendigo is said to drive nearby living creatures insane before tearing them apart

The greater Sprigs posed a threat, but the Wendigo made the Silent from the dwarven Underdeep seem tame. The cryptids sent a chill down Henry's spine, and even worse, they were undead, which meant the three Sentinels were likely controlling them with the Hold Undead spell.

Bharat stepped forward and removed the hood from his head. Even through his red aura, Henry could make out skin that looked sickly pale, almost green. Black veins crawled across the Sage's visage. "Haven't you done enough already? Can you not see the pain you've caused our peaceful goddess? Drop your weapons and prostrate yourselves before her benevolence."

"I would ask that you join us and help end the Sprigs that have been harassing your elves, but you don't strike me as the type to negotiate," Henry shouted while keeping his attention on both the elven contingent and Ghara's Sprigs.

Brown, yellow, and green magic swirled together in the Sage's palms. Bharat sneered at Henry. "I cannot allow you to harm her. Talji, Lata, Surat, attack."

The Wendigo bound forward, clawing up huge chunks of dirt and covering twenty feet in each mighty leap. The mass of skulls on the monsters' shoulders cried out in silent screams of anguish, like they were trying to warn of the approaching danger. Below the skulls, the Wendigo's mouths parted in a sadistic smile nearly as wide as the creatures themselves, revealing uneven rows of vicious black teeth.

Just behind the Wendigo, Bharat's magic spiraled up in the form of dozens of dancing orbs that swam through the air like a school of hungry piranhas sensing blood in the water. The orbs careened toward the skeletons and cast shadows on the monsters below, making their terrible forms even more menacing.

Buddy placed his palms together, then knelt and pressed them to the ground. "Dark magic has driven him beyond logic. These creatures should not exist." Ten feet deep and thirty high, a wall of earth shot from the ground directly in the path of the Wendigo and the magical orbs. The mass of dirt and stone shook and crumbled as the three brutes collided with the defense.

"That won't hold them for long," Henry said, eyeing the dark orbs that snaked over the wall and careened toward the group. Each orb homed in on its target, following like a hound chasing a hair. Buddy's flame-covered shields intercepted several of the magical attacks, and Beast blinked herself and Jai out of harm's way, but some of the orbs managed to connect with Henry and Ox. Like being hit with a ball of sludge, the dark magic washed through Henry's armor and adhered to his bones.

Status Effect: Necrosis (Severe): Healing effects reduced by 75%

Henry's Health dipped significantly with each impact. Because he was out of healing crystals, the Status Effect meant he needed to protect his Health even more.

Deep grunts from the top of the wall indicated there were more immediate problems to worry about. The Wendigo easily scaled the structure and gazed down at the skeletons, preparing to pounce. Buddy spread his hands, and the dirt and stone turned into mud. The three Wendigo lost their footing and sank into the melting wall, tumbling down to the skeletons' level. "Hit them before they can recover!" Buddy yelled.

"Can do!" Ox charged his hammer and swung with all his might at the struggling Wendigo. His maul connected with the churning skulls with such force that the mud and stone around the creature blasted away like a child had stomped in a puddle. Chunks of skull and meat went flying. The monster shuddered, though it didn't drop.

Ox continued to pummel his opponent. The other two monsters churned in the falling mud wall. Arrows and elemental blasts struck them, while Henry and Jacoby danced just out of range of thrashing claws, slicing with their swords but unable to do substantial damage to the monsters.

A cry like a dying rabbit rang through the vast cavern. The scream sounded like it came from the elves, but it carried in its tone a deep sorrow and anguish that Henry felt couldn't have come from a natural being. Now that the wall had fallen, Henry saw that the cry came from Lata. The elf ran up the path toward the Wendigo that Ox had struck. Blood streamed from claw marks on her face and ran down her white armor and fur. Her eyes had turned completely black, and she stumbled as much as she ran.

Lata tripped and fell in the mud with a splat. Ox readied his maul for another heavy swing, but the Wendigo lurched out of range and swept up the fallen elf with a clawed hand. The monster crammed the elf into its mouth and folded her into the opening with a bone-crunching chomp. Lata disappeared inside the black maw, and the wounds on the creature instantly healed. Another skull emerged into the mass on the monster's shoulders like a rotten qualigourd bobbing in a warlock's cauldron.

While Ox's Wendigo was feasting on the Sentinel, Surat collapsed in a violent seizure. He clawed at his face as his back bent enough to snap in half. The elf died on the spot, though his body continued to convulse and seize.

With Lata and Surat dead, two Wendigo were free of their controlling Sentinels. Henry hoped that would render them docile, but he was wrong.

Instead of disengaging from the fight, Ox's Wendigo and the one in front of Henry attacked with a fervor and tempo that a creature of that size shouldn't have been able to muster.

The sudden rush caught Henry off guard, and the monster would have eaten him like the other had Lata, if Buddy's force wall hadn't stopped it. Black claws as long as Henry's sword scraped against the invisible barrier. Each strike from the monster threatened to bring down the shielding, and Henry knew Buddy couldn't hold it back forever. Black and yellow saliva dripped from the giant maw, like every vile emotion in the world had been distilled into the excretion.

Blitz

Harden

Spark

Henry jumped back to gain his footing as the magical barrier flickered, then broke completely. His Vitus plummeted from the compound Abilities he was engaging, but he didn't want to give the monster a chance to get him on the defensive, which would quickly spell his demise.

He danced to the side, dodging and slicing, knowing that the creature was too strong and dangerous for him to parry, let alone block one of its attacks. Luckily, he wasn't alone. Blue fire blasted into the creature and kept it from rending Henry apart. Henry's Health dipped under the heat wave, but the Wendigo took far more damage from the direct blasts. Black bark-like skin burned away. Unfortunately, the magical attacks only intensified the monster's bloodlust.

Before Buddy's attacks subsided, Beast appeared behind the monster and delivered a whirlwind of slices. The blades weren't doing much damage, but her Void Ability took enough chunks out of its muscle to slow it down. Henry pressed the attack, searching for a critical opening, and managed to look to his right.

Even though the Wendigo was forcing him back, Ox held his own. The slope of the landscape kept Ox on the high ground. Henry could tell that even his massive Strength had started to falter under the relentless attack.

Oddly, the middle Wendigo had stopped attacking, and instead pawed at the ground and growled at Jacoby like an invisible leash was holding it back. Jacoby still brandished his golden shield of projective magic, and his sword radiated the same Effect. Henry glanced toward the elves and saw Talji holding her hands to her temples and shaking her head. *Could she be preventing the monster from attacking Jacoby?*

Henry didn't have much time to contemplate the strange behavior. Even with Buddy and Beast's help, he was hard pressed to keep the monster at bay. Beast must have realized the same, or maybe she had been waiting for it to weaken, because she buried her daggers in its back, and the two vanished in a puff of green and yellow aura.

Henry heard a snarl and a thud behind him and turned to see Beast and the Wendigo on the ground a few dozen paces from where Ghara sat with her Sprigs. A red fractal pattern resembling broken glass was fading just above where Beast and the Wendigo had landed. Still on her throne, Ghara held up a glowing red hand. Henry assumed the Primal had blocked Beast's Blink Ability in the same way Buddy used his force wall.

The Wendigo swung a heavy claw at the skeletal elf, but Beast had already Blinked to Ox's shoulders and began firing arrows at Ox's adversary. Ox continued to swing at the pressing Sprig. His movements jostled Beast enough that the alchemy bag at her hip came loose and fell to the ground. Glass bottles and reagents of all sorts tumbled into the dirt.

Henry prepared for the monster Beast had transported to charge back into battle. Instead, it turned to face Ghara, dug its wicked claws into the ground, and bound toward the Primal. The greater Sprigs rushed from Ghara's side. The giant bear and colossal tarantula met the cryptid in a storm of claws and fangs. A cacophony of roars, snarls, and hisses erupted as the three monsters tore into each other's rotten flesh.

Henry struggled to tear his eyes away from the cryptid-Sprig clash, but the sound of Beast and Ox in the heat of battle helped him prioritize. He rushed and prepared to thrust with his sword. Before he could strike, a pillar of lightning, fire, and ice engulfed the monster and blasted upward. The column of elemental magic burned the monster and tore chunks of the Wendigo's body away from its form, lifting them toward the cloudy ceiling of the cavern. By the time the magic faded, little was left of the monster beyond ash and bone. Buddy dropped to a knee. Henry ran to his side to help, but the mage signaled that he was fine.

The greater Sprigs had also wrapped up their battle, though both had received grievous wounds. Tarantula legs were scattered over the torn-up earth, and sword-sized incisors were buried in the cryptid's chest. Half of the grizzly was missing, though it had taken both arms off the Wendigo. All three lay twitching in the dirt.

"I can't . . ." Talji yelled, but it came out as a whimper. Henry watched the elf's ugly yellow aura fade, quickly replaced by the typical red iridescence. She had willingly cut off the connection, and nothing held back the last cryptid. Jacoby must have realized the same and pushed even more magic into his sword and conjured shield, forcing them to radiate a brilliance on par with daylight.

The Wendigo crouched and prepared to pounce on the Acolyte.

Bharat's voice reverberated through the cavern, halting the monster before it could attack. "Hold!"

CHAPTER 30

Command Link Present: 45,786/52,000

"Hold!" the Sage shouted. His aura shifted into the yellow spectrum and broiled around the elf. An unnerving quiet settled over the mound, only interrupted by the death throes of the tainted grizzly.

The notification in Henry's view told him that Bharat was using the Hold Undead spell, though it wasn't targeted at him. Because the Wendigo wasn't attacking Jacoby, Henry felt the Sage had taken control of the cryptid from Talji. Somehow, Henry's Harmony allowed him to view the link, even though it wasn't connected to him. He noticed that Bharat's control over the link had increased by several thousand points, but nearly as many were already devoted.

Oh no. Horror swept over Henry as he felt the connections throughout the vast cavern. He realized that Bharat wasn't just controlling the Wendigo, he was Holding Ghara as well. *That must mean Ghara is undead!*

Bharat sneered down at Talji in disgust. The Sentinel

collapsed and was vomiting, but there was an unexpected look of relief on her face when she glanced up at Jacoby.

"Just like Harshmira—not prepared to serve the greater good. Your failure is every bit as traitorous as hers."

Bharat calmly approached the battlefield like he was going for a midday stroll. The confident look on his face gave the impression he was utterly unfazed by the carnage that had just taken place. "You fools have no idea of Ghara's importance. Just like the pious Oxendines and the brash Degonharts who took their power for granted, you couldn't possibly fathom her significance."

Command Link Present: 48,240/52,000

Henry noticed the devotion points of the Command Link tick upward quickly.

No one responded as Bharat continued his rant. "The Primals—Celestials and Dragons, like the Giants and even the Archons—bestow power on their Remnants with the same regard as one would hand out candy to children—*rotten*, undeserving children. The Spriggans, however, chose to spread their blessings throughout the natural world and have never lowered themselves to designate a Remnant." The Wendigo fell in behind Bharat, following the sage like a chained dog. The skeletons moved aside, allowing the elf to approach Ghara. The Sage's eyes were wide and crazed, almost like Malek's had been when Henry fought him at the entrance to the Dragon Realm.

"Spriggans create life, not death. Ghara is even more unique. When all the young gods abandoned Jallfoss to search for grandeur or whatever else they desired, only our lady of the forest remained to comfort him. She is blessed in her selflessness." Bharat neared where the other Wendigo and the greater

Sprigs had battled. The Sprigs were both dead, and the cryptid had ceased its thrashing. Bharat barely seemed to notice them. Ghara watched on from her wooden throne, unmoving.

Bharat turned and looked at the skeletons. "What example would I set for my elves if I abandoned Ghara in her time of need. The dwarves and the Oxendines unleashed the Necromancer on us all because of their greed, but our faith in Ghara will restore her to her former glory."

Command Link Present: 51,090/52,000

"He has control of Ghara with the Hold Undead spell. Get ready," Henry warned the others.

The four huge limbs of the Magnolia shook and began to curl back toward the main tree, like fingers clenching in a fist. Bharat raised his hands, and his voice got louder. "You were a fool to think you could change the nature of the Oxendines, Mathis." More green, yellow, and brown magic swelled around Bharat like a miniature hurricane.

"Who is he talking to?" Ox wondered aloud.

"The one who killed this mountain," Buddy answered.

Ox cocked his head, but Bharat began to shout before the giant skeleton could ask any more questions.

"And now, I will serve as our Lady's punishing hand. I will strike you down and offer your broken bones to her!" Bharat's magic expanded, accompanied by a terrible wind. It ripped up dead plants and tore glowing leaves and branches from the Magnolia. Two of the largest branches curled above the Sage, like great antlers of a mighty stag.

"Receive your punishment, vile skeletons. Die, and die again!" The wretched hurricane swirled into lances of dark magic and shot forward. Henry expanded his dread shield while Buddy hastily erected a force barrier. Ox puffed out his chest, inviting the Sage's attack.

Command Link Present: 52,130/52,000 – Capacity Exceeded

The two giant Magnolia branches smashed into the ground with an earth-shaking wallop—directly on top of Bharat and the Wendigo. Black and red gore splattered across the surrounding earth.

The largest branch unfurled and struck the wall directly above the exit. The elven contingent scattered, and several were crushed by falling boulders. The crumbling wall caved in the tunnel, closing off the only avenue of retreat. They were all trapped under the mountain with an angry, undead Primal.

CHAPTER 31

Ghara leaned back on the wooden throne, her stoic expression still unchanged by Bharat's failed attempt to control her and his subsequent demise. The wooden seat grew and formed around the Primal, pulling her into its trunk until she had melded entirely, and only a semblance of her face remained. Henry tried to assess her again.

Haruspex

Name: Ghara
Type: Primal—
—Error

Once again, his senses were overloaded, and his efforts were rejected. It was like Ghara was all around him, and his Ability couldn't locate her. That's when he realized that Ghara wasn't the being that had been on the throne; she was the entire Magnolia. Henry focused his Remnant Attributes and spread his awareness through the wooden structure, then forced against the resistance blocking him. It pushed back, but with a final shove of his Might, it released.

Remnant Gateway
Haruspex

Name: Ghara

Type: Primal, Corrupted Spriggan

Tier: 190

Health: 892/892

Vitus: 459/523

Attributes:

    STR: 452

    MOB: 240

    FOR: 1056

    ACU: 212

    PER: 126

    RES: 84

Resistance: Physical, Magical, Environmental (Cold)

Weakness: Fire, Poison, Acid

**Lore: Thought to be descendants of the young gods themselves,
Primals are the embodiment of pure forces of nature. Spriggans
are creators of life and are generally docile, unless threatened**

Ghara's humongous Attributes overwhelmed Henry, and he
wished he hadn't forced Haruspex to work. Despite the shock,
Henry steadied his Resolve and forced his Perception to filter
through the connection. Ghara felt both alive and dead simultaneously, like pieces of the Primal were continuously dying
and being rejuvenated. There was a war going on inside the
massive tree. Ghara was fighting for her life, and she had been
slowly losing that battle over the last century as something dark
ate away at her. That balance between life and death was likely
why Bharat's spell could find purchase on the Primal, and why
it had ultimately failed.

That information was relatively useless, as Henry had no idea how they would overcome the Primal. With the exit sealed, escape and even survival seemed unlikely.

Before Henry could focus and warn the others, Ox stepped forward and addressed Ghara. The curled branches that had smashed Bharat and the last Wendigo lifted from the ground, revealing the mangled remains of the elven sage and the summoned cryptid. "Now that we've gotten that out of our system—"

Ghara's patience was gone. Like the crack of a bullwhip, one of the large branches snapped toward the undead.

Blitz

Henry surged forward and pulled Buddy and Muji just below the swipe. Beast Blinked herself and Jai out of the way. Jacoby raised a golden shield. The branch glanced off the man's Palisade, then he ran toward the scattering elves. Ox, unfortunately, caught the full brunt of the attack.

The branch impacted him flush and sent him flying like a rock leaving Jai's sling. He spun through the air and cratered into the cave wall, buried deep in the mountain rock.

The other branches joined in without warning and started relentlessly pummeling the mound. Buddy raised his hands and summoned a force dome just in time to reflect the attacks. His magical barrier turned aside the heavy branches, but the shield flickered with every strike. To make matters worse, dozens more berries broke free and dropped their contents in the dirt. Another horde of Sprigs rushed toward Buddy and Henry, threatening to overwhelm the magical defenses.

Beast appeared beside Henry. She didn't seem concerned that the contents of her alchemy bag were scattered just outside Buddy's force wall.

"Where's Jai?" Henry asked.

"I dropped him at the far end of the cavern. He wasn't happy, but he's safe from most of the Sprigs and branches," Beast replied.

The wave of Sprigs swept closer to Henry, Buddy, and Beast. The army of monsters would be on them in a few moments. Henry could use his xiphos to keep his Vitus charged, but his body would give out long before the skeletons could defeat the monsters and the Primal tree. "Buddy can't hold them back for long. Can you Blink us to the tree's base so we can fight Ghara directly?"

"No," Beast said, anger and frustration apparent in her voice. "There's some kind of barrier, and I can't transport through. We could run past, if the tree and Sprigs would let us."

"We'll have to fight our way through. Buddy, can you keep the branches distracted?"

Buddy lowered his arms, and the force dome disappeared with a flicker. A massive ball of blue fire swirled above his head, then flew toward the Magnolia. Just before it reached the tree, Buddy's magic exploded into a huge fiery blast. Several Sprigs below the impact disintegrated into ash from the heat of the explosion, while dozens more continued their charge. As the fire dissipated, Henry saw the red fractal pattern hanging in the air where Ghara's barrier had stopped Buddy's magic. Like watching a pane of glass break in reverse, the lines healed themselves and quickly disappeared.

The Magnolia branches recoiled from the fire, then renewed their attack on the skeletal mage. Henry and Beast darted forward. The force dome opened and reformed, allowing Henry and Beast to leave the mage's perimeter. They sprinted toward the dais and started cutting their way toward Ghara in a spray of black gore resembling a torrent sea's whitecaps.

Far down the slope, the elven Sentinels hadn't fared well.

With nowhere to run and little in the way of defense, the branches turned half of them into red, bloody smears. A curled limb descended directly above Talji. The elf may have sensed it coming, but after her bout controlling the Wendigo, she lacked either the Strength or the will to evade. Jacoby, however, was still primed for the fight.

The Acolyte stood above the elf and raised his conjured shield. The huge limb crashed into him, sending golden sparks blasting around the human. The Acolyte's defense held, leaving him and the elf unharmed. Talji looked up and gave a weak smile. Jacoby was too busy blocking subsequent attacks to notice.

Henry dodged more huge branches, looking for a path to the tree's base. A rumble and Ox's loud yell pulled his attention away. He glanced back at the hole in the cavern wall that Ox had created. Cracks and fissures formed on the vertical surface as Ox's yell grew louder.

"It's about time, big guy," Henry said, dodging another wild branch.

———

Ox shook his head, trying to clear the stars from his vision until he realized they were flashing glyphs. He allowed the display to show him the details.

Status Effects:

    Broken Ribs (Moderate): STR -10%, MOB -10%, FOR -5%

    Broken Arm (Moderate): STR -5%, MOB -5%

    Broken Skull (Minor): ACU -5%, RES -5%

    Dazed (Minor): MOB -10%

    Necrosis (Minor): Healing effects reduced by 25%

Ox had seen the massive limb speeding toward him, but he couldn't move fast enough to avoid it.

No, that was a lie he failed to convince himself. It was his pride that made him hold his ground. He felt his Strength could withstand the attack. In truth, only his dread armor had kept him from being smashed into skeletal dust.

Heal

His bones stitched back together, though much slower than expected due to the lingering Necrosis from the Sage's spell, even though the Effect had faded in severity over the last several minutes of fighting. The glyphs from broken bones went away. However, an old Status Effect now occupied the space directly before him.

Astral Covenant: Disabled

    Bond 1 of 3 broken: Resistance All -5

    Bond 2 of 3 broken: MOB -30%

    Bond 3 of 3 broken: ACU -30%

Who was on the other side of the Astral Covenant? No matter how strong he became, it wasn't enough to protect everyone. Ox heard the noise of battle, but it sounded far away. He shoved against the rocks that entombed him, barely getting them to move at all.

"G . . . ghakk," Gator squawked, still attached to Ox's shoulder.

"Yes, Gator, I got beat up again. Some emperor I am."

"Ghakk," the amalgamator replied with a bit of agitation.

"I know. I'm not the emperor of this mountain." Saying the truth out loud was a blow to his ego, but after getting wrecked in so many fights, he felt he didn't deserve to carry the moniker. Who was he fooling? The broken bonds were proof that time and time again, he'd failed those around him. Did he even deserve their company? Ox considered lying in the hole until his bones crumbled. Jaromak, the Acolyte, was far weaker than Ox, but the human wiped the floor with the much larger skeleton, as if he were playing a game. And just then, the elves had a monster that would have eaten him, were it not for Beast, Henry, and Buddy. To top it off, he just got beaten up by a tree . . . *a tree!* He gritted his teeth hard enough to crack molars. His friends deserved better. They deserved someone who could protect them and keep them safe.

"Ghakk!" Gator barked, and the force behind his voice shook Ox out of his self-pity. Did it matter if he wasn't an emperor? That wouldn't change the fact that the others were relying on him.

The amalgamator skull shook and grunted on his shoulders like he was trying to say, "Sit here and pout, you big oaf. I'm going back to the fight!" Ox had no idea what an amalgamator was, but somehow Gator had gone from a battle trophy meant to annoy Beast, to a faithful companion. How many others had fought by his side? How many had he failed? Too many.

"I won't let you down, Gator. I may not be the emperor, but until the real one shows up, I'm the best you've got. And I'm sick and tired of getting my ass kicked. That's it!" Ox's anger surged within him until he might as well have been engulfed in a red, rage-inducing aura. He flexed his bones and strained against the rocks that were crushing him. At the same time, he pushed through his mind and into his core.

The colossal glacier wound through mountainous peaks until it reached a crystal-blue ocean. A lazy deck of gray clouds hung over the ice sheet, obscuring the highest mountain tops. Huge chunks of ice broke from the glacier and slammed into the ocean as Ox summoned Vitus from his core.

Heart of the Jotun

Strength swelled through his bones, and he pushed with all the force he could, but the rock still failed to move.

Heart of the Jotun, Heart of the Jotun

Ox activated the Ability repeatedly. Each time the rock failed to yield, he got angrier, and his shouts got louder.

"Move, you dumb rocks!" Ox didn't care about the stone burying him, and he didn't care about some pretty tree god. He had to save his friends. Almost unconsciously, Ox flared his Affinity and forced open the channels that regulated his Vitus, allowing his glacial core to flow continuously into his bones.

With all his Might, Ox pulled from the well of energy deep within his core. The clouds above the glacier darkened and began to dump layers of snow on the glacier's surface. It swelled and cracked, forming giant fissures as it surged against the mountains and into the turquoise bay. The mountains rumbled under the force of the ice as millions of tons of earth, snow, and trees cascaded down their slopes. Huge icebergs broke off from the main glacier and forced their way into the salty water below. The water churned and broiled, mixing sapphire water and brown silt.

Ability Discovered: Heart of the Jotun II. Increase STR by 100%. Vitus cost slightly reduced

"Ghakk!" Gator yelled. The rock around them crumbled like sand.

Propelled by the massive burst of Strength, Ox rocketed out of the hole. He arced through the air and hit the ground, taking in the carnage. Henry had received a bit of a beating, but the Sentinels had taken the worst of it. Buddy had his shield up, though the mage could do little more than hold his defense together. Red fractures in the air around the Magnolia's base indicated Beast kept getting rejected as she tried to Blink near the Primal.

Ox's Vitus was draining fast, but he didn't care. He slammed into the earth mound and rebounded, launching himself forward. He saw the Magnolia take notice, and a branch swung at him. It was fast and going to hit him, but he was done getting pushed around by a tree.

Ox pulled at the glacier in his core once again, grasping for anything he could wrap his mental fingers around. He felt something below the glacier. It was deep under the surface and far more ancient than anything he'd felt before. He pulled again, and whatever was there ceded to his will.

Ability Discovered: Remnant Form, Giant. As the prog—

Ox pushed the message away and focused on the limb screaming toward him. He heaved from the glacier with all his Might until a rush of power shot through his body. Ox's bones began to swell and press against his armor.

Heal

Adapt

Instinctively, he forced Healing magic into the dread bones. He was also aware of Gator helping manipulate the armor. The branch drew closer and closer, but it seemed much smaller than before. Ox lifted his arms and brought them down. He kept moving—the Magnolia branch didn't. The limb exploded in a shower of red leaves, black ichor, and rotten wood. Ox kept charging and continued to pull from deep within his core.

He must have reached too far, because something pulled

back. It latched onto his psyche, and he felt his mind being drawn . . . hauled . . . forced . . . toward what remained of his glacier. No amount of physical Strength could stop it. White obscured his vision, and everything around him faded.

CHAPTER 32

Smacking into the frigid water and the subsequent plunge caught Ox completely by surprise. The freezing brine sucked the breath out of his lungs and forced him to gasp for air. Painful daggers of intense cold dug into his skin, sending him into a panic.

The water around him churned in huge waves, blasting icy spray into the air above him. A blizzard raged from above and blinded him almost as much as the water. Just in the distance, he could barely see the outline of a floating mass of ice.

Ox paddled for all he was worth, struggling not to choke on salt water. Powerful muscles tried to seize up under the freezing temperatures, and he had to force his body to propel himself forward. It could have been a minute, or it could have been an hour, but Ox finally reached the towering block of ice.

He faced a sheer wall of frozen water with nowhere for him to grab hold. Undeterred by the impediment, he smashed his fist against the ice to create handholds. The berg shook, and ice blocks fell on him from above, but he didn't stop. Twenty, thirty feet he climbed. His fingers were completely numb when he finally reached the top and flung himself over the ledge.

Instantly, the blizzard stopped and cleared, revealing a sapphire-blue sky.

Ox's chest heaved from the exertion, and he forced himself to stand, thankful to be on somewhat solid ground. He looked around and counted five suns in the sky. No, a sixth, just on the horizon. The sea had stopped churning, and there were icebergs as far as he could see. Thousands dotted the calm ocean and stretched to where the sky touched the blue water.

Ox's body relaxed, and the cold instantly became unbearable. He held his arms tight against the muscles on his chest and abdomen. That was the first time Ox noticed he wasn't a skeleton.

His skin was pale, light-gray, and his chest and arms were hairy. A short, thick brown beard covered his face. And his muscles . . . his muscles were huge. Like iron beams and dwarven hydraulics, the power that flowed through his body was insane. Only a shabby set of cloth trousers covered his hips. *Like Henry's path. The warrior was right,* Ox thought as he admired his own physique.

Ox pulled at the band on his pants and peered below his waist, smiling with satisfaction at what he saw, despite the cold water he'd just been in.

Cold was an understatement. His body soaked up the frigid temperature like a sponge in a bucket of water. It seemed to fill up every inch of his massive frame and forced his mind away from the recent addition of flesh and muscle. Ox looked around for something to warm himself, but found only snow, ice, and miles and miles of water.

"Th . . . this won't do at all. I should be f . . . fighting," Ox said, holding back shivers. He was even more useless on this iceberg than when he was stuck in the hole in the cavern wall.

"There must be s . . . something helpful here. What did Henry say?"

Ox remembered Henry mentioning something about the Remnant Attributes and how they allowed him to connect and manipulate certain things. *Fine, I'll try it.*

He shut his eyes and tried to listen. All he could hear was the steady beat of waves against his icy island. He took a deep breath. The air smelled of brine even as the chill stung his nose. All he could feel was the cold bite on his skin. His frustration started to boil over. He got angry at the cold, so he pushed back against it.

That's when he felt the connection. It wasn't cold around him; it was air, and cold was just one of its properties. He let out a breath and relaxed. Suddenly, he could sense the air in a way beyond touch. *Harmony*, he thought. *Henry also talked about how he was able to affect and change things. That must be Affinity.* Ox willed the air to speed up within itself, and it obeyed. He felt just the slightest give to the bite in the cold.

More. He forced the air to speed up. *Might! That's it!*

Like someone had lit a bonfire around him, his skin instantly warmed, though the snow under his toes strangely didn't melt.

At least now I can think. The bitter cold receded, and another sensation replaced the fleeting chill. Ox felt something similar when he'd entered Ghara's chamber, though the battle with the Sprigs and Wendigo had drawn his attention away from the Primal's presence.

A splash of cascading water roared from the ocean around him, and Ox instinctively ducked, ever ready for an attack. The splashing only got louder, and Ox poked his head up to see a shape emerging from the water. A head that looked larger than Ox's berg rose from the waves until Ox could see the head and shoulders of a massive man with a bald dome and a thick, white beard that hung into the water. The face was old, but the muscles under the skin looked more solid than the ice under Ox's feet.

Marooned on the frozen island, there was nowhere for Ox to go. Hopefully this . . . thing . . . was nicer than Henry's dragon. "Hey, you! What's going on?" Ox shouted.

The giant man's eyebrows twitched, and he looked down, slowly turning to glare at Ox. His eyes were such a light blue that they were nearly white, matching the snowy ice below Ox's feet. The man looked directly at Ox . . . and frowned, like someone had just told him that his dinner had been replaced with a combination of rotten didgaro gizzards and sadness.

The colossal watery being let out a blast of mighty wind from his nose. Then, with slow, drawn-out words, he started to speak. A deep rumble that sounded more like an earthquake than a voice shook Ox to his glacial core. "You again, Chokriot. It has been so long in the lifespan of a mortal. I had hoped you wouldn't return."

"Good to see you too . . . again, I guess. Listen, I'm in the middle of a fight, and I need to get back. My minions are relying on me."

"You're here because you need to be. Who are you fighting this time, tiny giant?"

"That's a cryptic response, and I'm not sure what you mean by tiny. You're just huge. But anyway, I'm fighting an elven tree god named Ghara—"

"Ghara . . ." the giant drew out the name long and slow. "So, you are still at Jallfoss after such a long time. Ghara is neither a god nor a tree. She is the Spriggan Primal charged with protecting that mountain. You should not be fighting her."

Ox held up his hands and shrugged his shoulders. "Not my choice. And if she's supposed to protect the mountain, she's not doing her job very well. A Necromancer did something to her, and now she's making corrupted animals and attacking elves. If you ask me, she's a rather poor hostess."

The giant shut his eyes and pulled in another deep breath. After a moment, his expression turned even more sour, and he furrowed his brow. "This is truly bad, indeed. Whatever the False Remnant did, he delivered such a blow to the lifeforce in the mountain that it corrupted her. Her power is weakening. She can no longer hold both the seal and her mind. In her state, a Remnant like you should be able to restrain her in your Primal form."

"You mean when I got big? As soon as I did that, I ended up here."

"Do not toy with me, Chokriot!" the giant shouted. Waves exploded around his colossal body, and Ox struggled to maintain his footing on the shaking iceberg. "You are tiny, but no fool. I have no patience for you playing one!"

Ox steadied himself, not at all pleased about being berated by whoever this soggy geezer was. "I'm trying to explain to you that I died a hundred years ago and lost my memory. Whatever the Necromancer did to Ghara, it cursed everyone to keep coming back as undead. I think. I didn't really pay attention when Buddy explained it to me. Regardless, you are familiar with me, but I don't have the pleasure of remembering you."

The giant let out a sonorous groan of frustration. "You've lost yourself again, Chokriot." He studied Ox for a long moment before switching to a resigned expression. "I am Giganthorp, Giant Primal, and keeper of the power of the young god Golos. Malek Vik'Taus is an archon Remnant—a most troublesome human. A short time for one such as me, but a hundred lifetimes ago for you, he tried to claim the power of Jallfoss for his own. All but Raynott thought him dead. If he has returned, you must stop him at all costs. First, you must repair whatever damage has been done to Ghara."

"She's being *uncooperative* at the moment. I'm good with the ladies, but I doubt I can calm her down. Any ideas?"

Giganthorp's frown grew even more dour. "Are there any other Remnants with you?"

"There's a human skeleton who keeps getting beaten up by a dragon. I think he met that Malek guy on his Path. There's also a regular human skeleton who's a darn good mage, and an Ikritian Acolyte. And also, two elves. One is a child and the other is undead, but she's very grumpy.

"An elf . . ." Giganthorp mused. "An elf will have to do. Very well, Chokriot. Once again, I'm forced to bestow power upon you that you don't deserve. You will control the memories of the giant Primals and hold sway over the creation of Remnants. The elf must kill Ghara, and you will do the rest."

"Say what? I have no idea what you're talking about."

"Though it pains me to grant you such an undeserved responsibility a second time, you are the closest thing to a giant that I have available. I charge you with our Legacy."

"Slow down, big guy. I'm not following." Ox held up his hands and took a few quick steps backward.

"You don't need to understand. You need to do as you are told . . . for once. Ghara was charged with containing the power of Jallfoss. Her seal has held through her corruption, so it should continue to last. Though how long remains unknown. You will find a way, tiny giant, because you must."

"Once again, I'm not tiny, you're just huge."

"Protect the elf with your life. Protect them all. And do not fail."

Ox tried to protest and keep asking questions, but everything around him faded to white.

CHAPTER 33

Ox's yell started as a child's tantrum, unrestrained and weak, but quickly grew to a focused rage that echoed through the cavern.

At least the idiot isn't dead, Beast thought while dodging a Magnolia branch and slicing the throat of a tainted boar. She took more notice of Ox's voice when the ground began to shake.

The Ox-sized hole in the side of the rock wall where the Magnolia branch had buried the skeleton started to grow and form larger cracks. Ox's roar reached a crescendo, and the huge skeleton burst out with the force of a dwarven solofurno.

Beast watched in stunned awe as Ox landed at the base of the Magnolia's mound and grew to nearly thirty feet tall. Somehow, his dread armor expanded around him and conformed perfectly to the colossal proportions of his skeletal body. His battle cry only grew in volume, echoing through the cavern as he charged the possessed tree.

The largest Magnolia limb pulled from the tunnel entrance and whipped toward Ox. The giant raised his hands and smashed it into the ground. The limb exploded in a shower of black sap and splintered rotten wood.

Not bad at all . . . Beast nodded with approval, but her admiration was short-lived. Ox's body went limp, and the giant face-planted directly into the dirt. Within a second, the broken branch and one of the other two that had been smashing into Buddy's shields began to pummel the giant armored skeleton.

Idiot, Beast cursed the dullard under her breath. She didn't have time to focus on Ox as several smaller branches and countless Sprigs surged toward her.

Blink

Beast felt the branches and the Sprigs were serving Ghara's will. If she could reach the spriggan Primal, she could end the entire assault. She tried to teleport next to the antlered woman. Once again, she reappeared, still fifty feet away, and rebounded off an invisible wall. Something was stopping her from Blinking any closer.

She tried to charge, but the branches only got thicker and faster as she neared Ghara, preventing her from getting any closer. Sprigs fell to her blades' keen edges, but the flailing branches were another problem. Even though her daggers were sharp, they could do little more than parry the solid wood, and she didn't have enough Vitus to use the Void skill on every branch. She needed a sharper blade or a better way to cut. The thought gave her an idea.

Another limb snapped toward her like a whip, threatening to smash her to bits. She focused the Void Ability to the edge of her blade, halving its width repeatedly until it was impossibly thin. With such a small area, she could supply a continuous stream of Vitus without draining her reserves too fast.

Ability Discovered: Nether Blade I. Hone your blades with an edge of infinite sharpness

Her dagger cut clean through the limb without resistance, then downed another four branches and ten Sprigs like she was dicing vegetables. Unfortunately, the branches regrew as fast as she could cut. She had to dodge back before the horde overwhelmed her.

She glanced around, hoping her companions were having better luck. Ox had gotten back to his feet. The branch he'd smashed had begun to reform, and he grabbed it and one other under his arms. He held the thrashing Magnolia limbs firmly, preventing them from crushing anyone else.

Buddy's shield persisted, and his evocation kept the last large limb and most of the Sprigs occupied, though the interval of his attacks grew increasingly large. The mage cultivated his power with every battle, but the limits of his Vitus could only stretch so far.

Henry had taken quite a beating and fought like a cornered badger. Black ichor sprayed like a fountain as he wound through the battlefield, but like Buddy's magic, every slice and dodge became slower than the last.

Nearly half the elven Sentinels had been overwhelmed and killed by stray Sprigs or Magnolia limbs, though a few had rallied and set up a slight resistance. Jacoby still stood over Talji and fought off both Sprigs and Magnolia with an impressive fervor. His Auric Palisade Ability was surprisingly effective as a defense, but he was restricted to close-range attacks. Because he found it necessary to protect the elf, he was mostly immobile. Beast had nothing but disdain for the elven Sentinel and would have preferred that Jacoby let her die so he could join the fight. *Stupid human.*

Jai had found a relatively safe spot behind a few large boulders, launching rock after rock from his sling and summoning extra-planar animals to fight for him. He was doing little more than distracting a few Sprigs, but at least the child was trying to help.

The one thing they all had in common was that each was showing increased fatigue . . . everyone except Ghara. The situation was starting to look grim, with little hope of either victory or escape.

"Grumpy minion!" Ox bellowed.

"What?" Beast Blinked around another flailing limb, annoyed that she had acknowledged him after he called her grumpy.

Ox struggled to keep his grip with the Magnolia dragging him across the battlefield, but his new mass allowed him to hold tight to the squirming branches. "You have to kill her!" he shouted.

"What do you think I'm trying to do?" Beast yelled back.

—

Henry heard Ox's shout—it was impossible not to. The volume of his voice matched his colossal size. Not even the roar of continuous Sprig waves or the violent song of twisting branches could dampen Ox's words. Henry yelled back at Ox, "We're all trying, but we can't get close enough to strike."

Ox strained against the Magnolia's force. "No, Herbie! A giant . . . ugh . . . a watery giant told me that Beast must be the one to kill her."

Henry opened his jaw to reply, then shut it and looked at Beast. So many questions went through his head, but he was low on options and decided to trust Ox. He shrugged and gave his orders. "You heard the emperor—Jacoby, with me. Let's get Beast as close as we can. Buddy, give us cover fire. Ox, break everything!" Henry wasn't as loud as his gigantic companion, but his direction got everyone moving.

Jacoby still stood over Talji. The elf hadn't recovered from whatever the Wendigo had done to her, and she struggled to prop herself off the ground. Jacoby fended off Sprig after Sprig, but with each blow, his magic dimmed. He made eye contact with Henry, then glanced at Ghara's throne and back at Talji. Henry saw a gamut of conflicting emotions run across his face. The man finally settled on one of determination.

The Acolyte dismissed his shield and scooped up Talji. The elf instinctively wrapped her arms around the man's neck and leaned her head into his chest, barely able to open her eyes. That was fine, as Jacoby had enough drive for them both. With a Strength and Mobility Henry didn't expect from the man, Jacoby sprang forward, vaulting above the strike of a tainted caterpillar with long curved pincers.

Like a mongoose in a pit of snakes, Jacoby dodged and spun, kicked and evaded, all while gently cradling Talji, until he arrived within the protective force wall that Buddy had erected. "Keep her safe," the Acolyte pleaded, lowering the elf to the ground. Buddy nodded in response as more heavy blows from the Magnolia assaulted the mage's barrier.

"Now, that's how you sweep a lady off her feet!" Ox arched his back, then whipped the limbs under his arms as hard as he could, sending a jolt through the tree that shook every leaf, branch, and tainted berry. Buddy dropped his shield and launched a barrage of elemental attacks, wiping out several dozen Sprigs between Beast and Ghara, and burning away some of the smaller, faster limbs.

Spark

Henry's sword lit up with lightning magic, and he spurred his team forward. "Now's our chance, let's go!"

Jacoby hesitated for a moment. He looked down at Talji, but the elf pushed him away. "Go!" That was all the man needed. In an instant, he and Henry flanked Beast, and the three sprinted up the dirt mound toward the base of the Magnolia.

Just ahead of their charge, an amber circle inscribed with various runes and sigils formed in the way of their offensive. Though the markings were foreign to Henry and their form was much more intricate than he'd seen previously, he recognized the source of the magic. "Keep going!" he urged.

A monstrosity, nearly the size of the Wendigo, popped into existence and led their advance. It had the stature of a gorilla with a rhinoceros' heavy plating and horns. Jai had truly surpassed his limits with the summon—not only with the creature's power, but based on the direct and focused intent of the summon, Jai's control over the contract had developed significantly. Henry wondered what the boy had to pay for the service of such a creature, but he hadn't the time to contemplate the spell's after-effects on the elf.

They neared the edge of the Magnolia's canopy, and the entire tree began to shake from a combination of the hundreds of smaller thrashing branches as another wave of hatching Sprig berries dropped their contents onto the ground. No matter how many Sprigs they slew, more fell from the massive tree. Fortunately, Jai's summon was as effective as it looked. The gorilla-rhino bowled through tainted creatures like they weren't even there, spraying green and black gore on both sides of the path. Magnolia branches snapped hard against the creature's plating, drawing blood, but only hindering the summon's progress slightly more than the Sprigs had.

"Everyone, protect Beast. Let's go!" Henry shouted.

With the gorilla-rhino at the front, and Jacoby and Henry

flanking Beast, they created a wedge that drove straight at the base of the corrupted tree. They made quick progress until Ghara took notice of the threat. The base of the tree where the Primal had joined with the Magnolia opened back up, and Ghara stepped out. Henry's Perception could make out much more detail this close to her. She was adorned with armor that looked like overlapping leaves, though if it was anything like the dread bones that came from the Silent, it would be much more resilient than even golem steel.

Remnant Gateway

Haruspex

Name: Ghara

Type: Primal, Corrupted Spriggan

Tier: 85

Health: 621/621

Vitus: 198/417

Attributes:

    STR: 68

    MOB: 125

    FOR: 79

    ACU: 75

    PER: 48

    RES: 42

Resistance: Physical, Magical, Environmental (Cold)

Weakness: Fire, Poison, Acid

Lore: The Ent form is the heart of the Spriggan Primal. The gentle mother of the forest is a friend to any ally of nature

Now that Ghara had separated her humanoid form from the rest of the Magnolia, and Henry was near her, his Haruspex picked up that her Attributes were substantially less than before.

Though still far above any of the skeletons, it gave Henry a glimmer of hope that there was a chance of victory.

Ghara's eyes locked onto the approaching party. From a distance, they appeared obscured by shadows, but up close, Henry saw they were as black as night. Her hands were the same jet black, with long, clawed fingers that came to sharp points. As they neared, those claws started to glow a brilliant red, then Ghara lifted a hand and closed it into a fist.

Instantly, the attacking branches swelled with vigor and spiraled toward them. Jai's summon took the brunt of the attack. Limbs wound and closed around the creature, lifting it into the air and ending its charge. It still fought and snarled, but the struggle was useless against the constricting branches.

Henry and Jacoby did their best to fend off the increased tempo and intensity of the flailing tree. The foliage stalled their charge just a dozen paces from the Primal, but they had opened a clear path for the elf. "Beast, take her out!" Henry shouted and flared Blitz, Harden, and Spark in sequence.

Beast vaulted over the last few striking branches, unleashing a flurry of slashing strikes. Henry hoped she would make quick work of the Primal, but that wasn't the case. Ghara was even faster than Beast, and her claws were more dangerous than the elf's frost daggers.

Ghara deftly parried Beast's attack and responded with a series of slashes that sent the elf tumbling out of the way. Beast tried to dance back in melee range, but Ghara would nearly rend her to pieces every time she got close and force her to retreat. A quick attempt at Blink found her rejected, and she rebounded off the red broken-glass shielding.

The Sprigs and branches took Henry's Health down by

a third. The damage only made him more determined to give Beast the opportunity to strike. "Jacoby, I need some space."

The Acolyte unleashed a spray of color that blinded the nearby Sprigs, sending them reeling and clawing at their eyes. Black flesh blistered and melted away under the heat of the Acolyte's spell. The man dismissed his golden shield and focused all his Vitus into his blade, then spun through the animated forest like a whirlwind, making Henry second-guess his desire to battle the man in an even fight. Jacoby's blade faded as the attack ended, and Henry could tell the man had drained the last of his magic. Henry now had the room he needed.

Sacrifice

Henry pulled the modified dread claw javelin from the holster on his forearm and pumped it full of Vitus until it was five feet long. It felt strong and well-balanced in his hands.

Blitz

He sent the weapon flying directly at Ghara with a quick, smooth motion. The Primal saw the attack coming and dodged, but it didn't matter. The spear buried halfway into the Magnolia's trunk, and Henry activated another Ability.

Taunt

As he had done with the dragon, Henry forced the mental attack through his connection with the Primal, and she responded accordingly. For the first time, the stoic expression on her face turned to anger. All the branches and Sprigs focused their attack on Henry, and a forest of angry limbs quickly swept him up. The branches were extraordinarily strong, squeezing him like an anaconda. Only his dread armor kept him from being crushed.

The dread javelin had served its purpose, and Beast didn't waste the opportunity Henry had provided. She caught Ghara in the chest with both her blade and her Void Ability.

Beast's blade rebounded off the Primal's armor, not leaving the slightest mark. Ghara swatted Beast with a backhand that sent her tumbling aside.

Drat, Henry cursed. Just like with the dread bones, Beast's attack couldn't pierce Ghara's armor. They were running low on options. If Beast had Henry's Blitz and Spark, she could maneuver inside the Primal's reach and do some damage with higher-tiered weapon Abilities. If only there were a way to give Beast his magic.

Maybe there was.

Henry felt a rib and an arm bone snap under the Magnolia's squeeze. His Health dipped further. He ignored flashing glyphs and instead spread his awareness, reaching toward Beast as he had done moments before with Ghara. Instead of attacking her mind with his Taunt Ability, he activated Blitz and channeled it into her body.

Bestow: Blitz

Ability Discovered: Bestow I. Transfer the Effects of an Ability to a single ally

Beast must have felt the boost to her Mobility, because she blurred around the Primal nearly as fast as if she had Blink available. The sudden assault caught Ghara by surprise, forcing her backward. Beast landed attack after attack, but they weren't effective against the Primal's armor.

With his Vitus nearing zero, Henry pulled the Health from his bones, turned it into magic, and then willed it through the connection with Beast.

Sacrifice

Bestow: Spark

Henry's bones crinkled under the force of the tree limbs that continued to tighten around him. His Health plummeted. His connection to Beast held . . . barely.

CHAPTER 34

"Beak?" the tiny creature chirped just inches from Talji's face, curious about her condition. The creature was right to be concerned if she looked anything like she felt. It wasn't a squirrel; she knew that for sure. And it definitely wasn't any type of varmint or rodent she was familiar with. Since it accompanied the skeletons, Talji could only assume it was something from the dwarven Underdeep.

She managed to look around. Jai's skeletal mage stood near her and was firing barrage after magical barrage at the waves of Sprigs that swarmed toward them. Huge branches smashed against the invisible dome the mage had erected above them. Protecting them—protecting her.

Talji's head throbbed like she'd been pounding it against a rock for hours. Holding back the Wendigo had been extremely painful both physically and mentally. She felt like the monster had nearly eaten her from inside her own mind, though she had no idea how that was even possible.

She had resisted the cryptid as long as she could. She didn't know why she chose to hold the Wendigo back from attacking Jacoby. Through the pain and madness, that was the only thing she knew was right. Maybe that's why Jacoby and the skeletons had chosen to protect her from the spriggan. *Would it even matter? Ghara was a god, and they were only undead.*

The scene around her looked hopeless. The elven Sentinels had rallied and were helping cull the Sprigs, but their numbers had been nearly cut in half by the pounding Magnolia branches. One of the skeletons had become a giant and held onto two whipping branches. There was no telling how long he could restrain the Magnolia. Jacoby had brought her under the mage's protection, then went with Harshmira and another skeleton to fight Ghara directly.

"Mira . . ." Talji said, just barely above a whisper. *Could it really be her? After all these years, had the traitor finally returned?*

"Beak," the squirrel creature chirped again, more forcefully this time. It stood on its hind legs, and Talji noticed it wore a leather harness around its torso with a Drift Amulet secured in the straps. Its Tier was **17**. *How is that possible?* she wondered.

"Muji requests your aid, elven warrior," an aged voice said. It took Talji a moment to realize it was the undead mage who was talking to her. She wasn't used to hearing the incorporeal voice coming from the undead. "My magic is useless against the Primal. Any assistance would be much appreciated."

"Magic won't work against her. She has the shield of the gods," Talji said, struggling to sit up.

"Then what *will* work?" the mage asked. "We only need her distracted long enough for Beast to deliver a fatal blow."

Beast. That's what they call Mira. Talji pushed the thought from her head and looked up at the giant red leaves of the Magnolia's canopy. "We need fire. Real fire," Talji replied. She looked around the battlefield, searching for dry moss or kindling— anything to help her create a blaze. As though Ghara herself had answered the elf's prayers, there it was—an alchemy bag lying on the ground just a dozen paces outside the mage's shield. She activated her Drift Amulet's Identify Ability and saw the high-quality ingredients scattered on the ground.

"I can do it, but I'll need you to protect me," she wheezed, holding back another wave of nausea as she fought to her feet.

The skeletal mage addressed the tiny creature between elemental blasts that tore apart the mass of swarming Sprigs. "Muji, she is our ally now. Help me protect her."

"Beak," the squirrel responded. Now that her senses had cleared, Talji was confident the rodent before her was the same creature that had attacked her and Bharat at the arena. It didn't matter. They had to survive.

Talji ran.

More stumbled than ran, but she made her way as quickly as her broken Mobility would allow.

Several Sprigs charged. The creature—Muji, the mage had called him—darted between and lured them away. Whenever a Sprig chased Muji, the monsters would erupt into either blue fire or lightning. The tiny creature even leapt onto the back of a wolf Sprig and bit into the monster's nape. Ghara's monster collapsed immediately. As her Drift Amulet indicated, he really was at Tier **17**.

Talji dropped to her knees near the scattered alchemy contents. She didn't need Assess to understand that what lay before her was a treasure trove.

"Witch's tail . . . scaldroot . . . billinger shroud," she mouthed the names of the reagents. There was a pestle strapped inside the bag, but she couldn't afford the time to utilize it. She muddled the ingredients with her hands, wincing as a spine from a double-finned mud whobbler dug into her flesh. Red gas started to form, and the mixture quickly began to heat, causing Talji to hold her breath to avoid breathing in the toxic fumes.

Blasts of fire and explosions of ice erupted all around her. She knew Muji and the skeleton were doing everything possible to hold back the Sprigs. Too engulfed in her work to try to defend herself, she had to trust the mage and the squirrel.

She mashed the ball of reagents together in her hands until there was only one more ingredient she needed. The sounds of battle roared around her. She ignored the chaos and opened her mouth to bite into the flesh at the base of her thumb.

She expected the copper taste of blood to hit her tongue. Instead, it tasted like rot. Hopefully, the aftereffects of the Wendigo wouldn't hurt her alchemy. She held her hand over her mixture and let her black blood drip into it. A glyph formed above her creation.

Scaldroot Grenade Activated: Detonation in 5 . . . 4 . . . 3 . . .

Talji stood and threw the ball as hard as she could. It exploded mid-arc and rained down streams of fire on the lower Magnolia leaves. Each torrent that hit a branch or leaf erupted into two more, shooting into the air in random directions. Some fell to the ground and fizzled in the dirt, but many more spread through the tree and began to climb the massive canopy. She thought she heard a low rumbling sound like the tree itself was writhing in pain.

Talji dropped to her knees. What had she done? Her entire life had been devoted to serving Ghara, and now she'd chosen to directly harm her god. She slumped to the ground. Before her eyes closed and she lost consciousness, she saw Muji's bushy tail. The squirrel creature stood between her and a rushing horde of Sprigs. As small as the creature was, it had a ferocious growl, giving no indication it would flee Ghara's corrupt army.

She didn't deserve whatever kindness was causing Muji and the undead to protect her, but if she survived, she would spend the rest of her life making amends for whatever damage she had caused.

—

Blitz Ability Available. Accept?

Beast was fast, but Ghara was faster. The Spriggan Primal had razor-sharp claws that could cut through Beast's bone with little resistance, showcased by the slash marks in her leather armor from several near misses. Amid her battle with Ghara, Beast ignored the glyphs in her view, dismissing them as soon as they appeared. One in particular wouldn't go away. Assuming it was another annoying notification, she accepted without taking a moment to examine it. Power swelled through the magical channels holding her bones together like she'd been gifted with actual flesh. Her Strength and Mobility soared, and she could somehow tell the boost was coming from Henry.

Blitz Activated: STR +25%, MOB +25%

Though she had been quick before, the boost to her Attributes from Henry's Blitz made her feel like everything around her had slowed down. She had no idea how Henry was doing it. Even though the Magnolia's branches nearly cocooned him, he could still grant Beast his Abilities.

Herny was a warrior; there was no denying that. His mastery over tactics on the battlefield was unmatched by anyone she'd come across in her afterlife and likely anyone she'd met before. She and the other skeletons trusted him to see them through each obstacle they encountered, but they also had faith in his mission to save the Jallfoss undead from their curse. Henry was naïve, a bit too trusting, but in a way that drew others to follow him. There was something more, however. Whatever he was experiencing in his visions, whatever connection he had formed with the Necromancer, he was destined for something far beyond the curse the mountain had bestowed on him.

He was also loyal to a fault. Even as the Magnolia constricted around his bones, Henry was forcing his Abilities into Beast to give her a chance of victory. Beast was determined not to waste that chance.

With her upgraded Strength and Mobility, she shot forward between red-tipped slashing claws and sliced with her frost-enchanted blades against the exposed Spriggan torso. Her daggers glanced off armor that looked like overlayed leaves, but it was far stronger than the dread bone that Henry and Ox wore.

Nether Blade

Beast enchanted her weapon with infinite sharpness and jabbed hard. Void magic met Primal armor, and the blade rebounded again, leaving Ghara completely unharmed.

"Minoa's blind ogre, why won't you die?" Beast cursed.

Ghara swiped at the skeletal elf, and Beast dodged back, barely avoiding the deadly claw strikes. The Primal's black eyes looked more vacant than the magic from Beast's Void Ability. If Beast could pierce Ghara's armor, maybe she could inflict some real damage, but her weapons and Abilities weren't up to the task.

Ghar was unbelievably fast, and her defenses were too robust for Beast to overcome. Regardless, Beast knew the antlered woman exchanging blows with her was not a fighter. Where Beast's attacks were precise and meant to flow into devastating combinations, Ghara's were wild and undisciplined. She was more an animal than a trained warrior, which had left Beast mostly unscathed by the deadly slashes from the Primal's claws.

Blitz made Beast faster than Ghara, though her attacks couldn't penetrate the Primal's armor. Beast tried to use her Drift Amulet to Assess any weakness. It failed to identify the armor, but she assumed it had to be at least Legendary-quality. That was something her Void and Nether Blade Abilities just couldn't overcome.

Henry's Ability cut off. Her Strength and Mobility dropped, and she suddenly felt sluggish. Another message flashed in her view.

Spark Ability Available. Accept?

Henry. That idiot was still channeling magic to her.

Beast mentally accepted the magic. From hearing Henry describe Spark, she knew that it increased the Tier of any weapon's Ability. Instantly, her daggers lit up with arcs of lightning. With Blitz gone, she was unsure if she could get in close enough to land the strike. Even if she could hit the Primal, Nether Blade wasn't a weapon Ability. She wondered how Spark would affect it.

Ghara wasn't about to give her the chance to think through the finer points of Henry's magic. The Primal lunged toward Beast as dozens of vine-like branches whipped toward her. Beast prepared to slice and dodge, but Ghara's assault was thwarted as the entire magnolia shook.

Ghara's black eyes widened into a look of surprise mixed with no small amount of anger as the area near the Magnolia's truck lit up with brilliant red and yellow flames. A large section of the giant canopy erupted in a fire that quickly spread.

Ghara turned toward the fire, obvious expressions of pain on her face. Beast attacked.

Nether Blade

Frost Blade

Beast lunged while activating the dagger's frost enchantment and adding in her Nether Blade, all stacked on top of Henry's Spark. Void, frost, and lightning magic surged from her weapons. Every last ounce of her Strength and Mobility propelled her forward. The Primal armor gave way under the combined magic of her and Henry, and she buried the blades deep into Ghara's chest.

Void

Beast used the last of her Vitus to expand the Nether Blade inside Ghara into her Void Ability. The Primal lifted black claws, and Beast knew she couldn't dodge; she could only pump more magic inside the monster.

Beast braced for the impact, but nothing came. Only the sound of crackling flames filled her ears. The creaking vines and racket from the army of Sprigs had silenced completely.

Beast saw Ghara's hands drop to her sides, and she looked up to find the Primal staring directly at her. That close, she could see the black in Ghara's eyes fade like someone had wiped frost from a glass window, revealing a deep emerald green. Ghara's expression softened, and Beast saw the faintest hint of a smile. Then the Primal's eyes faded completely to white, and she slumped to the ground.

Spriggan Primal Killed, Soul Essence Claimed, +3 Tiers
STR +3, MOB +5, FOR, +2, ACU +6, PER +3, RES +4

A wave of emotions flooded through Beast's mind. It was the most powerful sensation she'd ever felt after defeating an enemy, and it nearly took her to her knees. Ghara's last emotions were a strong sense of failure, then relief that her pain was over.

Hundreds of broken memories bombarded Beast so quickly that she had no hope of parsing through them all before they faded. There were visions of massive, chaotic battles followed by eons of peaceful sunsets. One memory clearly stood out: a creature adorned in bone armor that looked suspiciously like the Silent from the dwarven Underdeep. It filled the roots of the Magnolia with vile magic. Beast had no doubt it was the same Necromancer Henry saw in his visions.

Ghara's spirit began to fade from Beast's awareness. Strangely, Beast was almost sad to feel the spriggan depart.

"Not yet, beautiful tree lady. Get back here!" Ox's colossal yell shook the entire cave.

—

Ox knew he was strong, but his Strength was just plain ridiculous in his giant form. Unfortunately, so was the Magnolia, and Ox's Vitus was running very low. He held two of the tree's largest branches firmly under his arms, whipping him around regardless of his size and power. A third was relentlessly striking him and even started to damage his dreadmail.

Buddy had set up his defense on the other side of the dirt mound. The mage's shielding took a pounding from the fourth branch, and his magic was laying waste to the legions of Sprigs that endlessly dropped from the Magnolia's canopy. Both Ox and Buddy were too occupied to help with the primary battle at the base of the tree.

Henry, Jacoby, and Jai's summon were doing their part, but the smaller branches had them wrapped up. The only one that had gotten to Ghara was Beast, and that fight wasn't going well.

The battle had gone on long enough. The Magnolia would smash their bones to dust if they didn't end it now. It was time for the emperor to act.

Heart of the Jotun

Ox's Strength doubled in an instant. He released one branch and brought his hand down hard on the other. Wood exploded as Ox severed the limb. He didn't stop there. Another monstrous branch rushed toward him, and he wrapped both arms around it and pulled with all his might. The Magnolia groaned, and Ox started to run, bending the limb and pulling as hard as he could. The branch splintered, and Ox's Vitus dipped dangerously low. With a final push of Strength, the branch tore completely off the main body. The tree shuddered as though it were in physical pain.

Before Ox could celebrate, a fiery explosion lit up the Magnolia's canopy. Buddy and Muji had protected the beautiful lady elf long enough to somehow allow her to ignite the angry tree.

Heart of the Jotun faded, and Ox saw that he and Talji had successfully distracted the tree woman. Through the thrashing foliage, Ox watched Beast plunge her blade through the Primal's chest.

The grumpy minion did it, Ox thought with no small amount of pride. Beast had delivered a lethal blow to the spriggan, but Giganthorpe's words echoed in Ox's skull. He needed to act before Ghara's soul, and subsequently, all her power, got away.

"Not yet, beautiful tree lady. Get back here!" he bellowed.

Ox wasn't sure what he was expected to do, so he just did the last thing that worked for him. When he was freezing on the iceberg, he spread his awareness to the air around him. He did the same this time, but directed all this attention to Beast. He focused his Affinity and could almost see a portion of Ghara's Soul Essence funneling into the skeletal elf. There was more Essence, much more, that was leaving. The leafy tart was getting away, and Ox wasn't about to let that happen.

Though it was all in his mind, it felt tangible to Ox. He willed his presence to the fleeing Primal soul and grabbed hold of it. It was terrible, like a rotten deer carcass covered in gangrene. Skin festered and boiled, filling his nose with the stench of death. The soul struggled, thrashing at him with wicked antlers, but Ox didn't let go. Instead, he willed his blizzard aura around himself. Ox flared his Might. White swirled all around, freezing and ripping the flesh from the Primal's soul. It writhed and snarled, like a lion caught in the metal teeth of a bear trap.

The putrid flesh melted away, revealing a brilliant green light that emitted such a force that it felt like a year's worth of springtime sunshine had been compressed into a single point. Ox wrapped a mental hand around the ball of light and hauled it back. It had a heft to it that light shouldn't have possessed, like Ox was pulling the entire weight of the colossal Magnolia. Ox refused to fail a test of Strength. He pulled until the green light was just in front of Beast's body. She stood there, motionless, frozen in time. Ox pushed the light into her. It resisted at first, but Ox shoved again with all the mental clout he could muster. Like a thirsty camel at a trough after a month-long desert trip, Beast's body drank in the spriggan soul, absorbing it completely.

Legacy of Golos

Whatever power the water giant gave Ox came with just enough instinctual knowledge for him to activate an Ability. That Ability wasn't displayed in his Status, but when Ghara's soul entered Beast, a prompt appeared in Ox's display.

Bestow Remnant Status? Y/N

With a mental nod, he confirmed the selection.

Multiple Primal sources available. Choose one:
Giant
Spriggan

Only for a moment did he consider making Beast a giant. Though it would be hilarious, the stakes were too high, even for a joke that good. He selected *Spriggan*.

The power of the Giants flowed from Ox and into Beast. The magic from Giganthorpe allowed Ghara's spriggan soul to meld with the elf. For just a moment, Ox thought he could feel the water giant's approval, but that sensation faded, and only his words remained in Ox's mind: "A single remnant can only do so much against a primal, even a corrupted one."

Now they had two Remnants in the party. If Henry could get himself together, they would have three.

CHAPTER 35

Henry wasn't one to give up hope, but when his dread-mail began to crack under the squeezing force of the branches, he knew his bones wouldn't last much longer. With his Vitus all but gone and his Health approaching single digits, he could only hope he'd given Beast the chance she needed to slay Ghara. He diverted only a small amount of Vitus to his Harden Ability—just enough to allow him to keep Spark flowing into Beast.

Henry breathed a sigh of relief when the branches stopped constricting and glyphs began to flash in his vision.

Spriggan Primal Killed, Soul Essence Claimed, Tiers +2
STR +3, MOB +3, FOR +4, ACU +2, PER +3, RES +2, HAR +4, AFI +3, MIG +2

Ghara's last emotions were the most powerful he'd experienced yet. As strong as they were, there was little information beyond those sentiments. The flood of Soul Essence betrayed a vile anger that was quickly replaced by a deep sense of failure, followed by gratitude and satisfaction. A few memories came with the experience, but one that stood out was a vision of the Source Crystal.

When Henry had killed Jacoby all those weeks ago, the man's last thought was imagining himself reaching the bottom of the dwarven Underdeep and finding a large but simple gem that shone with a brilliant radiance. Ghara's mental image was much different than what the Acolyte had constructed in his mind. The Source Crystal was a monstrous gem-like growth inside a cavern nearly as large as the one where the Magnolia resided. Lava rivers ran through the cavern floor, and the crystal itself pulsed with energy. The mental image quickly dissipated, leaving Henry with nothing but the sensation of the branches still holding him firmly.

Though the Tier up had filled his Health and Vitus, he still had neither the Strength nor the magic to free himself. After several minutes in the Magnolia vine's tight embrace, he heard muted voices approaching.

"Where's Henry?" Buddy asked.

"Up there, but I can't reach him," Jacoby answered.

"Beast, I believe Henry could use your help," Buddy said. Beast didn't respond to the mage, but Henry soon felt the swish of her daggers slicing apart his wooden cocoon. The organic prison shattered, and Henry dropped much further than he expected. He caught a few stray limbs on the way down and slowed his fall so he didn't take any damage upon landing.

"Thanks, Beast. I was starting to get a bit claustrophobic." Henry took in the aftermath of the battle. Hundreds of Sprig bodies had turned to ash and started to flake away. Little was left besides the wooden husks from which the tainted creatures had hatched. The blanket-sized Magnolia leaves had turned from brilliant red to a dim green, and sections of the foliage had begun to curl upon themselves.

Fat rain droplets poured from the clouded ceiling, putting out the last tongues of fire that had consumed about a quarter of the canopy. The Magnolia no longer moved to attack them, stilled after Ghara's humanoid form had died. Bare branches seemed to almost reel in pain from the fading fire.

The battle had completely destroyed the Magnolia's base and the surrounding hillside. Now that it was raining, the downpour turned the churned-up dirt into a muddy mess. Henry welcomed the deluge that helped clean a week of grime from his bones and armor.

"It looks like we did it. Is everyone alright?" Henry asked, surveilling his companions. Muji was sprawled across Buddy's shoulders and dozed peacefully. Jacoby slowly made his way toward the group with Talji in tow. The elf had an arm around the man's neck for support. Her face was pale, and her footing was shaky, but she looked like she had recovered a bit from whatever the Wendigo had done to her. Jacoby carefully lowered her to the dirt. The elf kept her eyes low, purposely avoiding curious stares, especially Beast's hostile glower. At least eight other Sentinels survived. They huddled near the caved-in entrance, reluctant to leave their slain compatriots.

"Did you see what I did, Mira? That was my strongest summon yet!" Jai bounced excitedly around Beast, talking about the gorilla-rhino he had conjured.

"Your spell was . . . effective, but my name is Beast, not Mira," Beast replied. She tried to end the conversation, but Jai kept engaging her.

Ox stood close to Henry. He had returned to his normal size and replaced Torgga's ring to suppress his Temperance aura. He had his arms crossed over his chest and wore a smug look on his face.

"We're more than fine, Harvey. Assess me and the grumpy

elf," he said, spreading his arms wide. Henry activated the Ability.

Haruspex

Chokriot Chukrathik
Undead Half-Jotun (Giant Remnant)

Beast
Undead Elf (Spriggan Remnant)

The first time Henry used his divination Ability on Thorodd, the Dwarven Elder blocked Haruspex and scolded the attempt as rude. Henry now realized how his Abilities and Remnant Attributes—Might, Affinity, and Harmony—formed connections between him and the surrounding world. He was hesitant to use that connection to look beyond the names of his companions, but what he saw was enough to tell him there had been a significant change in both Ox and Beast.

"Who is Chokriot?" Henry asked.

"That is my old name . . . I think. I pulled too much from my core, and something pulled back. I fell into a freezing ocean surrounded by icebergs. The experience was similar to how you described your Desert Path. There, I met a giant named Giganthorp who told me that Beast had to kill Ghara. I'm still unsure why, but I figured out how to use the antlered woman's power to make Beast a Remnant. Not only am I a great warrior and humble emperor of this mountain, but I am also a Giant."

Jai's mouth dropped, and his excitement reached a crescendo. "Mira has Ghara's power? Does that mean she's a spriggan?"

Before Beast could give an angry retort, Talji answered the

boy in a shaking voice. "Bharat once told me that the other young gods flagrantly distributed their power amongst their underlings like a human sowing crops—flinging seeds about with little thought. Ghara never bestowed her power on an elf, choosing instead to fill the world with her creations. That made her blessings all the more precious. He said the Oxendines and Degonharts didn't deserve their gifts. Bharat's jealousy of the dragon and celestial Remnants blinded him to reason; that's obvious to me now."

"Just like Thorodd told us, Primals create Remnants," Henry remarked, pondering the implications. "Ox, you said you were responsible for Beast becoming a Remnant. Does that make you a Primal? And can you do it again?"

Ox stared at his hands as he thought for a long while.

"Ghakk," Gator squawked from his shoulder, stirring Ox from his musings.

"Good point, Gator. Though I am very big and strong, I am only a Remnant. The Giant from my Path reluctantly gave me an Ability called *Legacy of Golos*. I can't see it in my Status, and I think I can only use it under special circumstances, but I don't know what those are."

Henry considered Ox's assessment and wondered if the giant . . . half-jotun . . . could help him with his own Path. Each type of Primal had a very different way of interacting with its Remnants. Perhaps whatever Beast experienced with the spriggan could give him an advantage when confronting the dragon.

"Beast, did you have to go through a trial or a test? Are your Attributes degraded like mine, or did you get some kind of boost?"

Beast shook her head. "Neither. I just got a notification that I had been granted the Title of *Spriggan Remnant*, and I was gifted one strange Ability called *Barrier of Gaellus*. I can't get it to activate, and I have no idea what it does. There's no description for it like my other Abilities."

The gifts from the Primals were strange, though from Henry's experience, extremely useful if their purpose could be discovered. "What of her memories?"

Beast expanded her rib cage by unconsciously pulling in a deep breath. "Ghara saw herself as the protector of the mountain. What she was protecting, or what she was defending against, I haven't a clue. A monster came and poisoned her. It could have been the Necromancer, or perhaps this Malek character, but the memory didn't give me a clear view. The poison crept into her mind and gnawed at her sanity until only her mission to protect Jallfoss remained. Out of options, she started diverting the poison to her Sprigs. It worked just enough to keep her alive this past century."

Beast jerked a thumb toward Ox. "Whatever the oaf did to her, it stopped the poison."

Ox placed a massive hand on Beast's shoulder. "Ghara's soul tried to escape, but I tore off the corrupted part and put the rest inside Beast."

Beast pushed Ox's hand away with obvious derision. "I never asked you to do that."

"Of course you didn't. You don't understand the power of a Primal like I do. Giganthorp told me to leave Ghara alone . . . that she was protecting the mountain. When I told him what was going on, his guidance changed. He said that Malek had tried to claim Jallfoss for himself, and that we must stop him."

Buddy had been listening quietly to the account. "The details are still a bit fuzzy. Apparently, Ghara was holding back Malek's power. Ox's giant determined that removing the corrupted Primal from the picture was the best course of action. However, with Ghara gone, the barrier keeping Malek restrained will weaken, and he will eventually escape. I believe the giant Primal intended to instill Beast as the new guardian, though what that entails is beyond our knowledge."

Henry knew Buddy was right. Malek wanted to escape and had nearly succeeded at getting through the doors in Henry's Path. "When we go on a Path, we occupy two different worlds simultaneously. If Ox and I can exist in two worlds, so can Malek. I freed him from his prison, then blocked him from the Dragon realm. I think Ghara was the one keeping him out of this world."

Jacoby piped up, frustration and confusion apparent in his tone. "We have a crazy man from Henry's dreams trying to get into our world, and we also have a Necromancer sending Acolytes to stop us from saving the mountain. What are we supposed to do about either?"

"We stick to the mission," Henry declared. "Nothing has changed. More than ever, we need to revive the Empress and break the curse if we want to stop those two monsters."

A gurgling wheeze coming from nearby interrupted their conversation. The Magnolia's branches had destroyed the land-scape in its attempt to annihilate the intruders. The entire scene had been turned over and uprooted, like a giant, erratic plow had torn through the dirt hill. Henry walked toward the sound and found the bloody pulp of the Wendigo that the Magnolia had smashed. Next to it, covered in dirt and black blood, Bharat struggled to breathe. The Wendigo took the brunt of the attack, but the elf's old body was crushed and mangled nearly beyond recognition.

Talji slowly approached, glaring at the disfigured Sage. "I know I don't have the right to ask this, but can he be healed?"

Ox knelt beside the smashed elf and extended a white, glowing hand. Healing magic poured into the Sage, forcing

Bharat to wince in pain and spew blood. Ox looked back at Talji and shook his head. "My magic helps the body reconstruct itself. Bones are easy, but mangled organs to this extent are beyond me. If I heal him, it will just cause extreme pain and extend an inevitable death."

Talji nodded. "That relieves my guilt for not wanting to save him. I shouldn't be happy, but I am. The elves are ready for a change. With Ghara and Bharat gone, we'll have a chance for that."

Bharat opened his eyes. They remained unfocused as he stared toward the cloudy ceiling. Just above a whisper, the Sage spoke in labored words. "You've doomed us all. Ghara was the only thing protecting us from the Necromancer. Sprigs are nothing in the face of the evil you've set free."

"Joke's on you, old elf," Ox replied with a boisterous laugh. "We have a Spriggan Remnant, and we're on our way to revive the Empress and stop the Necromancer's curse."

With panic in his eyes, Bharat looked at Talji, then at Beast. "No. Harshmira, you mustn't . . ." The Sage's voice trailed off, and his body went limp. Bharat was dead.

The ancient elf's dying words clung to the damp air, leaving only the sound of fat raindrops splatting in the mud. Jai broke the silence. "I told you, Mira. You're my sister."

Beast grumbled but didn't reply. Talji spoke up. "I didn't know her well, but Mayur did. She was said to be the greatest Sentinel that ever lived. That made her betrayal even more terrible. Bharat professed her as responsible for releasing the Necromancer and corrupting Ghara. After the dark magic he used to summon the Wendigo, I think there's more to the story than he claimed."

Buddy knelt next to Bharat's corpse. "Your Sage died with many secrets, and what he said troubles me. Ox's Primal claimed Ghara was blocking Malek, but Bharat just said the Spriggan was stopping the Necromancer. We're confident those two, Malek and Stavros, are separate beings. How they are connected remains a mystery. And what is this?" Buddy reached inside a fold in Bharat's robes and pulled out a few sheets of faded parchment.

"What did you find?" Henry asked.

Buddy studied the parchment for several long moments before responding, "Hold . . . Raise . . . Create Undead. These are necromancy spells."

"We never questioned how Bharat created the circlets that allowed us to control the undead. Necromancy isn't common among elves. We just assumed it was divine inspiration." Talji said and lowered her eyes, obviously embarrassed.

"*Very* inspirational," Beast growled. Talji just continued to stare down.

"Where did Bharat get those spells?" Henry asked.

Buddy folded the parchment and placed it inside his metal tome. "These pages are identical to the ones we found on Smyrna's body. I'm confident they are the very pages that Skuttur retrieved when Smyrna transported him away from the Source Crystal."

"That means Skuttur is the Necromancer!" Ox exclaimed, confident he'd solved the mystery.

Buddy cocked his head like he was disappointed with Ox. "No. It means necromancy was involved at the Source Crystal *before* the Necromancer was released. I remember Thorodd saying that the Ikritian Emperor was interested in the Source Crystal, then Livadi attacked the mountain with his fire monsters. Maybe he gave this magic to the dwarves, hoping it would be used to free the Necromancer?"

"Bharat got these pages from Skuttur, so he's not the

Necromancer. Now we just need to figure out how Stavros and Malek fit into the Story." Henry looked around, hoping someone else could explain.

"You said Stavros is the Necromancer, but also that Malek was the enemy of the Oxendines. What if Livadi intended to release Malek, but something else got out instead?" Jacoby proposed, still supporting Talji. Henry didn't understand the man's loyalty to his former captor. He assumed it was some remaining Effect of the Hold spell. Either way, the Acolyte seemed concerned the skeletons would attack her.

Regardless, Henry agreed with the man's assessment. "I can think of no better explanation. Livadi mistakenly thought Malek was in the Source Crystal when he was actually imprisoned in the Primal Realms. Livadi wanted Malek's help to conquer Jallfoss, so he put in motion the events he thought would free the archon Remnant. Instead, the Necromancer got out, was banished from the mountain by Lady Destria, and eventually took over Ikrit. Ironic, but that doesn't change our mission. We're wasting time. We still have to get to the Empress."

Henry found no dissent among the group, and even Beast nodded in approval. They all agreed that continuing to the Empress was their best, and likely only, course of action.

While Buddy and Ox cleared the cave-in at the exit tunnel, Henry addressed Talji and the other Sentinels. "The Sprigs are gone, and the elves are safe. What's next for Amera?"

Talji gave the Magnolia a sad look. Only a relatively small portion of the tree's massive canopy had been burned away with the chemicals she'd mixed from Beast's alchemy container. Still, she had spent her whole life revering Ghara, and now she was complicit in the spriggan's destruction. "The piece of the spriggan that we call Ghara is dead, taking with it whatever corruption had been tainting her creations. The Magnolia's leaves have turned from red to green, but I feel our sacred tree won't sustain itself with such an integral part missing."

"I won't pretend to understand the relationship between Ghara and the Magnolia," Henry replied, "but the fact that Beast is now a spriggan Remnant must have some significance. Perhaps the Empress can help us figure out how to use that power to sustain the Magnolia and also fight Malek and the Necromancer." Henry replied.

Talji laughed, but there was no humor in her voice. "If Harshmira has Ghara's blessing, that makes her our leader. An undead forest elf is now our Great Sage."

"Just like I said, Mira. You're my sister," Jai said, pulling on Beast's cloak.

Beast crossed her arms and turned away. "I am not your sister. I am not this Harshmira. And I am not your Great Sage. Once we revive the Empress and get my body back, I will leave, and you all can sort out your own problems."

Jai folded his arms over his chest, mimicking Beast. "If you're leaving, then so am I."

"Not if you're missing your legs." Beast wrapped her boney fingers around the hilt of her sheathed dagger. Jai didn't flinch, but the exchange made two nearby Sentinels look very uncomfortable.

Talji laughed again. "If you're going to kill us, you should do it now. Otherwise, we'll return to Amera to fulfill your wishes, *Great Sage*." She emphasized the title with surprisingly more reverence than sarcasm. Beast only shook her head and grumbled.

"You should know, Mira, the contents of your alchemy bag are of extreme quality and rarity. You should take care of it. I took the liberty of mixing a few potions that you may find useful. Your Drift Amulet should Identify them easily enough,"

Talji said, handing the leather container to Beast. Beast took the alchemy bag and secured it to her waist without giving Talji a reply.

Henry was curious about what types of potions Talji created with the contents of Samos's container, though he didn't feel it was his place to ask. Instead, he addressed the Acolyte. "And Jacoby? What will you do?"

Jacoby had been watching Talji intently. He nodded slowly and gave Henry a serious look. "Stavros is the Necromancer. I know that beyond a shadow of a doubt. I must do what I can to fix the damage the Acolytes have caused, so I will join you. After that . . . who knows."

Henry held a skeletal hand out to the human. "Good. Next to me, you're the best swordsman we've come across in this mountain."

Jacoby's eyes narrowed. He gave Henry a grin and clasped the skeleton by the forearm. "When this is over, we'll test that claim."

———

Ox and Buddy cleared the path with minimal effort. Ox's Strength and Buddy's force magic moved the thousands of tons of earth as easily as children playing in a sandbox. The others scavenged what they could from the aftermath of the battle, but there was little to retrieve. Ghara's body had absorbed into the ground shortly after her defeat. Buddy collected a few of the smaller, healthier-looking green leaves and stored them in a pouch. Talji gathered some of the withered remains from the few plants the fighting hadn't destroyed.

With the exit tunnel cleared, the undead and the elves made their way out of Ghara's den and assembled at the mountain's base just as the sun reached its highest point in the sky.

The Sentinels laid the bodies of their fallen comrades on makeshift wooden drags, then gave Jacoby the armor and gear from Surat. He had tried to refuse, but they insisted that he take it. Besides Talji and Jai, the other elves appeared extremely grateful that they'd been spared from Ghara's wrath, and even more so that the undead hadn't turned on them after the battle.

Jacoby donned the armor and examined it.

Item: Elven Leather Armor (Superior)

Description: High-elven armor made from briarvex hide and boiled in troll fat. MOB +2, Slashing Resistance +5, Cold Resistance +2. Hardness 15, Structure 50/50

Lore: Standard elven armor for Guards of high elven nobility. Though meant for show, it is still functional and provides adequate protection from the cold

The elven leather was of much better quality than the Acolyte plate he wore—much lighter and more resistant to the cold. He still held the sword Talji had given him for the fight in the arena with Henry. He hadn't taken the chance to examine it yet.

Item: Sentinel Captain Sword (Epic)

Description: Weapon (Enchanted). Elven sword forged from ironoak and bolstered with ancient magic. Hardness 30, Structure 100/100

Lore: The forest elves of the high valley nearly revolted when Bharat ordered them to turn over their weapons and submit to his newly appointed Sentinels. After the first elf died under the claws of one of Ghara's tainted Sprigs, they became much more compliant

Abilities:

> **Heightened (Alteration – Passive): Spells cast while wielding this weapon are amplified by 10%**
>
> **Into the Light (Alteration – Passive): Damage +10 against incorporeal enemies**

"This is yours," Jacoby said, handing the sword to Talji.

The elf pushed it back. "We're returning to Amera to tell everyone what happened. With the Sprigs gone, I have no use for a sword. Keep it until you're done. Something to remember me by. Maybe you can bring it back when your mission is over."

"Maybe I can—"

"Alright, let's get moving," Ox boomed.

Talji gave Jacoby a shy smile, then turned to follow the other Sentinels away from Ghara's cave and back to the forest.

Beast Blinked in front of the departing elf, close enough to startle Talji. "Do I need to remind you of your promise in the arena?"

Talji collected herself and replied, "My days as a Sentinel are over, Mira, but I will continue to serve the Great Sage. Until your return, I will honor my contract and support Jai to the best of my ability."

"If you don't, I'll flay you alive and make you wish the Wendigo had ended you instead."

Talji only gave a weak nod in response. Beast returned to the other undead without another word to the former Sentinel.

Jacoby watched as the elf disappeared, then joined the skeletons in gathering their gear and preparing for the next leg of their journey.

"This way. If we hurry, we can make it to the top before nightfall," Jai said and started walking toward a weathered stone staircase. It was midday with a clear blue sky, though the air was still chilly due to the elevation.

"Where do you think you're going?" Beast appeared in front of the boy, though much less threateningly than she had just done to Talji

Jai stopped and gave Beast an angry look, then went to step around her. "Like I told Henry, I'm coming to help."

"No, you're not." Beast moved in his way again.

Jai looked at Henry, then back at Beast. "If you were my sister, I would listen to you."

The boy was determined to lead them up the mountain, and Henry found no harm in letting him join. "He's done his part. Let him come."

"Fine." Beast threw up her arms and moved out of Jai's way. The boy started back up the path with a swagger of defiance in his step.

Jacoby and Buddy followed close behind, but Henry held back with Ox. He'd wanted to talk to the giant for a while but hadn't found the right time or place to start the conversation. Then was as good as any. "Ox, when you went on your Path, did you find out what happened to your friends?"

Ox stared down at Henry but said nothing.

Henry continued. "Before we fought the Acolytes at the Ammerthall ramps, I overheard you talking to Buddy about your Astral Contract. I was hoping you found something on that iceberg when you met your Primal."

Ox shook his head. "No. Like your Path, it gave me more questions than answers."

Henry knew Ox was struggling in the same way he was. The flakes of memories from a past life, the Remnant Paths. It was a lot to handle. "Don't worry, Ox. If they're in this mountain, we'll save them."

Ox nodded slowly, and after a long pause, he said, "Thank you, Henry. Whoever they were, I'll find them. Even if I have to level Jallfoss to do so."

CHAPTER 36

Father, we've secured Lundarbrekka. The damage to Smyrna's hold was severe, though we've already started clearing rubble and building our fortifications. The exo-construct I created with the gnomes has proven its worth many times over at both moving boulders and fending off the influx of the Necromancer's dread army.

A single bridge leads from the lower Underdeep to Lundarbrekka's bottleneck, where the Silent have welled up from the deep reaches of Jallfoss. Their numbers are many, but still less than expected. We've seen iterations of the same three silent—dread claws, rams, and mantids—as Henry named them.

Without a doubt, Smyrna's golem was the single force holding them back. Now that the Master Flowsmith's automaton no longer guards the only choke point, it's obvious this is where they were coming through. The journey of dozens of Acolytes ended here as well, proving the Golem had effectively kept the lower Underdeep separate from the rest of Jallfoss for a century. With the guardian destroyed, the two worlds have now been reconnected.

We've learned the Necromancer's minions are cunning and will avoid overwhelming threats while setting up rudimentary ambushes. They can climb and fly, and they are fast and vicious when they strike. With great sadness, I must report that a surprise attack from the Silent saw our first, and hopefully only, loss. A score of dread rams pounced from beneath the stone bridge leading into Lundarbrekka. We fought them off, but not before they took the life of Hronngar. Tell his wife, Martta, and his boys that his death was not in vain. He fought with a heart of forged steel and took three dread monsters with him into a lava shaft. His sacrifice granted us entry into the stronghold. May his name forever ring through the halls of Hjardharfell.

The treasures we've uncovered are few, but amazing nonetheless—two uncharged magma blasters, epic-quality mining tools, and no shortage of flow crystals. We've even located the remains of Smyrna's Golem and have started its recovery. If we can fix the Golem's command array, we'll have another tremendous asset on our side.

Buddy and the others have given us a chance to reclaim the glory of Hjardharfell, and I won't see that opportunity wasted. The lifeless undead that haunt the tunnels have not recovered, so I know his mission is yet incomplete. Please watch for him and assist in any way you can. I feel his quest may be more important than ours.

Regarding supplies, we're working through our food and water. We'll need to start scavenging within the week, but we've no shortage of weapons and mining supplies. We also have enough solofurnos to bring down the entire mountain.

Rocks and Hammers,
Torgga

—

Torgga stuffed the parchment into the Farscroll and closed the cap. The magical device hummed and pulsed with a dim light, indicating the message had been delivered to Thorodd. Torgga placed the item in an open holster in her armor, then wiped several beads of sweat from her forehead. Though fresh, cool air was being pulled from the mountain tops and forced into the lower reaches of the Underdeep, it couldn't completely counter the oppressive heat surging from the lava field a hundred feet below her. The fact that she was encased in a thousand pounds of golem steel and gnomish hydraulics only added to her discomfort.

All around her sat a dozen inert golems. Some had seen better days, but she was confident the gnomish engineers who accompanied her could restore the automatons to their original glory.

Just a month earlier, she happily traipsed the winding caves near Hjardharfell with no more weighing her down than her Geist cloth armor, salamander leather boots, and silk undergarments. Her illusion magic and lone-dwarf tactics kept her hidden and allowed her to easily carry out her job of goading cave monsters away from the dwarven settlements.

Now she was thundering down those same tunnels wearing mechanical armor, accompanied by two cells of dwarven warriors and half that many neglected golems. The responsibility of her mission weighed her down more than any armor possibly could. Every Hjardharfell citizen's life was precious, and even a single lost soldier was too many. She vowed Hronngar would be the last soldier to fall under her watch.

Even as she swore to protect the dwarves, orcs, and gnomes that followed her into the Underdeep, she knew the mission at hand was far more critical than any of their individual lives. Every inhabitant would be in danger until she could stop the Silent from flooding into the upper Underdeep. Her father charged her with halting the flow of dread monsters into Hjardharfell and beginning the reclamation of dwarven territory—a mission that she refused to fail.

Though the task was critical and extremely dangerous, leading the dwarven cells through the Underdeep and taking Lundarbrekka had been much easier than she expected. She briefly considered continuing the charge all the way to the Source Crystal, once they established their stronghold.

Wouldn't that bristle my father's beard, Torgga thought with a giggle as she imagined fighting her way to the very cause of all their trouble. It was tempting, but she wasn't that brash—at least not until she'd properly scouted the lower Underdeep. The armor she and the gnomish artificers had created, along with her illusion magic, brought her and the two cells of Hjardharfell's finest warriors halfway to the bottom of the mountain. It was truly the adventure of a lifetime.

"Any word from the Elder?" Gallanni asked. The dwarven Lieutenant beside her served as her second in command. He wore black polished, golem steel armor with a matching tower shield and hammer. He wasn't as strong as Captain Craggitt, but he was still much more experienced in formation fighting and dwarven tactics than Torgga. While she had spent the better part of a century as a Geist, perfecting her illusion magic and warding off the dangerous monsters of the Underdeep, Gallanni had been fighting those same monsters with nothing more than inadequate weapons, old armor, and his fellow dwarves.

The monsters had nearly overwhelmed the dwarven defenses when Buddy—and the other skeletons, of course— had returned with the Magma Blaster and given them one last chance to save Hjardharfell. Her mind drifted to the undead, more specifically to the skeletal mage. Buddy had a way about him that she'd never experienced before. Even without a memory, he commanded a grasp of magic beyond what Torgga ever thought capable. His love of magic eclipsed even her own passion for the art, and she hoped to get another chance to pick his brain.

"Lady Torgga?" Gallanni said.

Torgga realized she'd been lost in thought, imagining various academic scenarios with the skeletal mage. She gave a quick smile and a giggle. "No. Nothing from my father, but he's never been one to respond quickly on the Farscroll. Any word from the scouts?"

Lundarbrekka was a single structure connecting the upper Underdeep to the lower expanses. It wasn't very large, with a diameter of a few hundred feet in total. It was a grouping of storage rooms clumped like grapes on a vine. Most had been destroyed, likely by Smyrna's Golem while fighting the Silent and the Ikritians. Various Acolytes had looted the rest. The original concept behind Lundarbrekka was its setup as a fallback position for the dwarves in the somewhat likely event that the humans attacked. There was only one way to get to Lundarbrekka from the upper Underdeep: over a heavily vulnerable bridge that crossed one of the massive air shafts.

What the dwarves didn't anticipate was that it would be used as a defense in reverse. Smyrna's Golem had effectively been the single force holding the Necromancer's Silent army at bay from the opposite direction of what was intended.

Just like from above, there was only one way to Lundarbrekka from below, a long but narrow cavern hosting a lake of lava. A single stone bridge, a hundred feet tall and several miles long, ran the length of its center. At one end of the bridge sat a heavily fortified portcullis that led to the dwarven storage and fortifications at Lundarbrekka. Torgga's dwarves hadn't yet gotten it working, but they were hopeful they could close the portal shortly.

The other end of the bridge held a small exit into a cave

that quickly branched into several large and dozens of smaller tunnels.

Torgga and Gallanni stood on the long, narrow platform that extended through a vast cavern. Far to their left and right were dozens of holes in the stone walls. Most released lava falls that lazily splatter molten rock into the pools below, like porridge slowly boiling over in a pot on a stove. Torgga surveyed the molten lake below and wiped more sweat from her brow.

"One scout has returned," Gallanni reported. "The other two are expected back shortly. Dozens of paths converge on the far end of the bridge, and it will take us weeks to map the area even without the threat of the Silent. I recommend we retreat to the bottleneck and focus our efforts on fortifying our defenses."

Torgga agreed with Gallanni. The bridge was the only way into the Lundarbrekka; if they could block that, they could protect Hjardharfell. They could also easily watch the long span to make sure nothing snuck up on them.

Torgga made to stand, but cries from the far end of the bridge caught her attention. Half a mile away, two dwarven scouts sprinted from the far tunnel, screaming their lungs out. From the distance, Torgga could only make out one word from their shouts: "Silent!"

That's when she saw the dread monsters.

Like hornets swarming from an agitated nest, the Necromancer's minions flooded onto the bridge in close pursuit of the fleeing dwarves.

"Lady Torgga, back to Lundarbrekka!" Gallanni shouted.

Torgga narrowed her eyes at the incoming dread monsters and started pulling Steam from her core. "Prepare the cells for a counterattack. I'll hold them back and buy you some time!"

Gallanni wanted to argue, but as a trained soldier, he knew

when to obey an order without question. He collected his shield and hammer, then sprinted back to the other dwarves in the storage rooms, shouting orders and trying to grab his soldiers' attention.

The scouts sprinted for all they were worth. They had a lead of a few hundred feet, but with every step, the dread rams gained on them.

Torgga engaged the powered metal shell that served as her armor. Flow crystals glowed deep purple as gears spun and pistons actuated solid metal limbs. Made from the surplus of black golem steel the skeletons had uncovered from the hidden room, her armor was a near-indestructible mixture of utility, defense, and weaponry. A giant blade shifted into position on her left arm, and a three-foot buzzsaw unfolded on her right. At its full height, the steel exo-construct made Torgga even taller than Ox, though size and power weren't the greatest strengths of her armor.

With a flick of two switches and a twist of a knob, the giant flow crystal seated in the center of her chest plate began to glow with a brilliant blue. The golem heart hummed with the power of ancient dwarven enchantment. The sound of grinding gears and flow crystal-powered engines roared all around her as a dozen ancient golems woke from their slumber and answered her call to duty.

Torgga lifted her legs and pumped her arms. Her armor responded and propelled forward far faster than a short-legged dwarf could ever hope to run. The golems followed close behind. Thousands of pounds of metal thundered over the stone bridge, but the sturdy dwarven construction had been built to withstand extreme force and weight. There was no give to the bridge under the heavy footfalls of the automatons.

The dread rams were gaining on her dwarves, but Torgga's

speed would see her to the scouts first. Fear replaced her hope as the thrum of mantid wings sang through the cavern. The agile monster lifted from the rush of dread rams and zipped toward the fleeing dwarves. Razor-sharp claws the size of great swords poised for deadly strikes as the monster dove toward its prey.

No, you don't. The buzzsaw on Torgga's arm began to spin. She clenched her fist and pointed toward the mantid. It was nearly on top of the scouts, and though her armor was fast and strong, it wasn't built to allow her to aim while running. She needed to be closer to ensure a direct hit, but she couldn't wait any longer. She released her fist, and the circular blade launched forward.

The mantid lifted its claws, just inches away from the scout. Torgga could see the terror in his eyes, begging for anyone to save him. The mantid's claws descended on the fleeing dwarf. Torgga's buzzsaw buried into the dread monster's chest.

The mantid slammed into the bridge and rolled to a stop as its severed foreclaws went flying. Sparks erupted from the buzzsaw, scraping across the stone and still deeply embedded into the dread mantid.

"Keep running," Torgga shouted as she leaped over the heads of the passing scouts, "Don't stop until you reach the stronghold."

When the gnomes created her armor, they included as much magical power as possible. Hundreds of flow crystals lined the construct and contained magical spells of every sort—healing, Attribute enhancements, curses, but mostly evocation magic derived from Buddy's spells. Torgga soared through the air and landed like a comet.

Detonate

A burst of force magic mixed with blue fire erupted from her point of impact and blasted the swarming dread monsters.

Black flesh ripped from dread bone and launched dozens of Silent over the stone railing on either side of the bridge like a tsunami.

The dread monsters continued their assault, driving through their fallen brethren and rushing toward the steel-covered dwarf with malicious intent. Torgga stood to her full height as her army of golems rushed past her. Metal-plated automatons smashed into the approaching dread monsters. Iron and bone collided like plows going through a rocky field.

The golems were strong, but Torgga knew a century of neglect had reduced their power, and they wouldn't be able to stop the hundreds of Silent that continued to pour out of the far tunnel and onto the stone bridge. A dread ram had already broken through the ranks, and its frantic eyes locked onto Torgga. The monster lowered its horns and blurred forward, aiming directly at the mechanized dwarf.

Flameblade

The sharpened metal beam on her left arm lit up in a blaze of red fire. Torgga met the dread ram's attack with a heavy downward strike. The epic-quality dread bone resisted the keen edge of her blade, but it couldn't withstand its sheer mass. The beam of flaming, sharpened metal obliterated the dread ram, smashing it as much as cutting through the monster.

The scene before her was pure chaos. Golems and dread monsters were tearing each other apart, though her metal army appeared to be gaining the advantage. *Dwarven engineering at its finest*, she thought with a giggle, then began to form another magical attack.

"Charge!" Torgga heard the rally cry of a dozen dwarven foot soldiers approaching rapidly from behind her. As expected, though against her orders, her company had gathered quickly and had come to join the fray.

Before the other dwarves could enter the fight, something unexpected happened. Like a school of fish, all the Silent turned at once and began to retreat. The move completely confused Torgga, as withdrawing was a maneuver beyond what she thought their simple intelligence was capable of.

Surely the Necromancer's forces wouldn't flee from such a short skirmish, she wondered. She didn't have long to contemplate. A faint rumble started to reverberate through the cavern. It quickly grew into a full quake.

The molten rock slowly dribbling from the holes in the side of the cavern suddenly erupted in violent spurts. Some of it shot as far as the stone bridge on which they stood, and her dwarves had to raise their shields to deflect the molten shrapnel.

Torgga had been in the mountain her entire life. She knew the sound of shifting earth. The subterranean sang with a particular resonance as it gave way to the tectonic forces far below. Like a chorus of rock and magma, the song of the world changing was as violent as it was serene. What Torgga heard was not that song.

The sound was the steady, rhythmic beat of something colossal. The Silent continued to rush back into the tunnel. Torgga understood then that they weren't running from her. They were running toward whatever was coming her way.

"Back to Lundarbrekka! Now!" Torgga shouted to the approaching dwarves. She directed the golems to follow as well. Whatever was coming, there was likely no advantage to fighting it on the bridge.

As the dwarves retreated, Torgga looked up at the ceiling. Stalactites broke free from the rocky dome and plummeted into the quickly expanding lake of lava.

"Buddy . . . hurry!"

CHAPTER 37

What started as a leisurely hike became substantially more taxing as the coterie ascended. After an hour of climbing, clouds began to roll in, and the light breeze picked up significantly. The stone steps grew more weathered the further they went, and certain sections were almost indistinguishable from the surrounding rocky landscape.

Henry found a flat area of stone overlooking the Amera Valley about halfway up the mountain and took a moment to rest. The Jallfoss range was a chain of peaks that stretched from North to South as far as he could see. Enormous castles were built along and into the range, but Henry could detect no signs of life among the various structures. Miles below him, clouds obscured the Ikritian plain. Jai explained that the human nation was a vast expanse of farmland and huge cities that stretched far beyond the horizon. There were thousands and thousands of humans within the borders of the most powerful kingdom in the world. In the opposite direction from Ikrit, the elven valley of Amera ran between Jallfoss and a distant, smaller mountain range. The vast pine forest looked like a green river, winding past the towering peaks.

At four separate spots along the range, geysers emitted clouds of steam and bouts of water in sporadic bursts hundreds of feet into the air. Henry remembered the massive columns in Ammerthall that he initially thought were holding up the high ceiling, but were actually dwarven utilities responsible for piping air and water throughout the mountain. After the dwarves started their forges, those utilities resumed circulating and now released excess heat into the upper reaches of Jallfoss.

Henry wasn't going toward any of those locals. Looming high above, still a few thousand feet away, the rocky summit stared down at him like an opposing foe. It looked like a dead volcano with a jagged, craggy rim at the top.

The ground began to shake, pulling Henry from his thoughts. What started as a slight rumble that could have been easily ignored quickly grew to a violent quake that sent loose rocks cascading down the steep cliffs.

After a moment, the tremor subsided, but something had changed in the valley below. Instead of spouting steam and water into the air, the mountain vents now belched out black smoke and jets of fire.

"Jai, do you know what's going on?" Henry asked.

The elf's face turned white as he stared at the black clouds forming above the geysers. "I've never seen that happen."

"Maybe the dwarves are working some issues?" Henry offered.

Buddy nodded in agreement. "Perhaps. That seems the most likely explanation. Once we've finished here, we should return to Hjardharfell and consult Torgga."

"If that is what we're calling it, then let us hurry to the Empress so you can *consult* your dwarf," Ox teased. Buddy gave the giant an annoyed look and started walking up the stone path. Henry and the others followed close behind, though

REMNANTS OF DUSK | 325

they kept constant watch on the erupting fires. The smoke and flames didn't appear to be threatening the greater valley, but there was no telling what noxious gases could be contained in the smog.

There was no life along the winding mountain path—no varmints or insects could be seen, and even birds remained far away. Jacoby and Jai's breathing grew labored, but that struggle wasn't limited to those with flesh on their bones. The skeletons also felt fatigued, though with neither lungs nor an accompanying Status Effect to explain the sluggish feeling, Henry credited the weariness to insufficient Fortitude.

After hours of trudging up the stone path, the sun began to dip toward the Ikritian horizon and cast long shadows over Amera. The top of the crag loomed several hundred feet above them, and the path led to a stone archway in the sheer mountain face.

"Buddy, do you have any flow crystals we could enchant before entering?" Henry asked.

"My bandolier is half full," the mage held a thumb toward the leather strap that crossed his chest and was lined with small pouches that held various flow crystals. Muji watched intently from his perch on Buddy's shoulder. "I was forced to spend most of them in the last fight. Several shattered under the force of discharging their contained magic. Muji and I have refilled all but two Legendary crystals."

"Can we charge them with healing?"

Buddy pulled two clear crystals from his bandolier and held them at his waist. The trogold scurried down Buddy's robes and plucked the shards from the mage's hand, then held them high in the air as he waddled toward Ox, his bushy tail swishing back and forth to keep him balanced.

"Of course, Master Muji. Gator and I are at your service."

Ox reached down and opened a palm nearly the size of the trogold.

Muji carefully deposited the crystals in Ox's hand, then looked up at the giant and chirped, "Beak." Ox closed his fingers, and Muji placed his tiny hands on the bone.

A white glow surrounded Ox's hand, and after a moment, he stood and tossed the newly enchanted healing crystals to Henry and Beast. "You already have a healing spell, human. You'll have to do without."

"I'll be fine," Jacoby said, not removing his gaze from the elven forest below.

"Thanks, Ox. Now let's find the Empress and get this over with." Henry led them forward.

The archway was twenty feet wide, thrice as tall, and looked more natural than built, but Henry couldn't tell for sure. They stood at the opening and peered in to find a chamber nearly a mile across. The inside was hollow with a flat floor and no ceiling. Massive oak trees, almost as large as the mushrooms of the Grunischwald, lined the exterior at regular intervals. Their canopies were barren of foliage, and only twisted limbs stretched to just below the jagged rim above them. The flat, rocky floor of the massive cavern was strewn with thousands of bones. No auras—green, red, or other—wafted from the mass graveyard.

"We're well above the tree line. Those oaks shouldn't be able to grow at such an altitude," Ox noted.

"The trees aren't what I'm worried about." Buddy motioned toward the center of the open chamber. Half a mile away, three figures sat around a blue campfire. They either didn't notice the skeletons approaching or didn't care. Either was equally likely.

"Acolytes," Beast hissed.

"Likely so. Hopefully not as strong as the group we fought at the Ammerthall ramps." Henry dropped his pack and dug through it, then turned to Jai and handed the boy the Flow Bracers. "Jai, keep these safe."

"What are they?" the elf asked with wide, curious eyes.

"Dwarven artifacts that should have the power to revive the Empress. We're counting on you to protect them, young elf," Buddy said.

Jai took the bracers and stared at them with awe, then gave Henry a determined look. "I'll guard them with my life."

"Please do. Stay back until we've pacified whoever these three are." Henry turned to the rest. "No more delays, we've got a mountain to save."

Four skeletons, a trogold, and an undead human made their way toward the center of the highest peak in the Jallfoss range. Henry's Perception allowed him to make out the three humans as they neared. All had the tell-tale red cloaks of the Acolytes. One was a woman with heavy armor and a large halberd. The other was likely a mage, as he was much smaller and wore little, if any, protection. Those two were several dozen paces away from the blue campfire that Henry realized wasn't a magical blaze. An apparition of a woman with pale skin and white hair floated within the light. Without a doubt, it was the Empress. Just in front of her stood another Acolyte. The man was only a few inches taller than Beast, and he had the most enormous sword Henry had ever seen propped against his shoulder with its tip resting on the ground. The blade was nearly six feet long and over a foot wide. It had a jagged edge, pitted with rust, and looked like it had been pulled from a neglected dwarven machine rather than forged by a blacksmith.

"They don't seem concerned with our approach. We should be wary of traps," Buddy said.

"No, this one doesn't need a trap. He's just that strong." Henry's Harmony screamed at him to run. Even in the company of a corrupted Primal, Henry hadn't felt such a powerful presence. The man before him was beyond dangerous. Henry sealed off his awareness but could still feel a horrible potency radiating from the Acolyte.

Henry and the others had grown used to resisting the Effects of the red auras, but that didn't make them any less noticeable. The swirling crimson radiance the center man exuded wasn't any different in size from the others, but Henry felt it had a certain weight that made it far more substantial. Shortly after awakening, Henry realized that auras were not a direct indicator of capability. With his Remnant Attributes, he had learned to gauge power levels more accurately than with Haruspex alone, which only gave him numbers that usually failed to tell the whole story. The two Acolytes that stood back felt similar in power to Samos and Jaromak, but the stoic man before the Empress was something far beyond the normal Ikritian soldiers.

Status Effect: Calamity (Minor) - Environmental Damage Resistance -2

The wind was stronger inside the cavern than on the climb and seemed to push against their advance. "Spread out," Henry ordered, and the group followed. He didn't know what the three Acolytes were capable of, but the prospect of finding out had him questioning his resolution. Even without the degradation from his Desert Path, he wondered if he would even stand a chance against that man.

A dozen paces away, Henry started to make out the finer details of the apparition. He didn't know what an Empress should look like, but the floating woman fit his expectations. She was by far the most beautiful woman he had ever seen . . . but he *had* seen her before.

Recognition hit Henry like a bolt of Buddy's magic. The woman before him was the same person carved into the yellow-stone doors he'd used to seal Malek from the Dragon Realm. She had to be. No other could possess such striking features. Her eyes were closed, and her face held a calm expression that gave him a sense of tranquility. That peaceful feeling was soon interrupted.

"I've become accustomed to the undead charging me upon sight," the center Acolyte, obviously the leader, said in a relaxed voice without taking his eyes off the Empress. There was apathy in his tone, but it also contained an undeniable amount of authority.

Henry pulled his attention from the apparition and replied, "We've learned to overcome that urge."

The man took his eyes away from the Empress for the first time and looked directly at Henry. A chill ran through the skeleton's bones as the Acolyte asked his question. "Then can I assume you're reasonable?"

"As reasonable as skeletons can be, but that would ultimately depend on your intentions," Ox answered, and Henry wondered if the giant was experiencing the same signals of danger. The serious tone of Ox's voice signaled the affirmative.

The man turned back toward the Empress, seemingly more focused on the ghost than the party of undead that approaching him. "My name is Cirilo. I am the Commander of the Bastion and leader of the Acolytes. These Master Acolytes are Eudora and Mersin, two of my most capable warriors. If you're here, that means you killed many good soldiers to get past the ramps."

A rush of wind bore into Henry, and he struggled to maintain his footing against it. "Jaromak, Samos, and a smattering of lesser humans. Yes, we killed them all."

Cirilo pulled in a deep breath, then let it out slowly. He looked back at Henry with deep sadness in his eyes. "Did they die a good death?"

"A warrior's death, and nothing less," Henry replied. He noticed the other two Acolytes were watching him closely, likely waiting for an order or a signal from their Commander.

Cirilo nodded his head and gave a sad smile. "And you, Jacoby. You're undead now. You killed two of your fellow Acolytes."

Jacoby stepped forward. "I regret that I slew one and nearly the other. Even worse, I don't remember them as brothers. I woke with rage and empty memories. I have no recollection of them . . . or you."

Cirilo studied Jacoby for a long while before he replied. "You have taken hundreds of Junior Acolytes through Jallfoss. You and I together have faced dangers beyond the comprehension of normal men, and we have shared enough whiskey to float a galleon. I was there for your wedding, and when your first son was born."

Jacoby's voice wavered. "I . . . I have a wife? And a Child?"

"Three children. A beautiful family, by any measure," Cirilo said. Jacoby could only stare at the ground and shake his head, struggling against the fog of his memories to parse any truth from Cirilo's words.

The Acolyte Commander reached toward the apparition and slowly moved his hand through her form. It swirled around his gauntlet like he was waving it through calm water. The light and shadows quickly formed back into the Empress's ethereal body, completely unaffected by Cirilo's touch. The Acolyte turned back to Henry with sad, lethargic eyes and asked, "You're here for the Empress?"

"If we can bring her back, maybe she can break the spell.

If there's a chance to save the undead from this endless cycle, or even the prospect of returning them . . . us . . . back to life, we must try." Henry felt like a child pleading with an adult to stay up past bedtime, knowing the request would ultimately be denied.

Cirilo slowly shook his head. "No. You can't affect this ghost. I've tried. No magic or weapon does anything beyond obscuring her image for more than a moment. Even if you could, I would not allow it. As undead, you're under the influence of the Necromancer. Whether it's a poor ruse or you truly believe you can save the mountain this way, I cannot let you succeed. Lord Stavros himself has tasked me with thwarting your efforts."

Status Effect: Calamity (Moderate) - Environmental Damage Resistance -5, Healing Effects -25%, MOB -5

A flash of light and the crack of thunder ripped through the vast cavern. Storm clouds started to roll across the sky. As the sun set, it lit up the growing thunderhead with brilliant reds and yellows.

"That's where you're wrong," Henry cried, losing his composure beneath the sheer power that Cirilo projected. "You are the one under the influence of the Necromancer. That evil being is one and the same with your Lord Stavros. He took Koş's soul so he could reach into our minds. Doubtless, I felt his evil."

For the first time, a look of hesitation crossed Cirilo's face. "I . . . was there when Koş died."

"Were you? What did you see?" Henry demanded.

There was a long pause before Cirilo responded. "No. I was just outside the door when the boy passed . . ."

Though Henry was numb to physical sensation, he was aware of the gusting wind's increased power and that the cavern's temperature had slowly begun to rise. "Stavros has to be stopped."

With the tip of his massive sword still on the ground, Cirilo pushed on the hilt until the blade stood vertically. Upright, the sword was a whole foot taller than the man. The Acolyte twirled the blade on the long axis, unconcerned that the tip drilled into the rock below.

Haruspex

Item: Kyalganat's Fury (Legendary)

Description: Weapon (Enchanted). This greatsword is constructed of an unknown metal. Damage +15. Hardness 50, Structure 107/150

Lore: Hewn from the armor of Kyalganat herself, this weapon channels the power of the fallen Dreadnaught

Abilities: Unknown

The Acolyte's greatsword was as mighty, if not more so, than Slyngur. Though Henry was more concerned with the man's Status.

Name: Cirilo Galantis

Race: Human

Tier: 44

Health: 489/489

Vitus: 498/512

Attributes:

    STR: 89

    MOB: 42

    FOR: 63

ACU: 59

PER: 38

RES: 98

Resistance: Unknown

Weakness: None

Henry knew that Tiers didn't tell the whole story. When melded with the tree, Ghara was at **190**, and even separated from the Magnolia, the Primal was still at **85**. Yet Beast slayed the Primal with a combined magical attack. The problem was that Ghara was a mystical being of nature, unaccustomed to combat. Cirilo was the Acolytes' Commander. The power he emitted clawed its way across Henry's Harmony, further enforcing the skeleton's intuition that there was much more to this man than just his high Tier and massive Attributes.

Cirilo grabbed the hilt of Kyalganat's Fury, and it stopped twirling. "Thirty years ago, I was a Junior Acolyte standing on the Ikritian front lines against an army of Skyknights. We sent a legion into the Brochet steppes to stop raiding parties from killing our Southern farmers. Lord Stavros absorbed the brunt of their attack. A thousand foul sorcerers descended upon him at once. I remember the sound of his screams as their magic tore into him. 'You will not harm even one more Ikritian family,' I remember him yelling as he turned their magic against them."

The wind picked up speed and drove against Henry. The myriad bones scattered through the cavern rattled and skidded across the ground, unable to resist the increasing gusts.

Thunder reverberated through the cavern, though it couldn't mask the force of Cirilo's voice. "The Great Lord loves Ikrit like a father loves his firstborn. He is the leader that none of us deserve. I would rip the hearts from the young gods themselves and pull the moons to the very plains of Ikrit, if he would but ask. No undead abomination will sway me from serving him. Jacoby, you were the best of us, but if you have joined the forces of evil, I will slay you the same as any other fallen Acolyte. I will not ask you to leave this course again."

Jacoby surprised Henry with his tenacity. "I don't know what I did before my death, but I know what Henry says is true. Somehow, the boy's passing brought me back to life. I felt the dark magic Stavros used. It was terrible, leaving me with no choice but to join these skeletons and their mission."

"You've chosen to side with them," Cirilo said, the tone of finality in his voice carrying a distinct threat.

Jacoby held Talji's sword tightly in his hand. "I won't fight you, but I know in my heart that these undead are on the side of what is right. I beg you to let them through so we can end this curse."

Cirilo ignored Jacoby's request and looked deep into Henry's dead eyes. The pounding wind and rain didn't seem to affect the man. "So, skeleton, we've reached an impasse."

"That we have," Henry replied and started dumping Vitus into his bones. Every instinct in his skeletal body began to scream a warning of the encroaching danger.

Cirilo rolled his shoulders and lifted his massive sword. At his full height, he wasn't impressive by stature, but his mere presence continued to send alarming waves through Henry's Remnant Attributes. It was more than just Henry's senses—the intensity of the elements surged into a full squall, and a tremor began to shake the ground.

Though his voice was calm, the single word from Cirilo's mouth filled the entire cavern, resounding over the wind, rain, and thunder.

"Calamity."

CHAPTER 38

Status Effect: Calamity (Severe) - Environmental Damage Resistance -10, Healing Effects -50%, MOB -10

Lightning ripped through the sky and struck the rim of the mountain crag hundreds of feet above. Another bolt connected to one of the dead oak trees. Bark and branches exploded in a violent burst of fire. Wind and rain tore through the cavern under the force of a tornado, turning tiny droplets into piercing daggers. The ground beneath Henry's feet trembled like the whole mountain was crumbling beneath him.

The battle for the Empress had begun.

With an unnerving confidence, Cirilo took a few deliberate steps toward Henry. The skeleton drew his sword and pumped Vitus into his dread shield.

Blitz

The Acolyte lifted his massive blade with ease. Though the swing was telegraphed, and Henry knew exactly where the sheet of metal would land, it was delivered with such speed, power, and precision that Henry could do nothing to stop it. There was no counter or parry he possessed to prevent such an attack. Only Henry's magically enhanced speed kept him alive.

The solid rock below his feet exploded under the force of Cirilo's sword, sending broken stones flying like ballista bolts. Henry dodged out of the way, but the attack was so powerful that it sent him staggering.

Cirilo lifted the blade out of its crater. The man was as collected as though he'd just cast a fishing line and was reeling it back in. "You are far weaker than I expected. How did you beat Samos and Jaromak?"

Henry didn't answer but took the opportunity to expand his awareness to the battlefield.

Jacoby had created distance from Cirilo. He made no move indicating he intended to join the battle, but he also hadn't fled.

Buddy was twenty paces behind Henry. Five golem-steel bucklers orbited around the mage, surrounded by various elemental magics. Henry also knew the mage had erected a force barrier around himself, but Henry wondered if it would stand against the power of the Commander's sword.

Beast and the man in the robes had begun to circle each other. Jai hid behind one of the far oak trees, poking his head out and holding his sling in a trembling grip.

Ox charged the woman in heavy armor. The female Acolyte lifted into the air, standing upon a lance. More weapons appeared around her, and she floated just outside Ox's reach. The giant and flying Acolyte exchanged banter, but Henry wasn't afforded the opportunity to listen to their words.

"Focus on me, skeleton, or this will be over before I can even warm up," Cirilo warned and cocked back his massive sword for another attack.

—

Beast and Mersin stared each other down. Though the man had no weapons or magic that the skeletal elf could see, Beast could tell from his deliberate movements that he was an expert fighter. He kept his eyes pointed to the center of her mass, using his peripheral vision to take in her movements.

"We used to call you *The Assassin of Ammerthall*," the man said with a high-pitched whistle.

"What?" Beast snapped.

"You've killed more Acolytes than any other being in Jallfoss. We've tied you up, torn you apart, and buried you. Still, you managed to pull your bones back together and continue murdering from the shadows. The only thing that could keep you restrained was the animal cages at the Ammerthall Coliseum. How appropriate that you've chosen *Beast* as a name."

The man's whistling voice grated into her senses, making her hate him even more. "I am far more than the skeleton that ripped apart your men. Samos underestimated me. Now he's in thousands of pieces, spread far and wide across Ammerthall. Your fate will soon match his.

The Acolyte shrieked in laughter. "His confidence was his downfall, as I always knew it would be. He thought he could become the Sorcerer Exalt with magical trinkets alone. I mourn his death, as I would any of my brethren, but I will not let pride get the best of me." A faint blue shimmer scintillated across his body, likely a magical shield of some sort.

Beast hissed, "I will end you just the same and add another Acolyte to my tally."

Blink

Beast teleported behind the man and jabbed with her dagger, aiming for his liver. Mersin was ready. He twirled and knocked the dagger aside. Though not as fast as Ghara, he was nearly equal to Beast in speed.

What followed was a flurry of blows. Beast struck with Void, Nether Blade, and her frost daggers, but the blue sheen around the Acolyte acted as a barrier, repelling both magic and metal whenever her attacks hit true. The number of blows Beast landed was far fewer than the number of attacks she sent his way.

Mersin only used his limbs, but fists and feet, knees and elbows, were as deadly as any forged steel. The Acolyte delivered a continuous chain of combined attacks, each meant to set up the next, until a punch slipped past Beast's guard and caught her square in the chest. She stumbled back. Mersin paused and slowly stretched his fingers. A sinister smile parted his lips. Beast felt Henry was as effective in hand-to-hand combat, but this man's Attributes were far higher.

Siren

Beast channeled Vitus into her throat and opened her jaws as wide as possible. Her scream rang out with enough force to cause visible waves of distortion around her. Mersin winced and blinked his eyes, but the scream didn't appear to affect the man further. Instead, his blue sheen slightly dimmed, then rebounded against her Ability. Beast thrust with her daggers, furiously stabbing and slashing as she searched for an opening. Her frustration only grew as every attack that wasn't blocked or parried by the Acolyte simply reflected off his warding.

"You are far stronger than I expected, but what is a *Spriggan Remnant?*" Mersin asked between effortless attacks. It annoyed Beast that the man had time to use his Drift Amulet's divinity on her while they fought.

"Assess this," she said and Blinked around him several times, slashing and thrusting between each teleport.

Mersin countered every attack and still managed to converse. "You are faster than me and will eventually wear me down. I can't have that."

Beast lunged, but the man blurred and split into two, then doubled again and once more, until five Acolytes stood before the elf.

"Petty illusions," Beast growled and dodged back, searching for an indication that would allow her to differentiate between the enemies.

"If only you were so lucky," the five men before her replied in chorus.

Beast realized too late that Mersin's words were no mere threat, and the five shades were definitely not illusions. All five versions of the Acolyte began to pummel her. Every attack dropped her Health lower.

—

Eudora's long red hair was pulled back in a tight braid. It waved like an Acolyte banner as the woman zipped through the air, just outside the reach of Ox's hammer. Weapons of all sorts, mostly spears, lances, and javelins, appeared from nowhere and bombarded Ox. Most bounced off his dreadmail, though there were so many weapons assaulting him that a few got through and damaged his bones.

"If your combat skills match your beauty, I'm in for a long night," Ox said with no small amount of gusto. The damage he was receiving was minimal and would have been manageable, even without his armor. Unfortunately, the Acolyte was far too evasive for him to reach with his limited Mobility.

"I'll make sure you don't last through the eve," she said with a wicked smile. More weapons appeared and zipped toward him, faster than any arrow, and now emitting a red glow. They bit into Ox with an intense heat and packed far more punch than the previous attacks. Ox charged and swung his maul, knowing there was little chance of him catching her.

"I don't suppose you'd consider a leg wrestling match? Loser buys drinks?" He powered his maul with force magic, then blasted a wave of summoned metal weapons back at her. She dodged easily with the grace of a hummingbird.

"There will be nothing left of you to enjoy a drink." The glow around Eudora's weapons increased, and the bombardment continued.

"That's unfortunate," Ox said, reaching into his glacial core.

"Ghakk," Gator confirmed.

Remnant Form: Giant

Ox's bones grew and pressed against the dread armor, but with a deluge of healing magic and some adjustments by Gator, the armor swelled around his bones, still fitting perfectly. In the span of a few heartbeats, he grew to nothing short of forty feet.

"Minoa's vacant sheath . . ." Eudora stopped and floated, slightly bobbing on the currents of her magic with her eyes wide in horror.

"I know. Impressive, right?" Ox roared above the thunder and wind.

Eudora bared her teeth and summoned dozens of weapons, flinging them all at the giant.

"I guess she's not a fan of sexy giants," Ox said, swatting most of the weapons from the air, while a few nicked exposed bones.

"Ghakk," Gator agreed, expanding the armor around Ox.

"Good call, Gator. Let's get her." Gator and the dreadmail

went left, Ox tumbled right. The weapons struck them both, but the duo rebounded and charged the Acolyte. Colossal animated dreadmail and giant undead skeleton batted at the soaring Acolyte.

Eudora danced between their fingers and barely escaped. Weapons chipped into Ox's bones, though his healing magic kept up with the damage. Eudora danced high above their heads, raining endless volleys of summoned metal down on them.

"Gator. To me!" Ox shouted at the amalgamator.

Gator ran at Ox and jumped. Ox caught him and stepped off to the side, spinning as hard as he could, then arched his back and launched his companion straight up and directly at the flying Acolyte.

Thunder and wind drowned out Eudora's surprised shout. The Acolyte barely dodged the amalgamator missile. Gator flew for several hundred feet straight up, nearly past the rim of the crag. While he didn't hit the Acolyte, the trajectory gave Ox an idea.

Heart of the Jotun

Ox slammed his fists into the ground. His immense Strength shattered the smooth stone underneath. He picked up one of the largest chunks and spun his body. "Catch!"

Ox flung the boulder as hard as he could. Eudora dodged and responded with a volley of her weapons.

"Ghakk!" Gator screamed as the dreadmail plummeted back toward the ground. Ox jumped and met the animated armor, and the amalgamator melded the dread bone around the skeleton.

Ox continued his attacks by alternating between breaking up the ground and flinging the resulting boulders at Eudora. The Acolyte was much more accurate with her summoned weapons, but Ox had Vitus to spare and could create endless projectiles. He was starting to enjoy himself.

———

Buddy watched the battle between Henry and Cirilo. The human's movements were slow and lethargic, though Buddy saw through the ruse. This would not be an easy battle, and the undead would need more than luck if they wanted any chance of victory.

Though the total magical power from the Spriggan and her deadly Magnolia had been much greater, the Acolyte Commander was by far the most dangerous enemy they'd faced yet. The man was proficient in melee fighting, but his magic was potentially more potent. Buddy needed to understand the full extent of the man's Abilities and whether there was any hope of stopping him.

Mystic Revelation

Waves of magic poured from the man like a blinding sun and reached through every inch of the environment, well beyond the massive cavern and far into the towering thunderstorm that had begun to form above them. The man's magic flowed toward the undead like conscious, swirling eddies in a churning river.

Not only was Cirilo causing environmental distortions, but his magic was also the source of the debilitating Status Effects. The Acolyte Commander could control the surrounding environment with a broader influence than even Buddy's evocation, and the negative Status Effects indicated the man could combine large-scale evocation with alteration magic in a very effective and dangerous manner.

Five golem-steel bucklers orbited around Buddy, enchanted

with a heavy combination of force and blue fire magic. Buddy reached deep into the volcano that made up his core and pulled out a considerable amount of Vitus.

Evoke

Type: Fire, Lightning, Ice, Acid, Wind
Vector: Bolt
Modifier: X30

Buddy formed magical clout into an array of powerful bolts and sent them, along with his flaming bucklers, careening toward the Acolyte Commander.

The man blocked a few, but several more impacted their target, creating an explosion of elements. The various forms of elemental magic raged against each other and blasted outward, pushing back Henry and stalling the fight. Henry's chest heaved, and even though the fight had only raged for a minute, Buddy knew that withstanding the powerful Acolyte taxed the full capabilities of the warrior. As quickly as the explosion erupted, the elements cleared. Cirilo stood unharmed, glaring at Buddy.

Evoke

Type: Force
Vector: Dome

The wind roared like a summer squall and blasted toward the mage. Buddy erected his force shield just in time to keep himself from tumbling across the cavernous expanse. A small funnel of wind mixed with bone and rock to form a tornado between Buddy and the two warriors. Flying debris grated against the invisible shield and threatened to tear it apart should Buddy stop pumping Vitus into it.

"Beak?" Muji chirped from inside the safety of Buddy's robes.

"No, Muji. Stay in there, the magic is too powerful for you to weather. I can't match the intensity of the Acolyte's magic. However, I have more Vitus and can endure the onslaught while drawing his focus. Hopefully, we can give Henry more than a fleeting chance to best the man."

Buddy pulled a substantial amount of Vitus from his volcanic core and continued to direct it toward his shield. The magic repelled the cutting wind of the cyclone that surrounded him. With his mind still hindered by pushing the bounds of his own limitations during the battle with Jaromak, he hesitated to demand more of himself until it was absolutely necessary. Until then, he could only draw the Acolyte's magic and hope Henry had what was required to withstand the man at the physical level.

Even beyond the current fight, one thing concerned him far more than the Acolyte Commander's power. Bharat, the elven Sage, had referred to him as *Mathis*. Buddy knew from his hours poring over the tome of the red mage that Tekşan greatly admired a powerful wizard under that name. Buddy couldn't consult the metal tome at the moment, but he recalled that a man named Mathis was referred to as the greatest sorcerer ever to live, next to Stavros, of course. More importantly, Mathis was Ikritian and alive during Jallfoss's fiery destruction.

Buddy had no idea what role he had played in the ruin of Jallfoss a hundred years earlier, but the mounting details were concerning at the very least. If he was truly responsible, his retribution would lie on the other side of the current battle.

CHAPTER 39

Henry was a crumbling embankment trying to hold back the force of an entire ocean. Like weathering the relentless waves of the sea, he could do little more than endure Cirilo's attacks. It wasn't the Acolyte's armor and weapons that gave Cirilo the advantage, as they were equal in quality to Henry's equipment. Nor was it Cirilo's fighting technique, which, although nearly flawless, Henry picked out minor weak points that if the skeleton were stronger and faster, he could exploit. It was the fact that the man had Ox's Strength, Beast's Mobility, and Buddy's magic.

Buddy was nearly a hundred paces away. Henry's Harmony picked up that the skeletal mage was preparing a magical strike. Cirilo paused his attacks on Henry and turned toward the mage. Blue flaming bucklers and magical bolts of every sort slammed into the man.

Cirilo blocked the first wave of Buddy's magic with the broad side of his gigantic sword like he was swatting away flies. He weathered the rest, and, through the explosion of elements, Henry could see the magic had minimal impact on the man.

Cirilo lifted a palm, and a tornado the size of Ox's giant

form gathered before the man. A twister of rock, bone, wind, and rain, along with waves of earth, skull-sized hail, and lightning bolts, tore through the battleground and met the wall of Buddy's evocation in a cataclysmic eruption of elements.

The two forces combined in an earth-shattering confluence that would have rivaled any natural disaster.

Status Effect: Calamity (Minor) - Environmental Damage Resistance -2

Thanks, Buddy. The mage had drawn the Acolyte's magic and given Henry just enough breathing room to get to work.

Blitz

Henry rushed forward, trying to maneuver himself close to Cirilo and slip his xiphos past the man's defenses. The Commander caught him with the flat side of his sword, delivering a bone-crushing strike that sent the skeleton skipping along the ground like a stone across the surface of a lake. Henry skidded to a stop fifty paces from the original impact.

Status Effect - Stunned (Minor): MOB -5%, ACU -25%

Cirilo's approaching form blurred as Henry steadied his gaze and recovered from the attack.

"Mage. Assassin. Giant. You have gathered the three unique skeletons from Ammerthall and brought them here. I wouldn't be surprised if you had recruited the Fiends as well. Sadly, I don't recognize you from the thousands and thousands of other undead. How did you come to lead this motley crew?"

Taunt

"I'm just a skeleton named Henry. I've killed humans as long as I can remember, and I'm damn good at it."

Taunt Failed

Cirilo only blinked as the unsuccessful Ability washed over him, still in control of his mind and unaffected by the spell. "Not good enough," he said, lifting the massive blade for another attack.

Blitz

Harden

Spark

Henry sounded his Abilities, one after the other, and lunged inside Cirilo's range. Lightning crackled around his shield. Henry lowered his shoulder and put all his Strength and magic into a bash. Cirilo crossed his sword and met Henry's bash with the flat edge of the blade. The impact felt like Henry had tried to ram a tree rooted to the center of the world. His teeth ground against each other, and the bones in his shoulder cracked under the force. The Acolyte Commander didn't budge.

Status Effect - Broken Shoulder (Minor): STR -10%, MOB -10%

Henry thrust with his sword, but the man turned Henry's xiphos aside like he was swatting away an annoying grigfly. They exchanged attacks, and Henry leaped out of range at his first opportunity. Before he could escape, Cirilo caught him with a sharp kick to the ribs. Henry dropped to a knee and clutched his torso. The Acolyte bore down with another mighty slash.

Status Effect - Broken Ribs (Minor): STR -5%, MOB -15%

Blitz

Henry exploded from the ground and thrust with a knee right for the man's jaw. Cirilo saw the attack early enough to parry, but too late to dodge completely. The strike landed in the middle of the Acolyte's chest.

Status Effect - Broken Leg (Moderate): STR -15%, MOB -25%

Henry felt his femur break, but he also felt the man's chest give just a bit. A normal human's body would have caved under the force of Henry's attack. Cirilo took the blow in stride, but Henry's Perception picked up the smallest wince from the man.

"Clever ruse, skeleton," Cirilo said with an amused smile.

Henry retreated again, just outside the range of the Acolyte's steel. That's when he saw something that confirmed his fear of Stavros. There was a dent in Cirilo's armor where Henry's knee had struck, but a faint hint of magical radiance came from that area. The scintillation shifted from sickly yellow and green to deathly brown—the same as Bharat's necromancy. There was no doubt in Henry's mind that whatever spell was radiating from the Acolyte came from Lord Stavros himself.

With his suspicions confirmed, Henry hardened his Resolve. He had no choice but to defeat the Acolyte before him. Henry might not be able to stop Cirilo, but if he could keep the man busy long enough, maybe the other undead would have a chance to claim victory and turn the tide of the battle.

Henry pulled the single Health Crystal from his belt pouch and activated it. The Legendary-quality shard held a substantial amount of Ox's healing magic.

Status Effects Dismissed: Stunned, Broken Shoulder, Broken Ribs, Broken Femur Healed

His bones knitted themselves back together enough to send away the Status Effects and brought his Health nearly to full.

Without another source of healing, Henry knew he couldn't take too many more attacks.

The brief respite from combat allowed Henry to collect his wits. He found it strange that the Commander was using his magic Abilities on Buddy and his physical attacks on Henry. Hopefully, the dual effort required more focus than the man was letting on. Either that, or the Acolyte was toying with them. Based on the sensations of power bombarding Henry, that was absolutely possible. The Commander held back Buddy's evocation as easily as the man blocked Henry's attacks, making him an almost insurmountable obstacle . . . almost.

Sacrifice

Blitz

Henry expanded the dread bone on his wrist to the size of a full tower shield and rushed forward. Cirilo held up his sword to block, which was easily the size of a shield itself. The impact shook Henry's entire body. It was like trying to ram down the mountain itself, and the man didn't even budge. Henry rallied his Strength and pushed again, but Cirilo pressed back and shoved him away easily.

Cirilo was on Henry before the skeleton could recover, and once again, Henry struggled to defend against the barrage of attacks. Just before Henry's Strength gave out, another round of magical bolts impacted Cirilo. The magic didn't damage the man, but it gave Henry a moment's reprieve from the fight— enough time to make out the shape of the mage through the magical storm of elements. Buddy was pushing back Cirilo's magic and still managing to help Henry.

Cirilo focused on Buddy, and the tornado's intensity rebounded. "I am impressed, Mage. With enough time, your magic would overpower mine. I refuse to allow you that advantage, but I must say that your magic is second only to

Stavros himself. Unfortunately for you, I fear it is a far second, like comparing the height of a blade of grass to that of a thousand-year-old grossoak." The tornado grew further and bore down on the mage, completely obscuring him.

Blitz

"Good thing Stavros isn't here!" Henry shouted. With his Vitus flagging, Henry thrust and, for the first time, attacked with a bit of hope. His theory was correct that Cirilo was focusing all his magic on Buddy. If Henry could occupy him long enough, the mage could triumph. The rush caught Cirilo off guard enough to allow Henry a slice that bit into the man's armor but did little more. The victory was short-lived. Cirilo spun faster than the tornado that fought Buddy and extended the huge sword. Henry saw it coming, but there was no way to dodge it.

Harden

Henry pumped all his remaining Vitus into his bones, knowing neither his Harden Ability nor his dread armor would stop the blow. Henry braced.

A shower of golden sparks erupted. The rusted sword slammed into Henry but stopped before cutting him completely in half. Jacoby stood between Henry and Cirilo, with the undead human's golden shield of blazing light halting the massive weapon mid-swing. Jacoby had blocked the blow and saved Henry's life.

Status Effects
Broken Ribs (Severe): STR -25%, MOB -25%
Shattered Pelvis (Severe): STR -30%, MOB -50%

Henry collapsed. His Health and Vitus were dangerously low, and if it hadn't been for Jacoby, he would be two half skeletons instead of a full Henry. He struggled to right himself, but had taken too much damage. More bones shattered when he tried to sit up. He could only watch as Jacoby stood defiantly before Cirilo, bathed in golden light.

Cirilo tightened his grip on his sword. "I wanted to avoid killing you, but you have forced my hand."

"I wanted the same, but Stavros has forced mine. I can see the magic coming from your chest is necromancy, and I can no longer stand idle in this fight."

The two met in a flurry of blows and an explosion of golden sparks. The former Acolyte fought Cirilo with the fury of a cornered animal, slicing and thrusting at a jarring pace. Jacoby was a great swordsman, but against Cirilo, he would fall in seconds. Every block and swing caused Jacoby's magic to dim significantly.

Cirilo's magic still focused on Buddy. Though bouts of blue flame, ice, lightning, and several other elements were starting to emerge from the tornado, Cirilo would finish Henry and Jacoby long before the mage could help. Buddy could beat the Acolyte's magic, but not combined with the Commander's sword and monstrous Strength and Mobility.

The battle was looking far less than hopeful. Beast had somehow gotten surrounded by a group of Acolytes, and Henry could hear her cries of frustration. Ox wasn't losing, but judging by his continuous banter, the giant was more concerned with flirting than fighting. All around and above the natural walls of the craggy mountain top, the forces of nature roared against the undead. Wind, rain, and even the trembling earth beneath their feet hindered their movements. Hail threatened to smash their skulls. Lightning cracked across the sky and blew apart another oak tree.

Henry watched the blue arc of electricity turn into a red

blaze and start consuming the tree. He knew what he had to do. If he wanted to beat this Acolyte, he would first need to confront a far stronger opponent.

Henry's only hope was to get back to his Path. With Buddy still enveloped in the raging tornado, Henry couldn't count on the mage to assist with his magic. He had gotten everyone into this mess. He had to get them out.

Henry calmed his mind and spread his awareness to the violent tempest above him. Though its power was immense, it reminded him of the raging storm that made up his core.

Remnant Gateway

It wasn't a single channel that opened between Henry and the towering thunderhead above; it was a flash flood that overwhelmed his senses, like he was trying to drink the magma that powered the dwarven forges far below him. The connection swelled, and electricity dumped into the channel, surging toward him.

Blinding light exploded all around Henry as lightning ripped through his bones.

Lightning Resistance Applied: 100/122 Damage Negated
Health: 9/79

The blinding column of electricity around Henry faded to black. He prepared for a fight.

CHAPTER 40

The scent of brine filled Henry's nose. The wind and ocean spray chilled his skin, and coarse sand worked its way between his toes. The colossal blue lizard before him opened its maw into a horrendous snarl filled with teeth as big as Cirilo's sword.

The dragon crouched low with its head just a few feet above the sand. It balanced on powerful winged forelimbs that spanned the beach between the cliff face and the white-capped water. Behind Henry, the beach stretched for a quarter mile before curving around a cliff and out of sight. There was no-where to escape, though retreat wasn't Henry's plan.

The dragon sucked in a huge breath, forming vortices of mist around its nostrils and expanded its massive blue-scaled chest. A white and blue ball with arcs of electricity formed in the back of the monster's throat. It opened its mouth and narrowed its eyes to focus on Henry. Yellow eyes with vertical slits like those of a monstrous snake let Henry know he was facing an apex predator—one that wasn't used to its prey being a threat. Henry had to prove that assumption wrong.

The blast of dragon fury was a heartbeat away, and that

short moment to prepare was all that Henry needed. Just like he had with the tempest above Jallfoss, Henry reached out with his Harmony and connected to the power within the dragon.

The monstrous lizard opened its mouth, unleashing a roar that shook the landscape and battered Henry's ears. A lightning bolt erupted from the back of its throat and hit Henry with the force of an entire thunderstorm. The intense heat seared his skin, and his blood threatened to evaporate within his veins. The muscles in his back contracted so hard that he felt his spine might snap. Henry ignored the pain as best he could, instead focusing his Affinity, forming millions of tiny channels in his body into a lattice and directing the lightning through his flesh. The pain waned, then stopped as the lightning routed around and within him. With a final flex of his Might, Henry locked the connection between the lightning from the dragon, the storm high above, and the tempestial core in his mind.

He opened his eyes and let his muscles relax. The monster's attack continued, but Henry felt the world around him had slowed, dragging out the seconds as the weaponized force of nature washed over him. The sand beneath his feet turned to glass, and huge chunks of the gray cliff behind him disintegrated into a shower of rock and dust. Even the moisture in the air around him boiled and turned to steam. Aside from his pants nearly burning away, Henry was completely unscathed.

As quickly as the blast started, it shut off like someone had pulled a sun globe from its sconce. Obscured by dust and steam, Henry regarded the dragon. The terrible lizard arched its mighty back and stretched. Languid, uninterested eyes looked out toward the ocean. The dragon . . . no, the Primal . . . didn't expect Henry's survival. Seeing a sliver of a chance, Henry took the initiative.

With every ounce of Strength and Mobility his flesh-covered

bones possessed, he sprinted away from the dragon and toward the curve in the beach. The power in his muscles surprised him as he accelerated at an incredible pace. He couldn't fight the dragon in the open and would need every bit of speed he could muster to gain whatever advantage was possible.

Henry's retreat didn't go unnoticed. Far behind him, a surprised grunt trilled into a deep growl. The dragon spotted him and wasn't pleased that its prey still lived.

Henry ventured to look over his shoulder and immediately wished he hadn't. The dragon roared and gave chase, tearing through the sandy beach. With a cliff on one side and churning ocean on the other, its movements were hampered. Its breath attack wasn't.

Lightning ripped into the rocky wall and along the beach. Aiming must have been hard for the monster while running, and Henry's head start had tripled the distance between them. Part of the blast grazed Henry, but luckily, what he had done to his body left him still protected from the element. The blasts still hit with enough force to send him tumbling. He quickly righted himself and sped forward without losing too much ground.

Up ahead, large, towering shapes emerged from the fog. Huge islands that jutted hundreds of feet toward the sky littered the ocean. There were dozens of them up to a mile away. They were close together, though Henry couldn't make out much more than their shape and location through the thick mist.

The curve on the beach drew closer with each step. Henry pumped his legs as hard as he could, hoping to maintain whatever distance he'd created from the angry monster chasing him.

Another lightning bolt ripped through the air as Henry rounded the bend. The beach stretched ahead of him and into the fog. With the turn in the landscape, Henry was now just out of sight of the dragon.

Henry gathered himself and leaped into the air. His hand found purchase on the rocky cliff, and he hoisted himself up the wall. The terrifying rumble of the approaching dragon got closer, and Henry climbed for all he was worth. He was exposed and vulnerable on the cliff, and if the dragon saw him, he would have nowhere to evade.

Henry's powerful muscles brought him fifty feet high before the dragon rounded the turn. The monster could have easily reached him if it lifted its head, but its body was low to the ground, expecting its prey to still be on the beach.

The incensed Primal sped across the black sand with an intensity only matched by Muji pouncing on a cave lizard. Henry planted his legs and pushed off the cliff as hard as possible. Cold, wet air rushed against his skin as he descended upon the yellow-horned monster. The blue-webbed hide that formed the bulk of the dragon's wings made for a soft enough landing. It was incredibly slick, forcing Henry to slide from the monster's wing and onto the iron-hard scales on its back. When he reached with his hands for a hold to slow his tumble, the scales ground against his flesh like sandpaper, but he managed to roll to a stop between the monster's shoulder blades. Immediately, the dragon spun. Its head hit the cliff, and its tail smashed into the ocean, sending a spray of water and a shower of rock down on Henry.

The dragon thrashed and snapped, trying to remove the unexpected rider. Henry held tight, gripping the edges of a shield-sized scale. He was still in awe that a creature could be so big and powerful, and it seemed even more impossible now that he was on top of it. It was well over a hundred feet long from horned snout to the tip of its spiked tail, and even wider were it to stretch out its winged forelegs.

Unable to remove Henry, the dragon bound clear of the cliff and picked up speed, spreading its wings and pumping them hard. Within seconds, the massive dragon lifted into the sky. Henry held tight and braced against the increasing speed of the wind that assaulted him.

Immediately, they were in the clouds. Whisps of nimbus rushed over the dragon's wings. The Primal turned and bucked, and Henry's senses became so overwhelmed with the gyrations that he lost all awareness of his orientation.

The clouds went from dim grey to brilliant white, then a surge of blue sky and yellow sun filled his vision. The sudden brilliance temporarily blinded him, but his eyes adjusted quickly. What he saw was amazing. Where not covered by the low cloud layer, an endless continent of forest, desert, lakes, swamps, hills, and mountains stretched ahead as far as he could see. To his left, islands dotted an ocean that lined dozens of miles of black sand beaches.

The dragon banked hard to its right. A mountain range snaked into the distance and away from the ocean. Though Henry hadn't seen Jallfoss peaks from the planes of Ikrit, he couldn't imagine them being any bigger than the high ridges before him. The tops of the range were still thousands of feet above, and the dragon's rate of climb brought them closer by the second—closer to the storm that Henry saw raging on the other side.

The dragon flew parallel to the range until it crested a high pass, then turned directly toward the tempest. Henry's unwilling mount continued to buck as they passed between two snow-capped summits. On the far side, Henry saw that the range was forcing the clouds high into the atmosphere. Henry held tight, squinting his eyes against the frigid blasts of air. The dragon soared directly into the storm, still pumping its wings and driving toward the upper reaches of the cumulonimbus.

Wind and freezing rain drove against Henry, and the on-slaught only got worse as the dragon took them higher. Ice started to build on Henry's bare chest, and he wondered how the dragon could keep climbing under the heavy accumulation. Through squinted eyes, he found his answer—the dragon's scales on the leading edge of its wings moved against each other and shed any ice before it could build up. The yellow horns and spikes along its body arced with electricity, producing enough heat to keep any ice from forming in the first place.

Henry wasn't fortunate enough to have the dragon's anti-ice and de-ice capabilities. His body began to freeze, and his limbs started to go numb. Hail from the storm and flying ice chunks from the dragon's scales pummeled his bare skin. Every second, his hold on the scale slipped just a bit more.

The dragon banked hard again. The sudden movement caught Henry unaware, and his hands slipped free. He tumbled to the side and across the dragon's wing. His hands found one of the spines that formed the skeletal support structure of the webbed skin, and he got just enough grip to stop himself from falling, though his hold began to fail quickly.

The cold continued seizing his muscles, and the thin air made breathing harder and harder. He couldn't hang on for much longer, so he did the only thing that had worked in the dragon realm for him up to that point.

Henry spread his awareness as far as he could. Strangely, his attention focused on the spine in his hand. That gave Henry an idea. He harmonized his body with the dragon's scales, then willed his skin to match its form. Henry felt Strength and warmth swell through his body, and when he looked down, he saw that his hands and wrists were covered in blue scales.

Not only were his hands stronger, but they had also grown resistant to the storm's cold. He had willed scales into existence, but he needed more. The dragon had an advantage in the air that Henry couldn't allow it to keep.

Henry spread his awareness further through the dragon and focused on its body as if it were a blueprint of a dwarven golem. He then overlayed that image on his own physique and locked the mental rendering into existence.

The muscles in his back twisted. The pain was excruciating, but he forced the change until wings ripped free from the confining skin on his back and expanded like sails in the wind. Unfamiliar muscles stretched, and the flesh of his wings caught the draft, nearly ripping him free from his mount. His scaled fingers held tight as the wind against his wings pulled him and the dragon's spine along with it. The dragon's wing deformed under the force, and with one lift device out of synch with the other, both Henry and his escort dropped several hundred feet before recovering. That gave Henry another idea.

He gripped the spine as hard as he could, then spread his wings. He angled his wings to use the lift he generated to force the spine closer to an inward one. Henry grabbed the other spine and pulled, collapsing the winged flesh between them. The dragon immediately plummeted and began to spiral from the sky. It roared and thrashed, but Henry held strong.

The dragon eventually gained enough control to settle into a hampered glide, but it was still losing altitude quickly. The monster tried to turn and snap at Henry, but it couldn't move its head enough to reach him without inducing another spin. Henry pulled on the spines and flared his wings, giving the dragon as much trouble as possible.

He had no idea where they were, but he hoped their flight

path pointed to where they would land in the ocean and not crash into the mountains. He was wrong.

Henry and the roaring, angry dragon burst from the thunderhead, pointed directly at the side of a towering peak. Henry released one of the spines just in time to give the dragon back control and a boost in altitude, but it still smashed the wing opposite Henry into the rocky slope. Massive bones snapped with a bang louder than the blast from a solofurno. Snow-covered rock tore through the flesh on the monster's wings.

Henry and the dragon tumbled past the range. With only one good wing, the dragon barely managed to slow its descent. They tumbled more than glided as the forest below turned into individual trees at an alarming rate.

Henry folded his wings against his body and clawed his way onto the dragon's back.

The impact was just as violent as getting smashed by Cirilo's sword. Trees snapped and shattered against the dragon's colossal body, but not without putting up a fight. The dragon, and subsequently Henry, spun and tumbled, taking nearly as much damage as they inflicted on the innocent vegetation.

Even the Strength imparted by Henry's scaled hands couldn't keep him attached to the Dragon's back, and the tumble ripped him from his perch. As he rolled through the forest, he thought for a moment that he should have ejected and used his wings to glide to safety. Since he lacked the confidence in his own proficiency to slow his rate of descent in a fall, he felt it better that he hadn't.

He rolled to a stop at the base of a mighty oak, covered in dirt and blood. After a second, the pain set in. He didn't know how many bones he'd broken, but he knew it was many. The good news was that he was still alive, and a quick survey of his body showed no bleeding beyond superficial. Unfortunately, roars and snarls close by indicated that the dragon was also alive and quite perturbed.

Everything hurt. Henry's broken body urged him to stay and hide. The last thing he wanted was to rally himself and keep fighting a dragon.

Henry! Echoes of the woman's voice screaming his name reminded him that he had a duty to attend to. His friends were facing an enemy of extreme power. If he didn't help, they would surely fail. He pushed away the weakness in his mind—giving up wasn't something he could allow himself to do. Through the pain, Henry forced himself to stand and start making his way toward the sound of the dragon.

Finding the Primal didn't take long, as most of the trees between them had been torn down. A blind man with a buried head couldn't miss the sound and thrashing.

Dark red blood covered broken yellow and blue wings. The dragon was hundreds of times Henry's size, and as it thrashed to right itself, it toppled more gigantic trees like they were tiny saplings.

Henry's powerful body was battered, but for the most part, he had little trouble quickly navigating the destroyed landscape. He pumped his wings and found it easy to use their force to heighten his jumps, then spread them out to carry him into a glide. He wasn't ready to try flying with an angry, injured Primal so close.

Within a hundred yards, the dragon noticed him. It arched its back and roared, but the sound had changed to one of a cornered animal, not a predator on the hunt. Henry refused to dodge and hide. He was tired of running—tired of being weak.

The dragon summoned another ball of lightning in its mouth and released a torrent of electricity. Though this blast was much weaker than the previous discharges, it still tore through the landscape and ignited the fallen timber. The fire gave Henry pause, but the lightning passed through him, leaving him completely unharmed. The crackling electricity almost felt welcoming to his injured body.

The dragon hurled blast after blast at Henry, each weaker than the previous one. Henry ignored the attacks and kept his steady, confident approach. As he neared, Henry sounded the familiar pattern of his Remnant Attributes. He connected to the dragon's mind and felt the depths of the monster's emotions. There was rage, anger, and hunger, but also fear. Henry latched on to the final emotion, then amplified the dragon's fear a hundred-fold.

The Primal reared back, struggling to create distance between itself and Henry. The forest and the monster's broken wings hindered its retreat.

It snapped powerful jaws that could have eaten Ox whole—a threat Henry ignored. Then, unexpectedly, the dragon stopped. It lowered its head just above the forest floor and closed its eyes. When it opened them, the yellow irises were replaced with a dark, brilliant blue. The animalistic continence took on a veneer of deep and ancient wisdom. The fear that sang across the channel between Henry and the dragon was replaced with a sense of calm. Henry felt that sensation flow through his body, almost like the experience of gaining a Tier. The pain and fatigue left him, and his body healed instantly. The same happened to the dragon. Boken bones unfolded to their intended position. Gory wounds patched themselves closed, and arcs of lightning seared away the blood.

The dragon studied Henry, then dipped its head ever so slightly in what Henry could only interpret as an approving nod. The monster turned and leapt into the air. Mighty wings sent broken trees flying as the Primal propelled itself into the clouds and out of sight beyond the tree line.

An eerie calm settled over the leveled forest. With the dragon gone, Henry was now free in this land—the Dragon Realm, apparently. However, he couldn't stay. The time for the real battle was upon him.

CHAPTER 41

Primal Guardian Defeated: Soul Essence Claimed, Tier gained x1: STR +2, MOB +2, FOR +1, ACU +3, PER +1, RES +3, HAR +5, AFI +6, MIG +6

Path of the Dragon Remnant: All Attributes +10%. Access to the Dragon Realm granted. Remnant Form I (Drake) granted. Resistance: Lightning (Immune), Cold +20 . . .
  Corruption Detected (Undead): Attribute bonus reduced to 5%, Fire Resistance -20

Strength surpassed first Threshold. Attribute bonus applied (STR +10%), Damage Resistance: All +1

Acumen surpassed first Threshold. Attribute bonus applied (ACU +10%), Vitus +1 per Tier

Mobility surpassed second Threshold. Attribute bonus applied (MOB +20%), -20% Vitus requirement for all Transmutation Abilities

Resolve surpassed second Threshold. Attribute bonus applied (RES +20%), Mental Damage Resistance +5, +5 Vitus regeneration per hour

Ability Discovered: Remnant Form I: Drake (Transmutation). You have earned the approval of your patron and now join the ranks of the great protectors. Never soar above the heights of your own reticence, humble Remnant. STR +5, MOB +10, Vitus -1 per second while in Remnant Form

Abilithy Discovered: Lightning Immunity I (Transmutation – Passive): Ignore all lightning damage and associated adverse Effects

Ability Upgraded: Remnant Gateway II (Enchantment) . . .

Ability Upgraded: Primal Urge II (Enchantment) . . .

Synergy Detected: Combining Primal Urge II, Taunt II, and Remnant Gateway II

Ability Discovered: Reverie of Dominance I (Transcendent): The mind bridges the gap between this realm and the others. You have mastered that expanse and can now exert your influence on the incorporeal. MIG +50% vs Primals and Remnants. RES +10, AFI +5, MIG +5, Mental Resistance +15

Henry returned to Jallfoss's highest peak. A rush of power flooded into his bones, accompanied by a pain so intense he could have sworn he brought his flesh from the Dragon Realm. The incredible bump to his Attributes and the change in his Path Effects from negative to positive were more intense than withstanding the full brunt of Cirilo's Calamity.

Magical power tore through his being like a ravenous pack of wolves. It consumed and rebuilt him simultaneously, and he didn't know whether his bones were knitting themselves back together or crumbling under the force. The power didn't stop at his bones. It rushed into his very core. Instead of harming him, the tempest within swelled and took in the energy, growing so massive that Henry wondered how his psyche could contain such a cumulus.

Henry could do little but weather the influx of power, and there was nothing he could do to stop himself from screaming. His jaw opened, and what he released wasn't his human voice. A dragon's roar reverberated from his skull. He shut his eyes tight to seal out the pain, but his Status still occupied his vision.

Name: Henry

Race: Undead Human (Dragon Remnant)

Tier: 17

Health: 169/169

Vitus: 273/277

Attributes:

    STR: 45

    MOB: 70

    FOR: 41

    ACU: 40

    PER: 48

    RES: 68

    MIG: 21

    AFI: 24

    HAR: 14

Resistances: Cold, Mental Damage, Physical Damage, Poison (Immune), Lightning (Immune)

Weakness: Fire

The pain slowly faded, as did his roar. Henry opened his eyes.

Cirilo's raging magic still filled the open cavern, but the Acolyte and Jacoby stopped their battle and turned their attention toward Henry. He was aware of the struggles Buddy, Beast, and Ox were fighting on the periphery of the battlefield. Everything seemed to slow just a bit as he processed what was happening with almost no effort—the bump to his mental Attributes left him with a calm, slow, and controlled awareness.

He dismissed the notifications in his vision. With his bolstered Attributes, his body, mind, and soul swelled with their new power. It was more than just increased Attributes—he felt like a hidden potential had been unlocked. The boost was insane. The rewards he'd earned for besting the dragon were apparently commiserate with the task.

Henry was no fool, and he realized that his Attributes alone wouldn't be enough to beat Cirilo. However, his new Ability just might.

Remnant Form: Drake

Henry watched tiny blue scales form over his hand bones. Yellow-tipped claws sparked with static yet kept a form dexterous enough to allow him to wield his sword. Covered by dreadmail bracers, he couldn't tell how far the scales went, but he felt like they stopped halfway up his forearms.

The dreadmail pressed against the shifting bones in his back.

Adapt

Henry activated the armor's Ability, allowing the back dread-bone plates to open enough to release his form. Bestial wings unfurled behind him, snapping like sails on a ship in high winds. Tipped with yellow spikes and covered in blue-scaled membrane between the spines, the wings filled him with a further boost to his Strength and Mobility. His Vitus was triple what it had been, but now, in his Remnant form, it started to tick down slowly. He only had minutes to finish the fight.

"Cirilo!" Henry shouted. His voice was human again, though it still carried a hint of draconic growl. It easily projected through the mayhem of the battle and almost seemed to push back the wind, rain, and hail that still assaulted him.

The Acolyte Commander gave Henry a cold stare. The man's presence was no less potent than it had been, but Henry turned it aside with a flex of his boosted Might. The corners of Cirilo's mouth curved up, betraying the slightest hint of amusement. "Degonhart . . . your status as their leader makes sense now. Legend says your like never quit. We'll see about that."

Blitz

Spark

Henry's new Attributes, coupled with the force of his wings, launched him forward like an arrow released from the taut string of a longbow. The tip of his sword crackled with lightning as he thrust for the Acolyte's heart.

As strong as Henry had become, Cirilo still had him outmatched in both Strength and Mobility. The Acolyte turned aside Henry's xiphos with the flat edge of his great sword and countered with a rising slash. Henry spun clear of the blade, but Cirilo had already focused on Jacoby. The Commander kept the momentum of his upslash and spun mid-air to bring a heavy descending attack down on Jacoby.

The undead Acolyte saw the attack coming. He was right in the path of the massive blade that plunged toward him with the intent of a guillotine. The speed of the attack left him little hope of escaping the full force of Cirilo's Strike. Henry forced his Vitus toward Jacoby and activated his favored attack.

Bestow: Blitz

Jacoby dodged by the narrowest of margins and returned a series of slashes. The unexpected rebuttal forced Cirilo on his heels, and, for the first time in the fight, Henry felt they had a chance. Unfortunately, with his Remnant Form engaged and his Bestow Ability pumping Blitz into Jacoby, the remaining minutes turned into seconds. He had precious little time to maintain the advantage. Henry rushed, and the three men met in a clash of steel, flesh, and bone.

Scaled wings pumped furiously, speeding up and extending Henry's dodges and pivots, allowing him to attack from multiple angles nearly simultaneously. Jacoby wasted none of the Mobility Henry was channeling into his muscles and kept up a series of irregular attacks. He wasn't inflicting much damage, but his pace kept Cirilo occupied enough that Henry managed to slip his blade through a weak spot in the man's armor.

Henry felt his xiphos sink into flesh below the man's thigh. When he pulled free, the blade was covered in bright red blood. It wasn't deep, but he had wounded the Commander and stolen a few vital Vitus points.

Cirilo bared his teeth and adjusted the grip on his sword. Before he could attack, a cry rang out.

Gator and Ox had finally cornered Eudora. In his Giant Form, Ox wrapped his hands around the woman and squeezed.

Cirilo roared. A blast of wind and heat burst from his body, propelling Henry and Jacoby backward. Cirilo spun and launched his sword like a giant arrow. It caught Ox in the shoulder, severing his huge arm and freeing the Acolyte from his grasp. Henry took the opportunity to force his new Ability through the mental channel between him and Cirilo.

Reverie of Dominance

"Focus on me, human, or this will be over before I can even warm up." Henry pushed against the oppressive mental force of Cirilo's presence. He felt the man struggle against the Ability and eventually turn aside the mental attack, though how close it had been to penetrating the defenses of the man's psyche, Henry wasn't sure.

Cirilo balled his fists. The wind, rain, and hail stopped, and the Commander's eyes flashed a brilliant crimson that spread over his skin, drowning out even his blazing aura.

Status Effect Dismissed: Calamity Dispelled

—

"I think there's a rule against throwing rocks at girls, but if you won't get close enough for a hug, I guess I have no choice." Ox launched the thousand-pound mass of stone as easily as if he were tossing an apple. Eudora zipped out of the way, and the boulder smashed into one of the huge oak trees, ripping a massive portion out of its side, then crashing into another.

"You're a bit too boney for me. I like a little meat on my men. You've not enough hair for me either," Eudora said with a smile before sending another volley of summoned weapons at Gator and Ox. Swords, axes, spears—blades and polearms of all sorts bounced off the amalgamator's dread mail. The weapons couldn't pierce the high-quality dread bone and golem steel, but they effectively kept the living armor from cornering her.

"You'd love my other body." Ox swatted dozens of metal spears out of the air. Several more found their mark and took chunks out of his elephant-sized bones. The gashes healed over before the weapons clanked to the ground.

"I doubt that." The source of Eudora's weapons seemed to be endless as she continued her assault. Ox's Health ticked down by the second, and only with a constant flow of healing spells was he able to keep himself together.

"Ghakk!" Gator cried from within a swirling mass of dread armor. The amalgamator had also picked up several of the destroyed skeletons from nearby, as well as many of the weapons the Acolyte had fired at him. He grew with every addition, but the bigger he got, the slower he moved.

Though Ox enjoyed the battle as much as the banter with the red vixen, he knew his fellow skeletons were having as much trouble with the Acolytes as he was. Beast was outnumbered, Buddy was inside a tornado, and Henry was getting manhandled by the Acolyte leader who exuded a presence that made Ox feel weak in comparison.

Ox couldn't allow the fight to drag on any longer. Two more lances and a broadsword impacted his massive rib cage, but he took the blows in stride and picked up another chunk of loose stone. Before he could throw it, a crack of lightning rocked the entire battlefield.

When Ox looked over, he saw that it had struck Henry. His concern turned to surprise when he saw that the lightning hadn't killed the skeleton. Sparks of electricity crackled off the warrior's dread armor. Henry looked down at his hands and released a roar that shook Ox more than the lightning bolt had. Suddenly, blue wings, like those of a bat, exploded out of Henry's back, and the skeleton launched himself into the melee with such vigor that the greatest warlords would have been jealous of Ox's minion.

"Looks like Herbie's got this. I need to attend to this angry woman," Ox said to himself, then shouted to his companion. "Gator, over here!"

Gator spun in place and rushed to Ox, now more a ball of bones and equipment than a humanoid form. Ox grabbed the mass and spun until the centrifugal force threatened to tear the abomination apart. Ox heard Gator scream as he released, and the amalgamator shot toward Eudora as fast as the tiny rocks from Jai's sling.

As quickly as Gator flew, Eudora was just nimble enough to dodge. Ox was ready for that.

"Gator. Expand!" Ox shouted. Gator turned from a tumbling mass to a flying web of bone and metal far too big for the Acolyte to dodge. She summoned more weapons and shields and attempted to bore her way through, but Gator constricted around the Acolyte and knocked her to the ground.

Eudora hit the crumbled stone rolling and sprang to her feet. Sheilds and swords appeared around her as she summoned weapons and armor to protect herself. Ox's huge hands shot through her shielding and wrapped around her torso.

"Ghakk." Half of Gator's body had been torn apart and scattered across the cavern, but he'd kept most of the dread mail together. He rose from the ground, reconstructing the plates back into his bone golem form.

"Die, you undead scum!" Eudora screamed.

"Too late. No hard feelings, but I've got a job to do. I'll make it up to you when we bring you back." Ox squeezed, and the woman's armor crinkled under his boney fingers. In his Giant Form, he had no trouble crushing the steel plate like a tin can. Eudora shrieked, and Ox only squeezed harder—not wanting to drag out the pain, yet knowing he couldn't allow her to live.

Suddenly, a flash of silver impacted Ox, and his arm was on the ground, still holding the woman.

The Acolyte leader had broken free of his fight with Henry and Jacoby long enough to save Eudora. Henry's wings must have helped because the battle looked far more even than it had previously. The tornado around Buddy was dying down, but the Acolyte leader had turned a red much more brilliant than that of a normal crimson aura. The Commander's ominous presence doubled its intensity and bore down on Ox.

Ox looked down to see that Eudora had escaped and was running for the giant sword that had taken his arm. Gator chased after her. She was wounded but still too fast for the amalgamator to catch.

"Gator, back to me. One more time." Gator stopped the chase and came churning back to Ox.

"You won't get me with that trick again!" Eudora warned as she lifted into the air, riding on Cirilo's giant sword. Dozens more weapons appeared in the air, orbiting around her.

"You should give up and join me. I can't go easy on you just because you're beautiful."

"I've got your chivalry right here," Eudora cried, unleashing another volley.

Ox would have grinned if he had the facial muscles to oblige. As it was, he could only end the fight quickly. He reached down, but instead of picking up his severed arm, he retrieved his maul. It was big enough to fit in his giant hands and still had several charges of force magic remaining. Ox activated them all.

He held out the maul, and the amalgamator wrapped himself around it, turning Gator into a giant hammerhead. Once again, Ox spun and sent the amalgamator flying.

Eudora went to dodge, and she would have easily, if Gator hadn't manipulated the force maul behind his soaring mass. The hammer's magic released and propelled Gator forward in a rippling explosion of force. He was no longer an amalgamator. He was dread-bone shrapnel. "GHAAKK!"

The Acolyte didn't have time to use her summoned

equipment as a barrier. She didn't even have time to scream. Bones, weapons, and armor ripped her apart.

"Looks like chivalry is as dead as I am." Ox's gloating was cut short. His Remnant Attributes screamed a warning at him. A new presence had arrived, one many times stronger than the power from the Acolyte Commander. Even stronger than what Ox had experienced with Giganthorpe. It originated from where Beast was fighting.

CHAPTER 42

J ai hadn't moved from his hiding spot behind the massive oak trunk. He couldn't. The strap in his hand shook, and the elf trembled, frozen in fear.

The fight in Ghara's cavern had been intense. Hundreds of Sprigs, a walloping Magnolia, and the corrupted god herself all tried to kill Jai and the undead who had accompanied him. However, Ghara was a being of nature. She and her Sprigs acted in accordance with the laws of the world, as any animal would. The Spriggan . . . Primal, as the skeletons called her . . . was not a warrior. These Acolytes were.

The three humans fought with deadly precision and intent. They were vicious and calculated, yet cold in their demeanor. The earth and sky fought on their side. The ground shook beneath Jai's feet. Lightning destroyed several nearby trees, and hail ripped through their dead branches. Even the wind and rain tore into Jai's exposed skin, forcing him to shield his eyes.

A mighty whirlwind enveloped Buddy, though the mage's blue fire still roared from within the cyclone. Henry had nearly died, and would have if Jacoby hadn't stepped in, though the human wouldn't be able to fight the Acolyte Commander for long. Ox was getting ripped apart by an enemy he had no chance of catching.

Worst of all was Mira's situation. Jai hated calling her *Beast* when he knew deep down that the skeleton was his sister, even though she was adamantly opposed to the notion.

The Acolyte Mira faced, Mersin, was a match for the skeletal elf in every way. Blink had been effective at first, but somehow the man and his clones had anchored themselves to her in a way that allowed them to transport with her with her conjuration magic. She couldn't escape, and even though she was faster than the Acolyte, his clones and constant physical attacks kept her on the defensive. The few times she had recovered or landed a blow, the storm seemed to turn on her, catching her off guard with a gust of wind or tremor of earth. Jai stared on in horror, realizing she wouldn't last much longer.

A crack of lightning hit the battlefield, though the tornado obscured its impact point from Jai. The thunder that came after sounded to the boy like the growl of a thousand trolls rather than the roar of a storm. The clap shook him out of his frozen fear. He looked around, frantically trying to find something that would help. His eyes settled on the Flow Bracers in his hand.

Buddy told Jai that the bracers were dwarven artifacts that could revive the Empress, and Henry charged Jai with protecting the items. No matter what, he had to honor that promise. Jai slid the bracers over his hands so he wouldn't drop them if he had to run. They would hinder using his sling, but what would a rock do against three Acolytes, anyway?

"Ahhh!" Beast cried out under the continued onslaught. Jai didn't know if her scream came from pain or anger, but he could hear her bones snapping, even from far away. They circled her, picking her apart like wolves attacking an injured elk.

Jai knew anything he could summon would be no match against the Acolyte, but he hoped that contracting a powerful enough creature might give Mira a few more seconds. Jai pulled from the waterfall in his core and sounded the familiar pattern. He desperately reached out for any monster or being powerful enough to help.

His magic flowed through his hands, but something happened when it got to the bracers. His spell became a tiny drop of water that dumped into an entire river of magic flowing through the artifacts. If his spell were a single pine needle, that power would have been the whole forest of Amera. Jai couldn't wrap his head around the unbelievable amount of magic before him, so he shut his eyes and released the spell with a simple request. "Save Mira."

Everything stopped. It wasn't just the atmosphere that halted; there were no sounds, not even his own breath or heartbeat. For a moment, Jai thought that maybe the bracers were so powerful that they had taken his life. He cautiously opened his eyes to find that he was still alive, but everything around him had frozen in time. The scene before him could have been a painting, as still as it was. Blue fire erupted from the tornado. Henry's lightning and Jacoby's golden magic met a deep red glow that had formed around the Acolyte Commander. Bones and weapons filled the sky where Ox and Gator fought the red-haired woman. Most concerning were the five Acolytes bearing down on the skeletal elf.

"What happened?" Jai asked, more to himself than expecting a response.

A voice louder than any crack of thunder echoed through his head. It sounded both close and far away at the same time. It could have been under the deepest ocean, or right before him.

You called, child, and I have answered. Such power as yours was enough to pique my curiosity.

The voice was deep, slow, and drawn out, like an old man telling a story to a captive audience. Jai could sense a presence, like his awareness had been supplanted into the head of another. The being, whatever it could be, was all around Jai, and he could feel its attention go to the Bracers. Jai clenched his fists and pulled them toward his chest. "You can't have these. I'm protecting them."

There was a laugh that sounded more like the crash of an avalanche.

I do not covet your trinkets, though I now understand the source of your power.

"Why did everything stop?" Jai asked. He didn't know if the being had shown up to kill him or help him, but he felt there was very little he could do to stop it, whatever its intent.

Time does not stop. It is our perspective that changes. I have pulled you into my Realm, for the moment.

"So, what are you doing here?" Jai asked. Another sensation of amusement bombarded the boy's senses.

The spell you cast is one of conjuration. I wanted to investigate who would cast such magic and where the power of the old god came from. I am quite surprised to find only a child of the Raven. Now that I have answered, I turn the question to you. What is it you seek?

The booming voice and overwhelming presence had nearly made Jai forget the spell he had cast. He looked at Mira and the frozen Acolytes that were descending upon her. "I need you to save my sister."

The being's focus went from Jai to the battlefield. It seemed to study everything that was happening. It spent a long time on the blue light containing the Empress's ghost, then finally settled on the skeletal elf.

What an interesting chain of events. Very well. I can save the undead you call your sister, but what do you offer in return?

Jai wasn't prepared for the question. In all his previous summons, the contract had been an understanding, but not a formal agreement. He didn't know what he had to offer besides his Vitus. The important thing was that Mira had Ghara's soul in her, and Jai had no doubt that she was his sister. He had to save her.

Without a second thought, he gave his offer. "Anything. You can have anything you want, even my life."

Another round of laughter, far beyond amusement, shook Jai harder than the Acolyte's earthquake. He almost felt the waterfall in his core shake and splash.

A foolish offer that one less benevolent than I would take advantage of. I accept your request, and I will collect what is appropriate in return. Be careful with your negotiations in the future, child of the Raven, lest you give more of yourself than is needed.

"Wait, who are you?" Jai shouted, but the presence had already left his mind. Dozens of amber spheres appeared and surrounded Mira. The battle before Jai resumed as though its fury had never waned.

Hundreds of long blue tentacles, no bigger around than Jai's arm, erupted from the amber summon gates and wrapped around the Acolyte and his clones. There was no struggle, no cries for help, as the arms constricted. Gore exploded from all five Acolytes, and then the tentacles were gone.

Jai tried to step forward, but he felt weirdly off-balance. His left arm was numb. He looked down and saw an empty sleeve up to the shoulder where the limb had been. He suddenly felt light-headed. Jai passed out and dropped to the ground.

———

Henry was grateful when the presence faded from his senses. The assault on his Remnant Attributes had been far more powerful than the energy Cirilo exuded, and it even dwarfed that of the dragon.

Whatever power appeared around Beast was gone, hopefully never to return. That didn't change the fact that there was still a monster of a man before Henry, and the fight with the Acolyte Commander was only getting more intense.

Cirilo's Strength and Mobility almost doubled when the Effects of the man's Calamity Ability receded. Some of Henry and Jacoby's attacks landed, but the red sheen around Cirilo provided protection beyond armor. Henry wondered if the combination of Spark and his Xiphos could penetrate the barrier. With his Vitus dwindling, he had to ensure he landed the blow.

Henry's Blitz bolstered Jacoby. The undead Acolyte and the skeletal Remnant were putting up substantial resistance. They were both master swordsmen, and each attack set up the next powerful blow. Against any other martial opponent, they would have overwhelmed them in seconds. Cirilo was no ordinary foe.

The man used his hands as shield and cudgel, turning aside the undead's blades and countering with such force and speed that the air around his limbs yielded to their potency. Henry's Harden Ability reinforcing his dread armor, and Jacoby's Auric Palisade were the only things stopping Cirilo's fists from crushing their bones to dust.

"This skeleton is telling you the truth. I have felt the evil in Stavros. The magic in you is his, and you know it's necromancy," Jacoby pleaded.

"Stavros is the Necromancer. We seek to break his curse on this mountain," Henry growled, draconic resonance still present in his voice.

"If the Great Lord is evil, I have already lost." Cirilo turned away from Henry to throw a wild back swing at Jacoby. Henry stepped in to take advantage of the Commander's blind spot. Before the man thrust, Henry's Perception drew his attention to the Acolyte's closest boot that pointed slightly away from Cirilo's target. Henry dodged just in time, avoiding a heavy spinning kick that would have smashed him in two. Henry and Jacoby both jumped back, still flanking the Acolyte Commander.

Cirilo looked at neither of them and instead held up his hands. Nearly a hundred magical bolts of fire, lightning, ice, and several other elements impacted Cirilo, enveloping the Acolyte with their power. Buddy had recovered from his fight with the tornado.

Cirilo stood calmly, staring at the mage. The red sheen faded to a dull glow.

"Don't let up!" Henry yelled. Before he could charge, Cirilo took the initiative. With a speed that rivaled Beast at her fastest, he lunged and grabbed Jacoby, then threw him at Buddy. In the same motion, the Commander charged Henry.

Blitz

Harden

Henry cut off his Bolster to Jacoby and sprang forward with his shield raised. Henry's draconic wings and magic-enhanced bones propelled him forward at a blinding speed. He and Cirilo met with such force that the stone under their feet exploded outward, leaving them in a shallow crater.

It was less like hitting a wall and more like trying to move the very earth beneath him, but Henry held firm enough to keep his bones together. He didn't budge . . . neither did Cirilo.

"I cannot let you succeed!" Cirilo cried. At that range, Henry noticed the red blaze of the man's eyes had been replaced with the sickly yellow-brown that Henry easily recognized as necromancy.

Sacrifice

Reverie of Dominance

"For the sake of this mountain and all within, I cannot fail!" Henry pulled all the Vitus he could afford from his bones and pumped it through his mental channels. Instead of sending it to Cirilo, Henry focused on the red sheen. It was a barrier, no different than the door in his Path. And just like that blockade, there was a way to open it.

Cirilo's will revolted against Henry's Reverie, but with a final push of Resolve, the blockade sundered, and the Acolyte's barrier dropped. That's when Henry felt it. Just the most minute give in the impenetrable wall that was Cirilo's stance. The Commander yielded the physical space of a hair's width, but that cession told Henry all he needed to know—the fight was his.

Spark

Blitz

Henry shoved again, then pulled his dread shield away and quickly thrust with his sword. Cirilo caught the blade. It bit into the man's fingers and coated the xiphos with blood, but the Acolyte's grip stopped the weapon just inches from his chest.

Cirilo reached with his other hand and grabbed Henry where a living being's throat should be. His hand wrapped around Henry's spine. The Commander went to tear Henry's skull from his undead body. Jacoby stopped the man.

The tip of a golden blade shot from Cirilo's chest, opposite Henry's xiphos. Jacoby stood behind the Commander with tears streaming from his eyes. Cirilo's grip on Henry loosened, and Henry pressed again with his sword. Slyngur's eversharp blade went right through Cirilo's chest plate and into the man's heart.

Henry was inches away from Cirilo's face. Deep brown eyes maintained a staunch look of defiance, but there was no hiding their resounding sadness.

Cirilo pulled in a gurgling breath. His lungs filled with as much blood as air. "I pray to whatever gods will listen that you're right, skeleton. For the sake of us all . . . please be right."

Henry felt the man's life fade. Then came the emotions.

Sadness at the loss of Acolyte life—not only at those Cirilo had brought in is coterie, but for the ones that the skeletons had killed, and the hundreds of fallen Acolytes who had died in Jallfoss over the last century. Then there was shame. Cirilo had let down Lord Stavros, the man he idolized like a father.

Cirilo's last thought was a flood of information. The skeletons were at the Empress's ghost and had the capability to revive her. Then Cirilo started thinking about each undead in detail. He only got to Henry and Jacoby before the sensation was cut off.

Cirilo's thoughts faded as the man died, and Henry's focus connected with Jacoby. An internal conflict created a great chasm in the man, separating his duty to his fellow Acolytes and his family, and that of the undead's mission to fight the evil Ikritian Lord. There was also the hint of longing for Talji that Henry felt was misplaced, but Henry considered it little more than the aftereffects of the Hold spell.

What came next caught Henry by complete surprise.

This was not the accidental meeting with Stavros that had

occurred before. This was intentional and guarded. Waves of dark magic bore down on Henry as the Necromancer tried to work his way into Henry's mind. It was a terrible sensation, like he was surrounded by lions, snapping at him for a chance to be the first to draw blood.

Henry grew angry. Stavros had destroyed this mountain and taken everything from him. So much death and suffering had resulted from whatever evil motivation spurred on the Ikritian Lord. Henry refused to balk before the mind of the Necromancer. He'd stood before a dragon—he would never back down from anything lesser.

Reverie of Dominance

Henry forced a challenge through the connection, daring the Emperor to come to Jallfoss. Then, Henry flexed his Reverie further and blocked out Stavros completely. Before the bridge between their minds collapsed, Henry gleaned two pieces of information from the brief exchange. The first was great sadness, not unlike that which came from Cirilo. Second, the Necromancer intended to do something terribly evil.

Acolyte Commander, Cirilo Galantis Killed: Soul Essence Claimed

CHAPTER 43

The menacing connection to Stavros fled Henry's mind like a snuffed-out candle. Only an eerie calm hung in the open cavern without a breath of wind. A few upper limbs on the burnt oak trees still smoked from where lightning had hit them, but the rain had put out the blaze before it too had faded away. A clear, starry night now draped overhead, and the full white moon, Ezerath, peaked over the craggy edge, casting shadows and providing ample illumination.

Henry noticed his Remnant Form receding. His hands returned to normal bone, and the blue-scaled wings shrank and pulled inside his dreadmail. He let his ribs expand, satisfying his body's natural urge to pull in a calming breath. Then, he relaxed the bones in his torso and let out a heavy sigh. Henry took in the destruction that surrounded him.

The once smooth floor of the massive cavern had been smashed and upturned, like the young gods themselves had taken a hammer to a pane of glass.

Blood pooled around Cirilo's lifeless body. The man's eyes were closed, and he almost looked peaceful. Jacoby stood over the Acolyte Commander. The solemn expression on the man's face left no doubt that he'd experienced the same evil intent from Stavros. Henry heard footsteps approaching and turned to see Buddy walking his way. "He's coming for us," Henry said flatly, leaving no doubt in the mage's mind he was referring to the Ikritian Emperor.

"He's coming for the mountain," Jacoby replied.

"Jai!" Beast's cry cut the cavern's silence like the sharp edge of her dagger. Near the entrance to the massive cavern, she knelt over the young elf's body, propping his head in her arms.

Henry rushed to their side with Buddy, Jacoby, and Muji close behind. Ox merged back with Gator and shed all but his original dreadmail. The sound of heavy footsteps indicated he was coming too.

"You dumb boy. What did you do?" Beast shook Jai's body as the others drew close. She was soaking wet with what looked like strands of seaweed stuck to her cloak. Jai also looked like he'd been dunked in a water trough.

"What happened?" Henry asked, kneeling beside them. Jai was wearing a single Flow Bracer on one forearm, but the other was lying beside him. The boy was unconscious, though still breathing. Most troublesome was his missing arm. Henry went to rip off the elf's clothing to bandage the wound until he saw that there was no blood, no exposed injury, only skin covering the spot from which his arm should have protruded.

"I don't know. What he summoned was far more powerful than anything I've experienced—more than Ghara, and even more than that Acolyte," Beast said, indicating with her head toward Cirilo's corpse.

Before Henry could reply, Jai's eyes fluttered open, and he started coughing uncontrollably. Jacoby offered the boy some water, and Jai collected himself after a moment. He studied his missing arm, then looked up at Beast with a huge grin. "I did it! My summon saved you, Mira!"

Beast stood and crossed her arms, giving the boy an angry scowl. "If that summon was your doing, then I'm impressed. However, I am still not your sister. My name is Beast. Not Mira. Not Harshmira. Beast." She turned her back and stormed away toward the crushed pulp of Mersin's remains.

Ox hunched over the group and looked down at Jai. "I agree, tiny elf. Whatever you summoned was more powerful than even my impressive bones." Then he quickly added, "though very close."

Henry helped Jai sit up. "Jai, are you alright? Your arm, what happened?"

"It wasn't all me. The Bracers made my spell so powerful. I don't know what that thing that I summoned was. It didn't say. I offered my life to save Mira. It laughed at me, then only took my arm. I guess I'm lucky to still be alive," Jai chuckled.

Buddy picked up the single Flow Bracer on the ground and held it close to his face. Muji scurried up his robes and perched on his shoulder, reaching out with his long fingers to help Buddy examine the artifact. "Beak, beak," Muji chirped in a serious tone.

"Astute observation," Buddy acknowledged. "Nearly three-quarters of the power in this Bracer is gone."

"I'm sorry. I didn't know what I was doing until it was over," Jai said.

Henry put a hand on the boy's good shoulder. "It's fine, Jai, but your arm isn't. Ox, can you heal him?"

"A boon I would grant to any of my loyal minions," Ox said, holding out one of his palms. White magic swirled around his hand, and a matching spiral appeared where Jai's shoulder should have been. The magic disappeared, but nothing changed. Ox then held up both palms and cast a much larger healing spell. Still, nothing happened.

Beast returned from the crushed Acolyte and stood close to Ox and Jai. The subtle movements of her skull showed a range of emotions—concern for Jai, and something entirely different toward Ox. It may have been curiosity, but without muscles and skin, Henry couldn't tell for sure.

"Hmm," the Giant Remnant grumbled. He knelt beside the elf, placed his hand on the shoulder socket, and cast the spell again. Once more, nothing changed.

"What's wrong?" Jacoby asked.

Ox grumbled again and shook his head. "My magic uses the body's memory of itself to restructure bone and tissue. It doesn't work on things like infections, or if the body has been destroyed beyond a certain point." He indicated to Mersin's remains." However, it's very good at patching wounds, forming bone, and regrowing limbs. I don't understand why my magic isn't working on the boy. It's like his body has no memory of the missing arm."

"It's fine. That was the cost of my summon. Saving Mira was all that mattered to me at the time. That's over with, and now we have an Empress to revive," Jai said, bringing himself to his feet and handing the Bracer to Henry.

Henry took the artifact from Jai, then looked toward the blue blaze surrounding the Empress's ghost in the cavern's center. "Let's get this over with."

Henry and Jacoby recounted their interaction with Stavros as they walked toward the center of the cavern. Buddy surmised that whatever necromantic effect Cirilo had been exuding, it was likely a spell that connected him to Stavros.

"Clever," Henry acknowledged. "They planned this contingency."

"They were clever, yes, but your challenge to the evil sorcerer was far less intelligent. If I were him, I would perceive you as the greatest threat," Buddy said. Henry couldn't ignore the warning in the mage's tone.

"We're all that's left to stand against him." Henry shrugged his shoulders. It wasn't the best idea to taunt the man responsible for killing thousands, maybe even millions, but Henry was over his fear. He had faced a dragon and would soon have the Empress on his side. How much worse could the Necromancer be than what he had confronted so far?

The group made their way to the Empress and stood before her. Henry hadn't gotten a good look at her when he was engaging Cirilo, but now that the fight was over, the sight of her nearly took his breath away. He couldn't imagine someone more beautiful than her, even in her dead, incorporeal state. Wavy blonde hair hung nearly to her waist, framing her body like a waterfall hugging a cliff. Her features were soft and delicate, though distinct in a way Henry couldn't quite place. She looked peaceful, like she had just drifted off for an afternoon nap.

Henry ran his hand through her ethereal body. Her shape distorted like he had dropped a pebble on the smooth surface of a pond. "I think this is her very soul, but it's anchored to something other than her body."

Buddy stroked his chin and circled the spirit. "If that is her soul, perhaps the memory of her body is there as well. Ox, would a healing spell work in this case?"

"Doubtful," the giant replied," but I've never left a woman wanting." Ox held up both hands. Whisps of his magic spun around the Empress, weaving through her body like dolphins breaching the ocean's surface. The magic disappeared as suddenly as it had started, and Ox clenched his fists.

He pulled back and cocked his head. "It's her soul, I can feel it."

"Is that how we bring her back? Just a healing spell?" Henry asked.

Buddy held up the Flow Bracer to Ox. "Not just a healing spell. A powerful one. Use this, Lord Oxendine. There's likely only enough magic left for one attempt." Henry handed the other Bracer to Ox.

The giant accepted the artifacts and slid them into place over his huge, skeletal hands. Smyrna's craftsmanship was such that links and plates easily expanded to accommodate Ox's large digits. He flexed his fingers, gave an approving nod, and motioned for the others to step back. "Keep your distance, minions. If this works, the Empress might be so grateful that she jumps my bones immediately. I don't want anyone to get caught in the crossfire of love."

Beast threw her hands in the air and released an audible groan. "Give me a break."

"You've only got one shot, Ox. You can do this," Henry encouraged.

"Of course I can, Harvey. Now watch and be amazed." Ox held up his palms, and the white glow of his healing spell appeared, then suddenly blinked away. Henry made to speak, but an explosion of white radiance silenced him.

The luster was brighter than the noon sun and engulfed both Ox and the Empress. There was no sound beyond Ox's strained grunting.

The light slowly began to dim and shrink. After a few seconds, it faded altogether.

Ox still stood with his palms out. With Henry's high Perception, he could see that the flow crystals in the Bracers were cracked and shattered. The artifacts had likely been rendered useless.

The state of the Bracers no longer mattered. Before Ox, a woman with blonde hair wearing a long black gown knelt on the broken rocks. Her head was down, and her long hair covered her face. Henry had become used to seeing auras surrounding beings, and when nothing existed around the woman, he hesitated, wondering if the person before him was alive.

He crept forward. In a quiet, soft voice, he said, "Lady Destria?"

The woman picked up her head and looked directly at Henry. Her face was soft and gentle but carried a scared, worried look. "Desi? Where is Desi?" She looked around frantically and tried to stand. Her legs wobbled, and she started to fall.

Blitz

Henry caught the woman before she could tumble and gently propped her up. His Ability had become more of a reflex, or a muscle movement, than a spell. "Are you not Empress Destria?" he asked.

She looked up at Henry but didn't recoil as one would expect a woman to act in the clutches of an undead. She reached toward his face but stopped just short of touching him. "No. Desi is my sister. My name is Estreya." The woman turned to the others, and a sad look rolled over her face. "It wasn't a dream. Desi is gone. No, no . . ."

"You're safe," Henry said, trying to comfort the woman.

Estreya started to shake her head and brought her hands to her temples. "No. No. It's so loud."

Beast stepped forward and snapped at the woman. "You've been a ghost for a hundred years. What happened to Livadi and Malek? Why are the undead—"

"Quiet! **QUIET**!" Estreya screamed, clutching her head. A blast of mental energy bombarded Henry and the others.

Status Effect: Psychic Devastation (Severe), 12 mental damage per second. You are stunned for the duration of the Effect, MOB -100%

Henry felt like his brain was melting. A channel formed between him and Estreya, and across it surged a power so intense that it drilled into his mind and turned his thoughts to mush. The pain was beyond excruciating, and it threatened to rip apart what little psyche he had cobbled together over the past few weeks. Henry almost gave in and let the mental barrage consume him, but the last bastion of his mind bubbled to the surface—his first waking thought, and the rock that had seen him through every tribulation. The woman's voice cried his name with a desperation that rocked the skeleton to his tempestial core.

Henry!

He forced every last point of his Resolve against Estreya. His mind revolted against his efforts, threatening to tear itself apart. Her scream burrowed into Henry like a dwarven drill churning through sandstone. He pushed back, creating just enough space in his mind to activate his Ability.

Reverie of Dominance

Ability Bonus Activated: MIG +50% vs Remnants

Like he'd barred Malek from the Dragon Realm, Henry slammed the channel shut, and the pain instantly stopped. Estreya was still before him, clutching her head and screaming. "QUIET! QUIET!"

Henry's companions were on the ground, convulsing and writhing in pain. He gripped the handle of his sheathed xiphos and began to draw it. He could have struck down the woman. Instead, he sounded his Harmony and broadened his awareness to the woman's magic. He could almost see the channels between his friends and Estreya. Golden light as pure as the sunrise flowed from her and into Henry's friends. Henry had to protect them.

He spread his mind across those golden channels and forced his Ability into it.

Bestow: Reverie of Dominance

Ability Upgraded: Bestow II. Transfer the Effects of an Ability to multiple allies. Vitus requirements are compounded for every target beyond the first

Henry's Vitus dropped, but his magic held strong. He sensed the connections between Estreya and the others blink out of existence. Estreya stopped screaming and fell to her knees. She grasped her chest and sucked in heavy breaths like she'd just sprinted until she dropped. The others slowly gathered themselves. Jai and Jacoby wiped blood from their eyes, and Muji softly whimpered from the safety of Buddy's pack. Even Gator's jaw clacked like he'd been violently shaken.

Beast was the first to reach her feet. She drew her daggers and pointed a frost-covered tip at the woman. "This was a mistake. We should kill her now."

Henry held up a hand and warded off the skeletal elf. "It's alright. She didn't do it on purpose."

Beast eyed Estreya suspiciously, then returned her daggers to their sheaths.

Henry helped the woman to her feet. Tears streamed from

her eyes, but they held a focus and surety that wasn't there before. Henry's breath caught in his throat as their eyes met. Estreya held Henry's gaze for what seemed an eternity before she lowered her head and spoke in a voice softer than the finest velvet. "Thank you . . . I . . . I'm sorry. All your thoughts overwhelmed me."

Beast spat with a venom that made the woman wince. "She drilled into our minds. She could have killed us."

"But she didn't. I've blocked the connection, and we're all fine," Henry said calmly.

Estreya clung to him for support, and Henry hadn't yet taken his gaze off the woman's face. "We're all glad you're better. I know this is a lot, but we have precious little time. We need to know what's going on here. The dwarves told us you died down at the Source Crystal."

Estreya steadied herself, and Henry took a step back. She lifted a hand to her mouth and softly bit the tip of her finger. Her eyes darted left and right.

"Only a hundred years. Yes, I was there. Malek Vik'Taus, Archon Remnant and ancient enemy of my family, was released from the Source Crystal. He killed Destria." Her voice trailed off, and tears streamed down her face. The woman rallied her courage and continued. "I fought Malek and Livadi . . . I can't remember exactly what happened. Everything is blurring together. I know they were too strong for me, so I did the only thing I could. I sealed Malek in the Primal Realms and turned Livadi's undead and his army of fire soldiers against him."

"The Primal Realms! That makes sense. That's where I found Malek," Henry said.

Buddy's stoic voice cut off Henry. "That doesn't explain why you've existed as an apparition for a century. Perhaps you could also shed some light on *these* . . ." Buddy held up the weathered pages he'd collected from Bharat.

Estreya lowered her hand from her mouth and delicately plucked the pages from Buddy's skeletal fingers. Her eyes looked at Buddy with a sense of familiarity, but her expression turned dour when she surveyed the pages. She flipped through them for several minutes, then nodded her head. "These are from Livadi's spellbook—likely the cause of this mountain's curse. As far as my suspension . . . I don't know. The last thing I remember is banishing Malek. Then I woke up, and you all were here."

Buddy nodded, studying and then accepting the woman's explanation. He turned up his palm and reached toward the woman. "If you're finished. The pages may be of further use to us."

"Of course." Estreya hesitated momentarily, then placed them in the mage's hand.

Buddy returned the pages to his metal tome and secured it at his hip. "If Livadi was the Necromancer, he must have passed his power to Stavros. The Ikritian Lord is on his way here as we speak. Thousands, maybe millions, of undead exist in a mindless state of rage. You are surely a great sorceress if you could resist both Malek and Livadi. Is there anything you can do to save the former inhabitants of this mountain?"

Estreya shut her eyes and clenched her fists. After a long while, she opened them again and shook her head. "I have the spell but lack the power to cast such magic. My core has withered to nothing."

"Can we give her the Flow Bracers? That worked for me and Ox," Jai said.

"No," Henry replied. "The Bracers are destroyed. Perhaps we could get the dwarves to repair and somehow recharge them?"

Estreya walked over to Ox, more gliding than stepping. Her movements were regal, elegant beyond what Henry could put into words. She grabbed Ox's massive hand that, when splayed, was nearly the size of her torso, and lifted the Bracer to her eye level. Her lips moved softly like she was reading the magic from the dwarven artifact. After a moment, Estreya's gaze left the Bracer and moved to Ox's hand. She slowly traced a digit along the giant's palm and followed it until their fingertips touched. For the first time since Henry had known the giant, Ox was speechless—almost afraid to move or speak, lest he startle the woman's grace.

"That seems unnecessary," Beast growled. The skeletal elf crossed her arms over her chest and stared daggers at the woman.

Estreya carefully lowered Ox's arm and shook her head. "If what you say is true . . . if all the inhabitants of Jallfoss are undead, the spell to revive them will require more magic than these artifacts could ever provide. If I am to resurrect Jallfoss, only one place contains a pool of magic large enough."

"And what would that be?" Beast asked, her voice tinged with suspicion.

"The Source Crystal. It is the heart of this mountain and the repository of all magical energy."

"A quest to escort the lady!" Ox cried, righting himself like he had been released from a spell.

Estreya smiled up at Ox. "No, giant. I haven't the strength to make the journey. Thousands of years ago, Raynott and Osyrian locked Malek in the Source Crystal. The dwarves opened the ancient geode with their engineering and released him back into this world. With Malek now locked in the Primal Realms, it is safe to access again. If you were to restore the dwarven technology, I could harness the

Crystal's power from here. It may be our only chance to save Jallfoss."

Henry pulled the pack from his shoulders and fished through its contents. At the bottom, he found the dwarven flow matrix that he'd recovered from the flowsmiths' bodies in the hidden cave in Hjardharfell. It was a cylinder, open at both ends, and filled with shattered flow crystals. He held up the item before Estreya. "Is this what we need?"

She examined the relic and nodded. "I think so. That looks familiar. Use it to activate the Source Crystal and allow me access to its power. Then, I can revive the undead and ward off the Necromancer."

Henry examined the crystal array. The last embers from the burning grossoak trees reflected off its shards and cast a prismatic rainbow on the cracked ground below him. "Back down?" he asked, not bothering to turn to the others. He already knew the answer.

Ox's shout affirmed the sentiment of all in the party. "To glory we go. Either to victory . . . or death!"

CHAPTER 44

A tear rolled down the Great Lord's cheek, glistening in the dim light. Stavros hung his head and watched the drop fall, almost slowing in time as it caught and reflected different angles of luminance from a melted candle in a nearby sconce. When the tear impacted the floor, it sent tiny droplets mixed with dust splattering across the pristine marble. Another drop landed beside it, then several more. They collected in a tiny misshapen pool and followed the contours of the tile until they came to its edge, then ran into the mortar trough between it and the next.

How many tears had he shed for fallen comrades? Every adventure took the life of another of his cherished friends. He never wanted to outlive any of them, but the world had forced his hand. Instead of dying in his old age, content with the nation he'd created, he would live on—he would destroy.

The Great Lord felt Cirilo die. His most trusted Acolyte had failed. The death curse he'd given the Commander allowed Stavros to connect to Cirilo's dying thoughts. The skeleton named Henry and the fallen Acolyte, Jacoby, had been there too. How they'd joined forces was beyond Stavros's knowledge, but they would have felt his intent. The undead had grown far more powerful than he could have imagined, and they knew Stavros would soon be headed their way . . . to tear the mountain apart.

Several days prior, standing over Kos's dead body, Stavros delved into Henry's mind. The skeleton had been weak, full of doubt and uncertainty. The being he just encountered was barely recognizable as the same undead. Henry had issued a challenge . . . a threat . . . across Stavros's spell. How could it have been the same skeleton? The confidence and power Henry forced through the channel was something Stavros had only witnessed a scarce few times in all his adventures. That taunt forced any doubt from Stavros that he had to destroy the undead menace.

As Henry and Jacoby had likely gleaned Stavros's intent, the Ikritian Emperor knew their subsequent actions. Estreya would be revived soon, if she hadn't already. There was no reason to deny the obvious—Estreya was free, and with her release, the greatest danger to his cause had been awoken once more. He had delayed too long already, hoping he wouldn't have to undertake what was no longer an option.

The old man wiped a final tear from his eyes. It rolled down his wrinkled hands, over the liver spots and purple, spidery veins, and soaked into the cuff of his sleeve. He placed his hands on his knees and pressed against them to stand. Bones popped, and the aches of age chirped in his arthritic joints. He pulled the hood of this thick traveling cloak over his head and went down the spiraling stone staircase to the dungeon below his Citadel.

The depths of the Ikritian palace were not pleasant, but no prison ever was. No tapestries or ornamental weapons hung on the walls—only the occasional shackle or spider-webbed sconce.

Rumors of brutal punishment and prisoners left to starve and rot for petty crimes were often whispered throughout Ikrit. Most weren't true, but Stavros found it convenient to have that fear exist. The bottom levels of the Citadel were not designed for cruelty—they were merely a symbol to maintain order in the greatest society that ever existed. What nation could thrive without the unspoken fear of its ruler? Stavros didn't consider himself a callous man, but fear was a powerful tool for maintaining a nation's lawfulness. Those rumors were mostly unfounded during peace. Unfortunately for the current prisoners, these were times of war. Times that required a pit deep enough that not even screams could claw their way out.

Buckets of excrement and implements of interrogation were strewn about the winding passages, leaving no question about the horrors that existed below. Stavros walked down winding halls and twisting passages that never seemed to end. Even one familiar with the dungeon could quickly find themselves lost in the stone mazes, were they not careful. Fortunately, the Great Lord knew the passages of his Citadel almost as well as he did the upper spires of the Oxendine castles.

The quality of the stonework degraded as Stavros descended. Loose and uneven masonry strained his muscles and reawakened old injuries. Old age had reduced his Fortitude to a quarter of what it once was—enough for the Great Lord to feel fatigued, but not sufficient for it to show.

Stavros arrived at a final doorway at the end of a long passage. The single iron door rested in the stonework, supported by massive hinges. Two guards stood ready on either side of the portal. They wore the red tunics of the Bastion, and the double row of interlocking circles at the bottom indicated their rank of Senior Acolyte. It was uncommon to use Acolytes as guards, but the prisoners on the other side of the doorway were no ordinary inmates.

The guards stood at rigid attention as Stavros approached, and he acknowledged them with a slight nod. "As you were."

"My Lord, as requested, the Vanguard of Varanasi, servants of tyrant Basti, are ready for questioning," one of the guards said with a deep bow.

When Stavros returned to the Citadel after his trip to the Bastion, he ordered the prisoners to be brought to the holding chamber. Stavros hoped he wouldn't have to interrogate them himself, but Cirilo's death left him no choice.

A week earlier, Stavros had been in his office, discussing strategy with his highest General, Commander Alicos. The General argued to press the attack on Varanasi while Ikrit held the advantage. Stavros went against the advice, choosing instead to provide relief to the border villages. He was confident that the Varanasi would destroy themselves inside their thick stone walls, saving him the trouble of a costly siege.

Something else tugged at Stavros's mind. What was that rumor that Alicos had thought credible enough to broach? Dragons under Basti's control? *Nonsense*. He trusted his Acolyte's intelligence, but they wouldn't know a dragon from the lesser wyverns or lindwyrms. The Emperor chastised himself for allowing his mind to wander when a task required his attention. Basti could wait. First, Jallfoss would crumble under Stavros's wrath.

"Open the door," he commanded, calm and stoic.

"Lord Stavros, if I may. These men are the most powerful warriors in Basti's arsenal. I would never be so ignorant as to doubt your authority, but could we not bring them to you one at a time under heavy guard?"

Stavros shook his head. "We haven't the time for that. Now, join me inside for a moment." The guards agreed without another word of dissent. Stavros had never disciplined a soldier for speaking up, but it was understood that once was the limit of that privilege. One of the guards pulled out a ring holding several skeleton keys and unlocked the metal door. The irony of such a token of access was not lost on the Great Lord. The guards drew their swords and led their emperor into the chamber. On their way in, they lit two torches and placed them in empty sconces on the walls.

The smell of filth and grime filled Stavros's nose as he entered the thirty-foot square room. Shackles enchanted with anti-magic Effects were anchored to the walls, restraining twenty men who looked like they'd been through hell. They were covered in dirt and blood. Many had deep wounds, treated just enough to keep the injuries from festering. Though they'd eaten very little since their capture, their eyes held a vigor and defiance that no dictator could conscript. The loyalty these men had to Basti would not falter before their deaths. Their snarls said they were ready to die and would prefer that death be a violent one.

Assess

Stavros surveyed Varanasi's most elite warriors. He was surprised to find that most of them had Tiers, and a few were even in the **20s**. Had they obtained some of his Acolytes' Drift Amulets? Or had Basti's wizards found another way to imitate the gifts of the Primals? He knew the men would never tell him, but that didn't matter. There were other ways to pry that information from their minds. Unfortunately for them, Stavros was there for an entirely different reason.

"Guards, your swords, please." Stavros held out his hands, urging the Acolytes to hand him their weapons. The men hesitated only momentarily, then drew their blades and placed the hilts in the Emperor's hands.

Stavros lifted their swords, then commented on their make. "Kordoba long sword—Superior quality—Composed of an alloy only available in the distant lands. While not as strong as golem steel or as resilient as dwarven eversharp, my guards' blades can pierce low-Tier magical warding. They are also enchanted with various transmutation and evocation Abilities. Kings would kill for a single one of these. I know Basti has been trying to open trade with Kordoba for years. Losing a war that he shouldn't have started will set those efforts back significantly."

"Ikrit grew fat on wheat and cattle, while Varanasi suffered in your shadow. Your smug sense of superiority was more than enough reason for the invasion. Be grateful for your monopoly on the treasures of Jallfoss. It won't last forever," growled a prisoner at the room's far end. The man stepped forward as far as his shackles would allow and spat.

Stavros ignored the man and instead addressed his Acolytes. "Any person who leaves this room is no longer a prisoner. You will not hinder their departure in any way. Now, hand me your keys and step outside. Do not reenter under any circumstances."

"Lord Stavros, I cannot—"

"Leave us," Stavros said quietly, but his words were spoken with such authority that the guards swiveled on their heels and walked out, only delaying long enough to hand their Emperor the shackle and door keys.

Ward

When the iron door closed, Stavros cast his spell on the portal. No sound would make it through to his Acolytes. He didn't want to tempt them to disobey his orders and come back in.

Stavros turned back to the standing prisoner and tossed both swords on the stone floor between them. The man hadn't stopped staring at the Great Lord, and he cast such a ferocious gaze that a lesser man would have cowered in fear. Stavros had seen the look a thousand times before. Monsters and men alike would try to intimidate their enemies with such a visage, but the Emperor had faced too many foes to submit to such a tactic. Instead, he threw the key ring between the man's feet.

"I am Lord Stavros, the Emperor of Ikrit. You are now free men. All that you need to return to Varanasi is to pass through me.

The prisoners exchanged uncertain glances, but it didn't take long for the man to unlock his shackles and toss the keys to his fellow Vanguard. They quickly removed their restraints and got to their feet as the first man approached Stavros. "I don't know what tricks you're playing, sorcerer, but you're about to learn why old men don't play young men's games." The man walked past the Acolyte swords and made to push Stavros out of the way.

"Ughck—" The man stopped. His eyes grew wide, and blood spurted from his mouth. He looked down to see Stavros's arm, elbow deep in his chest. Behind the man, Stavros's hand stuck through his back, clutching a mixture of heart, lung, and splintered rib bones.

Stavros looked deep into the man's dying eyes. "I've spent more time as a young man than anyone deserves. I was planning on letting you devote your youth to rotting in this prison, but I have a need for it." Vapors of a sickly yellow hue diffused from the man's body. His flesh shrank and collapsed on itself like Stavros was wringing out a sponge. The man spasmed, and harsh gurgles caught in his throat. Stavros dropped the shriveled husk to the floor.

The vapors swirled and coalesced into a waving stream that disappeared inside the Emperor's chest. Most of the liver spots on his hands disappeared, along with a few lines on his face and some of the gray in his beard. "One way or another, you will end this night as free men," Stavros promised.

Status Effect: Aged (Moderate): All Attributes -50%

Like a flag had been waved at the starting line of a horse race, the Vanguard charged the Emperor. Two men scooped up the Acolyte swords and thrust at Stavros. The rest attacked with either magically charged physical strikes or ranged blasts.

The wave of blades, fists, and magic slowed nearly to a stop as the Great Lord's Perception spread through the room. The attack was coordinated, almost as practiced as that of Ikrit's Acolytes. Stavros saw every threat as clearly as the four moons on a cloudless night. After ingesting the first man's soul, Stavros's Aged Status Effect had gone from Severe to Moderate, returning **25%** of his long-lost Attributes—far more than he needed.

He wove through the room, faster than any normal man could perceive. His fists shattered ribs and jaws, and his feet kicked through femurs like dry kindling. He sought to maim, not to kill . . . yet. The broken members of the Vanguard cried out in pain as Stavros dodged and struck. Basti's soldiers immediately realized they were outclassed and fell back, forming a defensive position around one of their members.

They're protecting their trump card. Very well, Stavros thought, catching a sword thrust in his bare hand, then directing the blade down and into the attacker's femoral artery. Blood sprayed like a fountain as the man dropped, and Stavros moved on to the next.

Magical attacks bounced off his warding like flies on a pane of glass. He lowered his defenses and slowed his movements, allowing the strikes to connect. They didn't hurt—the pathetic attacks didn't even drop his Health.

Less than ten men remained, and they'd formed a defensive V. Stavros saw white sigils and lines of intense magic spin and fold into geometric shapes. He recognized the spell as a form of evocation and conjuration that drew from otherworldly sources. It could be quite powerful when cast by an experienced mage.

"Charge!" The lead man in the defensive formation screamed. He brandished one of the Acolyte swords and ran toward Stavros. The others followed, bolstered by magical Effects. They weren't trained to the same level as his Master Acolytes, but they did have Tiers and were still very strong and adept.

Stavros spun and caught the man in the chest with a powerful back kick. The man's sternum crumpled inward and shot backward with such force that he bowled over several others. Stavros didn't give them a chance to recover. Punches and kicks broke bones without mercy. To say this was the thousandth fight in which Stavros had been outnumbered would not have been an exaggeration, and the Emperor tore through the Vanguard with lethal efficiency, until all but one lay on the ground, writhing in agony.

Stavros turned his attention to the growing coalescence of magical sigils spinning in the air. "You may have gathered that my patience is low. Cast your spell so I can get on with my evening."

The Varanasi mage grunted, and sweat poured from his dirty brow. His eyes were panicked as he hastily wove his fingers through the air. The pattern before him spun faster and faster, and the lines pulsed brighter with every movement. "Behold, the power of Lord Basti!" The mage thrust his palms forward like he was pushing his magic toward his target. The brilliant white turned to onyx instantly, and jets of pure black shot forth and collided with Stavros. Powerful magic bore into the Emperor, and the light from the torches winked out.

The only sounds in the room were the groans of pain from the maimed Vanguard and the labored breathing of the Varanasi mage as he struggled to regain his composure. After several moments, the man whispered, "I . . . I did it. I killed him. I killed the Sorcerer of Ikrit." The mage formed a ball of magical fire with the last bit of his Vitus.

The blaze illuminated the room, and Lord Stavros appeared inches in front of the mage's face. The man cried out in fear and stumbled backward.

Stavros smiled and calmly said, "Had I been at Tier 1, your weak magic may have singed my eyebrows. The Necromancer taught me to add the Essence of others' souls to my own." Stavros reached under his collar and pulled on a chain until he produced a Drift Amulet. On its surface above the blue and red halves, a number was filled nearly to the top with black. It read 208.

The Varanasi mage could only shake his head in disbelief. Stavros returned the item and smiled. "Out of necessity, I took the Necromancer's spell a step further. By absorbing the soul entirely, I have stumbled upon immortality. This is a power no man should have, a power beyond what the young gods gave to their Primals."

"Evil! Evil!" the mage shouted as he scrambled backward, finding the stone walls of the Ikritian dungeons halting his retreat.

Stavros grabbed the mage by his throat and lifted him into

the air. "Yes, evil beyond measure. If only this world stayed quiet long enough to let me die in peace, I would have departed years ago."

The man kicked his feet as Stavros tightened his grip. The broken men scattered throughout the prison cell began to convulse. Their muscles spasmed, and they cried out as Stavros ripped their souls from their bodies. A hue of vile, bitter yellow erupted from their shaking forms and poured into the Great Lord.

The mage in Stavros's grip shuddered, his flesh withering into a shriveled husk. The light in the prisoner's eyes winked out, then all was silent.

The prison cell was now a crypt for Basti's Vanguard. Stavros had no further use for the desiccated bodies before him. He covered his head with his hood, then opened the cell door.

The two Acolytes met him in the hallway, their eyes wide and mouths agape. "Lord Stavros, they're all dead. And you . . . you're young. Is this an illusion?"

Reframe

Stavros silently cast his most powerful mental occlusion on the men, forcing them to adopt his suggestion. "Nonsense, soldier, I am still a weathered old man and was never even here tonight. One of the Vanguard freed himself from his shackles and tried to summon a demon. Luckily, you, my faithful servants of Ikrit, caught them and had to kill them." It was another lie to stack on the countless others he'd had to tell. At one point, Stavros had been an honest man. Husband material, years ago.

"They were summoning a demon, but we caught them in time," the men repeated in unison as the flicker of light from the spell faded from their eyes.

"Now go, alert the others," Stavros ordered. The men rushed off without a moment of hesitation. Even Acolytes hadn't the Resolve to resist his magic. Stavros followed them but at a slower pace. His muscles no longer ached; in fact, he felt none of the pain and lethargy that an old man should feel. He acknowledged the glyphs as he walked.

20 Souls Completely Absorbed – Maximum Soul Essence Claimed

Status Effect: Aged Dismissed

His rejuvenated body quickly brought him through the lower reaches of the Citadel and to the upper spires, where his private chambers were. Treasures from far beyond the known world filled the room—trophies from past lives spent adventuring. He pulled back an ornamental rug near the chamber's center, revealing hewn masonry.

Flowstone

The granite swirled like a whirlpool, and a suit of red armor rose from the liquid stone like a specter from the shadows. A fire blazed in the nearby hearth, recently attended to by servants. When the armor emerged, the light in the room dimmed significantly. Crafted from the hide of an Elder Balor, the armor would absorb most magical emissions. The fullplate armor was sleek and light, but unbelievably resistant to damage. Small black spikes lined the edges of smooth red demon-hide plates, giving it an intimidating look. Stavros had first learned of the material's durability when he'd nearly died fighting the demon to which the hide had previously belonged.

Next to the armor, a metal stand held a black, ridge-spiked mace—the only weapon strong enough to pierce demon hide. Stavros donned the armor and secured the mace to his side.

As he turned to leave, a full-length mirror caught his attention. It was like looking into the past, and it caught him by surprise. He was young and strong and handsome again. At his full height, he was an intimidating warrior, but the access to power his younger form now granted him was far beyond that of a Primal—hopefully near that of the god he was about to fight. His face looked young and energetic, a sight that had thrilled many women over the years. But it was his eyes that gave him sadness. They were full of life—life that was not his—life he had stolen. Though he vowed never to use that power again, he had broken that promise. The events at Jallfoss forced the Emperor of Ikrit to use the Necromancer's power once again.

Stavros had been content to grow old and die. That was no longer an option. Even if it were, he knew he didn't deserve such grace.

Outside the window of his study, the last hint of sunlight behind Ikrit City's skyline faded to dusk.

CHAPTER 45

K os. The word was little more than an echo bouncing around Sigurjon's dead mind. Pangs of failure and regret faded like the dimmest stars at dawn, leaving no trace of their existence—only a blank fog hung where memories should have been.

The man could see, in the sense that what remained of his eyes took in the destruction around him. Had he been alive, Sigurjon may have been aware of the rubble that filled the plaza resting between what remained of the two ramps of Ammerthall. He also may have noticed that most of the flesh had been stripped from his bones, and his armor had been shredded and melted away. As he was, the undead only noticed the two green auras of his former students—the Junior Acolytes he led into battle and failed to protect.

A gray mist began to rise before him. It started as the slightest puff of smoke, just a few inches off the ground. The mist churned and spun, growing until it towered over him. It darkened to a black, opaque cloud, then just as quickly, it dissolved away, revealing a naked, emaciated body curled on the ground. Sickly purple skin with black veins stretched over jagged bone. Slowly, the body unfolded and stretched atrophied muscles.

Over several minutes—or several years, as far as Sigurjon was concerned—the man before him brought himself to stand on wobbling legs. He turned and took in the devastation around him until his eyes fell upon the undead Acolyte. The man's tight skin and sunken eyes turned his visage into a frightful mix of horror and mania. He reached up a shaking hand and touched a bit of charred flesh that hung from Sigurjon's face.

"Such pain . . ." the man croaked with a voice so weak it could have been his last words. "I feel your loss as though it were my own."

The man turned and looked at the remains of the two Junior Acolytes, then back at Sigurjon. "You lost so much. I wonder what you would give to have it all back." His lips opened into a facade of a smile. The few yellow teeth left in his mouth screamed a warning of danger that the undead Acolyte could not heed.

The frail man suddenly blinked and pulled his hand away like he'd pricked his finger on a sharp echinosta spine. His eyes darted across the rubble and up toward the cavern-city's stone ceiling. He grunted in pain from the sharp movement but seemed to disregard his protesting body even as his bones threatened to pierce his skin. After several moments, the man returned his attention to Sigurjon. A different smile appeared on his face, one of a man who had bested a rival at a heated contest. He stared through the Acolyte like the man wasn't even there, and his voice emitted the only semblance of strength he had shown yet. "You've succeeded, warrior. She is awake, and for that you have my gratitude."

Malek slowly craned his head and looked deep into what re-mained of Sigurjon's undead eyes. "Wait here, failed hero. I will return to grant your retribution." More black smoke enveloped the man, and when it dissipated, he was gone—not even footprints were left in the sand to testify the specter ever existed.

I hope you enjoyed reading Book 3 of the Dead Again series as much as I did writing it. New authors like me thrive on your feedback, so please go to Amazon, Goodreads, or wherever you prefer, and leave a review. You can also reach me directly at brucejamisonbooks@gmail.com.

If you enjoyed this book, please leave a review at your favorite online retailer's website!

Enthusiastic reviews from readers like you are incredibly helpful.

Thank you!

NEF HOUSE PUBLISHING

Discover more awesome fantasy and LitRPG at
www.nefhousepublishing.com